Sign up for our newsletter to hear
about new and upcoming releases.

www.ylva-publishing.com

BETWEEN THE LINES

KD WILLIAMSON

DEDICATION

To my Michelle, I may not be a romantic in real life, but loving you has opened my mind creatively. To MB, who always gives me the truth whether I like it or not; you are way too perky to exist. To my mother, I know you tried to teach me well, and it worked for the most part. My potty mouth isn't your fault. I put the blame on Trump. Thanks to Ylva and Jove Belle who helped to make this happen.

CHAPTER 1

"You heard this story how many times now? Ain't you tired of it?"

Instead of responding, Dr. Tonya Preston smiled softly. The leather chair groaned as she leaned back and continued to observe her client.

She and Oleta always started out this way. There would be a few more questions, a few more attempts at hedging the issue before they got to the meat of the situation. Oleta refused to look at her. Her gaze was frozen on some invisible point on the floor. Her hands trembled, and she tried to hide it by wringing them.

"You not fixin' me. What kind of doctor are you? That medicine don't work. Yah heard me?"

"Oleta, look at me." It was Tonya's turn to lead the dance.

Reluctantly, Oleta raised her head. Her eyes were red-rimmed and accusatory. "I know what you gone say."

"Tell me." Tonya's tone was firm but coaxing.

Oleta pursed her lips, making the lines around her mouth more prominent. She looked all of her sixty-seven years plus a few extra. "It's gone work when I'm ready fo it to."

Tonya nodded.

"But I'm fine e'ry other day…e'ry other month. Don't need 'em then." Oleta looked away, as if trying to outrun the lie. "It's been three years since I been back…seven since it happened. I ain't weak."

"No, nowhere near it," Tonya agreed. But, as July rolled in, Oleta stopped sleeping. Then she stopped eating. It was a potent combination and marked the beginning of a depressive episode.

Oleta yanked the left leg of her pajamas up and pulled the tube sock up as far as it would go. Her fingers were gnarled, dry, and a little swollen, hinting at arthritis. She repeated the process, as if fortifying her armor before battle.

Tonya watched patiently and hoped that one day Oleta would realize that they weren't on opposite sides and that the war she envisioned was within herself.

"Yes, indeed. Look atcha. Some pretty mixed girl all rich and shit. You could pass fo white if you wanted. Whatchu know 'bout it? Whatchu know 'bout sufferin' at all?"

Tonya didn't take offense at the anger or the terseness in Oleta's voice. "I only know what you've told me, but no, our experiences were not the same. I didn't lose my home, and I had the ability to leave," Tonya repeated for the third time in as many years.

Oleta started wringing her hands again, and the tremor increased. "I ain't neva known my street to be quiet like it was that day. I was used to that stupid music and all kinds of racket."

She glanced away, hands fisted, and when she looked back, there were tears in her eyes. Tonya took a deep breath and listened. She wondered how far they would get this time. This year.

"That water…roared like some kinda monster. It ate my baby and came for me. The devil is a liar and so is God." Oleta's chest started to heave, and her breathing hitched. "I was done livin'. She just started. Don't make no sense." She shook her head, and her tears fell in earnest. "Don't make no damn sense."

Oleta whispered the words over and over. She rediscovered that spot on the floor.

Tonya looked on for a little while longer, knowing that they'd hit a wall. Previously, Oleta had refused to give her granddaughter a name and avoided terms of endearment. That wasn't the case anymore, so they'd made some progress. Tonya reached forward to touch Oleta's knee. In turn, Oleta covered her hand and squeezed tightly.

It was only the second week of July, and there had already been several intakes. By the time the anniversary of Hurricane Katrina came around, there would be more.

She took her hand away and stood. "I'll get Stephanie."

Oleta didn't acknowledge Tonya as she looked toward the door. The mental health tech stationed outside finally turned and peered through the glass. Tonya nodded. A few seconds later, he entered, and a woman in scrubs stepped in behind him. The nurse, Stephanie Chambers, smiled at Tonya. She gave a slight tilt of her head in return.

Stephanie glared, rolled her eyes, and gave her attention to their patient instead. "We ready to go, Mrs. Oleta?"

Tonya almost smiled. It was strange that after almost a year, Stephanie still got irritated by what she termed Tonya's *shield of professionalism*. Yes, they were friends, but within these walls they functioned more as supervisor/supervisee, with well-defined boundaries. With three psychiatric nurses, four mental health techs, a social worker, twelve adult beds, and Tonya herself, they were in very close quarters during their shift, even though they had their own wing at Universal Hospital.

Oleta didn't say anything, but she stood.

The mental health tech didn't look at Tonya at all. He didn't speak either. His demeanor was a direct result of the behavior she exhibited daily. Tonya'd heard the rumors about herself, thanks to Stephanie. Most thought she was uppity and unable to mix with the common, less educated folk. They were all dead wrong, of course. Still, everyone worked together to do their jobs and treated each patient with respect. That was the most important thing.

Tonya went back to her desk and unlocked the bottom drawer. She pulled out her handbag and headed into her private bathroom. With a critical eye, she gave herself the once-over. Soft pink lipstick complemented her lighter skin tone and accentuated the full curve of her lips. Oleta was right. She could pass for a tanned white person at first glance, not that she would ever try. That just wasn't her thing. Tonya pushed the thought away. She'd always thought her nose was way too small for her face, especially with her glasses, which she rarely wore.

Unfortunately, today the glasses had been necessary as she was waiting on new contacts. Tonya wrinkled her nose in irritation, exposing a hint of dimples. She pulled the square black frames from her face and set them on the sink. She blinked and leaned closer to the mirror as she fiddled with her mass of professionally styled curls, natural just like her mother's. Tonya's appearance was immaculate, cool and unruffled. Her clothing was an important part of the façade.

Tonya's purse vibrated, which was unusual.

Call me when u get this.

She stared at the message for a couple seconds. Tracy didn't usually text her while she was working, so there had to be something going on. "Here we go. Should be interesting."

Her sister's phone rang twice.

"Okay. Three things. Men suck. I'm bored because some of my classes are dry as hell no matter how the professors try to spin them, and I have some good news!" Tracy's voice went up a couple of octaves.

Tonya blinked. "I'm going to ignore the first statement because you say that all the time."

"Well, maybe I keep hoping that your comeback will be that women are the same. Give me some hope that the struggle is real, even for you."

For a few seconds, Tonya was quiet, simply because she didn't know what to say. Her sexuality wasn't a secret from her family, but by unspoken agreement, it was something they didn't discuss. Her father had never said the word lesbian. It didn't feel right to even broach the topic with Tracy. Instead, Tonya side-stepped the subject. "What do you mean…even for me?"

Tracy scoffed, and Tonya could practically hear her eyes roll.

"Please, you're hot, even in those yesteryear glasses, and just because you don't talk about it, somebody has to be taking care of home base. It can't stay dusty."

Tonya's mouth fell open. "What did you just say?"

Tracy groaned. "Jesus, thirty-six isn't that damn old. Forget it. I know you know what I mean, so I'm letting it go."

"I'm fine with that. Getting back on topic…" Tonya hesitated. "As far as I know, no one ever said getting a Master's in Education was sexy, and should I be sitting down for the third thing?"

"Very cute and a little sloppy. I did say I was letting it go. Anyway, it's way sexier than psychiatry. Easier to spell and not as messy."

Tonya smiled slightly, thankful to escape further awkwardness. "I like my mess." Besides, everyone else's lives were a lot easier to deal with and a lot more interesting than her own.

"Yes, I know, and no, you don't need to sit down. I pretty much got offered a job. If I want to teach, LSU will keep me on."

That would be great if Tracy actually knew what she wanted to do. She'd gone from interest in the business world to school administration and now teaching. She was graduating in December, and she was still going back and forth. Tracy's indecisiveness was frustrating, especially since Tonya was footing the bill for her tuition.

While Tonya had achieved career and financial success, Tracy had the type of wealth she truly coveted: personal freedom. Tonya couldn't even fathom what that must feel like, and there were times when she really wanted to. A surge of jealousy uncoiled in her chest, but she swallowed it down. She didn't want to antagonize her younger sister or seem unsupportive. Tonya chose her words carefully. "That was nice of them. You've obviously made an impression. Did you tell Daddy yet?"

"I tried, but he didn't answer the phone. And you know he doesn't text, so I'll catch him later. But...what I just told you? It's a good thing, right?" Tracy didn't sound so sure.

"It is if you want it to be."

"That's not really an answer."

Tonya choked back a sigh. "Just think about it. Visualize yourself in that profession and weigh your pros and cons."

Tracy sighed loud enough for both of them. "That's a Dr. Preston answer. I want to hear from Tonya."

"I'm me. I don't know what you mean." Tonya did knew exactly what she meant, but sometimes faux obliviousness was easier.

"Fine," Tracy said in an exasperated huff. "I'm going to celebrate my ass off no matter what."

"Sounds like a plan." Tonya's voice sounded wooden to her own ears. "As long as somebody's having fun," she mumbled under her breath.

"What did you just say?" Tracy asked.

"I said it sounds like a plan."

"Noooo, the second thing."

"Nothing, don't worry about it."

Tracy grumbled. "Fine. I'll talk to you later."

Tonya didn't get the chance to say good-bye. She tossed her cell back into her purse, glanced at herself in the mirror, and sighed. "Okay, I know I shouldn't have said that."

As she walked out of the bathroom, trying to push the conversation to the back of her mind, there was a knock at her office door. She slid into her chair and put her purse where it belonged, finally able to focus. The shield of professionalism slid firmly into place as the tech brought her next patient in.

Chapter 2

Haley filled her mouth with Captain Crunch. She stared at the TV as she watched the final few cut scenes in *Mass Effect 3*. She stopped mid-chew and leaned forward. Her eyes, dry from staring at the screen for so long, widened nonetheless. Haley's heart did a little flip in her chest.

Commander Jordan Shepard was dead. This was FemShep. *Her* FemShep. Renegade all the way, and the ultimate goddamned badass. She'd built her over the span of three games, forging unforgettable friendships with her crew. Then there was Liara, Shep's partner and lover throughout. She'd stayed faithful despite other romance possibilities, and *this* was her reward?

"What? Noo!" Haley's voice was shrill and loud enough to wake the neighbors even though the central wall separating the double shotgun house was several inches thick.

She tossed the controller onto the coffee table kind of violently, not giving a damn if the thing shattered into a million pieces—the controller, not the table. All these months of waiting and hiding from spoilers got her *here*? If she'd known it was going to end this way, Haley could have saved thirty-nine bucks. She stared in disbelief and disgust as the way-too-upbeat music continued to play and the credits rolled. What the actual hell? Without thinking about the time, Haley reached for her cell phone. It was almost dead, but it had just enough juice in it to get by.

Nate Danvers's name was right at the top of her most recent call list. He picked up at the beginning of the fifth ring.

"You…okay? Ever…everythin' okay?" he slurred.

"Hell, no. I just finished it."

"Wha? Finished…wha?"

"The game!" Haley was getting a little impatient. She didn't mean to snap at him, but given the circumstances… "Wake up." Haley heard the rustle of covers and a murmured voice.

"Jesus Christ! I just looked at the time. What is *wrong* with you?"

At least he sounded more alert. "I just finished *Mass Effect 3*. She dies! I can't fuckin' believe it!"

"Did you…did you just drop an f-bomb over this?"

"I don't know. Maybe."

"Let me get this straight. It is 3:27 a.m. You're not bleedin', and no one is dead?" Nate was starting to sound a little teed off.

"Shep is." Haley cleared her throat. Yeah, so maybe calling him hadn't been such a good idea.

"A real person, Haley! This is what you did your *whole* day off?"

Well, when he said it like that, it sounded dysfunctional. "Yeah, so?"

Nate grumbled something, but it was muffled, as though he had turned away from the phone. "Jen wants to talk to you."

Haley rolled her eyes. "No, tell her to go back to sleep."

"Well, that's kinda hard since you're the one responsible for wakin' us up."

"I was upset."

"Yeah, I gathered." Jen's tone was sarcastic. "You need to stop givin' me the brush-off. Let me fix you up. There's this one girl that would be right up—"

"No, you know I don't do that relationship crap anymore."

"But you do the video game *crap*?"

"Yes, no drama."

"You don't think callin' us at 3:00 a.m. is drama? You need someone to help you join the real world, and who said anythin' about a relationship? Just add her to your list of fuckbuddies. Maybe she'll end up first in line."

Haley groaned. "I can take care of that myself, thank you. Whenever I want it."

"Whenever I want it," Jen repeated teasingly. "So the toned biceps and baby blues make *you* the cure for vaginal dryness."

Haley chuckled. "I didn't say it. You did."

"You're so sweet, but this gamin' thing? We need to find you another hobby."

"Your husband was into them too, back at Ole Miss, remember? Before you *changed* him," Haley emphasized gleefully. She smiled, waiting.

"You mean…when he became an adult?"

Haley could almost see the smirk on Jen's face.

"Is that what it's called?"

"Uh-huh, yes, adulting." Jen yawned. "Anyway. You warmin' up to your partner yet?"

Haley switched gears. "Meh, he's an offensive asshole who talks to me like I'm five."

"It's three thirty. Are you really havin' a whole conversation? This can't wait until the sun actually comes up?"

Jen sighed. "Did you hear him?"

"Yasss."

"You okay now? Or are you goin' to sit there in your underwear and cry into your cereal?"

"How did you—" It was a stupid question, but it came out anyway. "Yes, to both those things." The world was just better without pants.

"Yeah, that's what I thought."

"Why are you still talkin'?" Nate asked.

Haley laughed.

"Lunch later?" Jen asked.

"Hell no, I'll probably be asleep. Did you forget I've been up since yesterday? I'm startin' the night shift tonight for the next month."

"Mmm, fun."

"Yeah, really."

"Nate will call you later."

"Okay, goodnight."

"Uh-huh. If I can't get back to sleep, I'm callin' you."

"I'll probably be up for a while findin' solace in fix-it fic. I'm sure there's plenty."

"Well, you do that then. Bye." Jen hung up.

Haley's phone beeped at her and she threw it on the couch. For the first time in hours, she noticed the stifling heat. The wifebeater she wore was damp, and her boi shorts were sticking in some uncomfortable places. She reached out with her foot and kicked at the box fan to angle it closer to her, but it was just recirculating hot air. The wall unit in the living room was barely spitting out anything at all. She really needed to call the landlord about that. The ceiling fans twirled fast and hard with the occasional squeak. Still, in here was a lot better than the bedroom, where the heat and humidity made her feel like somebody was breathing all over her.

She stood and opened a window, hoping for a semi-cool breeze. Instead, she was hit by a wave of warmth and the smell of recent rain, which made things even more unpleasant. Everyone suffered in New Orleans in July. Sweat gathered at the back of her neck. A cold shower would probably relax her enough to fall asleep, fix-it fic be damned, but she didn't move from the window. She peered outside. Working streetlights were few and far between on St. Roch, which was smack-dab in the Seventh Ward, but that didn't keep the few stragglers away.

Forget New York, for Haley, this was the city that never slept—a large chunk of it, anyway. She had been coming here since she was a child. It had been her second home, and now it was her primary one. New Orleans wasn't the same city it was pre-Katrina. Crime rates were soaring, but Haley refused to let that hold her back. After seventeen weeks of training, she was now one of the officers in charge of protecting this city. The whole process would have been harder if Nate and Jen hadn't been there to anchor her.

Was she going to save the world by becoming a police officer? Or at least New Orleans? Hell. No. Haley was a realist. She was no super cop, and after a month on the force, she knew she wasn't even a super rookie. But it was the little things that were most important to her. In time, by dragging away the deadweight that kept this city down, she had the chance to give the community back to the people who deserved it most, to the families struggling for a decent existence. She wanted to help people, especially the community she'd fallen in love with so long ago.

Haley groaned. Thinking about work brought up her partner. Was he an ass for real or was he was just acting the part? Using her arm to wipe away the sweat about to dribble down her face, she decided on that cold shower after all. Haley stepped back from the window and closed it. There was no point letting in more stagnant air. She glanced over her shoulder. The game had switched to the main title screen. She scoffed at it and moved back toward the couch, then reached for the Xbox controller and turned the whole system off. Game time was over for now. Well, maybe. Haley picked up her phone and plugged it into the wall charger. Sure, it was late. She scrolled through her contacts and picked one anyway. Somebody would answer her call. Haley wouldn't mind getting dirty again after her shower.

CHAPTER 3

Tonya turned up the volume on the radio as she started over the Causeway. For the next twenty-three miles, the waters of Lake Ponchartrain surrounded her on all sides. At first glance, it looked kind of scary with only two narrow bridges in the middle of an expansive lake. For Tonya, it was like being the only person on an island. Even though other cars were beside, behind, and in front of her, they were all strangers she couldn't touch or speak to. Solitude turned to loneliness at times, but she was used to feeling that way, even around those who cared for her.

Several miles in front of her, a humidity-induced haze hung over the Northshore, the most convenient entrance into St. Tammany Parish. The outline of Mandeville was distinctive. It lacked the jutting, harsh landscape created by the high-rises that were prevalent in the Orleans Parish skyline. Farther on, past Mandeville into Covington, there were simply trees, the highway, and the occasional business, before she'd hit the more residential areas. Just the way she liked it.

It was quite the daily commute since it usually turned into an hour or more, but she enjoyed the peace the drive brought her. As her BMW 328i ate up the miles, she shed her professional persona, allowing for deeper personal introspection. Tonya wasn't naïve enough to think she could mask "the doctor" completely, but she had definitely learned, through the years, to dial things back. She had a tendency to scare people if she didn't. Tonya smiled. There was some part of her that enjoyed the look on peoples' faces, whether it was in the black or white community, when she revealed that she was a shrink. She couldn't believe there were people who still thought of her profession in a negative light.

The truth of the matter was, she didn't go around analyzing, diagnosing, and dispensing advice. Well, she tried not to, since it was entirely too much work. The little voice in her head derided Tonya, reminding her that she didn't have much of a life outside of the hospital anyway, so she might as well hone her skills and utilize her education around the clock. "Shut up." Tonya slammed the door on those thoughts and turned the radio up even louder. She started to sing along, rather badly, to a Justin Timberlake tune, but the volume of the music automatically lowered as a call came through. Tonya answered it immediately.

"What are you doing?" Stephanie asked.

"Driving."

"How far away are you?"

"At least ten minutes onto the Causeway. Why?"

"You should turn around and meet me for drinks. I'm bored, and do you really just want to go home? Don't you need a break in the monotony? If I'm bored, hell, you have to be comatose. We can even go somewhere lesbian-friendly. Let's do Good Friends. Old queens and show tunes? I'm in."

The request was tempting for all of ten seconds. "It's a work night. You know how I feel about that." Tonya cringed, realizing she'd just fed into Stephanie's argument.

"See. That's what I mean. It doesn't have to be the weekend for us to go out together. I'm a grown-ass woman. Nobody's gonna tell on me. Nobody's gonna tell on you either."

Tonya switched lanes. Stephanie sounded truly irritated. There had to be more to this.

"None of your other friends were free." Tonya's tone was playful and a little accusatory.

Stephanie paused. Then she chuckled. "Shut up. I hate you."

"Yes, you've completely changed my mind now. I'll be there in thirty," Tonya deadpanned.

For a few seconds, Stephanie didn't say a word. "You're not being serious, are you?"

"No!"

"Don't yell at me. I was just checking. Can't tell with you sometimes, especially over the phone."

"And what is that supposed to mean?"

Stephanie laughed. "You're dry like a fine wine?"

Tonya chuckled. "Good save."

"I thought so. Tsk, sometimes I really don't understand why we get along so well. I mean, we're total opposites."

"I would think it's obvious by now," Tonya said.

"What? You keep me from getting pissy drunk and phenomenally stupid, and I make you laugh?" Stephanie asked.

Tonya smiled. "That's an interesting way to put it, but more or less, yes."

"It's good that you can let go a little sometimes, but that doesn't keep me from worrying about you."

Tonya resisted the sudden urge to make up an incoming call. She'd just gotten out of her own head. She had no intention of going back in, even for a friend. "Steph—"

"I know. Just bear with me. In our field, you and I both know that it's good to have a sounding board. You're definitely that for me. I know. I *know* you like to keep things professional at work, and trust me when I say I understand that. But we've known each other for almost a year, and sometimes I really do feel like I'm just that crazy bitch you have drinks with."

For a moment, Tonya was speechless. Stephanie meant a lot to her. When Stephanie first started at the hospital, she'd instantly treated Tonya with respect as her boss, but she'd seen the person too. Tonya had gravitated toward that both on the job and off. "You're more than that. You have to know that by now. Why are you questioning it?"

Stephanie sighed. "Look, I'm sorry for laying all this on you right now, but I guess it's as good a time as any. Maybe I should have waited and said this face-to-face, but... You don't ever feel like things are one-sided?"

"No. Why? Where is all this coming from?"

"It's just that I come to you for just about everything, and you just," Stephanie paused. "You don't talk to me."

"Yes, I do." Tonya didn't want to take this sudden heaviness across the water with her. Instead, she pulled over into one of the turnarounds.

"Well, you did tell me you were a lesbian, but I have the feeling that was easy information for you to offer. You're settled into it, but as far as your love life goes—"

"I don't have a love life." Tonya sighed and closed her eyes. "It's complicated."

It really wasn't, but at this moment in time, she was fine with that. Although, she did miss sex. There had been times when at least that part had ranged from pretty decent to good. For her, though, relationships had been few and far between, and it wasn't just because most of the women she'd dated were lukewarm to begin with. In addition to the lack of sparks between them, they hadn't cared to be her dirty little secret. Tonya let her father wear blinders, and because she had a responsibility to her family, she didn't rock the boat. The Prestons were a small microcosm of don't ask, don't tell.

"Anyway, let's not forget the way you talk *at* me about your sister and your daddy. You talk about them like you're on the outside looking in or something. I don't think I really started to notice until your mom died. Tonya, I didn't even know she was sick."

The subject of her mother was a sensitive one. It felt like yesterday instead of eight months ago. "That's because there was a chance the experimental drugs were going to work. There was no point—"

"Jesus, sweetie. Do you hear yourself? Everything is so clinical. You can't be the doctor—"

"I'm sorry. I didn't know you felt this way." Tonya cut her off, hoping the statement was personalized enough for her. Stephanie's words were way too similar to her sister's comment about *Dr. Preston*. Her whole body stiffened, and she sat ramrod-straight, despite the comfort of the leather seats behind her.

"I'm sorry too. I feel like I threw my emotions up all over you. I wasn't trying to sound shitty or ungrateful for what we do have. I just want to make sure I'm doing right by you. This isn't a movie. I don't want to be the sassy, one-dimensional black friend."

A warmth settled over Tonya, making her feel cozy and comfortable. A big part of her was grateful for Stephanie's emoting. A smaller part of her wondered if she had it in her to give what Stephanie was asking for. At the end of the day, it was easy to listen and laugh, but it was a whole different category of things to give of herself. "I'll try, and I'll trust you to let me know how I'm doing?"

"Yeah, deal." The smile came through in Stephanie's voice.

"And one more thing," Tonya said.

"Yeah?"

"You're not black. Not even a little bit." In fact, she was blond, perky, and looked like a cheerleader.

"True, but that's such a minor thing," Stephanie said airily.

"Is it?" Tonya laughed, relaxed, and put the car in Reverse. As she waited to get back into traffic, Tonya looked out at Lake Ponchartrain. The water, greenish-brown in hue, was barely moving at all. It was serene, relaxing.

"Yes, it is in the scheme of things. I'm letting you go, but Good Friends on Friday?"

Tonya didn't hesitate. "Good Friends on Friday."

"And maybe you'll go with me again to torture myself at Oz? I love making it rain even if most of the guys are gay."

"We'll see."

"Uh-huh. See you in the morning."

Thirty minutes later, Tonya pulled her vehicle into her attached, two-car garage, which was one of the reasons she'd bought the house. The other was the wraparound porch. As she got out, a barrage of delectable smells hit her; her father was cooking. It was a passion of his, and now that he was home daily, he flexed his culinary muscles all the time. For a man in his mid sixties, he was very spry. The house was always clean, and the yard meticulous. It was his way of contributing and showing that he cared. Maybe it was even his way of atoning. He didn't have to. Wasn't it a child's job to look after her parents as they aged? Though in Tonya's case, her role had always been to take care of everyone, whether she wanted to or not.

Tonya opened the door that led directly to the kitchen and pasted a smile on her face. Her father looked up from the huge pot on the stove. Other than that, the kitchen was spotless like she'd known it would be. Dark granite countertops gleamed, as did all the stainless-steel appliances.

He smiled right back and lifted a spoon toward her with his hand underneath as a guard to keep it from spilling. "Hey, my baby. Here, taste this. I think it's the best barbecue shrimp I've ever made."

All that butter was going to require some additional time at the gym in the morning. Tonya moved forward, blew on the broth, and sipped. Her taste buds did a little dance. "Oh God."

"See. Told you. I added a little extra butter, garlic, and some tarragon, along with the regular stuff." Robert Preston's brown eyes sparkled with pride, adding to already handsome features complemented by dimples and an always bright smile.

Her father refilled the spoon and brought it to his own lips. He spilled some down his chin onto his goatee and wiped it away with the back of his hand. "Just call me the black Emeril, baby girl." He winked.

Tonya chuckled and patted him on the shoulder as she moved away, even though it felt awkward to do so.

"Fix me a cold drink."

Without a word, she pulled a glass from the cabinet and got a can of Sprite from the refrigerator.

"I was gone do crawfish, but the shrimp at Rouses looked too nice to pass up."

"A crawfish boil during the week?" Tonya asked.

"Talked to your sister. We're celebrating her job offer. I got some nice wine, and the French bread is soft. She can be here in spirit."

"Oh."

The word hung in the air.

Robert turned and gazed at her as he reached for his drink. Tonya gave it to him.

"You don't sound too excited. I thought you'd be proud of her."

"I am. I spoke to her this morning." Tonya swallowed down the hundred other things she could have said about Tracy and her chronic indecisiveness, knowing she had to pick her battles. Better yet, pretend like those battles weren't even there. It was her family's superpower, after all. She gave him a wide smile because that seemed to always work.

"Good. She wants to do right by you 'specially since it's on your dime." He grinned, but it didn't quite reach his eyes.

Tonya's stomach roiled. She hated when he talked like that. It seemed passive aggressive. Yes, she'd paid her sister's way through college. Yes, she was in the process of taking care of her mother's leftover medical bills. Thank goodness for wise investments and her ability to save. She'd bought this house when she got her first real job. Shortly after that, her parents had lost everything. She took care of them when her father could not. It used to rankle her, but Tonya had come to grips with that reality a long time ago.

Tonya stood there staring at the back of his shiny, bald head. Sometimes his mere presence made her uncomfortable. She didn't like feeling that way in her own home, but Tonya knew being tethered to her family could be a somewhat positive experience one minute and a negative one the next. Maybe some good stuff was right around the corner. If so, why did she suddenly wish she had turned around to have that drink with Stephanie?

Brenda closed the distance between them. "Don't chu wanna know what it feels like?

Tonya couldn't breathe. "What if somebody sees us?" She looked behind them cautiously, then glanced over her shoulder. There was nobody there, but still.

"They won't," Brenda promised.

They stood in the space between Brenda's home and the neighbor's, which was an odd place to be. But Brenda's brother was a pain, and her backyard was too open. The narrow strip of dirt was just wide enough to fit them comfortably and close enough to offer some privacy, especially toward the middle. Tonya had always thought it was strange that the houses were so close together, but today, she didn't question it. She was just thankful. Plus, it was a minor miracle that she'd been able to get out of the house.

Brenda pressed her against the siding; it was warm and smooth against Tonya's shoulders. Tonya's stomach knotted, and she felt hot all over. She closed her eyes. The first brush of Brenda's lips was soft and tentative.

Tonya whimpered. She didn't know what she had been expecting, but it wasn't for her body to catch fire in a mess of teenage hormones.

Brenda ended the kiss. Tonya opened her eyes. Brenda looked surprised. "Boys...don't feel like dis."

Tonya nodded. She had nothing to compare their encounter to.

Brenda put some distance between them, and before Tonya knew what was happening, Brenda palmed her breast. She arched forward, and this time when their lips met, it was sloppy and wet.

"Ohhh, what y'all doin! I'm tellin' Mama!"

They jumped apart. Tonya was breathing hard, and Brenda was as well. Before she could speak, Brenda ran toward the front of her house to her brother, who was laughing loudly.

This wasn't funny.

She stood there, frozen. Time dragged. When Brenda finally came back, her chest was heaving, and tears were streaming down her face.

Tonya gasped as an icy bolt of fear plunged into her stomach.

"You have to go. He told Mama!"

It was then that Tonya saw the red handprint on the side of Brenda's face. She reached out, but Brenda batted her hands away. "Go! I think she's gonna call your daddy."

Those words shredded her completely. Tonya sobbed. Each intake of breath hurt like nothing she'd ever experienced.

"I'll see you on da bus in the morning." Brenda kissed her again, hard and quick. Then she was gone.

Tonya wiped her face and slowly began to move toward the front of the house. She had no idea what was in store for her, but there was no getting around it. In the short walk home, she went from crying hysterically to grudging acceptance and back again. By the time she actually got there, her eyes were gritty and burning.

She opened the door. No one was in the living room. Tonya trudged forward slowly. When she got to the kitchen, her father's back was to her. Her little sister peered at her over his shoulder.

"You take care of your own. I take care of mine!" he shouted.

Tonya jumped at the volume of his voice. She jumped again when he slammed the phone down.

He turned then. His expression was blank, save the anger in his eyes.

"Why don't you go play in your room for Daddy, baby girl?" He sat Tracy on the floor, and off she ran without a word.

Tonya stared at him, but she still didn't see the slap coming. Her face burned where his palm connected.

She cried out. "I'm sorry!"

Then there was a clap of leather, followed closely by stinging pain on her arms, back, and legs. Tonya covered her head and squatted to the floor as blow after blow rained down on her. She did her best to stay quiet, yet she couldn't. She just couldn't. In between her own cries, Tonya heard him yelling.

"Fuckin' embarrassment!"

"I didn't raise you to be like that!"

"Not in my goddamned house! Yah heard me? You not bringing that shit in my fuckin' house!"

His words started to blend together, and pretty soon all she could hear was the thundering of her own heart.

Tonya reared up in her bed, gasping. She wiped sweat from her face, along with the tears. "God!" Tonya took deep, fortifying breaths and reminded herself that it was all in the past. She leaned toward the nightstand and grabbed her glasses. After turning on the lamp, she opened the top drawer and took out her journal. Unclipping the pen from the side, she scribbled the date on a page that was nearly full and simply wrote, "Brenda dream." Tonya set the journal aside and scooted back against the headboard, breathing through the residual anger and fear and filling her head with mundane things until she was able to relax. Eventually, Tonya eased back down in bed and let sleep reclaim her.

CHAPTER 4

Haley buckled her seatbelt and peered out the window as her partner, Tim "Tang" Hudson, pulled out of the parking lot of the second district police station on Magazine Street. He was from Alabama and sounded like it. His accent was thicker than hers. Haley didn't know what Tang stood for or how he got the nickname, and she didn't want to know either. The guy was a whole lot of ass, plain and simple.

The area around Magazine was peppered with single and double shotgun homes, trendy coffee shops, bars, quirky bohemian clothing stores, art galleries, and restaurants that ranged from Jamaican to Asian fusion. A lot of the commercial buildings were packed together so tightly that there was no space between them, but the colorful exteriors and signs distinguished one from the other. Tourists wearing fanny packs, shorts, and big hats, mixed in with native New Orleanians, crossed against the red light as if it wasn't there at all. The streets in the area were narrow but always busy.

So, just like everybody else, they waited for the crowd to go by. It was so hot that it felt like hell had spilled over, especially after the daily hard-ass rain. If the heat didn't keep people away, the water puddled on the streets and sidewalks wasn't going to either.

They came to another stoplight, and Haley felt Tim looking at her. She didn't bother to acknowledge him because she was sure something stupid and redneck was going to come out of his mouth.

"How you likin' the late shift? Gettin' used to it?"

The radio murmured and spit in the background as other cops talked to dispatch and each other.

Haley grunted and shrugged. It was a little late to try to be friendly. She could have fought for a new partner, but she was starting to think—no, Haley *knew*—that she had drawn the short straw. Tim was clearly some newbie rite of passage. The guy had been on the force for six years with no promotion, and every time he opened his mouth, Haley could see why. Tim was her trial by fire, and she was going to walk through it even if it felt like she'd been doused in gasoline. Other cops smirked at her when she walked by, and then there was the container of Tang powder she'd found in her locker. Haley couldn't believe that stuff was still being manufactured.

Tim sighed. A second later he leaned forward. "Look at all that ass. I'm so glad I'm a single man, 'cause I got jungle fever." He snorted at his own joke. "Not that bein' married stopped me before."

She rolled her eyes. He was a man with *strong* features… something like a horse that had been kicked in the face by a mule. The pornstache did not help matters any.

"This must be like pusstopia to you, huh?" Tim turned the car to the left.

Haley groaned. *He just said that out loud. He really did.* Okay, yeah. She had the butch walk and the look. It was all a dead giveaway, and she wasn't hiding. So was this a misguided attempt to be supportive? Or was he really that ignorant? Or he just didn't give a damn. Maybe it was a combination of all three, which didn't improve her opinion of him at all. But his statement did cause a lightbulb to go on in Haley's head. She understood his nickname perfectly now, especially if *poon* was stuck in front of it.

"I don't even know how to answer that."

Tim looked at her as if she'd grown another head. "Well, it's a yes or no question, but you can add some commentary if you want."

"I don't."

"You don't what?"

"Want." Haley was emphatic. She had to draw the line some-damn-where.

He shook his head and sniffed. "Fine. I was just tryin' to have a conversation."

"Let's just stick to the Saints and the weather."

"No need to be shitty."

"I wasn't bein' shitty." Haley watched the streetcars go by as they stopped at St. Charles and Felicity.

"What you call it then?"

"Keepin' to myself."

"You don't like me, do you?" Tim asked.

There was no point in lying. Haley looked him right in the face. "Nope."

He snorted again. "I don't much care for you either. Long as you don't let me get shot in the back, I don't give a good goddamn."

"Then we understand each other."

"Guess so," Tim said.

He continued to take them up Felicity Street. It was "neat" how the neighborhoods changed from beautifully restored single and double shotguns to ones that looked like they needed about ten coats of paint and a whole lot of love. At least there were no potholes on this street. No epic ones anyway, where tires and car suspensions meet their doom.

She gave him five minutes. He was not the silent type. They neared South Claiborne, and Tim turned into the extremely small parking lot at the Church's Chicken on the corner. The line was out the door.

"You can get a two-piece dark and a biscuit for 2.99," Tim said, as if she needed or wanted an explanation.

This was just another reason to dislike him. Haley was Popeyes all the way. She'd actually found a fried chicken recipe that came damn close to their greasy goodness. She shook her head as he bypassed the line completely and went in. Most of the customers on the outside pointed and stared at her as if she had something to do with his craziness.

Haley pulled out her phone and clicked on Nate's name.

Pusstopia: use it in a sentence n
front of Jen. I dare u.

It didn't take long for him to reply. He sent an emoji, the one crying with laughter.

That's not right, but still I just went
for a visit last nite. Hold on.

Haley waited.

Her phone vibrated.

*She says ur a horrible influence and we
shouldn't b allowed to play 2gether.*

Haley smiled.

She can't keep us apart.

Damn rite!!! How's work?

*Shite. Started my shift with pusstopia,
can't wait 2 c how it ends.*

LOLz

*We bonded I think tho over our mutual
dislike for each other, so there's that.*

Well thats something.

Haley looked up. Tim was sucking on a drink and walking toward the car.
Maybe it *was* something.

*He's coming gotta go. I should b
professional even tho he's not.*

*K dealing with the dinner
rush neway. Later.*

Later.

The smell of chicken wafted in as Tim opened the driver's side door. He sat
down and glanced at her. "Hope you didn't want anythin'."

"I'm good."

Tim put his box of chicken between them. "Saints are gonna suck this year
with Payton suspended for the season."

That was two things they agreed on. She hoped this wasn't going to be a pattern. "Probably."

Haley was wired even though she should have been tired. The night had been long and tedious and she still had about an hour left to go. They had answered noise complaints that ranged from loud music to real domestic disturbances in the Uptown area; dispersed a few groups of natives who were having too good a time at one o'clock in the morning near Tulane University; and investigated a couple of claims of breaking and entering in Hollygrove that turned out to be false. During it all, Tim had been a real peach. Haley knew what kind of police officer she wanted to be—the kind that exerted quiet authority unless she had to get loud. Tim was the exact opposite. He was always turned up to the highest level. There were times when she'd wanted to pull him aside, but instead she'd just glared at him while he did his best to scare all the body fluids out of whomever they encountered. To civilians, it probably looked like some weird version of good cop/bad cop.

Now it was past 5:00 a.m, and the city, the part that slept last night, was waking up. The sky was lightening little by little. They drove up Oretha Castle Haley Boulevard, then turned onto St. Andrew for the fourth time in the past couple hours. She perked up; there hadn't been any suspicious activity the last three times they'd been in the area. Something was up. She watched and waited. There were a few stragglers walking around and even a couple people sitting on their porches.

The police cruiser stopped abruptly, making Haley jerk forward violently. "What the he—"

Before she could finish her sentence, Tim was out of the car and running toward a young man. Haley had no idea what was going on, so she went with her instincts: secure the cruiser and give chase. She tried to radio Tim, but there was no response. Moving at top speed, she flew by the onlookers and took a sharp left through the backyard of the house on the corner in hopes of getting a better view. What she saw brought her to a complete stop. The suspect—or whoever he was—was brushing himself off, and Tim stood beside him. He didn't have his weapon drawn and his cuffs were still on his belt. In fact, the two of them looked to be talking, but she couldn't be sure. Their faces were all screwed up in aggravation.

When he saw her, Tim waved, and Haley jogged closer.

Tim sniffed. "I was just apologizin'. He looked like somebody I was supposed to pick up last month on a warrant."

Apologizing? That did not sound right coming out of Tim's mouth at all. Talk about suspension of disbelief.

The man's eyes moved from Tim to her and back again. "Fuckin' cops. Better be glad I ain't suing yo' ass. Yah heard me?"

"Sorry for the confusion, sir," Haley said to try to smooth things over.

The man glared, brushed himself off, and walked away.

"What kind of shit was that?" Haley asked when they were alone.

Tim shrugged. "Didn't you hear what I said?"

"Yeah, but you couldn't have clued me in?" She'd heard him, but it had to be bullshit. Haley didn't trust this guy at all.

"No time. I knew you'd catch up. Don't get your boxers all stuck up your ass. It's not a big deal."

Haley wondered if she could get away with tazing him a few times. He probably wouldn't remember. "Whatever, and you're doin' the paperwork for this," she told him as they got back to the car.

"Did you see me write anythin' down? I didn't even catch that kid's name. Far as I'm concerned, that shit didn't happen."

Haley shook her head and got in the cruiser. She just couldn't wait to see what fun the next night would bring.

CHAPTER 5

Tonya pulled her BMW into the gas station beside pump ten. It was early yet, barely seven. Traffic was still light and there weren't any other cars in the lot except a blue Toyota truck parked in front of the convenience store and a battered sedan near the dumpsters. This wasn't her usual place; the Shell station had been blocked by a refueling truck, but it worked in a pinch. Tonya could have waited until after work like she usually did, but it was Thursday. Tonight was her therapy appointment, and her work schedule was unpredictable, especially this time of year. She didn't want to be late if she could help it.

Tonya had a love/hate relationship with therapy, even though it had been helpful. She had been able to figure out that her family couldn't, or didn't know how to, express or discuss deeper emotions. Neither could she, but she had taken crucial steps forward on that front. Tonya now considered herself a work in progress. The sessions with Dr. Finn had also given her an outlet to deal with the grief, rage, relief, and acceptance of her mother's death, separate from her father and sister so that she could continue to be their rock. There were times when that role was exhausting, times when she desperately wanted to be someone else and enjoy a moment of freedom.

These were such odd thoughts to be having, but it was happening more and more as of late. "Get it together." Tonya opened her purse, fished out her bank card, and popped the gas cap before getting out of the car. The heat was oppressive and the humidity even more so. Within seconds, she was sweating. Tonya swiped her card quickly and started the pump, then got back in the car to enjoy the air conditioning. Minutes later, the nozzle clicked, and she got out to return the hose to the pump.

"Damn, ma, you fine as hell. I like my bitches redbone," a man said as he and his friend walked toward her.

Tonya whirled around, nearly spilling gas all over herself and the hot pavement. The sudden jolt of fear sent her heart into her throat and then back down to her stomach. It was broad daylight, but this was New Orleans.

"For real doe," his friend chimed in.

Tonya didn't trust her ability to speak as the rest of her went on alert. Her muscles stiffened to the point of pain. Her heart thudded as if it were trying to escape from her chest, and her stomach cinched into hard knots. These men were sharks, and they would be able to smell her fear.

"What? Y'all too stuck-up to speak?"

One of the men took a step forward.

His friend eyed the BMW and said, "Hell yeah she stuck the fuck up. Look at dat car." He caressed the hood. "Yo man get dat fo' you? I bet you doin' all kinds of nasty shit to him to pay him back."

The other guy laughed hysterically.

Tonya scanned the area, trying not to be obvious. There was a woman and her child moving slowly toward the bus stop and a few homeless people gathered on the neutral ground that separated the lanes going up and down South Claiborne. They all looked a little too fragile for a rescue or interference. A few cars passed but didn't even slow.

Both men moved closer. One reached out and twirled a strand of Tonya's hair around his finger. She couldn't breathe, and her mind went blank.

He pulled the strand taut. "Is dis even real, ma?"

Both men laughed this time. In her terror, they were starting to morph together. Tonya couldn't distinguish one voice from the other, and black and white turned to muddled gray. It seemed as if they'd been out here for hours, although in reality, it had only been a couple of minutes. Tonya was still frozen with fear, but as he yanked harder, she thawed. She knocked his hand away and stepped back. Self-preservation kicked into overdrive. She wasn't going to be a damned victim. She didn't want her face splashed on the news as another example of the rise in violent crime. Not if she could help it.

"Ohhh there we go. I knew there was some fire under dat hot ass."

"I wanna see what she did to earn dat car. Just put her in da back. We need to get outta here anyways." He lifted his shirt to reveal the butt of what looked to be a gun.

Tonya's entire existence narrowed to this moment. Her life didn't flash in front of her eyes, but she was suddenly acutely aware of everything she hadn't yet done; everything she wouldn't get to be. She didn't want to die. Tonya took another step away and bumped into the pump behind her. That was when she felt the weight in her hand.

She still had the nozzle.

Tonya had a choice. She could give in and hope somehow she'd come out on the other side with enough pieces to put back together, if they allowed it. Or she could fight and hope that she'd come out on top.

In the span of a breath, Tonya made her decision. She categorically refused to be a victim. Tonya tapped into her anger, used her fear, and compressed the handle. Gas spewed out, and she flung the handle at them. It hit one man in the face.

"Fuckin' bitch!"

"Hey! NOPD! What's goin' on here?"

The voice was commanding and deep, and those words were beautiful enough to bring Tonya to tears. She turned around to see a young white woman in plain clothes, holding a badge in one hand and a gun in the other.

"Shit!" The man with the gun started to run. As he moved, he yanked the weapon out of his pants and fired a couple shots at the store. His friend was a few steps in front of him.

"Get down!" the officer screamed.

Tonya hit the pavement but kept her eyes on the cop in front of her.

Instead of giving chase, the cop scanned the area as she unlocked the blue truck. She took out a cell phone and immediately began dialing. "This is Officer Haley Jordan. Badge number 1264, reporting a 34S in progress and an attempted 67A. The two suspects, both male, one black and one white, on foot heading south on MLK. Should I pursue?" She paused, listening to someone on the other end. "I'm with the vic at the DP on the corner of South Claiborne and MLK." Haley paused again, then said, "Will do." The officer shoved her phone in the pocket of her cargo pants. She then put the gun back in her ankle holster and stood.

Tonya watched in silence, concentrating on the woman's bright yellow T-shirt. She needed something to anchor her. The sudden sound of sirens was musical.

"Miss? You can get up. There was a cruiser in the area. They're in pursuit and more backup is comin'." Haley walked toward her and reached out a hand.

Tonya took it, but let go a second later and stood on her own.

"Are you okay?"

Tonya tried to smile, but it wasn't convincing.

"You wanna go try to get cleaned up?" Haley asked. Her voice was soft now, almost soothing.

Tonya peered down at herself. Her tan slacks and white shirt were covered in grime. Only then did she start trembling.

Haley reached out. "I'm gonna put my hand on your elbow, okay?"

Tonya nodded, but she still flinched. She let Haley lead her inside. Glass crunched under her feet. The bullets had shattered the door.

"I know this was a horrible experience, but you got through it."

Tonya focused on the only point of warmth seeping into her body: Officer Haley Jordan's touch.

"Is there anybody you need to call?"

Tonya sobbed as the weight of what had just occurred fell on her shoulders. It crushed her, leaving her closer to the ground than she'd been in a long time. She felt weak, drained. The logical part of her brain—the Dr. Preston part—whispered that this was all a normal response. For the moment, though, she felt disconnected from herself.

"Really, it's okay…" Haley's voice trailed off. "I refuse to call you ma'am, and you're gonna get tired of me sayin' miss."

Tonya looked at Haley then, and that warmth she was feeling began to spread as Haley's smile extended all the way to her blue eyes. "Tonya."

"Okay, Tonya. It's normal to feel emotional and outta sorts after a situation like this."

"I know," Tonya whispered.

They came to a stop.

"I'll be right outside if you need me." Haley opened the bathroom door and waited for Tonya to enter.

Tonya locked the door behind her. She turned and stared at herself in the mirror. In colloquial terms, she was a hot mess. Her eyes looked haunted, for lack of a better word, and her face was flushed, colored by the adrenaline still making its way through her body. No amount of lukewarm water and cheap soap was going to fix all of that. To compensate, she washed greasy residue off her hands.

She had been a step away from death, or at least serious harm. Tonya exhaled shakily. But she was alive, standing, and there wasn't a mark on her. She wasn't going to cry anymore, and she wasn't going to fall apart. Not here. Not now. There was no reason to feel sorry for herself. Part of her was elated beyond words. She closed her eyes and let herself revel in that for a moment. When she looked in the mirror again, the haunted look had vanished, replaced by an expression she didn't recognize. Just like that, the somber, shaky feeling was gone.

It would return, of course, but right now, she felt like a giant. A vulnerable giant with an exposed heart, but a giant nonetheless. Tonya took several deep breaths. Dr. Finn was going to earn her fee this afternoon, and then some.

Deciding she had loitered in the bathroom long enough, Tonya dried her hands and shook out her shirt, ridding it of loose debris. When she opened the door, there were two other people present. The seriousness of their demeanor and the fact that they were talking with Officer Jordan led Tonya to believe that they were police too, even though they weren't in uniform.

At that moment, Haley turned and smiled. She met Tonya halfway. Her shirt glinted like a neon sign, but Tonya supposed that was the point. It was distracting, as was the black handprint in the middle. The shirt was tight over Haley's chest and upper arms, drawing attention to her toned biceps. For the first time, Tonya saw the words clearly: "We Know."

"'We know.' What does that mean?"

Haley's grin fell, and her face scrunched up. She looked utterly confused. "Huh?"

Tonya had to swallow down the urge to laugh and reminded herself that giddiness was par for the course with trauma victims. "Your shirt."

"Oh! That. It's from the video game *Skyrim*. It's the Black Hand. They control the Dark Brotherhood, a secret society of assassins."

Interesting. Haley looked like she was barely in her twenties. Gaming made complete sense. Tonya stared. "So you're one of those people."

Haley nodded. "I am."

Someone cleared their throat. Tonya had forgotten they were not alone. The two men looked at her expectantly.

Haley rubbed a hand over the back of her neck, making the sleeve of her shirt inch upward and revealing a black tribal tattoo higher on her right arm. Haley smiled sheepishly. "Sorry. I was about to tell you that you could use my phone if you need to call somebody. You never answered me."

That was extremely thoughtful for a cop, especially the NOPD. "Thank you, but I can wait."

"You're welcome to it if you change your mind." Haley offered her a crooked smile. "And just to let you know, those guys were caught. These two detectives here are goin' to finish things up."

"Oh." The news caught Tonya a little off guard. She looked between Haley and the stern-looking men standing beside her.

Then, without waiting for a word of consent or welcome, they stepped in front of Haley as if she were nothing. Haley's blue eyes darkened and her lightly tanned face paled.

"What were you doing in this area so early, ma'am?" The man in the rumpled suit and five-o'clock shadow asked. He looked like a TV cliché gone wrong.

"Getting gas?" Tonya's hackles rose and sarcasm leaked into her tone. She generally wasn't quick to anger, so the sudden aggravation was out of character and a good indicator that she was all over the place emotionally no matter how hard she was trying to compartmentalize.

"Did you know the suspects?"

Instead of answering, Tonya glanced toward Haley, who offered her a small smile and a nod but couldn't mask the anger in her eyes. "I don't think it matters who takes my statement, does it?"

"Uh, no, but it would be bet—"

"Then I'd like to continue this with Officer Jordan."

Haley's smile widened.

The detectives turned to look at her.

Haley turned away abruptly and stared at the rack of pralines beside her. "If that's what you want."

"It is. Thank you, Officer."

He had a higher rank than that, but she had a sudden urge to belittle him just as he had done her and Officer Jordan. This kind of pettiness wasn't her.

"It's detective."

Tonya didn't acknowledge his correction.

A cell phone rang, and one of the detectives stepped away. The call was over quickly. He walked over to Haley, invading her personal space and trying—unsuccessfully—to tower over her. He was only a couple inches taller. "We're arranging a lineup to see if she can make a positive ID, just in case the cameras didn't catch everything. Get her to the station. You can complete your report there. I expect your notes to be thorough."

Haley nodded. She stood her ground and didn't look the least bit intimidated. "No problem."

Then they were gone.

"Well shit. I'm glad that pissin' contest is over. I was 'bout up to my eyeballs." The store clerk leaned forward and smirked in their direction.

Haley bit her lip, but it was hard to miss the smile she was trying to keep at bay.

Tonya had no such compunction.

"You can follow me to the station."

"Where are we going in case I lose you?" Tonya asked.

"Second district station on Magazine Street."

When Tonya got in her car, she finally looked at the time. It was just past eight, and technically she was late. She had three missed calls and a couple of texts from Stephanie.

She stared at her cell for what seemed like an eternity. She needed to return Stephanie's call, and she definitely needed to call her dad. But she wasn't ready to share. She wasn't ready to be vulnerable with either one of them. "I can't do this."

Instead, she sent Stephanie a text.

Running late. Don't know when I'll be in.
Call Dr. Gouri in case of emergency.

The reply came almost instantly.

What's going on? R u okay?

Yes.

I guess you'll tell me what's going
on when you're ready.

I guess.

With one short sentence, she knew she'd confirmed Stephanie's view on their friendship. Still, she turned her phone off.

The knock at her window nearly sent her into the backseat. Tonya took a calming breath and rolled down the window.

Haley looked at her with sympathy and concern. "You okay?" she asked for the second time.

Their gazes met. For a few seconds, Tonya said nothing. Then the words just fell out of her. Or maybe Haley compelled them. "No, I'm not, but I'm ready to go anyway."

CHAPTER 6

Haley used the fifteen minutes it took to get to the station as time to process. She and Tonya had something in common: they had never been shot at. Haley was making assumptions, sure, but she seriously doubted that a woman who looked that well put together and drove that kind of car had been in gunfights. Haley was proud of herself. It was her first shooting. Haley could've freaked the fuck out. Still, she'd held it together, and that made being appropriate to Tonya a hell of a lot easier. The woman had almost been the victim of a violent crime, and she required a little sensitivity—maybe a lot— which obviously Detectives Fric and Frac couldn't give her.

She stopped at a light. Her thoughts jumped back to the shooting itself. They all could have gone up in flames. Haley shivered at the prospect, but the fact that she wasn't a nervous wreck was an awesome sign. She couldn't do her job if she fell apart after situations like these, and she'd handled that five minutes of shittiness pretty well.

Haley glanced in the rearview mirror to make sure the white BMW wasn't far behind. Tonya was kind of a badass. There weren't many people who could have done what she had. It was a thing of beauty, and the looks on those guys' faces? Priceless. They were as shocked as Haley was. She smiled and shook her head as she drove onto the NOPD parking lot. All of this was going to make one hell of a story.

By the time Haley got out of her truck, Tonya was coming toward her. Haley held up her hand to shield her eyes as they walked toward the station together. The metallic sign hanging in front of the entrance was shaped like a badge and glinted in the sun. She could barely see the big black letters that advertised the second district station. Tonya retrieved the shades that she'd tucked in the V of her shirt and put them on. The lady looked like she had been dragged through the dirt, but she held her head high. It was impressive. *She* was impressive.

"I don't know how long this'll take, but hopefully things will go like clockwork. I'm sure you have other places to be."

"So do you by the looks of it."

"I was on my way home, actually. I'm workin' nights right now. That gas station is the only one I've found around here that sells chili lime Doritos." Why did she let that come out of her mouth? Smooth. Real smooth. And she'd forgotten her chips at the store.

Tonya smiled slightly as she entered the building. "Interesting tidbit."

It was a good thing that Haley wasn't prone to blushing. As they walked into the lobby, she pointed to the chairs in the waiting area. "Have a seat. If they're not ready for the lineup, we'll go ahead and start on your statement."

Sergeant Hartley smirked at Haley when she made it up to the desk. "Look at you. Enjoy your five minutes, Rook. Tang's gonna shit a brick when he hears about all the fun you had."

"Yeah, probably." Haley grinned. "Do you know if my lineup is ready?"

"Nope. We're not McDonald's, you know. Nothing moves that quickly."

Haley nodded. She'd figured as much.

A few minutes later, Haley sat in front of her computer, with Tonya on the other side of the desk. She typed in the information from her driver's license. "The Northshore, huh?" Haley figured more small talk would ease Tonya into the interview.

"Yes, I'm not a huge fan of living in the city."

"That's understandable. I'd move over there too, but the commute would kill me." Haley paused. "Occupation?"

"Psychiatrist at Universal Hospital."

Haley stopped typing and stared.

Dr. Tonya Preston stared right back. "You're looking at me like I said I was a hooker in the French Quarter."

Haley blinked. "No, sorry. I'm just surprised."

"Why is that a surprise?" Tonya crossed her arms and leaned forward in her chair. Her forehead scrunched and her eyebrows dipped downward. Her gaze was piercing. She didn't look happy.

Jesus Christ. What was wrong with her? Haley said softly, "I wasn't tryin' to insult you."

Tonya sighed. "You didn't. I think a lot of people go on alert because they think I'm going to pick their brain and find something wrong with everything they do and say. Look, I'm sorry for being prickly. You've been nothing but nice to me."

"You're allowed to be prickly, and I saw what you did to those guys. Only somebody used to a boatload of stress coulda had it in 'em to pull that off." Haley gave her a discreet once-over. Tonya was tall, curvy, and obviously worked out. She also had an elegance about her. "And you're definitely not like any hooker I've seen around here."

Tonya flashed a smile. It was deep enough to show her dimples. "Thanks for the compliment. I think."

"You're welcome."

"Not to be stereotypical, but after all the stories I've heard and seen on the news about the NOPD, you seem way too nice. So I'm assuming that you're new."

"Well, I'm glad to disappoint you. And yeah, I've been here just the other side of a month."

"I'm going to look at that as a good thing. You were in the right place at the right time. I'm sure I'd be in my own trunk by now, especially after what I did." Tonya's hands clamped around her handbag; she held on so tight her knuckles were flashing white. She was at ease one minute and ready to jump out of her skin the next.

"True, and it was actually the first time I've been shot at."

"Congrats? It's New Orleans. I'm sure that won't be the last, though it doesn't sound like something to put on a cake."

"Greetin' card either."

Their eyes met. There was amusement in Tonya's gaze as they shared a moment of dark humor. Someone in the room laughed loudly, catching Haley by surprise. She had shut everything and everyone around them out, and she hadn't even realized it. Haley glanced away and cleared her throat. "We should probably get started."

"Yes, yes, we probably should." Tonya's hands tightened on her purse again, and the glint in her eyes disappeared. She looked as disappointed as Haley felt.

"Do you need anythin'? A coffee or water?"

Tonya shook her head. "No, not right now."

"Okay, let's start from the beginnin'."

Tonya was exhausted both mentally and physically by the time she arrived at the hospital. At least she hadn't needed to do the lineup. The cameras outside the gas station had caught everything. That was a relief since she definitely wasn't looking forward to seeing—Tonya didn't know what to call them. Those men? Those criminals? Those sons of bitches?—even if they couldn't see her.

She pulled into her parking spot and glanced down at her clothes. She desperately needed a shower and a new outfit, but going home was out of the question. After such an experience, most people would have sought the comfort of home, the comfort of family. Tonya wasn't most people. She got out of her car and walked toward the elevator. Thankfully, she was alone.

Once inside the hospital, Tonya headed straight for the attending lounge on the second floor. Grateful that it was empty, she found some scrubs and headed toward the shower. Less than two minutes later, she raised her face to the hot spray and scrubbed the day away with a brand new bar of soap she'd found in the cabinet. Tonya wanted to wash her hair because *he'd* touched it. Instead, she had tamed her curls and pulled them into a ponytail before getting in the shower.

Rape—or even the threat of rape—was something she had helped hundreds of female patients deal with, but never thought she'd face herself. This was probably going to haunt her for a while, but she would work through it eventually. It could be added to the pile she and Dr. Finn had been diligently sifting through for the past two years. She didn't want to wallow, and she didn't want to hide from herself, which was going to be hard since that was her usual way of dealing with things. Progress. She had to remember and acknowledge that she'd made progress by admitting her issues and seeing them for what they were. It turned out that her mother's death had been a catalyst for many things.

Then there was the fact that *she* could have died. It made her question: Was she satisfied with what she had? Who she was?

Tonya lathered up for the third time, and her thoughts strayed yet again. What would her experience have been like if some other cop had been the one to help her? If the detectives' treatment of her was any indication, things would have gone poorly. They didn't *see* her. They just saw the crime. Officer Jordan was different. She saw Tonya as a person, rather than a victim to be pitied.

Haley was young and butch, or whatever the correct term was these days. Tonya smiled at that. The way she carried herself, and the short hair, artfully styled into a spiky fauxhawk, were not the dead giveaways. It was the look of interest in her eyes later, at the station, that made it obvious. Tonya hoped Haley didn't end up jaded, or ostracized by other officers because of her sexuality. Yes, it was 2012, and New Orleans had always been progressive. Until it wasn't. Tonya sent a good vibe out into the universe. It was the most she could do. She closed her eyes and commanded her thoughts to settle as she rinsed the last of the soap from her body.

It was well after noon when Tonya made her way to the mental health wing and asked for a brief update from one of the psychiatric nurses. She threw herself into work: auditing charts and adjusting treatment plans to be discussed during the next team meeting. She didn't have room to think on things she could do nothing about.

There was a knock at her office door. Tonya finished a notation and glanced up to see a somber-looking Stephanie peering at her through the glass pane. "Here we go," she whispered to herself. This probably wasn't going to end well. Tonya waved her in.

Stephanie took a few steps into the room. Her brown eyes were dark with concern, and her lips pursed. "I just wanted to lay eyes on you myself and make sure you were okay."

Tonya met Stephanie's gaze, surprised by her restraint after the outburst earlier in the week. "I'm okay."

Stephanie nodded and stepped back, her desire to say more clear on her face. Her eyes clouded over with hurt. "You know you can tell…" She chuckled, but there was no humor in it. "Never mind. I'll let you get back to it. See you during group."

Tonya held Stephanie's gaze. Her stomach constricted. Pain of any kind was something she never wanted to cause. Her respect and affection for Stephanie grew tenfold. "Steph?"

"Yeah?"

"Thank…you." Her voice thickened at the end as she tried to put what she couldn't say into the words.

Stephanie sucked in a breath. She smiled slightly and turned to go.

Dr. Finn opened her office door and hesitated when she saw Tonya, who was still in scrubs as opposed to her usual attire. She quirked a brow and waved Tonya inside. "Well, should I assume we have loads to discuss?"

Tonya took a seat on the plush couch and waited for Dr. Finn to take her place. Dr. Finn was a severe-looking, diminutive woman with dark skin and hawkish features set off by short, naturally styled hair that was peppered gray. She wasn't the first psychotherapist Tonya had been to, but she'd facilitated the most progress. Best of all, when Tonya made a breakthrough, her smile was bright and astonishing. Sometimes it was all the praise Tonya needed.

Dr. Finn looked at her expectantly.

"I don't even know where to start."

Dr. Finn remained quiet. She tilted her head and studied Tonya, who reminded herself that this was a safe place, a place where she could unburden herself.

"Extra time tonight?" Tonya asked.

"If that's what you need."

"I think so, yes."

Dr. Finn nodded.

"I'm a horrible friend, but I think I knew that already. People come and go. It's the natural order of things. Unless I just never facilitated the relationship enough for them to stay."

Dr. Finn looked thoughtful but said nothing.

"And I was almost carjacked this morning. I'm sure they were planning on assaulting me in some way."

Dr. Finn leaned forward. "Where we start is up to you. Which one do you want to tackle first?"

"They're both connected. I should've called my father and Stephanie after it happened, but I didn't. I sent her a brief text and didn't contact Daddy at all." Tonya paused. "What those men tried to do—" She balled her hands into fists and took a deep breath, allowing the anger and other emotions through. "I haven't felt that vulnerable since Mama died. I didn't want to feel that, and I didn't want to show Daddy or anyone that much of me."

"Connect the dots to the bigger picture for me. I know you can, despite what you've probably told yourself."

They stared at each other. Dr. Finn was right. She was always right.

"Mama was bipolar. The things she did, things she said, scared me, and they pretended that it wasn't there. I became a part of that whole lie for a very long time, until I couldn't anymore. When I figured out that I was a lesbian, he pretended *I* wasn't there, or at least that part of me. I don't want to go through that again, but hiding is ingrained in me. I know I've gotten better. I have more of a life now. A separate life, but it's there."

"Yes, and are you satisfied with the life you've carved out for yourself?"

Tonya looked down at her hands. When had she started wringing them? "I thought I was." Tonya shook her head and looked up at Dr. Finn once more. "I could've died. If it wasn't for self-preservation and a police officer who just happened to be there—" Tonya flashed to Haley, remembering her courtesy and warmth. She stopped talking and tried to gather herself. "How do I know that what I'm feeling right now isn't just a result of trauma? We both know it's normal to overcompensate after things like this."

"You didn't answer the question."

"No," Tonya whispered. "No, I'm not."

Dr. Finn smiled. "A catalyst is just a catalyst sometimes, Tonya, but we will see in time, just like after your mother's death. I'm glad you weren't hurt." Her eyes were full of compassion. "Now let's talk about coping skills that have helped in the past, because they may assist you if PTSD becomes an issue. And by the end of this session, I want us to derive or revisit at least one baby step you're willing to take in order to move forward with yourself and subsequently your family and friends."

Chapter 7

Haley's cell phone rang just as she pulled into the restaurant parking lot. She smiled and fought off a yawn as she answered. "Hey, Mom."

"Mornin', sweetie. I just wanted to check in and see how you were doin' with the new shift change and everythin'."

Her mother was worried. Maybe she shouldn't have told her about the shooting. Unfortunately, it was something they were both going to have to get used to, no matter how crappy or how dangerous. "I was gonna call you on Sunday," she said softly.

"Yeah, I know, but I beat you to it. No biggie," Cathy said flippantly.

"It's goin' as well as it can be. The overnights don't bother me, and I'm *fine*. Psych cleared me. It's just somethin' I have to do after shootouts even if I wasn't the one who fired. Okay?"

"Okay, just be as careful as you can."

"I will, Mom." Haley thought it was best to change the subject. "Guess what? I think me and Tang have come to an understandin' of sorts."

"Ugh, just the nickname alone sounds backwoods to me."

Haley laughed. It wasn't hard to visualize her mother making a disgusted face.

"Did you figure out what it stood for?" her mother asked.

"You don't wanna know. Trust me. Can't believe it took me a month to figure it out."

"That bad?"

"Let's just say it fits him well."

"Well, my day will definitely go better without some weird visuals. You on your way home?"

"No, I stopped by Savoie. Jen and Nate are fixin' me breakfast."

"That's sweet. Are they doin—" Her mother stopped talking abruptly, and she'd either turned away from the phone or put her hand over it. Her stepfather's voice sounded in the background.

Cathy sighed. "I'm back. Sorry 'bout that."

"It's o—" Haley started to say.

"What? You can't be that big of an ass, Jeb! Don't you see I'm still on the phone?" Her mother didn't bother to hide her side of the conversation this time.

"Well, who is it? Who's callin' ya this early?"

"I am a grown-ass woman, Jeb Taylor. I can talk to whoever I want. Besides, it's just Haley."

Right about now, her mother was probably all red-faced, indignant, and messing up her perfectly styled salt-and-pepper hair by pushing her hands through it.

"Did she find a church home yet?" Jeb asked.

He sounded closer.

"Have you ever seen her go to church, goddammit? You ask me about that at least once a month."

Haley rolled her eyes. It was true.

"Watch yer language. I won't have ya talkin' about Him like that in my home. I thought we discussed this."

"This is my house!" Her mother's voice was starting to get all high-pitched and screechy.

"We're married. There's nothin' 'round here that just belongs to ya, and I'll ask ya about it twice a month until I get the answer I want."

"That work for you yet?"

Jeb grumbled something Haley couldn't hear. If this was *Jerry Springer*, the audience would be drooling.

"Mom."

"Hey, sweetie. I didn't forget about you," her mother cooed.

Backwoods? Tim and Jeb were neck and neck. The whole thing was somewhere between hilarious and pathetic. This was marriage? It was a question she had been asking herself for years.

"I know you didn't." Haley pushed the phone closer to her ear. "I don't like him, for you." It wasn't the first time she'd said so, but one day she hoped her mom would actually listen.

"I know you don't, but you haven't liked anyone since Ted. Trust me, Jeb can be sweet when he's not mouthin' off."

That was always her mom's answer. She should have learned by now not to say anything. Ted. She did miss that man. They were still in contact from time to time, but not consistently. She also visited her biological father's grave and left flowers when she was in town, but that was it for contact with her mom's exes.

Haley heard Jeb mumble something. Then there was the sound of a wet kiss and her mother's laughter.

She rolled her eyes. "I'll talk to you next week, Mom."

"Okay. I love you, and I'm proud of you. Send Jen and Nate my love."

Haley smiled. She would never get tired of hearing that. "Okay, I will. Love you too."

Savoie was packed, which wasn't unusual since they'd moved to North Carrollton, smack dab in the middle of Mid-City. The rent was higher since the business was on a major thoroughfare, but the money Nate and Jen were making made up for it. Haley scanned the restaurant and found Jen waving her over to a table in the back. The place was loud and the smells were enough to make her mouth water.

Haley pulled out a chair on the other side of the bistro-style table, ruffling the checkered tablecloth. "Hey, where's Nate?"

"In the office on the phone. What? I'm not good enough for you?"

Haley smirked. "Hell no. He was mine first. Don't forget that."

"That sounds so wrong comin' from you." Jen chuckled. Her green eyes were bright as she smiled.

"I know, right?"

"Give me just a sec. I'm makin' changes to the menu."

"You're addin' stuff?"

"No. Tinkerin' with a couple prices to balance things out," Jen answered.

"Mmm, okay. My mom sends her love, by the way."

"She's sweet. How's Jethro?"

Haley laughed. "That's such a genius nickname, and it fits him perfectly. Every time I talk to her or see them, he says somethin' stupid."

"So you keep tellin' me."

"Well, you don't come up with zingers that much, so I gotta make sure I praise you when you do." Haley reached across the table, snatched up Jen's glass of water, and took a long sip.

Jen glanced up. Her eyes narrowed. "You might not want to do that. I just gave Nate a blowjob," she deadpanned.

Haley choked and water dribbled down the front of her *Vader for President* T-shirt. She coughed a couple times to get rid of the burn in her nose and throat, glaring at Jen the whole time. She pushed the glass back across the table.

Jen's smile was wide. "I don't hear any praise."

"You suc—" Haley snapped her mouth shut.

Jen threw her head back and laughed.

Haley had walked right into that.

Someone nudged her shoulder.

"Oh shit. What did I miss?" Nate asked as he sat down.

Haley pointed at Jen. "She's a disgustin' woman."

Nate grinned. "I know."

Haley pushed him, hard. He wasn't a big guy, but he was solid.

"Ow! I'm givin' you free food."

"Yeah, yeah, that's still no excuse for her puttin' those type of images in my head."

"God, I'm scared to ask," Nate said. His eyes widened as he glanced from Haley to his wife and back again. His expression made him look more boyish than usual. Although his eyes were brown, he and Haley had the same mop of dark hair, full lips, and high cheekbones. People often thought they were related. They might as well be.

"You should be. Let's just never speak of it again." Haley gave a mock shiver.

"So dramatic." Jen chuckled.

"Can I get food now? I'm starvin'."

"Aww, Tang wearin' you out chasin the poon?" Nate asked.

"Cue dramatic sigh, right here." Jen propped her elbows on the table and waited.

Haley pointed an accusing finger at them. "I hate you both. Just put me in a food coma so I can go home."

Nate smiled, showing her a lot of teeth. "You want the omelet or the banana nut pancakes?"

In a perfect world, Haley would have said both. "Omelet."

Jen signaled one of the waitstaff, who was beside them in an instant.

"More andouille than crawfish."

Jen held up a finger, signaling the waitress to hold on.

"Extra cheese." Haley paused. "Oh and can I get some jalapeño on it, along with extra home fries?"

Jen and Nate stared. The waitress shook her head.

"What?" Haley asked. The waitress scribbled, then turned and walked away.

"I need a side of gravy too!" Haley called after her.

Haley leaned back in the chair and groaned.

"You still make me sick. After all this time, I still don't understand how you're able to eat so much and look like that." Jen's gaze was accusing but playful, one blond brow perfectly arched.

"Clean livin' and dragon's blood." Haley patted her abs.

Nate snorted. "You can bench one-hundred and fifty pounds."

Haley rolled her eyes. "So?"

"My weak ass can barely do one-twenty."

"Sounds like a personal problem to me."

Jen smiled at her husband. "It's okay, baby. You're strong in other areas."

Haley threw her napkin on the table. "Okay, ew. Don't even go there with me right now." She waved her hand in their direction. "Too soon." Still, she smiled as she watched Nate look at his wife all starry-eyed. "Since I'm not goin' to see you guys much with my schedule, I guess we have to do this more often. At least until I go back to days."

"It hasn't been that long. You miss us already?" Jen asked.

Haley didn't hesitate. "Yeah, I do. It's weird, you know? I have lesbian 'party friends.'" She made finger quotes. "But that's all they're good for, goin' out. Otherwise, I'd be knee-deep in drama." Haley took a breath. "I was shot at, and I'm fine. I really am. You guys know that." Momentarily sidetracked, her thoughts snapped to Tonya, and she wondered briefly how she was doing. "I'd tell you if I wasn't, but I don't know if I would be if I didn't have y'all to fall back on. I mean, Mom's just a phone call and a drive away, but it's not the same."

Nate eased his arm over Haley's shoulders and pulled her closer. She squeezed his hand in acknowledgment. "Y'all always give it to me straight. Just don't stop that. I probably need it nowadays more than ever."

Jen leaned forward. Her eyes were alight with affection. "Count on it." She smiled slowly. "It's inevitable, like taxes and Mardi Gras. We'll be here to kick you in the ass."

Haley smiled back and started laughing.

Tonya regulated her breathing as she increased the setting on the elliptical. She glanced at the large series of flat-screen TVs on the wall but didn't give much attention to them. It was Saturday morning. Just like she did every weekend, Tonya extended her workout by fifteen minutes, though today she had more of a need to clear her head.

It had been a very long week, and Tonya was grateful that it was over. So far, there had been no nightmares, but she was easily startled. When her father had come up behind her in the kitchen, she'd very nearly jumped to the ceiling. He hadn't touched her. He hardly ever did anyway. But his presence was enough. He'd looked at her strangely after that. Then there was Stephanie. Tonya had cancelled their Friday night plans because she was tired. A few hours of sleep in a forty-eight-hour period wasn't good for a person in her position. Stephanie had said she understood, but Tonya could hear the disappointment in her voice. She would make it up to her.

She still hadn't told anyone about the other morning, though she had every intention of at least informing Stephanie. Her family, not so much.

Tonya refocused on the TVs, and what she saw stopped her cold. It was strange seeing herself on television. The video was grainy, but she was still identifiable. The faces of her attackers weren't visible from that angle. There was closed captioning at the bottom of the screen.

"Instead of succumbing, this woman turned the tables on the perpetrators, and it was beautiful to watch."

The anchor replayed the segment and informed the viewing public that the video was available on their website. Tonya decided she hated those homespun morning shows and their human-interest pieces. *Good Morning New Orleans*, indeed. Didn't they need her permission to splash her face on television like that? Couldn't she do something? Tonya took a breath and decided that route would probably just bring more attention. She definitely didn't want that.

Inadvertently, Tonya slowed her workout to a crawl as her mind bounced from thought to thought. This was unavoidable now. There was no box to stuff it back in, and there was no hiding from it. Tonya grabbed her towel and wiped at the sweat dripping down her face. It was suddenly hard to swallow, and apprehension prickled at the back of her neck.

Her father wasn't going to take this well, but she wasn't sure if he was going to be more hurt and angry about what had happened to her, or the fact that she'd kept it from him. She mentally justified her actions once more. Her father couldn't be trusted with her feelings, and Tonya had had to learn to function around that. It had been a difficult, drawn-out process, but a necessary one. She couldn't control his actions, but she was in charge of her own.

Bottom line, Tonya needed to be ready for the fallout.

She stopped the elliptical and spread her towel over a nearby bench before sitting down on it. Tonya leaned back against the wall. She wasn't sure how long she sat there, but the phone strapped to her bicep started to chirp. Tonya peered down to see her sister's name splashed across the screen.

Tracy had to know. Tonya wasn't sure how she'd found out so quickly, but there was no reason for her to call otherwise—not after their last conversation. Tonya pulled open the Velcro strips around her arm and stared at her iPhone.

After a couple more seconds, the ringing stopped and Tonya pulled the earbuds out of her ears.

She wasn't sure why she hadn't answered. Tracy would be easier to deal with than her dad. Her reaction was sure to be mild and only slightly accusatory. Tonya's phone chirped again, but this time it was a text.

Call me plz. ;)

The winking emoji helped her to breathe a little easier. What was the point? "I need to get this over with." Before she could make the call, Tracy's name flashed again.

"Hello?"

"So, there are a million things I could say right now, but I'm going with: Why didn't you tell me you're a ninja?"

Tonya was speechless.

For several seconds, no one spoke.

"I, uh, stream some of the local shows since I can't get them on TV here, and *Good Morning New Orleans* is one of them. The lead anchor is cute. They have the video embedded in their website too. You don't have as many hits as you should, but I guess people want to see victims get the shit beat out of them rather than the other way around. Did you know that videos of neighborhood and school beatdowns get thousands of hits per day?"

Tonya took the phone away from her ear and stared at it, pleasantly shocked by her sister's response. Maybe Tracy understood her more than Tonya had realized, and she just wasn't ready to see it yet. That knowledge took root inside her. It was heavy and warm, and she wanted it to gestate and grow.

"I always knew you were a badass," Tracy said softly.

Tonya bit her bottom lip and closed her eyes. This...what was going on between them was refreshing, and Tonya had barely said a word. "Thanks."

"You haven't told Daddy, have you?"

"No."

"He's going to freak out, and not in the smooth way, either, like he did when we were kids."

Tonya smiled. It was strange to be nostalgic about such a thing, but there were moments of simplicity woven throughout the complexities of her childhood. "Where he just stared until one of us cried and confessed?"

Tracy chuckled. "Exactly." She paused. "I was going to come home for the weekend, but—"

"What's stopping you?"

"Nothing now. I wasn't sure, but now I am."

"I don't understand what the issue was." Tonya pressed the phone to her ear, using her shoulder. She removed the band holding her hair in a ponytail and raked her fingers through it, freeing damp curls.

"Because I'm getting to talk to my sister. Not Dr. Preston."

The warmth expanded a little. Tonya gasped. She wasn't sure how to respond to Tracy's words. "Okay. I'll see you in a couple hours."

"Okay. See you."

She could hear the smile in Tracy's voice.

Tonya looked down at her phone. Last session, Dr. Finn had encouraged her to pay attention, reminding her that while she had been battling to stay afloat, others could have been doing the same. She exhaled slowly. Dr. Finn was right, as usual.

Tonya's thoughts and Tracy's response galvanized her into action, and before she had time to overthink it, she texted Stephanie.

Are you free 2night? You can pick
where we go.

Stephanie responded in less than a minute.

Yeah, I am. Anywhere huh?

Yes. Tracy will b in town. She may
want to go.

Haven't seen her in months! Love 2 have
her along. I'll pick u guys up at 8.

That seemed a bit much.

*You don't have 2. We can just
meet in the city.*

It's fine, just b ready 2 go.

Stephanie added a kiss emoji.

Tonya stared at her phone for a few seconds and typed, *Ok.*

CHAPTER 8

Tonya went home to shower and change, thankful her father was absent. Needing to do something productive, and wanting to get out of the house, she decided on errands and a brief stop at the hospital to finalize some paperwork, which she could have done from her laptop at home. Tonya wanted to string together as many moments of peace as possible before she had to face her father.

Tonya's cell phone rang, and this time, she answered it without hesitation.

"I made a few stops along the way, but I'm here. Not that I'm expecting a red carpet or anything, but if it was night, I'd hear crickets."

"I'm taking care of a few things," Tonya told her sister.

"You mean you're trying to stay out of Daddy's way. Good move."

Tonya wasn't sure if she should be irritated or amused. She settled for somewhere in the middle. "Do you have to reinterpret everything I say to fit the situation?"

"Uh-huh, I do," Tracy sassed.

"Well then, feel free to stay and run interference tonight."

"What's that supposed to mean?"

"I cancelled on Stephanie last night, so I'm making it up to her and stepping away from the situation for a while."

"Hell no. You're not leaving me with him. To be honest, I don't know how he's actually gonna deal with all this. He plays it close...so do you. I'm probably the most open between the three of us, and that isn't saying much."

Tracy was right. Tonya was planning for an explosion when there was more likely to be bobbing and weaving. "I guess we'll see." Tonya paused. "Stephanie's picking us up at eight."

"Wait...why? We could just meet—"

"That's what I said. She insisted."

"Where are we going?"

"I'm not sure. I told her she could pick."

Tracy groaned. "Not Oz. They're all so pretty, but kind of like window displays. I can look all I want, but if I touch, I'll get yelled at."

Tonya chuckled. "Let's just hope for the best."

"Do you have earrings I can borrow?" Tracy walked into Tonya's bedroom and headed straight for the dresser.

"Probably." Tonya watched from the adjoining bathroom.

"Found some." Tracy turned and looked at her. "I love that top."

"Mmm." The shirt in question was red, elegant and understated at the same time, exposing delicate collarbones, the smooth length of her neck, and hinting at strong shoulders. It looked more expensive than it actually was. She'd gotten it on killer sale at JCPenny. She splurged for work, but for play, not so much. It was tiny sacrifice to ensure her family was taken care of. The shirt was form fitting and went perfectly with the jeans she'd picked out, which highlighted the curves of her hips and thighs instead of hiding them. She was nowhere near model thin and proud of it.

"It would be even better if you showed a little more cleavage."

Tonya glared.

Tracy grinned. They looked a lot alike. Same smile, nose, lips, and eyes. Tracy kept her hair short and sleek. She was also more petite, and her skin tone was darker.

"Just saying. With a honeypot like that, who wouldn't buzz the hell out of you?"

"Tracy!"

Tracy laughed, but there was a softness in her eyes. "It's been a long time since we've been like this. I'm just trying to enjoy it."

She meant before it reverted to weekly phone calls, standard niceties, and token encouragement. Things between them had been easier that way, and maybe Tonya wasn't too satisfied with that either. She stepped out of the bathroom and met her sister's gaze. "I'm sorry." Her words were quiet, almost not there at all.

"Yeah, me too."

Tonya's phone dinged with a text notification. She cleared her throat. "That's probably Stephanie."

A few minutes later, Tonya locked the front door after setting the alarm. Tracy had already gotten into the backseat of Stephanie's SUV when their father pulled up into the driveway. He got out quickly, but that was just enough time for Tracy and Stephanie to appear by her side.

"Hey, Daddy! Tonya's had a long week, so we're taking her out. Let's catch up in the morning."

Robert opened his mouth to speak. His forehead was wrinkled and his eyes were stormy.

"I'll be here until Sunday night," Tracy added.

His mouth closed.

Tonya stared at her sister.

"Yep, girls' night," Stephanie chimed in.

Tonya's gaze swung in her direction. She didn't know what to make of this…any of this. Before she had a chance to even start figuring it out, Tonya was in the front seat of Stephanie's car.

For several minutes, the only sound was the radio.

"Sooo…that was some La Femme Nikita–type shit you did the other day." Stephanie glanced in her direction while she paused at a red light.

Tracy laughed from the backseat. "Told you!"

Before Tonya could even contemplate building walls, Stephanie reached over and patted her knee. "I'm glad you're okay."

Instead of saying anything more, Stephanie turned up the music.

Tonya glanced at her friend, then in the rearview mirror at her sister in the backseat. They didn't meet her gaze or even acknowledge it. Tonya couldn't remember the last time something or someone had surprised her. Now she had two instances in one day. She wasn't sure if it was situational or long-term, but Thursday's mess may have set off some type of chain reaction. Some of the aftershocks had been pleasant, and some…well. Tonya would have to see.

"Shit! I don't have enough change for the toll. Anybody in a giving mood?" Stephanie asked as she poked around the compartments on the dashboard.

Reaching for her clutch, Tonya fished out three dollars and handed them over.

Stephanie smiled.

Tonya smiled right back.

"Where are we going?" Tonya looked out the passenger-side window at the people crossing the road to get to the streetcar. Stephanie was driving on Carrollton, going nowhere near the French Quarter.

"I was about to ask the same thing." Tracy asked.

"GrrlSpot."

"Who?" Tonya and Tracy asked simultaneously.

Stephanie chuckled. "You'll see."

"Uhm, is it a strip club for lesbians or something? Because that name..."

Tonya turned to look at her sister.

"What? I was just asking. If the drinks are decent and the music good, I'm in. Might have to stop and get some ones, though," Tracy said playfully. "Good thing my phone is charged. I have to get plenty of pics of you with ass shaking in your face."

Tonya sputtered. "I would never—" She took a deep breath and peered at Stephanie. "It's not, is it? A strip club?"

"If I say yes, will it keep this conversation going? I have to tell you, I'm very entertained."

Tonya glared.

Stephanie laughed. "No, from what I've read, it's like a roving club. The owners contract with local bars to use their space and advertise the location on Facebook. It's supposed to be all-inclusive."

Surprised, Tonya said, "I've never heard of it."

"Because you so have your ear to the ground about this kind of thing?" Stephanie asked.

Tonya didn't. She really didn't. Good Friends suited her just fine. It was sedate and personable.

"I haven't heard of it either," Stephanie admitted. "It actually looks like it's for a younger crowd."

Tracy snorted. "Well, this should be interesting. Especially for Grandma over here." She poked Tonya in the shoulder.

Tonya sighed. "I don't know—"

"See!" Tracy capitalized on her sister's hesitation. "Knock the dust off and live a little."

Tonya gave Tracy the finger. Customarily it wasn't her way of dealing with things, but it was succinct and better than saying the actual words.

Tracy and Stephanie laughed.

"You're on a roll," Tracy continued. "Don't stop now. I'm sure you can find somebody there to get the sand out of your vagina."

Stephanie was practically howling.

Tonya's mouth fell open. What was going on? "Have you been drinking?" She turned an accusing eye toward her sister.

"Not yet!"

Madigan's, GrrlSpot's venue for tonight, was moderate in size. The red-brick interior should have made the inside stark and cold, but it didn't. Instead there was a warmth punctuated by laughter and jovial voices, the pool tables and pub-style tables and chairs contributing to the overall atmosphere. Within fifteen minutes of their arrival, Tracy was already mingling on the other side of the bar.

From their table, Tonya watched her sister smile and laugh with strangers. She squashed down a pang of jealousy and reminded herself that she knew her own limitations. She just wasn't the overly outgoing type. Tonya nursed what was probably her only drink for tonight, a vodka gimlet, and noticed for the first time that Stephanie was drinking what appeared to be Coke.

"Is there rum or something in that?"

Stephanie shrugged. "Nope. I'll have a real drink later, but knock yourself out. I'll play designated driver. Go wild. Have two drinks." She grinned.

Tonya still didn't know what to make of all this. "Why this place?"

There was no DJ, but the jukebox was in play. Something by Britney Spears warbled through the speakers. It wasn't loud. Tonya could still hear herself speak.

"Wanted to be different. This didn't seem like a piano-and-singing-queens kind of night."

Maybe it wasn't.

As Tonya and Stephanie talked and laughed, Tracy stopped by a time or two to add to the conversation, which was wholly superficial and just what Tonya needed. Sometime later, she decided on that second drink, but the place was much busier than before. Knowing it would be a while before waitstaff came their way, Tonya got up and went to the bar for another vodka gimlet and a Coke, this time with rum.

There was a small space between patrons, and Tonya made her apologies as she leaned in, brushing against one of them. She held up a hand to signal the bartender and caught his eye almost immediately. He smiled and nodded.

The back of Tonya's neck started to tingle, but she pushed the feeling aside as she waited patiently. A couple of people bumped her as they walked past, leaving her hypersensitive. Tonya felt someone behind her. She glanced over her shoulder.

"I'm still not gettin' the hooker vibe from you." Haley smirked, then her lips curled further, forming a wide smile.

Tonya blinked. A wave of heat started at her toes and eased its way up, giving her a buzz like she'd had that second drink already.

"Officer Jordan." Tonya couldn't keep the surprise from her voice.

Haley's brows shot upward but her grin remained. "Dr. Preston." She inched a little closer, and her expression turned serious. "How are you?"

Tonya met Haley's gaze. She expected to feel aggravated by the question, but she didn't. "As well as I can be, I suppose. You have another shooting under your belt yet?"

Her blue eyes lightened to gray, and that crooked smile was back. "Not yet. Hopefully the next one won't be at a gas station."

Tonya smiled slightly. It felt good to make light of the situation, especially with someone who had been there. "Only banks and fast food restaurants from now on, yes?"

"Let's hope. Sounds excitin'."

"Let me know how that goes for you." The words were out of Tonya's mouth, and her brain took a few seconds to catch up. Flirting. It sounded like flirting, even though that hadn't been her intention. Tonya stepped back, but Haley hovered. She was a little taller and a lot stockier.

Haley chuckled. "Uh-oh. Do you want me to forget you said that?" Her gaze didn't waver, and it held a curiosity that was hard to miss.

"Do whatever you like with it." There it was again. Words just falling out of her mouth. Tonya looked away.

"Hey, lady? Did you want something?" the bartender asked.

Thank goodness the universe granted her a reprieve. "Uhm, yes. Vodka gimlet with Belvedere and a Coke with spiced rum."

The bartender nodded. Tonya expected Haley to quietly slink away. Instead, she was looking at the board above the bar where the specials were written.

"I'm starvin'. Have you ever eaten here?" Haley asked like the last few seconds hadn't happened.

"No, I haven't. This is my first time here."

"I looked on Yelp before I came, but you can't always trust that." Haley paused and glanced at Tonya. "It's your first time at GrrlSpot too."

"It is. You're a regular?"

"Yes, plus, you'd be hard to miss." Haley shoved her hands in her pockets. Their shoulders brushed and that buzzed feeling returned.

Tonya swallowed down the compliment and decided to move past it. She glanced at Haley's T-shirt. "What's *Warehouse 13*?"

"Geeky TV show on Syfy. Does some great things with history."

"You have a closet full of those kinds of shirts, don't you?"

Haley grinned. "Sure do."

A small group of young women eased up around Haley. One of them nudged her. "What's taking so long? There's twenty other people waiting for pool tables. So the sooner I start kicking your ass..."

The other women laughed. Haley's forehead scrunched. She looked irritated. "Well, start without me, then. I'm still waitin' to order."

Tonya watched them quietly. Haley hadn't even indicated to the bartender or waitstaff that she wanted anything. Tonya turned and glanced toward her table to get Stephanie's attention, but she wasn't there. She looked around and found Tracy and Stephanie standing together staring right at her. That wasn't good. That wasn't good at all. The questions and the teasing…so much fun. Tonya turned back to the bar, but their gazes burned a hole between her shoulder blades.

"Fine. Whatever, just hurry up," one of Haley's friends said.

Haley shrugged, and a few seconds later, the group walked away.

"Was that your entourage?"

"Unfortunately. You wanna save me?"

Tonya couldn't help but laugh. Officer Jordan was laying it on a bit thick. It was getting hard to breathe, and not in a good way. "I know you haven't been a police officer for long, but it's probably best that you don't save people and then hit on them later."

Instead of looking offended, Haley's expression was thoughtful. "I didn't save you. You did that yourself. I was just along for the ride, so to speak."

"Interesting justification." My God, was she going to have to go pour her own drinks?

"Isn't it? And I won't apologize for hittin' on you. I didn't think I'd ever see you again, so I took this as a sign."

"I'm sure there are plenty of other women here—"

"Obviously." Haley smiled.

"You know what I mean."

"I do." Haley fluttered her eyelashes.

"That's a vodka gimlet and a rum and Coke. Sorry 'bout the wait." The bartender interrupted with his ever-perfect timing. He sat the drinks on the counter in front of Tonya.

This girl was a clown, but that still didn't make her any less intriguing. Tonya reached for the drinks and had every intention of saying her good-bye's and leaving. "I'm sure you'll find a few that listen to Linkin Park, play video games, and tweet until their thumbs are sore," she said instead.

Haley nodded and raised a brow. "Probably, but who's Linkin Park?"

Tonya stared and just barely kept a smile from forming.

Haley held up her hands in surrender. "Okay, fine. I know a few songs, but they're so passé. Should I be insulted that you reduced my generation to a sentence or two?" Her eyes flashed. She crossed her arms over her torso, making her muscles appear more prominent.

"No more offended than *I* should be, considering how we met. Flirting with me doesn't feel a little weird to you?" Tonya answered. She recognized the challenge in Haley's gaze and in her stance.

Surprisingly, Haley shook her head. "Nope, but maybe I shoulda just started out with offerin' to buy you a drink."

"You're old enough?" Tonya couldn't help herself.

Haley's eyes narrowed. Then she threw her head back and laughed. "Yeah, yeah, I am." She didn't look insulted at all. Her gaze was heated but soft at the same time. "I think runnin' into you and this conversation are gonna be the most interestin' things to happen to me tonight."

Tonya tightened her grip on the drinks. Their coolness provided contrast to the warmth that pierced her. She wasn't sure how to take Haley's response. "Was—"

"It was a compliment…definitely. I think I should probably get back to my friends." Haley backed away.

Suddenly, Tonya really didn't want this to end. "I thought you were starving?"

Haley smiled, teeth and all. "I am." She cleared her throat. "It was nice seein' you. Have a good one."

Tonya held her gaze and offered a tight smile in return. "You too." She watched Haley walk away, disappointed to see her go. Tonya barely had time to take a breath before Stephanie and Tracy closed in on her.

"Okay…okay, what was that? Better yet, who was that?" Stephanie asked. "It's been a while since I've seen you chat anybody up."

"For real! Never had the pleasure of seeing you on the prowl at all. So you like 'em butch. I don't blame you, especially if they look like that. And did you see her arms?" Tracy grinned. She looked impressed.

Tonya was used to Stephanie's poking, and she was used to giving mundane answers in return. But her sister's curiosity she found interesting and a little disconcerting. Tracy never pressed, and Tonya gave nothing in return. In fact, she could count on her hands the number of times Tracy had been out with them…period. Then again, they usually went to places like Good Friends and Oz, so the possibility of Tonya being approached was always slim.

"I wasn't prowling. This isn't the jungle, and I'm not a damn cat. It's not what you think. She was the cop from Thursday morning, and she was just saying hello."

"Mm, looked like a hell of lot more than hello to me." Stephanie studied her but didn't say anything else. She took her drink out of Tonya's hand and sipped.

"Fine. Let it get rusty. See if I care. Next person down there is going to need a sandblaster," Tracy told her.

Stephanie laughed. Tonya shook her head. Really, what was with this sudden interest in her sexual exploits?

Feeling slightly offended, Tonya asked, "So…did you think I was just going to drag somebody to the bathroom or go to their car?"

"Shit. Why not? I would," Stephanie said.

Tonya glared at her.

"What? I would. Live a little." Stephanie stirred her drink and took a sip.

"I would never do something like that, just to make that clear to both of you, no matter how crappy my day has been." Tonya looked from her sister to her best friend.

Stephanie seemed to deflate a little. Her shoulders drooped. "Fine. Okay, maybe that was a bit much. I was just trying to help, especially after the week you had. Plus, I kinda like this GrrlSpot thing. It's not as pretentious as I thought it was gonna be."

"Maybe." Tonya wasn't sure what to make of it yet. She could feel Tracy's gaze on her and glanced her way. "What?"

"Nothing. I'm…still liking all of this."

The night, so far, continued to be full of surprises. Tonya was seriously thinking about a third drink; without realizing it, she'd almost drained the one in her hand. The back of her neck tingled again, and before she could stop herself, she was looking around. Haley was easy to spot. She stood by one of the pool tables. The cue was in her hand, and as she polished the tip, she stared right at Tonya.

When their eyes met, Haley smiled like she knew a secret. Then she leaned forward, stretching her torso across the table. The muscles in her arms stood out in sharp relief. Her first shot was powerful. The balls scattered, and several made their way into various pockets.

Tonya needed another drink. The remains in her glass were nowhere near enough to alleviate the sudden dryness in her mouth.

CHAPTER 9

"You like it?" she asked Darla, or was it Dawn? Haley couldn't remember.

"Fuck yes!" Her fingernails dug into Haley's shoulders, setting her skin on fire, but Darla wasn't faring any better. The grip Haley had around her waist was going to leave bruises, but she continued to tighten it, controlling every movement and drawing Darla in to match her own rolling hips. Her breasts bounced in Haley's face. She flicked one with her tongue.

"Fuck! I'm—"

A tiny bolt of pleasure shot through Haley, but it was just enough to call this whole thing satisfying. She shortened her thrusts but kept them deep. Haley shook her head violently to keep more sweat from falling into her eyes, but it didn't help much.

Darla stiffened and then went wild, growling and trembling as another orgasm caught up with her. Haley loosened her hold and guided Darla's hips into a slow, rhythmic grind.

"Yesssss." Darla went limp, and her damp red locks trailed over Haley's face as she leaned forward.

After a minute or two passed, Haley gave her an affectionate pat on the ass and squeezed.

"Mmm." Darla lifted her hips, and Haley was free. She slid off Haley's lap, but not before giving her a light kiss. "You got any beer?"

"There's a Kentwood Springs water cooler in the kitchen. Cups are already on top." No. No more drinks. Haley didn't want her staying any longer than necessary.

Darla chuckled as she looked around for her clothes. "This was fun, Haley, but don't get all nervous. I don't wanna cuddle or have an early breakfast."

Naked from the waist down, Haley sat back and breathed a sigh of relief. She spied a pair of panties under the coffee table. Using her big toe, Haley pulled them from their hiding place. "Hey, Darla, you lookin' for these?"

"What did you just call me?"

Dammit. Haley knew this was going to happen. "Uh, sorry."

"It's Dina, by the way, *Ha-ley*." Dina's eyes narrowed. "I know what this is…" She pointed at herself, then back to Haley. "But you can at least be personable about it."

Haley agreed. She was usually more on top of it than this. She held Dina's gaze. "You're right, Dina, I'm sorry." Haley stuffed as much sincerity into her tone as she could.

Dina's mouth opened like she was about to say more, but her eyes widened instead. She probably wasn't expecting an apology. She looked a little sheepish. "Thanks."

Haley grinned. "You're *very* welcome."

Dina's expression warmed, complete with dark eyes and a satiated smile. Several more minutes went by before her guest was completely dressed. Dina smiled wickedly as she looked down and tweaked the head of the dildo still standing proud between Haley's legs.

"Later," she said.

It was enough to make Haley smile again. "Later."

Then she was alone. Her smile fell and Haley realized that she'd been right: seeing Tonya had been the most exciting thing to happen to her all night. She had no idea what to do with that information.

"You were a mistake! There's no way I'd have a child this useless!"

Tonya stood her ground. Her head was down, and her fists were clenched. The tension in her body was the only weapon she had against her mother's words. In the back of her mind, Tonya knew they weren't true, but each syllable scalded her and left welts like boiling-hot water.

"Just tell me what you need, Mama."

Nicole's face was flushed with anger. Her dark curls were frizzy and all over the place like she had been pulling at them. "I did! Ten times already. I shouldn't have to keep saying the same—"

"No, you didn't." Tonya's tone was soft. She took a step forward.

Her mother's expression shifted to utter confusion. "That wasn't you in my room just now?"

Tonya shook her head.

"Oh! I'm sorry. We have a guest, then."

"I think she just left."

"That's a shame."

Just like that, her mother calmed down. The redness in her face went away, leaving her pale once more, and her green eyes didn't look as wild as they had a few seconds ago. She was beautiful again.

"But Daddy and Tracy will be home soon. Why don't we get cleaned up? I know how you like to look good for him."

Her mother nodded and smiled. "I do, and Tracy's so pretty." She took a step toward Tonya. "You both are."

Tonya reached out to her, but there was only empty air.

From behind, someone's hand tangled in Tonya's hair and pulled hard enough for tears to spring to her eyes.

She gasped and then cried out as she was slammed into the wall. Tonya recognized the man's face immediately.

He grinned. "You gone show me what you did to get dat car, ma."

His partner appeared. They looked at each other and laughed. "Look at her. She not all dat. I can get a better piece of ass on any street corner in da East."

"No!" Tonya lashed out at the man closest to her, scratching at his eyes.

"Leave. Her. Alone!"

Tonya whipped her head around at the sound of the familiar voice. Haley stood a few feet away with her gun drawn, and beside her stood an angry-looking Nicole Preston ready to pounce.

Gasping, Tonya bolted upright. She was drenched in sweat, and the covers were tangled around her legs. After several deep breaths, she was more aware of where she was, though her heart continued to race. This was her bedroom. Tonya turned on the bedside lamp to further confirm it.

After putting on her glasses, she scanned the area, looking toward her feet first. Those were her pale purple, five-hundred-thread-count sheets, one of many sets, and the down comforter she'd purchased just last year. Her gaze took in the rest of the room, painted in soothing, warm earth tones. Her heartbeat slowed, taking with it the last vestiges of fear and anxiety.

Dreams about her mother were common. Some were memories and others were her subconscious fabricating the mother she wanted…a mother who fought for her. The rest of it was certainly not what she was used to. *So it begins.* "Great. Just great," Tonya whispered. She'd been through a traumatic event, and there were bound to be some repercussions. Hopefully, nightmares would be the worst of it. Tonya leaned toward the nightstand. She pulled her journal from the drawer, then paused and stared at the photo album that remained. Tonya swallowed, closed the drawer, and began to write the details of her dream. In frustration, she scribbled out the first few lines. They didn't capture what she wanted to say. She needed to be candid and clear. Dr. Finn would want to know everything. Several minutes later, sunlight began peeking through the windows.

Tonya stopped writing when she got to Haley. She was involved in the whole ordeal. Her appearance couldn't be that unusual. Tonya recalled the fierceness in her eyes. No one had ever looked at her like that…no one had ever looked like that *for* her. It was just a dream. Maybe it was because she had been drinking. Maybe it was because she'd seen Haley. Maybe it was because of the impending confrontation with her father. Tonya didn't know. The one thing she *did* know was that she wasn't going back to sleep. When she finished writing, she put her journal away. In the process, Tonya glanced at the one picture of her mother she kept beside her, taken just a few years ago. Nicole's dark, curly hair was peppered with gray, and her haunted green eyes looked even brighter due to the paleness of her skin. She'd heard her father joke one time—back when he did joke—that she was the palest white woman he'd ever seen. Both she and Tracy had inherited their mother's good looks. She sighed and got out of bed.

The smell of coffee wafted up as she made her way to the stairs. Her father was up. When she entered the kitchen, sure enough, he was sitting on one of the stools that lined the island. He glanced up at her as he turned a page in *Gambit Weekly*. Instead of smiling, he looked back down at his paper.

"Morning," Tonya said anyway.

Robert got up then and went to the cabinet, pulling out another mug. Quietly, he poured a large portion of mocha-flavored creamer into the cup before filling the rest with coffee. He pushed it toward her and sat back down. That wasn't how she liked her coffee, but she didn't say anything.

"Sit."

She did and started drinking from her mug. Tonya tried to read him, but all she saw was the tension in his body. Each movement was slow, like he needed to wind up before he could complete it.

Finally, he sucked in a deep, audible breath. "You could've been really hurt. At least maybe NOPD woulda called. Let me know something."

Tonya set her mug down. The sound it made was loud, almost jarring. She swallowed. "But I wasn't. I didn't see a point—"

He slammed his fist on the granite countertop.

The resulting smack made Tonya jump.

Her father glared at her. Hurt and confusion swirled in his eyes and all over his face. It was the most emotion she'd seen from him since his wife, her mother…

"What is wrong with you?" Robert asked softly, enunciating each word carefully. It would have been better as an indignant scream.

Tonya stared at him. Something coiled in her chest. She had to clench every part of her body to keep it from springing forward. "Nothing." Hiding, denying…they were knee-jerk reactions.

"That's some bullshit!"

"I am not a child. You don't get to talk to me like that…" Tonya let her words trail off as she tried to get a hold of the sudden surge of emotions.

"What, in *your* house? Is that what you were gone say?" He stood.

Tonya blinked and deflated a bit. "No…what?" His resentment was clear. It wasn't her fault that he'd lost the store and the home she grew up in. How much had he been holding on to? Was it all going to come out right here and now? She took a breath. "This is your home too. I would never say otherwise."

He looked away and rubbed a hand over his bald head. "No matter what, you still my child." His voice was hoarse.

That other thing was probably something he wasn't ready to tackle, and that was just fine with Tonya. "I know that, Daddy."

"After all we been through the past couple years, what you did was like a slap in the face."

They had been through a lot more than he was willing to admit, but Tonya stayed quiet. Maybe this was what they needed. Maybe things needed to be broken even more in order to fix them.

He was still standing, and his hands were fisted at his sides. "You don't think I care. Do you?"

This was a very loaded question. He did. Tonya knew he did, but she'd been waiting for what seemed like forever for him to show it in some concrete way. She'd watched him with her mother. She'd watched him with Tracy. He had always been so different with them. More demonstrative…more everything. Tonya looked heavenward. She smiled, but there was no humor in it. "I know you do." But how could she share her emotions—how could she share herself—with someone who had discarded and ignored them for so long?

"Then why—" He blinked. "You…you think this is funny? What's *wrong* with you?" he asked for the second time. There was fear in his voice, and she knew why.

"I'm not turning into Mama. You can calm down." Tonya was very matter-of-fact.

His expression hardened, and then there was nothing there at all. "I don't get you, and I don't get any of this."

Tonya looked down into her coffee cup. Of course he didn't. "We're not okay. That's all I need you to get right now."

He picked up his mug and turned away, but not before Tonya saw his hand shaking. There was a loud yawn, followed by the sound of footsteps coming down the stairs.

Wiping her eyes, Tracy walked into the kitchen. She stopped abruptly and glanced between them. There was no way to miss the strain in the air. It was close to suffocating.

"Shit." Tracy covered her mouth. "Um, sorry. Do I need to—"

"You don't need to do nothing," Robert told his younger daughter. He smiled and motioned for her to come closer. Tracy did. He wrapped an arm around her. "It's good to see you, and now I get to say congratulations in person."

Her sister's grin was all sunshine and rainbows. "Thanks, Daddy."

For a moment, Tonya literally could not breathe, and when she did, the pain was horrifying. The jealousy that followed right behind it was a nasty chaser. Her whole body was trembling. Did she want things to continue like this? She couldn't force things to change around her, but she did have the ability to remedy her response.

"You're really okay with us being like this...aren't you?" Tonya stared at her father, refusing to let him run away.

Tracy's eyes widened.

"We're not doing this." His expression was flat and so was his tone.

"It's just a question."

"No, it's not."

Tracy backed out of his arms. "I'm gonna go shower."

At first, it didn't seem like he was going to let her go, but he did.

Now they were alone. They stood across from each other, squaring off like it was a gunfight. Only this time, Tonya was quicker and willing to take risks she hadn't before. She was ready to draw whether he was going to or not.

His eyes were hard. There was a flicker of something else, but it was gone before she could decipher it. "I'm not gone repeat myself. Yah heard me?"

"And I'm not letting this go." For a moment, Tonya let the hurt she felt guide her. Then, mentally, she retreated to tend wounds both new and old. She watched her father do the same, in his own way: He closed the paper he was reading and turned to pour himself a new cup of coffee. Without another word, he walked out of the kitchen.

CHAPTER 10

"He had to know." Tim glanced at Haley as they stopped at an intersection.

"That's just speculation."

"Bullshit. Just think about it."

"I am! Payton can't be everywhere. There's gotta be a shitload he doesn't know about his team or the rest of his coaching staff." Haley threw her hands up in aggravation, but she had to admit that the conversation was stimulating. Things had settled between them a little bit. Haley still found him offensive and ignorant more often than not, but he had his moments.

"The folks that run the Saints have to talk to each other or nothin' would get done. They have to communicate constantly."

That was a big word for him, but she didn't call attention to it. One thing at a time. "The past few seasons have been up and down, and they had some really big losses. I think that pretty much says they don't communicate all that well."

Tim sighed, but it sounded more like a growl. "The balls are gonna always know what the dick is doin. They work together."

Haley stared. That actually made sense. Appalled, she pressed the heels of her hands to her eyes, hoping that applying some kind of pressure to her head would jar her brain. It didn't work. But it was early Thursday morning, and the weekend wasn't that far away. So at least there was that.

"But there's an asshole too. It operates all on its own." Haley blinked. She couldn't believe that had just come out of her mouth.

Tim glanced at her. He pressed his lips together, and one side of his mouth lifted. Haley wasn't sure if it was a grimace or…no. It was a smirk.

He grunted. "True. I need to think on that one."

"You do that." She was not going to smile at him. She wasn't.

"You ever go to any of the home games?"

"Nah, I'm a fan, not a *fan*, and I don't have that type of money. I just watch them on TV sometimes. I've even been known to go to a bar if Nate's free. It's much more fun that way."

"We should go to one before they really start suckin'."

"Maybe," Haley said. She wasn't going to rule it out. He'd probably be a hoot to hang out with once she'd had a shitton of drinks.

Tim stopped at the intersection of Earhart and Carrollton. Two homeless men holding cardboard signs with "Anything helps. God Bless" written on them took advantage of the red light to weave their way around the cars. It wasn't unusual. On most days, there were one or two men and sometimes women at the corner of every stoplight from Earhart to Uptown. They were like postal carriers in a way, out in the sweltering sun or pounding rain; it didn't matter. Panhandling was illegal, but really? She wasn't going to be an asshole, and thankfully Tim wasn't either.

A loud ring filled the car, almost drowning out the voices on the radio. Tim reached for his phone, and after a couple of yeahs and okays, he hung up.

"You got somewhere you gotta be this mornin'?" Tim asked.

He didn't look at her, but in profile, his expression looked the same as always. Haley still stared at him. "Not…really," she said slowly.

"I gotta make a couple stops before we go back to the station."

Tim wasn't asking her permission per se, but he wasn't just doing what the hell he wanted either. Progress came in weird forms sometimes. He made a U-turn on Earhart and headed toward the parish line. Haley looked out the window. NOLA Box Supply stuck out, huge, puke-green, and pristine. Maybe it just looked that way compared to the boarded-up, graffiti-covered houses and the Church's Chicken right next to it.

Fifteen minutes later, Haley rolled her eyes when they pulled into the Krispy Kreme drive-thru. "Really? You drove all the way to Metairie for this?"

"What?"

"Donuts!"

"Whatever." Tim let down the window and barked out his order: half dozen crullers. A couple minutes later, he shoved the still-warm box in her direction.

Haley sat it on her lap. God, the smell made her mouth water. She was going to take one whether he liked it or not. Who the hell could eat six donuts in one sitting anyway? Haley opened the box.

"What the fuck you doin'?"

"What's it look like?"

Tim snatched the box away. "Did I say those were for you?"

"You don't need all six."

Tim closed the box as best he could and put it in the backseat. "I didn't say those were for me either."

Haley stared at the side of his head. "What are you doin' with 'em, then?" Her mind was working a mile a minute, and none of the scenarios were pleasant. They were all vaguely sexual. It was Tim, after all.

"Don't worry 'bout it."

She didn't say another word. Haley really didn't want to know. It was after six when they got to their second destination, which was thankfully Uptown. The sky was bright, and it was already humid. Tim pulled into the driveway of Crest Manor. He got out of the car almost immediately.

A woman in scrubs opened the door. So this was either a nursing home or some kind of assisted-living facility. The nurse didn't let Tim in, but they knew each other. She smiled and nodded and he did that grimace-smirk thing again before handing her the crullers.

He was still grinning when he got back in the car. Part of her wanted to know what or who put that look on his face, but that would mean she was invested in him somehow. The guy was a cartoon character. Haley just couldn't…didn't want to believe there was more to him.

"Shots fired on Belfast and Eagle with at least two gunmen involved. Eight forty-seven needs assistance. Eight twenty-two, are you in the vicinity?"

Tim groaned. "The fuckin' Zoo." He picked up the radio receiver. "ETA ten minutes." He flicked on the siren and glanced in Haley's direction. "Good thing you got some real-life practice under your belt."

"Yeah, for real." She hated that Hollygrove was called the Zoo. NOPD had to be the ones who'd started that. Haley couldn't believe that anybody would think of themselves as caged animals.

They sped down Claiborne to get to Earhart, ignoring traffic signals and swerving around cars that just refused to get out of the way.

Haley's heart jumped in her throat, and she deepened each breath. Despite the sudden surge of adrenaline that sent her heart into double time, calmness was the key.

She was preparing for fight mode.

Flight was not an option.

Haley rolled her shoulders. The bulletproof vest was bulky and awkward, but right now, it had never felt lighter.

Tim turned onto Eagle. The cruiser bobbed up and down as he drove over potholes. "Keep your eyes open."

The other police car was in the middle of the road. There were no officers present.

Haley didn't hesitate to find out why. "This is Officer Jordan. What's your location? Is the scene secure?"

There was a crackle of static.

"That's a negative, Jordan, but no casualties. They shot through someone's windows, but no one was home." He was out of breath. "We are in pursuit on foot and there is no sign of the shooters. We're making our way back to the car to search the other side of Belfast."

"What are we…" Haley stopped mid-sentence as a black man in a basketball jersey and shorts ran past them. There was no way to miss the gun in his hand.

"Shit!" Tim scrambled out of the car, Haley right behind him.

"We're in pursuit of one of the gunmen. I repeat. We are in pursuit, heading east on Belfast!"

Haley ran like her ass was on fire. She passed Tim and was on the heels of the shooter. She expected bullets to whiz past her head, but he was either out of ammo or too scared to fire on the police.

He was probably just out of ammo.

They zigzagged between houses. The air was stagnant, hot, and overwhelmingly humid. Sweat dribbled down Haley's face, stinging her eyes.

Dogs barked angrily.

Haley waved and yelled at the few people who were actually standing around watching. "Get down!"

The gunman kept glancing over his shoulder. His eyes were wide. Haley was gaining on him.

Seeing an opening, Haley lunged, and they both dropped to the grass. His gun went flying into the yard.

He tried to struggle, but Haley kept a knee in his back as she forcefully pulled his arms behind him.

The man cried out, but that didn't keep Haley from cuffing him.

Haley stood. Hearing a racket behind her, she glanced over her shoulder to see another man slightly bent over and sucking wind, but it was the gun in his hand that gave her pause. Shit.

With a quickness she didn't know she possessed, Haley unholstered her Glock. "Drop it!"

He straightened and looked up. His eyes went wide with panic, but he raised his weapon anyway.

Haley held her ground. She concentrated on her breathing once more. It heightened her awareness.

"Nigga, shoot this white bitch and let's go!"

Time slowed, and Haley heard every second as it ticked by. The man's shiny silver 9mm somehow seemed bigger, closer. Haley aimed at his chest. She was poised to shoot.

Tim appeared out of nowhere, smashing the man in the back of the head with his weapon.

He didn't even cry out in pain as he crumpled to the ground.

Haley met Tim's gaze. Slowly, she lowered her gun.

"You all right there, Rook?" Tim was red-faced and breathing hard, but there was a glimmer of concern in his eyes.

"Ye—" Haley's voice was husky, thick. She cleared her throat. "Yeah, I'm good. Thanks for—"

"Yeah, you're welcome." Tim nodded, but he stared at her for a few more seconds before pressing the button and talking into the radio on the shoulder of his shirt. "This is Hudson. We got your shooters."

By the time Haley left the station, it was well past ten. She yawned as she weaved through the parking lot to get to her truck. A sense of satisfaction and accomplishment settled over her, but fear was there too.

Haley refused to let it overtake her. She couldn't. Death had stared her in the face again, and it was closer than before. It was a hell of a thing to have to deal with, but the constant threat to her mortality was a reality of her job. She couldn't let herself get used to it. That meant complacency. That meant sloppiness. That meant a step closer to being jaded. Haley didn't want to be any of those things. So, while she didn't let fear overwhelm or incapacitate her, she acknowledged it, and was going to keep on doing so in order to stay sharp…in order to keep sight of her own humanity.

Then there was Tim. She'd been so sure she had him pegged. Yeah, what he did was his job as a cop and her partner, but the concern in his eyes had her thinking he wasn't the fuckwit he presented himself to be. There was more to him, and maybe no one else bothered to look deep enough to know what it was. Maybe she needed to be the first.

Haley's stomach growled. She could go home, eat a bowl of cereal, and sit half-naked on her couch, but she didn't want to be alone. Nate and Jen were probably dealing with the morning rush, but they would never turn her away. She needed to laugh. She needed to feel warm. Hell, maybe she just needed to celebrate life.

Twenty minutes later, Haley found Savoie's parking lot bursting at the seams; she was lucky to find a space on a side street. Haley pulled the door open and let exiting customers out first. She saw Nate almost right away when she walked in. He was laughing and talking with the hostess.

It didn't take him long to spot her. Nate waved, smiled, and started to move toward her. As he got closer, he tilted his head slightly to the side and his eyes narrowed.

"You're a couple hours late…no big, but what's wrong?" Nate nudged her slightly and started walking toward the tables in the back.

Haley followed.

"Well? Spill." Nate sat down. The easy smile he usually flashed was gone. He looked worried.

"Just a shitty good time at work. We kept busy all night, but the crap that went down right before the end of my shift took the cake."

Nate's eyes darkened, and he pressed his lips together, making them look thin. "Somethin' Tim did? I swear to God. I don't see how you—"

"No, Tang's…" She paused. "He's actually the hero in this piece."

"Say what?" His mouth dropped open.

"I'm serious."

"Okay, well… I gotta hear this."

Haley told him everything, from the weird situation with the donuts to the foot chase in Hollygrove. By the time she was finished, Nate had gone from red-faced to ashen.

"Jesus, Haley." In those two words, Nate expressed both his concern and his relief.

"I know."

"This is gonna sound corny, but you don't have to hide behind those video games to play the hero anymore. You get to be one every day, and that kinda blows me away."

There were a trillion other things he could have said, but he gave her praise. All of a sudden, it was hard to swallow. It felt good as hell not to be torn down for who she was or who she aspired to be. But then again, he had always been her cheerleader. After five years of friendship, his pom-poms had gotten huge. Haley stared at him.

"You're the shit. You know that?"

Nate smiled. He raised his hand and slowly tilted it from side to side. "Kinda, but I don't wanna seem arrogant."

Haley chuckled. "Yeah, yeah." She was thankful to have somebody like him around. "Where's Jen?"

"On the phone." Nate paused. His expression turned thoughtful. "Now that I think about it, and since the whole video game thing was brought up, Tim would probably fit right in as a character in *Gears of War*."

Haley looked at him as her mind wandered. "I'll be damned. You're actually right."

Nate laughed. "We need help. This isn't normal."

"You got that right too."

"You gonna tell your mom?" Nate asked.

Haley thought about that for a minute. "No. I told you about it. That's enough."

A little bit before noon, Haley was finally on her way home. She was pleasantly stuffed and emotionally renewed. As she drove, Tonya came to mind. She replayed their interaction at GrrlSpot, and it still brought a smile to her face. Sure, the recent excitement at work had her girding her loins, but her meeting with Tonya twisted them a little bit…in a good way. Haley had Tonya's phone number, address, and other identifying information, but using it without permission was a little too stalkerish in her opinion. Besides, Tonya was out of her league. Haley squashed the little voice in her head that reminded her she liked a challenge.

Too bad.

Not to mention that thinking about her was kind of pointless. It wasn't like they were going to see each other again. New Orleans was small, but it wasn't *that* small.

Tonya looked away from the computer monitor and rubbed the bridge of her nose. It did nothing to soothe her headache, but Goody's hadn't worked either. This week had been challenging, to say the least. It was difficult both dispensing and receiving the silent treatment in her own home, but at least it was honest. In the past, she had been able to close her bedroom door and find some peace, but now, tension permeated the very walls of the house. It didn't help matters that she'd refused to say good-bye or even acknowledge Tracy's departure Sunday night, despite Tracy's attempts to reach out to her.

Tonya had reached her limit. She was too hurt and too jealous to talk, to smile, to pretend. Tracy had called several times and sent text messages. There was one that stood out the most.

I want my sister back.

The words had an impact, but at the moment, Tonya couldn't honor that request.

In addition to all that, she was still having the nightmare. But her mother was no longer featured at the end, and Haley had started taking center stage when Tonya's attackers appeared. Standing beside her, Haley would become larger than life as they worked together to take the bad guys down. That part was interesting, to say the least. The nightmares didn't occur nightly, for which she was thankful; but when they did happen, sleep eluded her afterward.

The bright side was there had been no flashbacks otherwise and no anxiety. But due to a death in the family, Dr. Finn wasn't available this week. This left Tonya with the one way to cope that she knew worked. In order to separate one mess from the other and get some distance from everything that was going on, Dr. Preston had to be front and center. This wasn't the healthiest, but it got her through the workday and beyond somewhat successfully.

Someone knocked on her office door. Tonya glanced up to see one of the mental health techs with a patient in tow. She glanced down at her watch. They were a few minutes early. Tonya held up her hand to signal the tech to wait, then moved quickly to her private bathroom and studied her reflection. There were a few unavoidable wrinkles in her shirt, but her appearance was otherwise impeccable. Tonya leaned forward slightly and peered into her own eyes to make sure none of her personal turmoil was hidden anywhere in her features. She couldn't help anyone else find peace if she was broadcasting her own misery. Satisfied, she backed away and went to open her office door.

Minutes later, she was studying the man across from her. He was a new patient.

"We gone do dis or what?" He was young, in his midtwenties, and slouched in his chair with an air of nonchalance.

"We are," Tonya answered.

A little smile lifted his lips at the corner. It transformed his face, but his eyes were still flat and lifeless. "On da desk or on da couch?"

Tonya ignored his attempt at negative-attention-seeking, but maintained eye contact with him. Quiet stretched between them.

He was the first to look away. "All right, damn. Y'all just throw some kind of pills at me and let me go. Ain't no pernt in doin' dis."

"You mean therapy?"

"Yea, whatever."

"It's required. In order for you to be discharged, I have to make sure you're stable." Tonya's tone was crisp, professional.

"Don't I look it?" He opened his arms wide and glanced down at himself.

"Lee, what's your perception of why you're here?" Tonya leaned forward.

He pursed his lips and looked down at his hands, which were back in his lap. "I'm over it," Lee mumbled.

"That may be true, but it could only be temporary."

After a few seconds, his gaze met hers again. His eyes were sad, haunted. "Just 'cause I wanted to die don't mean I'm crazy."

"I agree." Tonya softened her voice. Lee needed her to do so.

His eyes widened in shock. "You do?"

"I do, and I don't like that word, *crazy*, so let's not use it in here, okay?"

Lee nodded. "I don't like dat word *depressed* either. I know that's what you gone say."

"We can call it whatever you want."

He stared at her. His face scrunched up.

"I'm serious." Tonya smiled at him.

Lee shook his head, but he smiled back. "Malcolm. Let's call it Malcolm."

"Malcolm it is."

Later, there was another knock on her door. Tonya wasn't surprised at all when she saw who it was. Stephanie stared back at her. She didn't look happy. There was no smile, no twinkle in her eyes. Tonya couldn't blame her, really. Right now, Stephanie was collateral damage, and she had been receiving the same treatment as everyone else. It didn't matter that she didn't deserve it.

It was just…easier.

Tonya didn't wave her in. She already knew this wasn't going to go well. Stephanie's gaze was unwavering. She walked in and stopped at the chair in front of Tonya's desk, but she didn't sit in it. Instead, she stood behind the chair. Finally, she looked down, brushing the leather. Her touch seemed soft, delicate.

"If I sit here, will you talk to me?" Stephanie's voice was thick, breathy, like it was painful to speak.

Tonya swallowed and looked away, but Stephanie continued. "I know I shouldn't do this here, but this is the only place I can pin you down. I'm tired of the prefab texts." She sat in the chair.

Tonya looked across her desk at her friend. There was a tightness in her chest that she couldn't ignore. "Steph—"

"No...no." She pointed her finger at Tonya. "I'm sitting here, and now you have to listen."

Tonya could only nod. She deserved that and so much more. This woman had been one of the only lights in her life the past year.

Stephanie's relieved exhale was loud, shaky. "I know you...as much as you've allowed me to know anyway. I know when you need space, and I've been trying to give it to you. I have no idea what happened at your house this past weekend, but I can tell it's really got a hold on you."

That was an understatement of huge proportions. However, her words were spot-on. Stephanie paused and looked at her, studied her, and apparently saw what she needed to keep going.

"The people you care about have hurt you, obviously. Your family, I mean... and I get it."

Tonya's fingers dug into the arms of her chair. She wasn't ready to discuss this, but she knew she needed to be, for Stephanie's sake.

Stephanie leaned forward and moved the chair closer to the desk. "But that's not what *you* do. That's not who *you* are." She reached her hand across the desk. "I'm not them and neither are you. Don't repeat their mistakes."

And there it was. The band around Tonya's chest loosened. Her heart was racing, and there was no way to ignore the warmth that started at her fingertips and spread.

"I'm here, Tonya, like I've been all along. I need you to recognize that and give me credit for it."

Yes, it was high time she did.

"I'm having dreams about the attack." The words shot out of Tonya's mouth, and they felt *right*. She wanted to share, needed to. She knew Stephanie would listen. Tonya had *always* known that she would. It was just a matter of her opening herself to it.

Stephanie's expression went from guarded and sad to worried. "Onset of PTSD?"

"Not sure. It's only happened a few times, and there's been no other consistent symptoms."

"Well, that's good, then."

But Tonya wasn't done. "Haley…the cop from the gas station is in them. We usually fight them off together."

Stephanie's eyebrows rose high on her forehead. "Ohhh my." She eased back in the chair, pulling her hand away.

Tonya had forgotten it was even there. She reached out, covering Stephanie's hand with her own. "Just about every night, I dream about my mother and my childhood."

A myriad of emotions chased themselves across Stephanie's features. There was confusion, anger, concern. She squeezed Tonya's hand. "Things were hard for you growing up, weren't they?"

Tonya smiled, but even she could feel the sadness in it. "I'm sorry. I didn't mean to hur—"

"I know, and I am too, for breaking your work rules." Stephanie's eyes were shiny, but there were no tears.

"We can't let any of this become a habit between the two of us. There was no reason to freeze you out."

"Yeah, I agree," Stephanie said.

CHAPTER 11

"I hate you!"

Her mother's eyes were wide, bright, and frantic. "Mama?" Tonya stepped into the bedroom and set the tray of food on a nearby dresser. She squashed down her own anxiety and moved forward slowly with her hands up in surrender. There were times when she could reason with her mother, and Tonya hoped that this was one of them.

"Don't call me that. I know why you're here."

Tonya inched closer to the bed. "Why, Mama?"

"To take everything that's mine," Nicole hissed. "You can't have it, and stop calling me that! You're not my Tonya. She's taller."

Tonya swallowed as her apprehension mounted. "I don't want anything from you. I brought you something, though." The home-health nurse had told her that her mother had refused lunch. She had to be starving by now.

"Why would I take anything from you?" her mother asked. "You can't make me do anything I don't want to!" She crossed her arms over her chest and turned away like a petulant child.

Changing course, Tonya shuffled toward the closet. It didn't hurt to be creative when her mother was like this. Quickly, she slipped out of her sneakers and into a pair of heels that were a size or so bigger than normal, but they made her taller. "I just wanted to give you a snack. You're not hungry? Tracy's at dance practice, and Daddy probably won't be home for a while."

Her mother turned slightly. Instantly, the wild look in her eyes was gone. "Tonya? Baby?"

Tonya nodded.

"What did you bring me?"

Tonya picked up the tray again. "Chessi ham and cheese with mayo."

Nicole smiled, and for a second, everything almost felt normal. "I'm starving. Thank you, my baby."

Tonya wavered. With a tentative smile, she stepped closer and laid the tray across her mother's lap. As she pulled away, her mother's hand shot out and grabbed her upper arm. A couple of her fingers dug into the meaty part of the muscle. The pressure was uncomfortable at first, but jumped to painful as she squeezed harder and harder.

Tonya gritted her teeth and tried her best to wriggle away. When she broke free, Tonya stumbled backward and pressed her hand against the throbbing spot on her arm. She looked down to see angry red marks that were more than likely going to be bruises later. Warily, she glanced at her mother.

She was eating her sandwich.

Turning to go, Tonya stopped as her mother started to speak.

"I knew it was you all along, Tonya. It's not nice to play games like that with your mama."

Suddenly weary, Tonya didn't bother to respond. She pulled the door open, intent on escape, only to see her father standing on the other side.

He stared down at her. He had to see the finger marks on her arm. He had to see.

His face was unreadable. Tonya waited for him to say something. She waited for him to show concern. Several seconds passed, and there was nothing.

He turned and started to walk away.

"Daddy?"

He didn't stop.

"Daddy?" Tonya moved quickly. She grabbed his arm and yanked as hard as she could. He jerked away, but he'd stopped and was looking at her.

"The pills don't work. All they do is make her sleep. Can you tell somebody? Maybe if she had better medicine—"

"She'll be fine." He started walking again.

Tonya stood there and watched. Her heart was pounding, and the ache in her chest felt like it was going to swallow her whole. Then she peered down at her feet. The shoes were so big on her. She was surprised that she hadn't hurt herself. Tonya kicked them off. She'd left her sneakers behind in her mother's room. They were her favorite, and even though she had other shoes, Tonya decided to go barefoot for the rest of the day.

Tonya woke up suddenly. There was no scream on her lips, but cold beads of sweat rolled down her face. Her heart was slamming against her rib cage, and she was breathing raggedly. She sat up in bed and kicked the covers away. Tonya scanned the room, acclimating herself, and when she was done, she reached for the journal in her nightstand. With shaking hands, she wrote as quick as she could.

These weren't repressed memories. Tonya remembered her childhood just fine, both the painful moments and the better times. At one time, she'd been convinced that it was some kind of cruel twist that she relived everything in her dreams. Now, she knew better. They were a reminder that she still had pain to deal with, a reminder that she could either let those feelings consume her or let go and forgive.

Tonya wasn't sure which one she was going to do today, especially where her father was concerned. She'd forgiven her mother long ago. Her behavior… her illness empowered Tonya to read and learn, as well as advocate for Nicole. Eventually, she did get better medicine and she did improve. It wasn't by leaps and bounds, but it was enough to where she had more lucid moments…where there was some normalcy.

Tonya took a cleansing breath. At least something good had happened this week. Those men who assaulted her had pled guilty. There was no need to testify or see them ever again. Yes, at least there was that. She glanced at the clock. It was just past 4:00 a.m. What was an extra hour of sleep anyway? Tonya got out of bed, removed the scarf covering her curls, and started getting dressed for the gym.

The sun was peeking through the clouds and lightening the sky when Tonya returned home. When she entered the kitchen, her father was sitting, enjoying his coffee and leafing through the latest edition of *Gambit Weekly*. It had been two weeks, and they had barely said a word to each other. Tonya and Dr. Finn had agreed that in order for a stalemate of this level to end, a series of confrontations needed to occur. In short, she had to fortify herself against more pain and more denial, and at the same time, Tonya had to be ready to voice her own emotions on the matter. They both needed to listen. They both needed to be heard. She just didn't know if that was possible.

Robert glanced up briefly, then went back to his routine. Tonya got a bottle of juice out of the refrigerator and headed toward the stairway.

"You can go on be mad at me for whatever reason, but your sister didn't do nothing. She told me how you been ignoring her."

Tonya stopped. She didn't turn around just yet. She could hear him shuffling the paper nonchalantly, like this was a normal conversation. Tonya's hand wrapped around the banister. The wood was cool and unyielding, just like he could be. Slowly, anger infused her. It started at her fingertips and moved swiftly to the rest of her body, making her tremble.

There was no way he could be that blind.

She stepped back and moved toward him, but he didn't even acknowledge her with a glance. When she got to the kitchen island, Tonya reached across. In a gesture of controlled violence, she yanked the paper away from him.

He looked at her then. His eyes were wide and shocked. He covered it quickly into something blank and unreadable.

"I haven't forgotten anything that happened. I'm sure you wanted me to." Tonya's voice was soft, deceptively so for the amount of anger boiling underneath. He looked away, but his jaw clenched. "Good, I'm going to take your silence as acknowledgment."

"All that happened a long time ago. Just let it be, dammit." Her father's gaze met hers briefly before it skittered away.

"I wish it was that easy. I really do."

"Your sister did."

Tonya's emotions flared so hot, she could barely contain them. She had to take several breaths to put out the fire raging in her chest. "She didn't see half of what I did, and she sure as hell didn't have the same experiences I did! You're not a stupid man. You have to know that adds up to something."

"Why you gotta be so disrespectful?" Robert stood and glared at her.

Tonya glared right back. "I'm not disrespecting you, Daddy. I'm just so tired. I can't pretend anymore. I don't have the energy. Mama was sick. She didn't know what she was doing, but what was your excuse?"

His lips thinned, but he said nothing.

"Were you that angry at me? Was it to punish me?"

His expression morphed into confusion. "What you—"

"Because of who I am!" Tonya slammed her hand against the counter.

Her father jumped.

His reaction deflated Tonya a little. "When Mama first started showing symptoms, I wanted to help out. It made me feel special, but it got to be too much. Everything was just too much." Tonya shook her head as memories bombarded her. "Nothing made me feel good anymore, and when I thought I found something…someone that made me feel right, you beat the shit out of me and my life became a nightmare."

"You damn right I did. Look at you now. You a doctor. You did something with yourself."

"That was despite what you did, not because of it!"

"That's bullshit, and I'm done talking about it." He grabbed his coffee mug and threw it in the sink. It made a loud clang, and she could tell the cup shattered. Then he marched through the living room and out the front door.

Tonya watched him leave. She didn't bother to go after him. There was no point. Twenty plus years, she'd been dealing with this. Was it any wonder she was exhausted? Whoever her father thought she was, Tonya couldn't be that person anymore. That much was clear.

She was too many people already.

Her thoughts shifted to her sister and then inconceivably to Haley. Tonya wondered what it would be like to be young again and get the chance to be carefree, or at least have some semblance of that feeling. Maybe, just maybe, it was time to find out.

Tonya took the cap off her juice and drank. Her father was right about one thing. She needed to stop closing Tracy out.

With disgust and awe, Haley watched Tang demolish a huge, bone-in fried chicken breast in record time. "How can you eat that? It's nothing but grease."

"Bullshit. Church's spicy is way better than Popeyes, and the pieces are bigger. It's like their chicken is anorexic or some shit." He wrapped the leftover bones in a napkin and dropped them in the Church's box.

He did have a point. "True," Haley grudgingly agreed. "I like to stay loyal, though, or try to."

Tang licked his fingers and stared at her. "To chicken?"

"When you say it like that…"

He snorted. "Tomorrow we're gonna do a blind taste test."

Haley rolled her eyes. "Whatever."

"Uh-huh, you say that now."

Haley smiled. "Just drive."

"I got a couple extra biscuits in a separate bag. I know you like 'em. You can duck down when we pass Popeyes so they won't see you and keep most of your loyalty."

"Fuck you." It was true. She had developed a love for their biscuits over the past couple weeks. Without saying a word, she picked up the bag and dove in.

Tang chuckled. "Welcome to the Dark Side."

Haley glanced his way as she finished off one biscuit and started on another. Things had settled between them. She wasn't sure what the actual turning point was because there had been a few of them. He was still an asshole, but he had some depth. The man was funny, and sometimes it wasn't in that offensive, hide-your-face way. "You a fan?"

They stopped at a red light, and Tang looked at her like she smelled like hot garbage.

Haley smiled. "I guess that's a yes."

"It's a fuck yeah. What the hell's wrong with you?"

Haley shrugged. "Not everybody's into it."

"Then they're not American."

Haley laughed. "For real." Suddenly, she got curious. "You a gamer?"

He gave her that look again.

She pressed her lips together to keep from smiling. "Console or PC?"

"PS3, Rook."

Haley was shocked. "I just lost my faith in humanity."

Tang snorted again. "I have a 360 too. Just play the PS3 more."

"Mm-hm."

"Too many damn kids on 360. What's your tag? I might log on now that I got ahold of someone decent and over ten."

"BadassJordy87."

"All right, then, Rook. *Call of Duty*?"

"You're on." Haley paused. "You play *Gears*?"

"Fuck yeah," Tang sputtered.

Haley laughed.

"What?"

"Nothin'. Just somethin somebody said."

"One of your girlfriends?"

Haley sighed. "No, why—"

"Be honest. How much ass you get?"

She groaned. "You were doin' good. Do you actually think about shit before it comes out your mouth?"

Tang shrugged. "Does it matter? Million different ways to say things. Might as well just cut to the chase."

"Piss more people off that way."

He shrugged again. "You don't look pissed to me."

"I'm not." Haley didn't say anything for a few seconds, but she viewed this as an opportunity of sorts to get to know him. "I tell you what. Answer my questions, and I'll do the same for you."

Tang turned on Toledano, and in the process gave her a side-eye. He grunted, and Haley assumed it was a yes. She decided to start out with something simple. "I know you're from 'Bama. How long have you been here? You leave any family back there?"

"Seven years all together, I think. I met my ex-wife here. We divorced last year, and now I'm payin' her lazy ass alimony 'cause she can't keep a job. As far as family goes, naw, it's just me and my uncle. He pretty much raised me." Tang paused. "He's gettin' up there, though. Needs someone to watch over him all the time. Goddamn Medicare won't pay for a nurse 'round the clock at home."

It was like somebody shined a fluorescent light in her eyes. "He's at Crest Manor and he likes donuts?"

"Yeah. It's a private-owned rest home. It's not cheap, but it's nice. Most of the others are shit. A lot of the time he doesn't remember me, 'specially if I'm in uniform. That mornin' we went he had a hard time the night before. I didn't wanna rile him up more."

Haley was floored. She cleared her throat. "So…me and ass?"

Tang chuckled. "Yeah, you and ass."

"I get my fair share."

He glanced at her. There was a little smile on his face. "No shit?"

"No shit."

"I do all right too. Even with this ugly mug."

Haley stared at his profile. "One more thing?"

"Yeah?"

"Why don't you just use *poon* instead of *tang*. It would be easier to figure out. At first, I thought you got it because you like that stupid orange drink."

He looked at her like she was slow before turning his attention back to the road. "'Cause Tim 'Poon' Hudson sounds stupid."

Haley had to bite her tongue to keep from laughing. "Yeah, I see your point."

"Good. Now, one more thing I gotta do before we start makin' rounds. Just take a few minutes."

Haley sighed. "Fine."

Tang stopped in front of a shotgun on Washington. As he got out of the car, a black man was already walking out of the house. Haley turned in her seat so she could see everything that was going on. She decided it would be rude to roll down the window, but she was tempted. They stopped midway up the sidewalk. Tang stood in front of the other man, making it hard to see.

They didn't shake hands. They didn't hug. They just stood there, talking and standing at least a foot away from each other. Tang nodded his head a few times, and after a few minutes he turned slightly to peer over his shoulder at her. It was enough to give her a view of the man's face. He looked kind of like the guy they chased a couple weeks ago over on St. Andrew.

That didn't make sense.

Haley craned her head to try to get a better look, but she couldn't. She had to know. The weird flutter in her stomach told her so. She was about to open the passenger side door, but Tim was on his way back to the car. The other guy had already disappeared into the house.

Tang got in and put on his seat belt. Haley stared at him. There was no need to mince words. "Was that the same man you chased down over on St. Andrew?"

"What?" His voice went up an octave. "No! What kind of sense would that make?"

That's what she'd thought. "Who was he, then?" Not that it was any of her business, but she had to ask anyway.

"Damn. Nosey much?" He sounded irritated but not angry. "He's just somebody I check on from time to time."

"Things didn't look too friendly." Haley really needed to shut up, but words kept falling out of her mouth. She wasn't sure why she was so suspicious.

"I'm not a hugger, and that kid's business isn't mine to tell. Can we go to work now? Or do you wanna know who's blowin' me too?"

Haley glanced at him. His expression gave nothing away, but that didn't mean anything. Well, now she felt like shit. She'd jumped to all kinds of conclusions, or at least partway there. Haley cleared her throat. "Sorry."

Tang grunted in response.

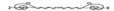

"Just got a call from intake. We have an involuntary committal, a male. One of the police officers who brought him in refused to let our guys escort him up. They're bringing him themselves," Stephanie said.

That sounded ominous. Tonya glanced at her watch. They still had time to make sure he was comfortable or get him that way before shift change. She nodded. "Okay, I'll check to see if his information is viewable yet. Give me his name. I'll look it over and be out in a minute."

"Will do." After dispensing needed information, Stephanie flashed a tired smile and left Tonya's office.

Tonya typed quickly, and when she found what she needed the words "possible psychotic break," "violent outbursts," "destruction of property," and "threats toward others" stuck out like the red flags they were. She minimized the program and stood. Even if most of them didn't like her, Tonya would never make her staff do what she wouldn't. If they had to be out there, so did she.

A few minutes later, the private elevator that led to the mental health floor dinged. The hospital staff escort stepped to the side to allow the occupants to exit. Tonya looked up. Something deep in her stomach fluttered. The universe had to be playing tricks on her.

"Oh my God," she whispered.

Their newest patient had his head bowed and his hands in cuffs behind his back. He moved docilely toward the main desk. He wasn't who caught her attention. It was one of the officers behind him.

Haley Jordan's eyes widened slightly, but her expression was serious.

Tonya had forgotten how blue her eyes were. The flutter in her stomach became something a little bit more.

Haley tore her gaze away and leaned forward to say something to the man they had in custody.

The man nodded, and the other officer walking beside Haley rolled his eyes.

Someone nudged Tonya from the side. "Is that the cop that…?" Stephanie whispered.

Tonya shushed her. Haley appeared more intimidating in uniform. The gun, taser, and pepper spray attached to her belt only added to the mystique. She looked dangerous. Haley said something else to the man, and he started to cry. She squeezed his shoulder. *Dangerous* was far from the right word.

When Haley and her companions got to the desk, Tonya was still standing there staring. A few seconds passed. It was Stephanie who stepped forward, which was enough to galvanize Tonya into action. Everyone was looking at her. She could feel it.

Haley reached out her hand, and Stephanie took it. "I'm Officer Jordan. If this break in procedure caused any problems, I apologize. Al felt more comfortable with us bringin' him up."

"There's no problem at all," Stephanie assured her.

Haley glanced at Tonya, who decided it was time for her to take charge of this situation. "His evaluation at intake led us to believe the situation would be more volatile."

Haley nodded. "He was, but once things calmed down, he wanted to come."

Tonya had a feeling that Haley had a lot to do with that. "Thank you for the additional courtesy."

Haley's smile was full, wide, and it changed her entire face just like Tonya remembered. Her lips curved upward, accentuating her prominent cheekbones, and her eyes seemed much brighter. This look suited Haley, and the ease with which she did it led Tonya to believe that this was a more natural state of being for her.

"You're welcome, Dr. Preston." Haley's gaze lingered.

"We'll take it from here," Tonya said. This prompted her team to action, but she stayed front and center. Haley was intriguing. On the outside, she looked hard, or that's what she attempted to cultivate. On the inside, there seemed to be a wealth of warmth that she wasn't afraid to show or to share.

There was no danger here.

"Y'all just stand here and chit-chat." The other officer glanced at Haley, then back at Tonya. "I'll make sure he gets to his new digs."

Two techs led the way, and the other psychiatric nurse trailed behind them. Stephanie coughed.

Tonya ignored her. Something was happening, and she wasn't sure what.

Haley's smile softened, but it was still just as effective. "Can I call you?"

Stephanie coughed again and elbowed Tonya in the ribs.

Haley's eyes went wide, and she rubbed the back of her neck. "I mean...to check on him."

"Yes." Tonya's voice was higher than usual, but her response felt right. It felt *good*, and she hadn't really experienced that in a long time. She wanted to start rectifying that, and today was as good a time as any.

Tonya saw the same challenge and amusement in Haley's eyes that she'd seen at GrrlSpot, and she wondered if she'd been expecting to get rejected.

Haley's partner walked around the corner. He didn't speak to them, but he nodded in Haley's direction.

"Have a good night," Haley said as she turned to go.

Tonya watched them as they moved toward the elevator. When they were halfway there, Haley looked over her shoulder. Her expression was playful, but there was an intensity in her eyes that was impossible to miss.

Tonya inhaled sharply at the sudden heat that coiled through her. It was quite the rush. After a few more seconds, she tore herself away to go check on their new patient. Stephanie was on her heels, but thankfully, she didn't say a word.

Later, in the process of getting ready to leave, Tonya wasn't surprised when her office door opened. Stephanie entered and leaned against it.

"Oh. My. God." She bounced around like a cheerleader. She had the look. It fit.

Tonya glanced up. "Couldn't hold it in?" She couldn't help but smile.

"Hell no!" she whispered loudly. "I'm sorry. You know I don't usually act like this, but I don't usually see what I just witnessed. Technically we're off work, though, so I can say whatever I want."

Tonya had an argument for that. "But, we're still—"

"No, don't even go there." Stephanie pointed her finger at Tonya. "Now, you do understand she was asking to call to talk about *you*, not the patient? Although I wouldn't be surprised if she did that too."

"Neither would I," Tonya agreed. "And yes, I'm not an idiot."

"Then why aren't you excited? Actually, I've never really seen you *be* excited, so I'm not at all sure what to look for." Stephanie looked thoughtful.

"I…" Her voice trailed off. Yes, why wasn't she? There *was* a giddy warmth buzzing inside her.

"It's okay to be excited, Tonya."

Their gazes met. "I know that," she said quickly.

"Do you?"

Tonya let her emotions take over. She'd started the morning wanting to do…wanting to feel something different. Everything that had happened in the last thirty minutes was a step in the right direction.

"Yes." She smiled. "I do."

CHAPTER 12

All it took was a phone call and some begging, and Haley agreed to meet the gang for Ladies Night at The Country Club. She was off tomorrow anyway, so they didn't have to twist her arm that hard. So she laughed, had a few drinks, took a dip in the pool. A little over an hour had passed, and she was already ready to leave.

"I think I'm gonna go."

"What? You just got here," one of her friends protested, drawing the attention of the others.

Haley shrugged. "So? I came. That's what matters, right?"

They grumbled but didn't try to stop her a second time.

Haley was at the door when someone grabbed her arm. She turned around.

"Hey! I've been calling your name for, like, a full minute. I just got here, and you're leaving?" The woman grinned.

She looked familiar. Blonde, short, curvy, and with a killer smile. Haley racked her brain. "It's Julie, right?"

Julie nodded.

"I'll call you." Haley wasn't going to do any such thing. She didn't even know if she had Julie's number.

"Anything I can do to get you to stay a little longer?" Julie's smile turned wicked.

Well, shit. What do you do when you get an invitation like that? Haley stared. This could be a lot more stimulating than her last hookup.

She grinned. "Lead the way."

Haley ignored the knowing looks that other women were giving them as they went into a bathroom stall together. She locked the door and leaned against it. Julie sank to her knees.

Now she remembered her. Julie wasn't afraid to get a little dirty.

Julie held her gaze as she unzipped Haley's pants. She reached in and pushed Haley's underwear aside to pull the black toy free. Julie wrapped her hand around it and pumped softly.

She swirled her tongue around the head.

Haley rolled her eyes. She was bored, but there was no need to be rude. She pushed the growing hollow feeling aside and kept going.

Julie looked up at her. Her gaze was predatory as she swallowed down a large portion of the shaft.

Haley smiled tightly. She brushed the hair away from Julie's face and touched her cheek. "Come up here."

Julie stood. Her breathing was loud and uneven. Haley kissed her until she whimpered and clung to her. Then she slid her fingers under Julie's skirt. She wasn't wearing any underwear, which made teasing her slit a hell of a lot easier. She was already wet.

Julie moaned.

"Turn around for me."

Julie didn't hesitate. She lifted her skirt and leaned forward, putting her hands on the toilet tank.

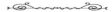

There was a pleasant burn in Haley's muscles still, despite having finished her workout thirty minutes ago, but it was a hell of a lot more satisfying than last night. She sucked down the rest of her Gatorade and opened the door to her home. She walked through the French doors that led to her bedroom and threw her bag on the queen-sized bed before heading toward the bathroom. After throwing the empty Gatorade bottle in the trash, she pulled her shirt over her head. It was designed to wick away sweat, but the damn thing was damp and clammy as hell.

Haley groaned in pleasure a few minutes later as hot water rushed over her. She hummed a Foo Fighters tune in celebration. It was Friday, her day off, and as of a couple days ago, she was officially done with night shift—for right now, anyway. Her humming became all-out singing by the time she started to lather up. She really needed to get one of those shower radios to sing along with so she'd sound better.

She was looking forward to playing catch-up with Nate and Jen. Their normal weekly routine of dinner, drinks, and TV had been thrown off big-time. With Nate and Jen's own changing schedule, they'd only met up once the past month besides the breakfasts, and Haley didn't like that at all. It left Haley feeling a little off-balance. Not that she was the type of person to need much grounding. It just felt good knowing she had a place to unwind, gripe, laugh with people who knew who she was and appreciated it.

Haley stepped out of the shower and toweled off, then walked back into her bedroom and pulled on a T-shirt and boi shorts. Now wasn't the time for pants.

For some reason, her thoughts wandered to her mother. They really hadn't had the chance to talk much the past week. Haley fished her cell phone out of her bag. It was just a little before seven, but her mom was an early riser.

The phone rang twice.

"Yeah?" Jeb greeted.

Haley cringed. "Where's Mom?"

"Went to the twenty-four-hour Walgreens ta get half-and-half. She left her phone."

"Really? You saw it was me; what was the point in answerin'?"

Jeb huffed. "See, this here is why we don't get along. You're so damn disrespectful."

"That's not the only reason. Hard to respect somebody who isn't very acceptin'."

"Well…when ya change your ways, we'll have somethin' to talk about."

"Ditto, Jethro." She was taking her taser next time she visited.

"Who? What did ya call me?"

"Nothin'. Just tell her I called."

"That's what I thought y—"

Haley hung up. She wasn't a kid, and thank God she didn't live at home anymore. Haley understood that a child, even an adult one, shouldn't have a say in a parent's love life. But she didn't get it. What kind of woman marries a man who's against someone she loves? Through all her mother's other marriages, Haley had felt that at least she mattered. She was really beginning to wonder if that was the case anymore. Her good mood went down a peg or two.

She plopped down on the couch and fired up her Xbox. Haley smirked. Tang was online, and as she loaded up *Modern Warfare 3*, her thoughts scattered, then zeroed in on something, someone, else. Tonya. It had been two days, and she couldn't get Tonya off her mind. It was starting to wig her out.

Instead of logging on to the server, Haley picked up her phone again. Yeah, it had only been a couple of days. Wasn't there a three-day rule or something? Screw it, that was probably something men made up anyway. Haley glanced at the time. It was after seven o'clock, and she was sure Tonya was on her way to work.

The phone rang five times before going to voice mail. She listened to it but hung up before the beep. Haley stared at her phone and made the immediate decision to call back.

Tonya answered on the second ring. "Hello?"

"I didn't think you were gonna answer."

"I wasn't."

Well. Haley didn't know what the hell to say to that, so she winged it. "Yeah, most people don't answer unknown numbers."

"I knew it was you. It's very rare someone calls my phone that's not already a contact." Tonya's tone was crisp and kind of aloof.

This was an interesting start. Not. Haley was crashing and burning without even taking off. "Okay. Why, then?"

The seconds ticked by.

"Maybe it would be better if you focused on why I answered instead," Tonya said, softer, hesitant.

Haley gripped the Xbox controller tightly as her stomach did an unexpected flip-flop. "Why?"

"You seem genuine and open. It could have more to do with your age, but—"

"Don't. Don't do that. I'm not twelve and tryin' to make friends with the big girls."

For several seconds, no one spoke. Haley wondered if she'd gone too far, and then decided she'd gone just far enough. Age wasn't going to be an issue—not for Haley, at least. Tonya was going to have to find something else to poke her stick at.

"I'm sorry. I wasn't trying to…sorry." Tonya cleared her throat.

She was nervous. Haley wasn't sure why that made her heart beat a little faster, but she accepted the apology. There was no reason to dwell. She'd made her point. "Okay…so how are you? I know you've probably been asked that fifty million times."

"Not really, but I'm okay. There were some positives and some negatives to come out of the whole thing. Either way, I'm sure I'm doing much better than they are."

"I have to agree with you there. You gonna go to their sentencin'?"

"I think I'll pass."

"Don't blame you."

"Where are you from? People from here don't have Southern accents." Tonya wasn't subtle about changing the subject, and Haley decided to just roll with it.

"Gulfport. We used to come here a lot when I was a kid. Just made sense to settle down here. It's like a second home. I live in a double shotgun at the corner of North Claiborne and St. Roch. I'm not far from Melba's and her fried chicken, and I'm positive that I'm right next door to the frozen-cup lady. The kids line up. She does these cool-lookin' rainbow patterns. So the area is all right compared to some of the others close by."

"The 7th Ward?"

"Yeah."

"That's mighty bold of you. I'm sure you stick out."

"I do, but I'm not the only one. There's a white guy who lives on the opposite corner. I've lived here over a year, and everyone has been neighborly for the most part."

"I grew up in a house over on Elysian Fields. We had a candy lady at the end of the block. So I heard."

"No kiddin'. Was there a huge difference in the neighborhood when you were a kid, you think?"

"Yes…I didn't get out much." Tonya's voice went from strong and enthusiastic to soft and tentative. This was obviously something else she didn't want to get into, and Haley saw no reason to push.

"That happens. So, tell me, do you like your snoballs plain or with condensed milk?"

"I'm sorry…what?"

Haley repeated the question.

"Piña colada and cherry with condensed milk and wedding cake with evaporated milk." Tonya sounded sure again.

"Piña colada, huh? I'm more partial to bubblegum and cotton candy." Haley paused. "No kid jokes, please."

Tonya chuckled.

Haley smiled, and her heart picked up speed again. "You like your po' boys dressed?"

"Yes, oyster fried hard or shrimp extra pickle and with hot sauce."

"Well, of course. Can't forget the hot sauce." Haley sat the Xbox controller on the table and got comfortable on the couch. Tang could wait. "Gumbo with ok—"

"No. Okra is a throwaway food. It adds absolutely nothing to a dish."

"You sound passionate about that. Not even fried?"

"Not even hot and pickled. It's not the taste of it, really. It's the texture."

"Well, aren't you special." Haley laughed.

"Maybe."

"You suck the head?"

There was total silence on the other end.

Haley coughed to cover it up. "On crawfish."

"Oh…*Oh*! I'm from New Orleans."

"Yeah, that was probably a stupid question. So, how's Al?"

"I can only speak in generalities, but he's stabilizing. I'll let him know you asked about him."

"Thanks. I just wanted to ask, but this is more about you than him."

Tonya didn't respond, and Haley wondered if it she was flustered, embarrassed, or just plain uncomfortable. She didn't want to know. "Okay… this is the most important question. Popeyes or Church's?"

"Raising Cane's." Tonya's reply was quick.

"What? That's not even chicken; it's just bits." Haley sat up and her voice rose about three octaves.

"Now who's passionate?" Tonya teased.

"You're laughin' at me. Aren't you?"

"A little bit, yes. I was just kidding. Popeyes, but when I eat it, I add an extra fifteen minutes to my workout."

"I work out too." Haley rolled her eyes. Like nobody could tell that from a mile away.

"I haven't noticed."

"I'll make sure my T-shirt is tighter next time."

"I appreciate that." Tonya paused. "I meant…thanks for informing me."

Haley grinned. "Uh-huh, and just to let you know, I was gonna erase and block your number if you said Church's."

"How do you know I'm going to be the one calling next time?"

"Doesn't matter, as long as I get to talk to you."

"Yes, well, I'm at work, so…"

"This was nice," Haley said softly. "Thank you for answerin' the phone. Have a good one, Tonya."

"Um, you too."

Haley held the phone until she heard it click. That was *really* nice, and she was more wigged out than before. She didn't usually do things like this, but Haley liked the hell out of it.

Tonya nodded hello to some of her crew as she got on the elevator. She took a deep breath and let it out slowly, but her heart was still quivering in her chest. She had enjoyed that entire conversation, even the awkward parts. Haley was funny and bold one minute and sensitive the next. It was a nice combination, and talking to Haley was the easiest thing she'd been a part of in a long time. It was nice to have something be simple even if it was just for a few moments. It was great to feel that flutter again. It had been a while. Not that it had ever ended with anything to shout about. Tonya pushed those thoughts away. She was being presumptuous.

It was just one phone call, but dear God, it felt incredible to just…be. Maybe this was her chance to grab hold of something just for herself, to enjoy life for once. The idea was scary and exhilarating all at once.

The elevator dinged and opened.

She was jumping ahead of herself. This could all just be a case of some young butch trying her hand at an older woman. Tonya dismissed the thought as soon as it came. It wasn't like the age gap was astronomical. Plus, she wanted to see all of this as a positive, and that meant not creating or fishing for the negative that could be nonexistent.

Tonya headed straight for her office. Before she could get it open, Stephanie appeared.

"You didn't answer my text. Does that mean you were on the phone?"

"I was driving," Tonya reminded her. It wasn't exactly a lie, but it wasn't the whole truth either.

"Have you heard from her yet?"

Tonya entered her office, Stephanie right behind her.

"We'll have to talk about this later."

Stephanie screeched. "I knew it!"

"Jesus, we're at work." Tonya tried really hard to keep her smile at bay and barely succeeded.

"Oh please. No one can hear us."

"Still."

Stephanie huffed. "Fine."

Tonya thought that was the end of it. She turned to put her things away. Her purse started to chime, and it wasn't just once. There was a succession of sound. She opened her bag and pulled out her phone.

Four texts, all from Stephanie.

Her phone sounded again. Tonya turned and glared.

As if feeling Tonya's gaze, Stephanie looked up. "What? It's the perfect solution. No one can see or hear."

Tonya sighed. "I'm not going to text you. You're standing right in front of me."

"But we have to keep up the shield…you know? Of professionalism."

Tonya smiled. It was too late to pretend like she hadn't.

"I saw that!" Stephanie said.

"Fine!" Tonya sat down, scrolled through the texts, and answered them all.

Did she call?

Yes. This morning.

Were you nice?

Yes.

She was dead set on answering as many as she could with a yes or a no.

What did you talk about?

Snoballs and po' boys.

Did she make you laugh?

Yes.

Are you gonna talk to her again?

Yes. I think so.

Sometime 2day I'm gonna need more than one word answers. Details girl!

Was she that predictable? Tonya looked up. Stephanie was smiling and her eyes were twinkling with amusement.

Obviously, she was.

"Fine," Tonya said, but there was no vehemence to it. She actually wanted to share everything with Stephanie.

A couple hours later, Tonya was putting the finishing touches on a progress note. When she was done, she glanced at the time at the bottom of the computer screen. It was at least twenty minutes until her next patient. Buoyed by the events of the day, Tonya opened the desk drawer and got her phone out of her purse. She didn't want to put this phone call off any longer. "This isn't going to be easy."

Tonya scrolled through her most recent missed calls. Tracy's name was front and center. She pressed her thumb against it.

Her sister picked up almost immediately. "I'm in class. Let me step out."

Tonya didn't reply. She just waited.

"Okay," Tracy said a few seconds later. "You called me." She sounded surprised as well as pleased. "I mean…I know we've never been all that close, but I don't understand this. Did I do something wrong?"

Tonya leaned back in her chair and pressed the phone closer to her ear. She had no idea where to start or how much she could let herself say. Either way, she needed to dole out an apology first. "I'm sorry, and no…you didn't. You're more of a product of your—our—environment. I think I lost sight of that."

"What? What do you mean?"

"Just, what do you remember about Mama and the stuff that went on in our house in general?"

"Not much from when I was young, but when I got older, I thought the whole thing was weird. Not being allowed in her room most of the time. You and Daddy were like the police, and then there was the shouting I'd hear her in the middle of the night sometimes. When I did get to see her, I could tell something was really wrong just by the way she looked at me and acted. I tried to talk to Daddy about it, but he would shut me down every time. I was scared to ask you because, hell, you were weird too. When it gets down to it, Mama didn't exist to me for a long time, and then, it just seemed like one day she was better. There was a lot of lost time to make up for. Didn't count on cancer interrupting that." Tracy paused. "I wish…never mind."

"No, tell me." Tonya got lost in her sister's words. It hurt to know that she wasn't able to protect her from it all.

"I wish everything that happened brought us closer, but you were invisible a lot of the time too. It carried over even though we're not kids anymore. I've tried to close the distance between us, but nothing has ever worked. It just seems like you tolerate me like I'm some problem you have to…fix." Tracy's voice broke on the last word.

Tonya closed her eyes.

"Why? Why are we talking about this now? We should've done it a million years ago."

Tonya tried the swallow down the lump in her throat, but it refused to go anywhere. "I don't know if I can answer that without sounding like I'm just giving excuses."

"Let me guess…" Tracy sounded tired and fed up. "It's just the way we are. We talk around things. Am I right?"

"Pretty much."

"I don't think I want to anymore."

"Me either, or at least, I'm trying," Tonya said softly.

"This thing between you and Daddy, though…"

Tonya stiffened. "It's in a category all by itself."

"Yeah, for real. He's hurting. I can hear it in his voice, and I know he loves you. It—"

"Why can't he tell me that, then?"

"Why can't you?" Tracy asked.

"I'm trying, but he hasn't even bothered."

"There's a lot for him to take in—"

"He's had plenty of time to swallow," Tonya said firmly.

Tracy sighed. "Okay…okay. You're right." She paused. "But we're sisters. No more of this surface shit between us. We need to talk more, be more."

"I want to try that too." Tonya meant what she said. She wanted to make the effort, but she hoped she wasn't going to be spreading herself too thin. It didn't matter. She had to make concessions for the important things.

"Good. I'd better get back to class."

"Okay," Tonya said.

"You're going to answer next time I call?"

"Yes."

"And text?" Tracy asked.

"Yes, I promise."

"Okay, bye. I lo…later."

Tonya didn't call attention to the way Tracy stumbled over her words. One step at a time. "Later."

Haley shoveled a forkful of pasta into her mouth as they started another episode of *Fringe*.

Jen groaned with pleasure. "You put capers in this?"

"Mm-hm."

"How do you think to do things like that? I mean, it's just crawfish pasta."

"It's jazzed-up crawfish pasta," Haley said.

"You need to cook more. You're really good at it."

"Shhh!" Nate waved his hand at both of them.

"We've seen the whole season already," Haley reminded him.

"I know that. I don't remember this episode, and we have to be ready for the final season."

"Ugh, don't remind me that they're cancellin' it."

"I'll just lie to you, then," Nate said.

"You do that."

"Shhhh!"

"You know we can pause it, right? That's the beauty of binge-watchin'."

"I know that. Hell, we practically invented binge-watchin'. Remember those *Battlestar Galactica* DVDs?" Nate asked.

Haley laughed. "Yasss, I think a whole weekend passed before we knew it."

Jen rolled her eyes. "God, you two were stuck together like someone dipped you in extra-strength superglue." She chuckled. "With you lookin' the way you do, Haley, I can totally understand why his parents thought he was gay."

Haley grinned. "Before they saw my tits."

Nate groaned.

"Hey, those were your dad's words, not mine.

He reached for the Xbox controller and paused the show, then stood.

"Where you goin'?" Jen asked.

"To get another beer and a glass."

"I'll get it. I want some more pasta."

"Bring me one too. Beer glasses are in the dishwasher," Haley said as Nate sat back down.

"Does the type of glass matter?" Jen asked as she entered the kitchen.

"Yes!" Nate and Haley said at the same time.

They looked at each other and grinned.

"Oh…my fucking God." Jen's words were muffled.

Nate jumped up. "What's the matter?"

Haley's grin widened.

"You need to come see this. I'm not touchin' it."

Nate looked at her, and Haley shrugged. He went to go check on his wife, and within a few seconds, Haley heard laughing.

"It's not funny! She's gettin' back at me for the blow-job joke."

"What blow-job joke?" Nate asked. They walked out of the kitchen with beers, glasses, and Jen's refilled bowl.

Jen sighed. "Just never mind." She glared at Haley as she sat back down on the couch. "Did you really have to assault me with your detachable penis?"

Nate laughed again.

"Yes…yes, I did. It wasn't premeditated or anythin'. I remembered it was in there when we were talkin' about glasses."

Jen stabbed at her food. "You suck, and not in a hot-chick kinda way. More like a slug kinda way. Does it have to be so realistic?"

"Hell yes, for her pleasure."

"You're a ridiculous human being."

Haley batted her eyes at Jen. "You still love me."

"Debatable. You normally wash it like that?"

"Only after I use it. I only wear it when I go out. It's dishwasher safe. It's been in there a few days. I've been lazy about unloadin the dishes. Been usin' the same plate, fork, and pot and rewashin 'em."

"If I had a sister, I wouldn't want her sex life slappin' me in the face. You're the next best thing, so, no, I don't need those images in my head."

"Aww, I'm like your sister?"

Nate was howling. After a few more chuckles, he quieted down. "It's a good thing mine doesn't come off."

Jen leaned toward her husband and brushed his shoulder. "Good thing for you maybe."

Haley covered her ears. "See…no. Consider us even." She glanced at the TV. "Look at that. You paused it on a Peter and Olivia scene."

"God, I love those two together." Jen thankfully jumped on the new subject.

"Me too, but I've read some online stories with Astrid and Olivia. I could totally see them bein' a thing too." Haley poured her Abita Andygator into a glass.

"Good grief. What's the point of readin' about other people havin' sex?" Jen asked. "You obviously get plenty."

"That's beside the point. It's not all sex. Some stories expand on what's written on the show, and they can be really good. I like the romance of it."

Jen laughed. "*You* like the romance of it?"

Haley shrugged, but she knew she'd just stepped in it. "Yeah, so?"

"Your idea of romance is drinks, tellin' a girl she's pretty, and screwin' her brains out."

Nate snorted. "She has a point."

"It's the better alternative, and it's worked for me so far." True statements, though she found she had no desire to turn Tonya into a woman on standby. It didn't feel right.

"Oh c'mon, even your mother married a few of the guys she was messin' around with, for better or worse," Nate said.

"Mostly for worse."

"Not all of them," he reminded her.

This discussion was starting to make her a little pissy. Haley picked her beer up off the table and took a long drink. It didn't help. "What's the point of doin' all that work when you end up growin' apart eventually anyway? It didn't work for me, not even once." She thought about Tonya. What was she doing with her? What was she trying to prove?

"You're right. That can happen, but it's a chance to get to know each other again and possibly end up closer than before," Jen said, but she was looking at Nate the whole time.

Haley felt a twist in her gut as she remembered when they'd come damn close to a breakup and sent them all into a tailspin. She didn't want to dwell on that. Haley stood and gathered up empty bowls. Quietly, she walked into the kitchen.

Okay, they were right about everything, and it made her feel hopeful even for someone with a wandering gene. It should have bothered her that she was starting to flip on the subject so quickly, but Jen and Nate were bona-fide evidence that things could actually work out. Was she 100 percent sold? No, she wasn't. She could end up dishing out a world of hurt. Wouldn't be the first time.

Haley put the bowls in the sink and rinsed them. She was jumping way ahead of herself here—way, way, *way* ahead. Then there was the question of why she hadn't said anything about Tonya yet to her best friends.

Why indeed. Haley needed to rectify that.

When she went back into the living room, Jen was sitting in Nate's lap and they were kissing. Haley smiled. It was nice to see. "I don't care how much in love y'all are, there better not be any screwin' around on my sofa bed tonight."

Jen shot her the finger.

Haley laughed, shook her head, and blurted out, "So, I kinda met someone…" She did not intend for it to come out that way, but in for a quarter, may was well give up the whole dollar.

The kissing stopped almost immediately. Nate and Jen turned her way. "What?" they said at the same time and stared.

"I, um, met someone?" Haley reached around and rubbed the back of her neck.

"Are you askin' or tellin'?" Nate asked.

"Yeah," Jen chimed in.

"Tellin' definitely." She then proceeded to drop the whole story on them.

"Is she hot?" Nate asked when Haley was done.

Jen swatted him.

Haley smirked. "Oh yeah. Curves for days, and she has these dimples. She doesn't even have to smile for them to show."

Nate and Jen glanced at each other before looking back at her.

"Well, she's gotta be somethin' to hold your interest for more than a few minutes."

"Yeah, what Jen said."

"I haven't even asked her out yet."

"What? What is wrong with you?" Jen asked. Her face was all scrunched up in disbelief. She looked like an angry blonde pixie.

Nate nodded. "What Jen said."

Haley rolled her eyes. "I was just—"

"Do it right now. It's just a little after nine." Jen smiled in excitement. She was still in Nate's lap.

"What Jen—" Nate started to say, but Haley interrupted him.

"Stop it! Just stop it." Haley glared.

Nate grinned.

She walked around the couch and plopped down next to them, reaching for her phone. She was nervous, which was ridiculous. It wasn't like she didn't know what she was doing.

"Hurry the hell up!"

She gave Jen a hard stare. Jen stared right back, looking impatient.

The nerves returned full force. Haley's stomach slithered. "I can't do it with you guys lookin' at me!"

"For God's sake, we're not watchin' you pee," Nate said. He sighed. "Just go outside, then."

Jen gasped. Her eyes widened and her mouth dropped open.

Haley got up. It was a good idea. She opened the door and closed it behind her before sitting down on the stairs, so focused that she didn't see her neighbor unlocking her door.

"Hey, friend."

Haley jumped slightly and turned toward the voice. She waved and smiled. Apparently it was enough because she went inside a few seconds later. Haley rolled her eyes and urged herself to just get on with it already. She was way too invested in this, and she wasn't sure if that was a good thing yet. Haley tapped Tonya's name with her thumb.

"Hello?" Tonya sounded surprised.

"You answered."

"Are you going to be shocked every time I do?"

"Probably." Haley grinned. She couldn't help herself. "Sorry for callin' so late."

"Yes, it has been a long, emotional day, so…"

Tonya wasn't being subtle. Haley could respect that. She just needed to get straight to the point. "I like talkin' to you."

Tonya didn't respond, but Haley pushed on, projecting confidence. It wasn't like she was going to say no. "We're pretty good at it. I think it'll be even better to do it in person. Say…next weekend?"

Tonya sucked in a breath. "I—"

Haley's stomach dropped and not in the good way. It was too late to backtrack; she'd already put herself out there, and she was flapping around naked and unprotected.

"I like talking to you too, but no, I can't. I'm sorry. There's just too much going on in my life right now."

Even though she was expecting it, Tonya's words were a hard punch to the gut. Haley didn't know what to say, so she just went on autopilot. "Um, okay. I'm gonna let you go, then. Have a nice night."

"Haley?"

"Yeah?" It helped a little that Tonya sounded disappointed.

"I really am sorry."

"So am I. G'night."

"Night," Tonya said softly.

Haley sat out on her stoop for a little while longer. Finally, she got up and went back in.

Nate and Jen were laughing. They stopped and turned to look at her like they were expecting the world on a platter.

"Damn, dude. I'm sorry." Nate was the first to speak.

Jen rolled her eyes. "Just hold on. What did she say and how did she say it?"

"What's the point?" She was pouting; she was damn sure allowed to. She sat down.

"Because it's important."

Haley played along for shits and giggles. She told Jen everything.

"She sounded disappointed? You sure?"

"Yes, I'm sure," Haley whined. She didn't whine.

"Okay, well, obviously she wasn't lyin' to you about bein' sorry, so this may not be a lost cause."

It was Haley's turn to roll her eyes. "This is part of why I don't do the datin' thing anymore, or any shit like this."

"Rejection is a fact of life. Get over yourself," Jen said.

Haley huffed and glanced at Nate. "You gonna let her talk to me like that?"

"Yep." He nodded.

"Gettin' back to what I was sayin', she likes talkin' to you, so why don't y'all just do that for now?"

Haley leaned back on the couch. "I don't know."

"Oh c'mon! It's the next best thing, and the more she talks to you, the more she's gonna like you. You're smart, funny, and genuine." Jen smiled and bumped her on the shoulder.

Haley's lips quirked. "You're biased."

"I am. I freely admit it, but you barely know her and look at you. There's somethin' here, and you'll kick yourself later for lettin' it pass you by. It's not like you to give up so easily."

"Maybe." Jen was right. Haley just didn't want to deal with the possibility of back-to-back rejection.

"Make your decision fast before she puts up an even bigger wall."

Haley groaned, but she sat back up and stared at her phone. Before she let doubts get hold of her again, she reached for her cell.

Tonya answered the call a lot faster this time. "Haley?"

"I don't wanna stop."

Tonya gasped. This time, Haley's stomach did the good kind of flop.

"So I'm gonna call you, and we can talk about how horrible the potholes are, or if coffee is better with or without chicory. Okay?"

Tonya sighed. "Okay, but it's better with chicory."

"I agree, but later?"

"Yes, later."

Haley hung up and stared at absolutely nothing. She had no earthly idea what she was doing, but she was doing it anyway. She swallowed and glanced up.

Jen looked smug. "Just let her see the Haley we see."

"That was fuckin' awesome! We need to get our own reality show." Nate's smile was huge.

Jen squeezed her husband's knee. "No, baby, just…no."

Haley laughed.

CHAPTER 13

"You all right to stop by Crest Manor before we get some lunch?"

Haley looked at Tang and nodded. "It's fine. I can just hang out in the car."

Tang glanced in her direction before his attention went back to the road. "Naw, I wantcha to come in and meet 'im. When I talked to his nurse this mornin', she said he was a little more there than usual."

Before Haley could let the words settle, she found herself asking, "Why would you want me to go in?"

Tang shrugged. "I kinda wanna see if he'll have problems figurin' out if you're a man or a woman." He threw a smirk her way.

Haley laughed. "Ass." But there had to be more to it than that. "Any of your other partners meet him?"

"Fuck no! They all acted like I had the plague. You've stuck around the longest, and it's been what? Two months and some change?"

"Yeah, I think so." Haley looked at him and smiled. "You do have the plague. I think it just rubbed off on me too."

"You're all right, Rook. I mean…Haley."

Her smile felt like it was going to split her face, and her heart swelled with affection. "You're all right too, Tim." Hell, if he could give that much, she could too. "Not this time, but after I give 'em fair warnin', we can eat free at my best friends' restaurant. The food is really good."

"Really? Well, who am I to turn down a freebie of any kind?"

Haley rolled her eyes. "That would be un-Amercan."

Tang laughed. "There you go. You catchin' on."

About fifteen minutes later, Tang parked in a designated visitor's spot outside Crest Manor. They didn't talk as they walked up the sidewalk.

Tang rang the bell.

"I see you, Tim. C'mon in," someone said through the speaker on the door.

Haley heard a buzz, and then they were inside. She expected the place to smell like a hospital. There was a faint tinge of alcohol and antiseptic, but the scent of apples and cinnamon took over, making it more homey. The lobby was airy and bright. The floor was linoleum, but that was the only thing cold about the place. The furniture consisted of cream-colored leather couches offset by dark brown chairs she could probably lose herself in. A glass coffee table sat on top of a rug that looked more like a piece of art than carpet. To the side of it all was a fancy cart that held a Keurig and a boatload of snacks.

Tang smiled as they reached the front desk. A real, honest-to-God smile. "Hey, Charlotte."

It was the same woman she'd seen last time, but this time she was in regular clothes.

"Hello, my love. I see you brought a friend." Charlotte got out of her chair, walked around the desk, and hugged Tang.

He returned it with enthusiasm. "Yep, this here's my partner, Haley."

Haley blinked. Maybe he was the hugging type but only in special situations.

"You never brought anyone here before," Charlotte said.

Tang cut his eyes toward Haley. "Yeah, I know."

"Mm-hmm, well hey, friend Haley."

"Hello, Ms. Charlotte."

Charlotte held out a hand and Haley gladly took it.

"Well, I won't keep y'all. Let me get Mary." She moved toward her desk once more and picked up the phone.

"Thank you, Charlotte."

Haley had no idea Tang could be so well mannered. It was a sight to see, and he didn't seem uncomfortable at all.

A door opened, and another woman stepped out. She smiled in their direction and leaned against the door to let them through.

"He's still pretty lucid, Tim."

"Thanks, Mary."

He didn't hug this one, but he was respectful. They walked through what Haley assumed was a common area. There was a huge flat-screen TV on the wall; couches and chairs in the same style as the lobby; and tables set up for chess, checkers, and some stuff she didn't recognize. There were people peppered about. Some were in wheelchairs, others used walkers, and a handful were on their own two feet.

They went through another doorway and past the elevator. When they were halfway down the hall, Mary stopped and knocked loudly on one of the doors.

"Yeah, c'mon in. Ya don't haveta beat it down."

That sounded like somebody related to Tang, all right.

Mary opened the door. A tall, stocky man was making his way toward them with the help of a cane. His hair was white and thick on the sides of his head, but the top was bald and dotted with liver spots. His face was pinched and sour-looking. Thin lips were drawn and pursed, but his eyes were alert and intelligent.

"Look who I brought for you, Mr. Milton."

Milton looked Tang up and down.

"I don't see no donuts."

Tang grinned and shrugged.

Milton chuckled, but it sounded like he was gasping. His face changed then, becoming more alive. "Don't just stand there; git over here, boy."

Tang did what he was told and they embraced in a quick hug.

"Who's this fella ya brought?"

Tang hooted with laughter.

Haley wondered if she was too deep in this relationship to taze him.

As they were leaving, someone pulled Tang to the side, toward an office farther down the hall. Haley waited for him. It wasn't long. When he came out, he was balling up a piece of paper. His face was bright red, and he was muttering. Tang stuffed the paper in the pocket of his uniform and walked right past her.

Even an idiot could see that something was wrong. Haley waited until they were back in the car to ask, "You okay? What's up?"

He grunted. "I don't wanna fuckin' talk about it."

Haley knew by now that his bark was much worse than his bite. "Okay, whatever you want." She paused. "Parkway Bakery and Tavern for lunch? I'll call it in. We can get one of those fancy po' boys with duck fat or whatever."

Tang grunted again.

That meant yes.

For a time, the only sound in the car came from the radio. Haley sipped on her drink, and her mind started to wander. It didn't go far, just to Tonya. A light, giddy feeling rushed through her. They'd talked a couple times a day since the weekend. Haley had regaled Tonya with tales of Tang, along with her own college exploits. She'd even thrown her mom and her numerous relationships in the mix.

Tonya laughed so hard at times, it made Haley wonder if she'd ever laughed like that before. Tonya hadn't revealed much about herself so far, but it was all about quality, not quantity. She wasn't part of the party scene in college, didn't even join a sorority. Working two jobs took up plenty of her time, and when she graduated she went straight through to medical school. Translation: Tonya could be focused and dedicated.

When asked what she did for fun growing up, Tonya got quiet but admitted that she didn't get out much, which meant she probably didn't have much of a childhood at all. She talked about her friend Stephanie more than she did her sister and father. In fact, she barely even said their names. This led Haley to believe that she was closer to Stephanie than to her own family.

They also talked about everything from politics, movies, and music to the Saints. Haley was slightly disappointed that Tonya wasn't into football, but looked at that as a challenge to tackle as soon as possible. Haley had barely scratched Tonya's surface, and she was dying to know more. Hell, she wanted to know it all. Those phone calls had already become the highlight of her day. But she wanted to look Tonya in the eyes, see her smile, and watch her face change when she laughed. Most of all, Haley wanted to touch her, just to make sure she was real.

And she was still trying to figure out what it was about Tonya that grabbed her and kept her wanting more, when she usually had the romantic attention span of a mosquito. Maybe there was no rhyme or reason to it. Maybe her interest, her attraction to Tonya just…was. Was all this a little scary? Haley had to admit that it was. She wasn't sure if she could handle it, and she didn't know if she was going to somehow screw things up. The only thing she knew for certain was that she usually went after what she wanted, and Haley wanted Tonya.

"I owe them money."

Haley heard him, but it took the words a minute to compute and for her mind to change course. "What? Who?"

"Crest Manor. I was hopin' I'd have more time before they said anythin'. If I'm not caught up by September, Uncle Milt has to leave."

Haley felt like a ton of bricks were sitting in her stomach. "I'm sorry. Wish I could help."

"Don't need your fuckin' apologies. I need money. They fuckin' hiked up the rent to my apartment, and the rates to the rest home went up too a couple months back. Thought I could handle it." Tang stomped on the gas as the stoplight on Earhart turned green. The tires screeched. "Fuck the apologies."

Haley didn't say anything. There was no need to.

After several minutes, Tang cleared his throat. "Sorry."

Haley glanced at him. "It's all right." Those bricks were still sitting there.

"I'm tired as hell. Been working a second job doing security at Ochsner. I need to see if I can bump up my hours."

Concerned, Haley asked, "When you gonna sleep?"

Tang snorted. "Never again? If the lack of sleep don't get to me the stress will."

"You got time to get a beer after work?" Maybe she could help a little with the stress.

"I got an hour and a half and as long as it's just one. You buyin' this time?"

This going out after work thing had picked up some momentum, and they usually had a good time. "That's long enough, and yeah, I'll buy."

Dr. Finn stared at Tonya as she sat down. "You look unsettled."

Tonya gave her a tight smile. "I suppose that's as good a word as any."

"Things not going the way you want them to?"

Tonya laughed. "Do they ever?"

Dr. Finn didn't answer.

"My father is way more stubborn than I thought he would be." Tonya sighed and admitted to herself that she couldn't browbeat him into submission. "But Tracy and I talked—actually talked. It was scary and refreshing at the same time. I got some things out in the open—not everything, but it's a start."

"The jealousy?" Dr. Finn asked.

"Good guess. No, I didn't go into that. I'm not ready, and there are times when it still feels so petty."

Dr. Finn leaned forward. "Not at all. We've gone through this before. With the way you grew up, it's normal to feel that the grass is greener on other peoples' lawns."

Tonya smiled.

"So, are you ready to try something different where your father is concerned?"

For several seconds, Tonya just looked at her. "You knew my anger wasn't going to get me anywhere." She wasn't asking.

Dr. Finn nodded. "You did too, but it was time that he heard about the pain you've gone through even if he isn't ready to listen yet."

Tonya tried to beat back the sudden feeling of desperation. Her hands tightened around the arms of the chair and her fingers dug into the leather. Her heart rammed against her chest. Despite everything they'd been through, he was still her father. She wanted to fix this. He wasn't getting any younger. Besides Tracy, she had no other family. "He's had years to get used to everything."

"So have you, and with help you've fared a lot better. He hasn't had that."

It was true. "What's your suggestion?"

"No more cold shoulder. Let him see the parts of you that you are willing to share. If you let down your guard somewhat, he could be willing to do the same."

Just the thought of that made her fearful. Tonya's hands squeezed tighter. They were actually starting to cramp.

"It's a risk, but it could pay off and be the start of something much larger."

Tonya swallowed. "I'll have to think about that."

"That's understandable." Dr. Finn paused. "Are you still having nightmares?"

"I have my normal dreams, but the nightmares not as much. They've changed somewhat. Haley's still in them." Her heart thudded for a different reason now, but she relaxed a little. Tonya cleared her throat. "We still win at the end. I haven't written anything new in my journal."

Dr. Finn smiled. "I like how you've taken charge of your nightmares." Her tone was thoughtful and proud.

Thoughts of Haley swam around in Tonya's head. It wasn't until Dr Finn called her name that she realized she'd missed something. "Oh, sorry."

Dr. Finn tilted her head slightly and studied her. "Is there something else you want to share?"

Tonya held her gaze. "Yes. I was going to anyway. I just got a little distracted."

Dr. Finn waited quietly.

Before Tonya could pick and choose what she wanted to tell, the words were out of her mouth. Several minutes later, she ended with, "She asked me out, and I turned her down. It was selfish of me to even reach out to her in the first place."

"Why is that selfish?"

"I wasn't doing it for the right reasons. I wanted to feel good. I wanted something for me, and with everything that's going on with my family, I don't think I'm really emotionally available."

"Hasn't that been an issue all along? You putting your life on hold or on the shelf for your family?"

"Well, yes, but I think something good could come out of it this time."

"Do you like her?"

Tonya looked down at her hands in her lap and back up again. "She's different from what I'm used to, less reserved and younger."

"Does that bother you?"

"No. I've teased her about it, but no. She's, well, even after I turned her down, she wanted to stay in contact. We've talked just about every day. I like it this way. There's no pressure."

"So that's a yes you do like her?" Dr. Finn's eyes were bright and amused.

Tonya didn't answer.

"Is there any difference in this situation compared to other women you've been involved with?"

"The few there's been have been nice, enjoyable...like a warm bath."

"Interesting." Dr. Finn smiled slightly.

"Yes, well, I was trying to be accurate."

"Mm, that doesn't really answer the question. How does Haley compare so far?"

"I don't have enough information to go on yet," Tonya said.

Dr. Finn studied her again. "I think you do, Tonya."

She was right, of course. The heat that buzzed right under her skin when she thought about Haley wasn't the norm.

"If we're being accurate." Dr. Finn smiled again.

Tonya stayed quiet. What could she possibly say?

"I suggest you give that a chance too. We all need something to counterbalance the negative."

"I guess I have a lot to think about."

"I agree. You do."

Haley walked out of the bathroom rubbing a towel in her hair. The sound of her cell phone ringing the whistled tune from *Kill Bill* made her drop the towel and head straight for her nightstand.

"Hey, you there?"

"I am. You answered just in time. I'm pretty sure your voice mail was about to pick up."

"Lucky me, then, and the fact that you're callin' *me*? Bonus."

"Is that a problem?"

"No, just pointin' it out as a good thing. It means you're invested."

"Oh? Is that what it means?" The amusement in Tonya's tone couldn't be missed.

"Yes, me and the universe say so."

"The entire universe is on your side?"

"Mm-hm, think about it. Look at how we met. Look at everythin' that happened afterward. It's gotta be the universe."

"So we have no choice in this whatsoever?"

Haley smiled and sat on the edge of the bed. "You made your choice when you agreed to the phone thing."

Tonya was quiet for a few seconds. "I guess I did."

"Any regrets?" Haley had to ask, but she really hoped Tonya wouldn't answer. Still naked, she got comfortable on her bed. She held her breath and waited.

"Yes…just one. That it took me being worried to call you."

Haley took a deep breath. The big-ass butterflies in her stomach were going to town. It made it hard to breathe for a minute. "You were worried about me?"

"I usually hear from you earlier. You are a cop, and in New Orleans, after all. I'm very curious. What made you want to go into law enforcement anyway? Hero complex or adrenaline junkie?"

"Neither. I don't wanna wear a cape, and I definitely don't like a gun being pointed in my face. I kinda stumbled around a bit tryin' to figure out what I wanted to do after college. I have a bachelors in sociology. Not much to do with that if you don't specialize. I remember what this place was like pre-Katrina, and I just wanna help get it back there."

"And you thought being a cop would do that?" Tonya's tone was skeptical.

"It's a start. I didn't wanna go into social work. Bein' on this side of things is way more satisfyin'. I get to sift through the bad seeds."

"And put them somewhere else so everything else can grow? I think I get it."

"Exactly." Haley was relieved, but only for a couple seconds. "I do need to ask you. Does what I do bother you?"

"That doesn't matter right—"

"Tonya?"

"Yes and no. I respect your reasons, but you have a dangerous job."

"Is that a dealbreaker?"

Tonya was quiet. "No, it's not."

"Good. I like this, and I like you."

"Stop. You don't even know if—"

"No," Haley said softly.

Tonya swallowed loudly. "Do you always just come out and say what you're feeling?" She was a little breathless, and that did weird things to Haley's insides.

"Most of the time, yeah. People who know me appreciate it."

"I think I'm starting to. You're just so different."

"You've said that before. I'm startin' to think it's a good thing."

"It is. We wouldn't be doing this otherwise."

"What is *this*, anyway?" Haley decided she'd push the envelope a little tonight to see what oozed out.

"We're talking and getting to know each other." Tonya's tone was hesitant.

"To what end?"

"I can't answer that right now, not with anything definite."

"Mm, can I tell you what my end would be? I wanna make sure you understand where I'm comin' from."

"Yes, okay." There it was again, that breathlessness in Tonya's voice.

"I'm goin' to be honest. I don't do stuff like this. I don't chat…I don't get to know. Christ, I don't know what it is about you, but I wanna try like hell to figure it out. We can go slow or we can go fast. I'm willin' to do both if it gets me somewhere with you. I'll bide my time with this phone thing, but in a little while it won't be enough for me, and, whether you admit it or not, it won't be for you either."

There was a slight hitch in Tonya's breathing.

Feeling cocky and more than a little heated, Haley said, "You liked that. I can tell."

"I did."

"Don't be afraid to say it, about anythin'." Haley hoped that by opening herself up a little more, she would inspire Tonya to do the same.

"I'll…keep that in mind." Tonya paused and cleared her throat. "No tales of Tang tonight?"

Haley smiled. She would give her the subject change. "Nope. He was a little outta sorts today. He's got a lot goin' on. We went out for a beer after work. Then I went to work out longer than usual. It's why I'm so late."

"You're a good friend."

"I try to be," Haley said.

"I'm working on it."

"It's easy when you got good people around you."

"Yes, I'm learning that."

"Well since I have no Tang stories for you tonight, why don't you chip in?"

Tonya laughed. "I'm sorry, but my life just isn't that interesting. Ask me something."

Haley had to think about it. She didn't want the tension between them to shoot up again so soon, even though by God it felt good. It had to be something broad but deep enough to make Tonya dig a bit. Whatever came out, Haley was going to add what she learned to the unfinished puzzle. "What was it like for you growin' up 'round here?"

"Do you mean because I'm biracial?"

"Yeah."

"There were some black people in my neighborhood who had an issue with me. It took me a while to figure it out. There were a lot of whispers behind my back. One of the neighbor's kids finally spelled it out for me. My hair looked different. My skin was much lighter, and I didn't talk the same. I wasn't black enough." Tonya went quiet. "That actually still happens to me to this day."

"Does it bother you?"

"Yes and no. Yes, because I'm a part of the black community, whether it's liked or not. I know our history, and it doesn't make sense that we'd do that to each other. No, because I don't let it hold me back."

"I can understand that. What about the other way around?"

"Racism from white people?"

"Yes."

"You sure you want to hear that?"

"I didn't do it, so..."

"There's plenty coming from the other side. I've never met my mother's family. There's times that it bothers me and times that it doesn't at all. Can't miss what you never had, right? My experiences on that end of the spectrum are a little more in-your-face."

"Someone hurt you?" Haley bristled at that. Maybe she didn't need to hear this.

"Nothing I couldn't brush off. There was this one thing that sticks out for me. I was at Walmart with my father. He let me go to the toy section by myself while he was in automotive. He made me promise to stay right where I was. I was playing with the toys on display and three boys walked up. I didn't even know they were there until they started talking. I didn't think anything of it, and we were all playing together. One of them kept staring at me. It made me uncomfortable, but before I could say anything, he was calling me a fucking nigger. It was the first time anyone ever said that to me. He said he could tell I wasn't really white because I had big lips. I was a lot younger when this happened, and I just didn't get it. One of the boys had a light tan, and I thought I looked just like him. They started pushing me, and I started crying. Something snapped, I think, and I started throwing punches. Daddy found me like that, crying and swinging.

For some reason, the boys didn't run. They just stood there while I told him what happened, and then they tried to call me a liar. Daddy saw through it. He didn't get loud, and he didn't get violent. I don't know what he said to them—I was still crying—but they took off running. Daddy was my hero back then." Tonya mumbled the last part, and Haley almost didn't catch it.

"Jesus." Haley couldn't clamp down on the anger burning her stomach. "That pisses me off just hearin' about it. How do you not just hate people in general?"

"Probably because I had some good experiences to counter the bad, and I can't deny part of who I am. I handle things more intelligently now. I ignore them when I can, but I also figured out that there's nothing more satisfying than insulting someone when they don't know it's happening. Sometimes all it takes is a couple of words."

Haley chuckled despite the heaviness of the topic. "You might have to show me that trick."

"I've used it on you, actually, that night at the bar."

"I know."

Tonya laughed. As she quieted, she asked, "I know this is probably a stupid question, but my race doesn't bother you? At all?"

"You mean because I'm from Mississippi?" Haley tried to make light, but Tonya didn't laugh. "Sorry, bad joke."

"Mm."

"No, it doesn't. All I know is, you're one of the hottest women I've ever seen."

"And you've *seen* a lot of them?" Tonya sounded amused.

"If you wanna call it that. Wait, you're not takin' what I said seriously, are you?"

"Not at all." Tonya laughed.

"Well, why is that?" Haley really wanted to know.

"Because."

"C'mon. You gotta do better than that. Because why?"

"It's hard to explain."

Haley couldn't believe that no one had ever told her she was beautiful, so that couldn't be it. Maybe, then, she didn't always believe it. "You are." Haley put as much softness and sincerity behind the words as she could.

"Haley…" Tonya gasped sharply.

"Yeah?"

"Thank you."

"You're very welcome." Haley's stomach growled. "I'm gonna take you in the kitchen with me. Hold on." She put the phone on the bed and pulled on underwear and a T-shirt.

"What are you cooking?"

"Robért's has a pretty good mac and cheese. I'm gonna throw in some sundried tomatoes, milk, and butter. Don't have energy for anythin' else. I have to have the time and be in the mood to really cook. I meant to ask you before. Do you cook?"

Tonya laughed. "A mean Zatarain's out of the box. My dad is the cook in the family. As a matter of fact, I was about to raid the refrigerator as we speak."

CHAPTER 14

Tonya's phone rang, interrupting the music. She expected the caller ID to splash Haley's name across the display. It was an interesting twist to see her sister's instead.

"You're up early."

"Not really. It's my usual putter-around time before getting the day started. I figured now would be the best time to call so I won't interrupt your workday. Just trying to be courteous."

"Well, I guess a thank you is in order, then?"

"If you say so," Tracy answered.

They both went quiet. It had been like this since they'd ripped the Band-Aid off that old wound they'd been nursing. Tonya didn't expect it to be easy, but she couldn't recall them ever going through this level of awkwardness.

"Is everything okay?" Tonya didn't let the silence drag on for long.

"I found out yesterday that, with the teaching job they offered, I'd only be allowed to teach low-level classes. Something about policy, until I get more experience and possibly a doctorate."

Tonya had no intention of stumbling over this conversation this time. "If that's what you want to do, then you'll have to get a doctorate."

"I don't know if I have it in me to do that right away. I need a break from school."

"The only stress you'd have would be academic. I'd take care of everything else if you make that cho—"

"No." Tracy was emphatic.

"What do you mean no?"

"I mean, if I go for a doctorate, I'm paying my own way. My grades are good this time around, and I could end up getting a fellowship. It's not like undergrad. I wouldn't lose it. Learned my lesson about partying too hard, even though it took me a minute."

"That's not necessary, Tracy. I have the money."

"You don't think part of our problem is that you take care of everything?"

"It's possible," Tonya agreed. "But it's a very small part compared to everything else. We're family, Tracy. Aren't we supposed to take care of each other?"

"Yes, we are, but you do all the caring. I don't think it's right for me and Daddy to just live off your dime. I know it bothers him."

"Yes, he can be very passive-aggressive about it, as with everything else he doesn't talk about." Tonya rode the wave of anger that hit her, breathing through it instead of letting it overtake her.

"He lost his store, Tonya. He loved that place, not to mention the house. That has to make him feel useless and probably embarrassed. He's always been the provider. He—"

"Did it to himself. He had a business. It wasn't a free-for-all to extend credit and take IOU's from everybody. The fact that they didn't pay him back time and time again is what did him in. He was already in debt before Mama got sick, but that made the situation worse. I know he holds it against me that his oldest daughter has to take care of him."

Tracy sighed heavily.

Did it bother Tonya that Tracy was still so firmly in their father's corner? Yes, yes, it did. She was tired of fighting about him. She was tired of fighting with him. "How did we get on this subject anyway?"

"I don't even know, but I meant what I said. You know I went through the summer so I can graduate in December. The fall session is the last—"

"You know that's taken care of already, Tracy. I'm not sure—"

"Maybe it's time for me to grow up and do things on my own for once. If it doesn't work, I'll come limping back asking for help, so don't worry."

"That's an image."

"I bet it is."

"Look, let's just table this discussion for now."

"Yeah, okay. I didn't mean for us to dig all this up. I thought we were trying to patch up this, whatever, between us and we keep ending up in these heavy-ass conversations. I didn't think things would be this awkward between us. It was easier when we were pretending."

That was actually very accurate. "Isn't that why we were doing it? Because it was easy?"

"More than likely." Tracy paused. "Maybe we need to stick to the lighter subjects. Get to know each other as we are now and have that pave the way for everything else."

Tracy's insightfulness made Tonya smile. "That's a good plan. Are you sure you don't want to come work with me in some capacity?"

Tracy chuckled. "Positive."

"Too bad."

"Uh-huh, so what's new in your world?"

Just then, Tonya's phone beeped. Her heartbeat increased when she saw Haley's name. "Uh, hold on a second." Why Tonya was trying to sound nonchalant, she wasn't sure, but she wasn't succeeding. To her own ears she sounded frazzled.

"You have to go?"

"No, just hold on." Tonya clicked over.

"Hey, mornin'."

Tonya heard the smile in Haley's voice and visualized it on her face. It made her insides tingle. "Same to you."

"You okay? You sound out of breath."

"No, it's the wind. Can I call you back? My sister is—"

"That's fine. Talk to you in a few."

"Okay, thank you." Tonya didn't know why she said it. The words just came out.

"Nothin' to thank me for. You sure you're okay?"

"Yes, later?"

"Later."

Tonya switched the calls back over. "Sorry that took so long."

"Why do you sound out of breath?"

"That's the wind." Tonya recycled the same white lie.

Tracy laughed. "You don't have a convertible, and no way are you driving on the Causeway with your windows down."

"Today could be the exception."

"Oh girl, please. Don't stress. If you don't want to tell me, it's fine and totally understandable."

There was disappointment in her sister's voice.

"It was Haley," she blurted out.

"Haley? Is that somebody at work?"

"No, she's the cop who—"

"Ohhhhh the one with the nice arms?"

"Yes…her." That was easier than Tonya thought it would be. She wasn't sharing some deep, dark, painful secret, but something that brought her the opposite—joy.

"Are you seeing her?" Tracy sounded hopeful.

"I'm not sure what to call it right now."

"Christ, you two would be hot as hell together."

"Tracy!"

"What? It's true. Look, I know this isn't something we talk about, so I'm happy to be a part of the conversation. That means I get to make up for lost time, starting now. I saw the way she looked at you. Go for it. And if you're not looking for something deep, you need to run to that one anyway. Have some fun. You're not dead yet."

"I'm not sure what to say to all that."

"You don't need to say anything else to me. Hang up and call her back."

"I need to concentrate on family right—"

"Hold up. We're all adults, and we're allowed to do adult things. I know I do, no matter what's going on. I just pace myself these days. So don't even go there. I'm hanging up now. Stop using me as an excuse."

Before Tonya could say anything else, Tracy was gone. Needing to compose herself, she hesitated for a few minutes before returning Haley's call.

"Hey, that was pretty quick. I hope you didn't cut things short on my account."

"No, she just kind of hung up."

"Huh. I know you haven't come out and said it, but I've picked up that you don't exactly get along with your sister and father."

"Not exactly, no," Tonya admitted. It felt good to get that off her chest. She wasn't trying to keep it a secret from Haley, but who wants to hear about family drama?

"You don't have to talk about it if you don't want to, but I'm on the outside lookin' in. You'll get no judgment from me. Besides, I wasn't kiddin' when I said I wanted to know about you."

"You sure?"

"Tonya, yes, I wouldn't bring it up if I wasn't."

"My mother plays a huge part in this, but I'm just not ready to go there yet with you. My father pretty much takes up the rest. As a family, we're kind of coming to terms with a lot that happened in the past."

"Like what?" Haley's voice was soft, like she sensed that the whole situation was fragile. It was, but Tonya wasn't. She'd conquered that hurdle long ago.

"We don't talk a lot in my family. I think my father thought if no one spoke about it…whatever it was didn't exist. I've never been Daddy's little girl. I was always in the middle, I guess, until my mother got sick. Then I wasn't anywhere."

"What do you mean?"

"I mean, I was a kid with way too many responsibilities that even some adults couldn't handle. I got away when I could, and there was this girl down the street. She made me feel good, and I can't even tell you how much I needed that. He found out, and, then, I really knew what it was like to be invisible. My sister took center stage. I was there to play nursemaid. I don't know how else to explain it. It's taken a long time, but things have finally come to a head. Tracy and I are trying to mend things between us, but my father—"

"Refuses?" Haley asked.

"Yes. To repair something, you have to admit there's a problem in the first place."

"Jesus, I can't even comprehend what that must have felt like, what that feels like even now for you. I've never been in the closet. My sexuality wasn't always accepted, but I didn't care."

"I lived my life. I just did it discreetly and didn't advertise."

"Okay, I see your point, but I tell you what. The strength it takes to get through even most of that had to be for the record books. If you can survive crap like that, those guys at the gas station didn't stand a chance in hell."

Haley's words made Tonya smile. "When you put it that way…"

"I'm just glad you didn't have a lighter. That woulda been messy."

Tonya chuckled.

"Hey?" Haley's voice had that fragile quality to it again.

"Yes?"

"Thank you for sharin' all that with me. I can tell you don't open up easily. It means…it just means a lot."

"You're easy to talk to."

"I try. It's good that you and your sister are tryin' to work things out, and it's a damn shame your father is missin' out on you. I'm greedy, though, so that's more for me, I suppose."

A sudden burst of heat spread from Tonya's chest to her stomach, and she marveled that she could go from such heaviness to this lightness. "That's an interesting way to look at it."

"If you say so." Haley sighed. "I'm almost at work. I'd rather keep talkin' to you than sit through roll call."

"That's sweet."

"You're like a bowl of Wheaties."

Tonya laughed. "What does that even mean?"

"You fortify my day?" Haley was smiling. Tonya could tell from the sound of her voice.

She laughed even harder. "No, I'm not vitamins."

"Well then, let's just say you're essential to my mornings."

Tonya felt a flash of that same heat, but this time it burned hotter. Haley's words were over-the-top, but that didn't stop her from feeling every single one. "You meant that, didn't you?"

"I did."

Tonya heard other voices. "You have to go."

"I have to go," Haley agreed. "Talk to you tonight."

"Okay."

Tonya hadn't expected this ache, and the feeling grew each time they talked. It energized her and left her elated. Tonya wanted more of it. If Haley was able to do this to her over the phone, in person her response would be ten times more powerful. There was nothing lackluster about Haley. The part of Tonya that savored the memories of Brenda jumped for joy, but the rest of her was still undecided. "What did I get myself into?" she mumbled quietly.

Apparently, the attendant had spotted Tonya coming down the hall; she was already unlocking the elevator designated for the mental health section of the hospital. Tonya nodded as she stepped in. It wasn't unusual for her to be the only one on it this early, but it was nice to see her staff show some initiative.

"Hold the elevator!" Stephanie yelled.

The attendant pressed the button so Stephanie could enter. Tonya smiled at her. "Are you going to make this a habit?"

"No, trust me. Once or twice a week, tops." Stephanie all but groaned. "I do have some good news, though, sort of?"

"Are you asking me?"

"Telling. I'm definitely telling, just don't kill me."

"You're being dramatic."

"I knoooow, but I've just gotten so popular all of a sudden. I should've told you, and then it slipped my mind, which isn't a good sign—"

"Still dramatic, and you're not making sense."

Stephanie scowled. "Anyway, I have a date, so I need to cancel our Good Friends thing for this week. I was going to reschedule for Saturday, but then I met this guy at CC's. He looked like the man with dreds on *CSI*, the one that got fired for being addicted to something or other. He started talking, and I just got sucked into his eyes, and before I knew it, we had made plans. If he turns out to be an ass..." Stephanie leaned toward her and whispered the word. "I'm all yours on Saturday. Friday, too, if that one doesn't bowl me over."

Tonya didn't begrudge Stephanie's fun, but she didn't like the idea of being stuck at home with her father for the weekend. Maybe she could convince Tracy to come home. That probably wasn't the best of ideas. It would probably just complicate matters. "I suppose I'll survive."

"You could do a lot more than that if you hadn't turned down—"

"Ahem." Tonya cleared her throat and glared.

"Ohhh, I see. Its okay for me to talk about my love life in public, but not you?"

"Yes, since you started the conversation anyway."

The attendant snorted, and Tonya had the feeling she was very entertained.

For like the thousandth time, Haley glanced at Tang. He looked rumpled. His uniform was wrinkled all to hell like it had been balled up on the floor. His mustache was usually the only facial hair he sported, but today there were whiskers that looked like they would snag her skin if she touched them. Not to mention the bloodshot eyes, and the fact that he yawned every ten minutes or so and had barely said a word to her all morning.

He reached for the humongous cup of coffee that had to be ice-cold by now and sipped from it, then set the cup back in the holder and turned toward her slightly as he stopped at a red light. "What?" His tone was flat, as if it took too much energy to muster his usual bravado.

"You look like shit, man."

Tang snorted. "No, tell me how you really feel, Rook."

"Did you even sleep last night?"

"Does it fuckin' look like I did? Shit."

Haley wasn't fazed by his attitude. She just waited. He'd say more when he was ready.

Soon enough, Tang said, "Worked a twelve-hour shift last night at Ochsner. I gotta get some extra hours in to save money. I barely had an hour's sleep before I came to this shitshow."

She could have told him to slow down and pace himself. But when it came down to it, he had to do what he had to do. "You still up for lunch at Savoie? Now may not be the time to throw new people at you."

"Naw, it'll do me good to laugh and get some decent food. All I had this morning was a bag of Flamin' Hot Cheetos and that nasty coffee."

"Why didn't you stop by McDonald's or somethin'?"

"Had to gas up my car. Seemed like as good a place as any to get food."

The morning was uneventful, which Haley was thankful for. The most exciting thing they dealt with was a woman reporting that a trampoline and a swimming pool had been stolen from under her house. It was boring as hell, but she'd take days like that when they weren't both firing on all cylinders.

They'd just finished another sweep of Hollygrove—the Zoo, as he liked to call it. Tang was driving back down Earhart toward Uptown. There was construction, and the right lane was off-limits because of it. A few people stood on the neutral ground separating the road. They had Dollar General bags and took advantage of the standstill to cross between the cars to the other side of Earhart. It took several minutes, but traffic started moving again, though it was crawling.

A car pulled into one of the designated turnarounds to make a U-turn. Tang slammed on the brakes. The space was big enough to fit a whole car, but the driver had decided to stop with his ass end sticking out in traffic. He completely blocked the road.

"Son of a bitch! How fuckin' stupid do you have to be!" Tang slapped his hand against the steering wheel.

She rolled her eyes. New Orleans was indeed the home of the worst drivers, and this was evidence. She was about to make a joke about it. When she glanced at Tang, his face was bright red and he was sucking wind. Before she could say a word, he put the car in park and jumped out.

This was not good. Not good at all.

"Do you see what you did? You can fit what? Three fuckin' cars in this space, and all you got in it is your goddamn headlights! Are you stupid, or do you just want attention?" he yelled.

Haley had to end this, quickly, before things really got out of control. She grabbed his cell phone and got out of the vehicle. Some cars drove around them. Others stopped and watched. One guy was recording the whole thing with his phone.

"Don't just sit there and fuckin' look at me! Move your car up, or I'll have the piece of shit towed!"

The driver looked terrified, which was probably why he didn't move.

Haley approached Tang from behind. She got close enough to touch him but didn't. It probably wouldn't have been a good idea. Neither would berating him in front of a crowd. Tang must have sensed someone behind him, because he glanced over his shoulder. Haley hoped that seeing her would be enough to divert him, but no such luck. He turned back and continued to stare that poor guy down.

"Tim?"

"What?" He didn't look back this time, but he answered her. That was good.

"Your phone rang."

"So goddamned what. I'm workin'."

"Your caller ID said it was Uncle Milton."

Tang whipped his head around, and for the first time, he looked at what was going on around him. He rubbed a hand over his face and muttered as he deflated a bit. He started back toward the car.

"Go on, sir. I'm sorry you had to go through that."

The man just sat there with his mouth open.

"Sir," Haley said firmly. That woke him up. He threw an angry glance toward Tim and made his turn when he was able. She ordered other bystanders along, and after everyone dispersed, Haley walked back to their car.

Tang hadn't gotten in. He leaned against the driver's side door. His arms were crossed, and his head was down. The man could be a dick, especially during an arrest, but this was another thing entirely.

"Give me the keys," Haley said with authority.

Tang glanced up, and he looked more haggard than he had earlier. He gave her the keys without argument. In return, Haley put his cell phone in his hands.

"Nobody called, did they?"

"No."

He nodded and moved around to the passenger side.

Haley waited until they were farther up the street before she spoke. "I'm not gonna sit here and waste my time on tellin' you what you did wrong and what coulda happened. You know that already. You got a lot of shit goin' down. But if you go off the deep end tryin' to shovel it all, who's gonna be around to take care of Milt?"

For a long time, Tang didn't say anything. He sniffed a couple of times, and she hoped to God he wasn't crying because, while that meant they had really established trust, it also scared her.

"You're right." Tang's voice wasn't quivering or anything, so she figured she was wrong about the tears.

"I know I am. You just better hope that man doesn't file a complaint or that video doesn't end up online."

Tang didn't say anything to that. What was there *to* say?

"I'm gonna call Nate and cancel lunch."

"No, don't. I know what happened was shitty, but it took the wind outta me. You don't have to worry about me showin' my ass with your friends. I'll be on my best behavior. Don't have the energy for anythin' else."

Haley was still hesitant. "What's the big deal?"

Tang shrugged. "You're the only one who stuck around, and you want me to meet your people. That's a big deal."

He just had to go and get sentimental on her. "Yeah, okay." Jesus, was she going to have a story to tell Tonya tonight.

Haley sipped on her sweet tea and watched as her friends and Tang interacted. It had been touch and go there for a minute, but she'd expected that. Haley hadn't exactly sung his praises at first, and Nate and Jen could be very protective. Hell, Jen was still watching him like a hawk, leaning back in her chair with her arms crossed over her chest like she was going to get all *Goodfellas* any minute.

It was almost comical, but it made her warm inside.

Nate took a bite of his sandwich and wiped his mouth. He held up a hand to get everyone's attention while he chewed.

"Okay." He grinned. "Pusstopia…is that an alternate reality you cooked up?"

Haley and Jen groaned.

"That's not even a real question. Did you pull that out an alternate reality too, or out your ass?" Jen asked.

Tang chuckled and glanced at Haley. "You told them about that?"

Haley shrugged. She wasn't sorry. "You were like some science experiment at first. I got help to figure you out."

"How ya doin' so far?"

Haley held up a hand and rocked it back and forth. "Meh."

"Bullshit. I think you're gettin' there." He looked straight at her and grinned.

Nate snorted. "Took you, what? A little over two months to work things through? Wonder how long it's gonna take with Tonya?"

Jen glared at Nate, but at least her body language was more open now. Her hands were on the table, and she leaned toward the conversation instead of away. "Like you understand anythin' that's goin' on."

"What do you mean? Of course I do. I know romance! I do romance all the time," Nate defended. His face was all screwed up. Haley couldn't remember the last time she'd seen him looking so disgruntled.

Jen reached across the table and took his hand. "You try, baby. You try."

Haley laughed.

Tang chimed in. "Wait. Who's Tonya?"

"What? She hasn't said anythin' about her? It's all we hear. I swear, I'm best friends with her by proxy," Jen said.

Tang cut his eyes to Haley. "Haven't heard a thing."

"They were there when I was tryin' to lay the ground work, and I guess I just wanted to keep more of her to myself." After all the stuff he'd told her about his uncle, his ex-wife, and failing the sergeant's exam twice, she actually felt bad for not confiding in him.

The table went quiet.

"Awww, take notes, sweetie," Jen said to Nate.

"What? I say sweet shit all the time! Even when I don't want to."

"Ohhhh," Haley said. She was going to give him a few seconds to realize his mistake.

Nate flushed red and as if on cue, "Uh, sorry. That came out wrong."

"Uh-huh," Jen said.

Tang just laughed. When he finally stopped, he asked, "When, where did you two meet?"

Haley grinned. "Durin' a shootout."

Tang stared at her. She saw the lightbulb come on.

"No way. The woman at the gas station?"

"Yep. You met her at the hospital. She was the doctor."

He looked impressed. "That right there makes you the king of Pusstopia far as I'm concerned."

"What an honor," Haley deadpanned. "Don't you mean queen?"

Tang snorted. "No."

Nate, who'd been silent for the last couple minutes, let out a loud bark of laughter. They all looked at him. He shrugged. "What? It was funny."

CHAPTER 15

"I'm surprised you don't feel like you're too old to play tea party with Mama."

Tonya glanced up at her mother as she stirred in milk and sugar. "I'm seven, Mama, not twenty."

Nicole laughed. "Okay, baby, sorry." She lifted a tiny plastic bowl. "Lemon?"

Tonya held up her purple plastic cup embossed with pink flowers. "Won't that taste nasty with the milk in it?"

"Give it a try." Her mother smiled.

Tonya believed just about anything when she smiled like that.

Nicole fanned at imaginary tendrils of heat coming from Tonya's teacup and then squeezed lemon into it. "Go on."

Tonya brought the cup to her lips and took a dignified sip. Afterward, she made a slight gagging sound. "It's not for me, Mama. Next time we should have the kind with ice. It's hot outside."

Her mother smiled, laughed, and gazed at Tonya like she was the most precious thing ever. "You think Barbie or Ken might want some?"

They both turned to look at the dolls propped up in chairs that were way too big for them but just right for Tonya. "I don't know, but I think it's only fair that they try it too." She paused. "Wait, I have to fix Barbie's hair again." Tonya untied the bow around the doll's blond hair and did her best to get every stray tendril perfect. When Tonya put her down, she and her mother worked together to pour the tea and put in the sugar, milk, and lemon.

"Mama?"

"Yes, baby?"

"How come they don't make Barbies with skin like mine or dark like Daddy's?"

"Oh, they have black Barbies and Kens, but they just haven't gotten it right yet. When they do, I'll buy you all you want, okay? I tell you what. Mama will call them and try to help out a little and tell them to speed up making Barbies that are light brown like you." She wrapped her arm around Tonya and pulled her close.

"And dark like Daddy?"

"Yes, exactly.

Nicole disappeared, and Tonya was no longer a seven-year-old sitting in her childhood bedroom. She recognized the upstairs area in her own home, but before she could get a grip on what was going on around her, Haley appeared in her police uniform.

The fierceness in Haley's gaze made Tonya's stomach drop down to her knees. Her eyes were like blue crystal, translucent but still multifaceted. In them, Tonya saw hunger, intensity, and so much more. She reached for Tonya but instead of meeting her halfway, Tonya stepped back until the wall stopped her from going any farther.

Haley grinned and moved forward.

She pressed her body into Tonya's.

Tonya's response was immediate. Her breathing hitched, and her heart skipped a beat before it started ramming against her chest.

The heat between them was staggering.

Haley placed her hands against the wall on either side of Tonya's head.

Tonya was floating, in need of something to anchor her. She grabbed hold of Haley's biceps. Her muscles flexed and Haley trembled.

Haley leaned in, ghosting her lips across Tonya's cheeks and nipping at her chin.

Tonya whimpered, and the arousal that was already singing in her blood set fire to her.

Instead of finally kissing her, Haley stopped short and smiled.

"He's down there. You hear 'im?" Haley whispered, and each word spilled over Tonya's lips like an actual caress.

Tonya blinked. She was confused. Why were they talking?

Then she heard it, banging in the kitchen.

"You're a bad girl for havin' me up here."

Tonya's hands slid upward over Haley's shoulders, clutching at them. Her breathing was loud, ragged.

Haley urged Tonya's legs farther apart and pressed her thigh against Tonya's sex with enough pressure to tantalize and promise.

Need coiled so tightly within her that she broke. Tonya cried out. She didn't care who heard.

Haley groaned. The sound rumbled through Tonya's entire body, making her vibrate.

"You wanna be a bad girl. Don'tchu?"

At this moment in time, she wanted so very many things, and that was definitely one of them. "Yesss."

Tonya moaned as Haley's lips brushed against her own.

Haley's tongue slid into her open mouth and light exploded around them.

Tonya woke up with another moan falling from her lips. She sat up and leaned against the headboard. Pressing a hand against her racing heart, she whispered, "Jesus."

She swallowed a couple of times and squeezed her thighs together. That was where all the moisture had gone. Even her nipples stood at attention, pressing almost painfully against her clothing. Tonya took a couple of deep breaths and turned on the lamp. She reached for her glasses and her journal, then documented that the dream was repeat of *Tea Party with Mama*. Just thinking about it made Tonya smile. Her pen hovered as she tried to decide if she needed to include the part about Haley. A shudder racked her, and she wiped away the sweat beading her forehead.

"Jesus," she said again.

It was just a dream. Surely, it wouldn't be that potent between them? Maybe because it had been a while for her? Who was she kidding? She couldn't remember anybody who caused that kind of reaction.

She smiled.

There was no need to add anything else. She was satisfied with keeping it to herself. Tonya wanted to hold on to this feeling, and the thrill that came with it, for as long as she could.

A few hours later, after the sun came up, Tonya made her way downstairs. The smell of coffee greeted her. When she got to the kitchen, she went straight for the pot, ignoring her father, just as he was ignoring her.

She sipped from her cup, watching him. From his profile, he looked so much older than he had a couple weeks ago. Something fiery and painful gripped her heart before settling in her stomach. Tonya reminded herself he wasn't immortal, even though there were times he seemed to be. Desperate to make the hurt go away, she decided to reach out with softer words and less anger. It wasn't going to be easy. There was still a large part of her that wanted to scream that she refused to be invisible anymore.

Tonya closed her eyes and tried to center herself. When she opened them again, her father was looking at her.

He turned away quickly.

Tonya set her cup on the counter. "Daddy?"

His gaze stayed on his paper, but he had to be listening.

"You and Tracy are all I have left. We've talked, and we're trying to build something real between us." She paused. "You're my father. I wouldn't exist without you." Her voice was soft, reverent. "I don't want to be like this anymore. I can't go back. I know it's a lot, but to be able to get through this, we have to acknowledge the truth. Mama said and tried to do terrible things to me. You knew. I told you. I showed you."

He stiffened and swallowed loud enough for Tonya to hear.

"I should've been able to be a kid some of the time. There was too much on my shoulders. You could've helped more." Tonya tried to breathe, but it hurt.

Tears burned her eyes and she let them fall. "It only got worse after Brenda. It was like I didn't even exist except to play nursemaid. I watched you with Tracy. I watched you hug her, kiss her, smile at her. I never knew anything could hurt like that. We should've tackled this a long time ago. We'd both be better for it. I love you, Daddy, but it's hard to get to those feelings when there's so much anger."

Finally, he met her gaze. Instead of his usual blank stare, there was a lightness in his eyes.

"Da-ddy?" Tonya's voice broke. She stepped forward and reached out to him. She was terrified of his rejection, but she couldn't turn away.

Then, just like that, the brightness in his gaze was gone.

Tonya faltered. The brick wall she'd just slammed into had knocked the wind out of her.

"I said it before. Don't know why you keep bringing all this up. You turned out fine. Nice house, nice car, good job. You even taking care of your family." Robert pursed his lips. "Only thing you need to do is get some sense and find you a husband before I'm too old to enjoy my grandbabies." He looked at her expectantly.

Something broke open inside her. Tonya tensed her entire body to try to contain it. Exploding would get her nowhere. Regardless, fissures opened and emotions leaked through. Tonya wiped the tears away. "Are you that blind to think I've been celibate all these years?"

He stared. His expression was furious.

"Just because we didn't talk about it, just because you didn't see it, doesn't mean a damn thing. There've been other women, Daddy. Deep down, you know that. I don't want you to die living in this lie. There'll never be a husband."

Her father stood, a defiant expression on his face. He was about to run.

Some of her rage fizzled then, and that's when she started to pity him. "Do you make up stories about me to tell your friends? Do you make me into this perfect daughter?"

He tilted his chin up. "I do what I have to. They don't need to know all my business."

Tonya shook her head. She didn't know how to respond to that, so she didn't. This time, she was the one to walk away.

By the time Tonya got back upstairs, she felt like she didn't belong in her own skin. It hurt too much to be there. For a moment, she wished she could go back to sleep and revisit her dreams, but she was done with running. She took slow, deep breaths to try to calm her thundering heartbeat and loosen the coils in her stomach. She wasn't very successful. It took her a few minutes to realize that she needed to talk, to vent, and maybe get a little validation. Tonya paused as she reached for her cell phone, still plugged in on the nightstand. Talking meant she had to trust. It meant she had to reveal all the things she had been holding back. Right now, she was okay with that.

After selecting the contact, Tonya brought the phone to her ear.

"Hey! I was just about to call you. I actually slept in this mornin'."

Tonya closed her eyes. It was good to hear a friendly voice.

"Tonya?"

"I'm here. Can you just talk? I don't care about what."

"What's wrong?" Haley's tone was urgent and concerned.

It warmed Tonya and melted the ice encasing her where it mattered most.

"Please? Just for right now. Talk. When I'm ready, I'll talk back."

"Okay, okay, gotcha. So I took the work wife to meet my friends…"

Haley went on about lunch with Tim and her friends. There were parts where Tonya couldn't help but smile and even laugh.

"They already know about you. In fact, they're part of the reason I didn't give up when you tried to give me the brush-off. It's like I have my own li'l cheerleadin' squad."

Haley's words settled and spread to the deepest parts of Tonya. She could count the people on one hand who'd refused to give up on her, and now she could add Haley to the illustrious group that included Tracy as well as Stephanie.

"My mother developed mental health issues not too long after Tracy was born. The woman I knew for the first ten years of my life was gone. She was replaced by this mean, violent, and moody woman, and sometimes she scared me. I wanted to help. I was young and thought that seeing me help her and be there for her would snap her out of it."

Haley was quiet. Tonya took the phone away from her ear to make sure they were still connected.

"I'm here, Tonya."

Yes, she was.

"Things got progressively worse. She was on medication, and all it did was put her to sleep, but she'd wake up the same. When my sister got older, I did my best to deflect and keep her away from it, but I don't have superpowers."

"Where was your dad durin' all this?"

Tonya laughed, but the sound held no humor. "In denial? I tried to tell him the meds weren't working. I tried to tell him about the things she said, the things she did to me. I even showed him the bruises. He'd look right through me. He only spent time with his own wife when she was somewhat lucid, which did happen, but she was always quick to cycle downward. I spent most of my childhood and teenage years taking care of her and watching my sister grow up as Daddy's little girl. Then, when I figured out who I was, what I was, it just all went to hell."

She told Haley about Brenda and the consequences of her momentary happiness.

"Jesus Christ! I'm so sorry that happened to you. You didn't deserve to be treated that way, and whatever he's doin' now, you don't deserve that either. You're a better person than me. He's what? Livin' in your house, and you're pretty much supportin' him? I don't think I could do that, Tonya. The fact that you're able to blows me away. It's his loss for shuttin' you out like that."

"I agree. It took me a long time to get to that point. But it's my loss too. He's my father. I want a relationship with him, but it can't be on his terms like it has been. I can't hide who I am or how I feel about everything that's happened anymore."

"No, you shouldn't have to."

"One of the good things that came out of all this was when I was old enough, I started doing my own research about psychotropic medications and my mother's diagnosis. It took a while, but I finally got her doctor to listen to me about how her meds weren't helping. After that, there were times when she seemed like her old self. When she wasn't, she still didn't turn into…whatever she was before." She missed her so much. That hole her mother's death had left in Tonya's chest wasn't as big as it used to be, but it was still there. It still hurt.

"It's why you became a psychiatrist," Haley said.

"It sounds clichéd."

"No, there's nothin' clichéd about you and what you went through."

"I want things to be better, but I just don't know what to do anymore. I've tried, and I don't know if I have it in me to keep trying, especially since he just stops me cold every time."

"That man has got to feel a lotta guilt."

"I wouldn't know. He won't talk to me." Tonya ran her hand through her hair in exasperation.

"Is your sister at the house this weekend?" Haley asked.

"No."

"So it's just you and him?"

"Yes. Why?" Tonya was confused by the question.

"I don't like the idea of you bein' alone with him, especially if y'all just had an argument."

"If that's what you want to call it."

"I'm serious. I'm comin' over."

The thought, the gesture made her tear up again. "That's sweet, but no."

"Then you can come here. I don't care which. I'm at 1530 St. Roch."

"No, I just needed to vent. I don't need you to come save me."

Haley was quiet for several seconds. "No, you really don't, do you?" she asked softly.

"I don't, but it's nice to know that you want to. It's nice to know that you're here for—"

"Anytime, Tonya."

"Thank you." This connection between them was the one simple, easy thing in her life, and she was tremendously grateful for it. "I think I'm going to the gym. It'll help clear my head."

"If it's okay, I'm gonna call you in a couple hours and check in?"

"You don't have to ask, Haley."

"Just take care of yourself. Okay?"

"I will." This time she had to put herself first.

Haley puttered around the house with cleaning and laundry. Her thoughts were never far from Tonya. It wouldn't have taken much to find out which gym she was a member of, but that would be a tad—well, more than a tad—much. She'd felt out of sorts and useless after their conversation, but realized later that it was selfish to focus on herself when she couldn't even imagine the range of emotions Tonya was experiencing.

Her life had been all rainbows and kittens compared to Tonya's, and honestly, she was infinitely thankful for that. Haley had no idea if she possessed the strength to go through what Tonya had without being beaten down in the process. Her admiration and respect for Tonya was way up there, and the fact that Tonya trusted her enough to invite her into her world like that? Haley was floored. It was a hell of an honor. All of this gave her hope that they were going in the right direction. In a short period of time, Tonya had gotten under her skin.

For all she knew, it had started on the first day they met. Hell, maybe that morning changed them both somehow. Here she was, gung ho about jumping into a relationship when she hadn't ever been in one that actually worked for more than a minute. She didn't count her teenage years because being fifteen and screwing around with the neighbor's daughter was just reckless shit. But she was chasing after a woman and getting herself in deeper every day, and drama? It was sitting right in her lap. The kicker? Haley wanted…*wanted* to help Tonya sort through it all. Not just because it brought them closer.

Did she have some kind of weird hero complex? She *was* a cop, for Christ's sake. Haley slammed the door to the dryer shut. No, she didn't think so, and that was because of Tonya herself. She wasn't some damsel in distress. She didn't *need* Haley to come save her and help her escape from the tower her father put her in, but she *wanted* her nonetheless. It felt good to be wanted that way.

So, yes, she was willing to jump headfirst into this thing between them. Despite all the family craziness, her feelings for Tonya and her hopes for them felt like the most sane thing ever. It all had been as easy as breathing. She could do this. She could totally do this, and sooner or later, Tonya would realize that she could too. Haley pushed it all to the back of her mind, and to keep it there, she decided to make a gym run of her own.

A couple hours later, Haley stepped out of the shower. She felt refreshed, and her muscles were still buzzing from her workout. After drying off, she pulled on a T-shirt and boi shorts, then reached for her phone and immediately thought about calling Tonya. At the last second, she decided to give her a little more space and called Nate instead.

"You busy?"

"Yeah, but it's you, so what's up?"

"Nothin' much. We still on for Sunday night?"

"Yeah, I think so. In fact, I'm tryin' to wrap some stuff up so Jen can have the day off completely tomorrow."

"Aww, you're a good husband."

"And I know it. You goin' out tonight?"

"Yeah." Even Haley had to admit she sounded distracted.

"Well don't sound so enthused."

"Mm."

"Talk to Tonya today?" Nate practically sang the words. It was cute and irritating at the same time.

"Yasss." Haley smiled. "Of course I did."

"And?"

Haley wiped a hand over her face. Suddenly, she felt like she'd been hit by a runaway speeding truck. "I think I'm in trouble, Nate."

He laughed. "What was your first clue?"

"I mean...I just...how did this even happen? I actually spent a good part of the mornin' tryin' to figure it out."

"Didja?"

"Hell no!"

Nate laughed even harder. "Shit happens. What can I say?"

"I don't get it. Why her? Why now?"

"It's just your time."

"What? Isn't that what people say when someone dies?" Haley's voice went up an octave or two.

"Oops? Sorry. I think you're right."

"Asshole."

Nate chuckled.

"I should be scared. I mean, I am…a little, but it's not enough for me to run the other way. I want her, and I don't want any of it to stop. She's told me things that shoulda shaken me up. I ended up wanting to help, and I swear there's been times when my phone almost spontaneously combusted or somethin'."

"Jesus, Haley. Let me sit down." He was quiet for a second. "It's only been a few weeks."

"I know. I knoooow."

"Damn. I don't even know what to say."

"Jen would know." Haley walked into the living room and threw herself on the couch.

Nate snorted. "Probably."

"No probably about it."

"This is makin' you a little crazy. I think it's a good look for you." He sighed. "And you haven't even had sex with her yet."

Haley groaned. "Not even a kiss."

"Well, you can't do that through the phone."

"No shit?"

"When you finally do, y'all are probably goin' to put the world in nuclear winter."

Haley laughed. "Have to get to that point first."

"Hang in there. She'll come around when she figures out she can take you seriously. Let things happen naturally. Don't jump the gun."

"That's what you had to do with Jen, wasn't it?"

"Yup," Nate answered.

"Mm, but what if I really am like my mom and can't make it work?"

"She made it work with your dad, didn't she? Everybody else has been… not him."

He had a point. "Well, yeah. She still talks about him."

"There you go."

Jen said something in the background, her voice muffled but distinctly recognizable. It was time for Haley to end the call. "Kiss your wife for me."

"I will. You want me to have her call you?"

"Nah, it's okay. You're enough sometimes. You know?"

"Yeah, I know what you mean. I'll catch up with you later."

"Okay."

Haley hung up and immediately made another call.

"Hey, honey!"

Haley smiled. "You alone?"

"For the moment. Somethin' wrong?"

"No, not really. I was just talkin' to Nate. He said somethin' about my dad, and I just wanted to call you."

"You're so much like him, and you know, not only in the looks department. He was sweet, kind, but didn't take shit from nobody."

Haley grinned and lay down on the couch. "I know. I remember you tellin' me."

"It's the truth."

"It's been hard to find somebody to fill his shoes?"

Her mother went quiet for at least a full minute. Then she cleared her throat. "Maybe."

They talked for a few more minutes before Jeb made an appearance, and Haley definitely didn't want to go there after their last conversation. She'd been scared before that she was losing her mother, but now, she figured that Cathy was only busy trying to find herself. Haley got up off the couch to go fix lunch. While walking toward the kitchen, she sent a quick text to check on Tang. It would probably be good for him to know somebody cared.

How's it hangin.

It took a few seconds to get a reply.

Long and to the left. How's urs?

Haley laughed. She knew he was going to make this into something dirty.

U at work?

Fuck yes.

U get ne sleep?

Most of those energy drinks r not bad. Did
hav one that tasted like stale cum.

Haley knew he was just trying to distract from the question, and she'd give it to him this time. That didn't keep her face from scrunching up. The man could be disgusting. She didn't know why he always had to go there, but now that they were, she had to dance around with him.

And u kno this how? Smthng u need 2 tell
me?

Nope just using my imagination.

Scary.

Could be. Gotta go. Ty for checkin n rook.

Later.

Haley sat her phone on the counter and opened the cabinets. She pulled down some pasta and then went to the refrigerator for veggies, butter, and garlic. She glanced at her phone. In her opinion, enough time had passed. She needed to talk to Tonya. She put her back to the counter while she made the call.

"Hello again." Tonya sounded better than she had earlier.

"I was just thinkin' about you. Just wanted to—"

"I'm okay, Haley. My father was hiding in his room when I got home from the gym, and I'm out running errands now." Tonya's voice was soft.

"I know you are. If we could do this phone thing all day, I would totally be onboard."

"Honestly?"

"Oh yeah."

"I think I would be too," Tonya said.

Haley was floored for the second time today.

Relief wasn't a strong enough word. Her father's truck was gone when Tonya got home. This whole thing with him was getting more uncomfortable every day. It was hard to keep reaching out, especially when her hand was constantly smacked away. There had to be a way to ease the situation between them, but she was rapidly giving up hope. Tonya pushed down the feeling of desperation. She refused to let it hollow her out.

She wondered for a moment what her life would have been without all the upheaval. What or who would she be if her struggles hadn't defined her? Tonya slammed the door on that kind of thinking. She was who she was because of the path she forged, not because it was forged for her.

The living room television droned on, but she barely heard it. There were hundreds of channels, but the only thing interesting was on HGTV. Even that, she was beginning to find tedious.

Tonya's cell phone rang. It was Stephanie. She didn't even get the chance to say hello.

"I'd say we're on for tonight."

Not that she minded, but Tonya was curious. "It's the middle of the afternoon. Did he cancel?"

"Nope, I did, but he had a hand in it, or should I say a dick in it."

"I'm sorry, what?"

"He started sending me dick pics about an hour ago. Don't get me wrong, he was impressive, but I'd call that a red flag that his dreds are a little too tight."

Tonya laughed.

Stephanie joined in.

"Yes, you could be right about that," Tonya agreed.

"So, anything interesting happen in your life today to trump that?"

Tonya sobered quickly, but she chuckled anyway. "Where do I start?"

"Oh, sweetie, if you're willing to talk about it, wherever you want to."

Tonya opened her mouth and spilled out her heart, including everything that had hurt it past and present.

By the end, Stephanie was sobbing softly.

Tonya was immensely touched.

"How...how did you come out of that and be the person you are? I mean, you know how wonderful you are, right?"

Tonya knew her own value. That didn't mean that validation was unnecessary. "I—"

"Because you are."

"Thank you."

"Don't thank me. I'm just glad we're at this point. I was scared that there was this big chunk of you I was never going to get to know, and can I say, I want to smack your daddy? Because what he's doing is horseshit."

"It's something all right." Tonya paused. "I have to apologize again for not being a very good friend to you."

"Girl, stop. Just stop. It's okay. We're here, aren't we?"

"Yes, we are."

"Good, then I'll see you tonight. I'll pick you up at seven thirty. I'm feeling Copeland's tonight. Let's do the fancy one that has valet service."

"Okay, I'm in."

Chapter 16

Tonya dressed simply in her favorite pair of jeans and a white, button-down shirt that hinted at elegance. She put the finishing touches on her makeup. There was no need to go overboard. There never really was. Her skin was blemish-free. It was just enough to make her look natural and soft. Tonya squinted, giving herself one final look over. She fluffed her hair even though it already looked perfectly windblown. She pursed her full lips and made a duck face. Her eyes twinkled back at her and Tonya couldn't help but smirk. That look did no one justice. She looked closer still. There was something different about her, but she couldn't quite put her finger on it.

Maybe it was just a trick of the light.

Tonya's cell phone chimed. She looked down at it. Stephanie.

Came a lil early to rescue u just in case.

Tonya smiled. No, she didn't need saving, but it was nice to know that two people wanted to.

I'm fine. He's not even here.
B down in a min.

True to her word, Tonya was scooting into Stephanie's SUV five minutes later.

She turned to Stephanie and was immediately wrapped in a hug. Tonya felt warm all over. Her breathing stuttered in her chest. Stephanie squeezed her hard, and Tonya returned the embrace equally.

"I love you. You know that, right?" Stephanie whispered into her hair.

Tonya nodded. "I—"

Stephanie pulled back. "It's okay. I know." She paused and studied her. "You look nice, but there's something…"

So it wasn't just her imagination.

"Huh, there was one thing we didn't really talk about. How are you and Haley?"

Tonya smiled before she had time to even think about reacting.

"Oh…oh holy shit. There it is. You really like her, like a lot."

There was no need to hold back. "I do. She's, I don't know. The whole thing is so effortless. That's what I like about it, about her. But it's all just a little too perfect."

Stephanie pulled away from the curb. "Oh Jesus Christ, I wish I could complain like that. Maybe she chews with her mouth open or snores."

The thought of getting to that point caused her spine to tingle. "That wouldn't be enough to bother me."

"Maybe she's bad in bed."

"God, I hope not."

Stephanie glanced at her and roared with laughter.

Tonya almost blushed. "You know what I mean."

"You said what you meant."

"Shut up."

Stephanie laughed again.

There was an intensity to Haley, a heat, and Tonya had the feeling that it all translated very nicely into the bedroom. But she was jumping way ahead of herself. They hadn't even gone out on a date. And that was her fault. She needed to stop straddling the fence and figure out if she wanted to straddle Haley instead. That thought made her smile. It had Stephanie's influence all over it. On impulse, she made a decision.

"Let's go to GrrlSpot tonight."

Stephanie reached in her purse between them and pulled out some ones, presumably for the toll. "What? Are you serious?"

"Yes, I think I am."

"Then I'm so fucking proud of you."

Tonya turned and smiled at her. "That's extremely proud."

"It is!"

She was quite proud of herself as well.

During dinner, Tonya had checked GrrlSpot's website to see that they were at Phillips Restaurant and Bar tonight. Now that they were in the parking lot, anxiety settled in. She wasn't sure why she was nervous. They *knew* each other. All the talking, the laughing, hadn't been for nothing. They had jumped right past that awkward phase.

"There's no reason to be nervous. You guys already know each other," Stephanie said.

Tonya chuckled. "I was just thinking that."

"Well, hell, what do you need me for?"

Tonya reached out and covered Stephanie's hand with her own. She squeezed but said nothing.

They got out of the car and made their way in. Tonya entered first. The inside was decorated sleekly, and everything was symmetrical. The furniture was all square; even the couches had crisp lines. The seating areas were peppered with tables. Some had small glass tops, and others were long and granite-based. Music piped in through the stereo system, but it wasn't overwhelming. The place wasn't packed, but it was a good turnout so far. Men and women of various ages were present. Some were holding drinks, and some were digging into appetizers.

Tonya scanned the crowd for Haley.

"You see her?"

"No."

"I'm gonna go get us some drinks. Keep looking. I'll find you."

Tonya nodded. Her heart was in her throat and her stomach knotted in anticipation. She had an idea where Haley was. Sure enough, as Tonya got closer to the back, she spotted her. Among a crowd of young people, Haley still stood out. She was tall, striking. It wasn't surprising to see a woman stuck to her side and touching her arm. The girl, because that's all she was, was hanging on Haley's every word, watching as she tossed back the last of her beer. Tonya had no right to feel jealous, but she was human, so she did. Tonya leaned against the wall. She waited. It wasn't long.

As if Haley sensed her, she looked up. The smile that spread over her face robbed Tonya of breath. It was wide, bright...and in her eyes there was such surprise and excitement. That girl next to her? Tonya knew now that she didn't matter.

Haley moved away from the crowd surrounding her and made her way toward Tonya. All of Tonya's nerves fled. Haley stopped in front of her, but her eyes still moved, drinking Tonya in. There was that intensity, that hunger. She'd heard it over the phone, but to see it? Was so much better.

Tonya couldn't turn away from it. She didn't want to.

There was no awkwardness, no hesitation. So Tonya wasn't surprised when Haley pulled her into a hug. Haley's body was flush against hers, but it suddenly felt like she wasn't close enough. Then the smell of her, something citrus and spicy. How had she missed that before? Tonya pressed her face into Haley's neck.

Finally, Haley spoke. "Hey! I didn't expect…this is…just really nice."

Tonya hummed in agreement.

Haley pulled away slightly. The wattage of her smile went up a notch, if that was even possible.

"You doin' okay?"

Tonya nodded.

"You not speakin' to me?"

Haley caressed her cheek.

Tonya sucked in a breath.

"I really like those dimples."

Tonya's stomach did a flip, and her body warmed even more.

"But still no words."

What could she say? She'd known seeing Haley would have a potent effect, but not like this. She hadn't expected to be shaken. "Hi."

Haley grinned. "Hey. It's good to see you."

"You too."

"Now that we have a conversation goin'."

Tonya chuckled. She glanced down at Haley's T-shirt. "So tonight you're a Tool."

Haley laughed. "It's a band."

Tonya grinned.

"Something tells me you knew that already. You just wanted to call me names."

"Maybe."

Haley stepped back, and Tonya immediately missed the blanket of warmth.

"There you are. I wish I was a lesbian or even bi. I just got three numbers." Stephanie held up Tonya's drink and turned her attention to Haley.

She looked Haley up and down, paused at her T-shirt and laughed. "Given the conversation we had in the car, I certainly hope she has plenty of tools."

"Oh my God, will you shut up!" Tonya glared at her.

Stephanie smiled. "What?" She turned back to Haley and held out a hand. "I know we kind of met at the hospital, but just to remind you, I'm Stephanie."

Haley grinned. "I'm not even gonna ask what all that was about, but I've heard a lot about you."

"Hmm."

"It was all interestin'," Haley said.

"Well, good. I've heard a lot about you too. Not sure what words I would use, but definitely nothing bad."

Tonya watched the two of them. Already she was glad she'd taken this chance.

"I guess I should probably introduce y'all to my crew. I'm sure they're burnin' a hole in my back by now."

They all looked toward the pool table to the left. Haley was right; a few of them were studying them curiously, and that young thing that had been hanging off Haley scowled. Haley made introductions. There were handshakes, nods, and forced smiles. They were not the most personable bunch.

Tonya sipped on her gimlet, Haley on one side and Stephanie on the other.

"You ever play pool before?" Haley asked.

"No, never learned."

"I could teach you. They should be finished with this game in a minute."

"Okay." Tonya was on board if it kept Haley close and deepened the scowl on that girl's face.

Stephanie snorted. "Well if that isn't lesbian cliché number forty-seven."

"And how exactly would you know?" Tonya asked.

"Because it's straight people cliché number forty-seven too."

Haley laughed. "I like her."

Stephanie smiled.

A few minutes later, Haley was handing Tonya a cue.

"Okay, you get comfortable with this while I rack up the balls."

Tonya watched as Haley removed the triangle thing and set a white ball on the table. Haley turned back to her.

"You've seen enough TV to know the basics, right?"

"You know I'm not big on TV, but I use the white ball to scatter them. I know that much."

"Yep, but that's easier said than done if you don't know how to use the cue. So, let's get started." Haley's eyes were twinkling. "I'll help you with your grip and stance."

Stephanie was grinning like an idiot.

Haley moved behind her. Their bodies were flush again. This time back to front.

"Spread your legs a little bit, just enough to be comfortable," Haley whispered in her ear. She was close enough to make Tonya's hair move when she talked.

All the air disappeared in the room. Tonya gasped trying to find some.

"You doin' all right?" Haley asked.

Tonya nodded.

Haley smiled. Tonya could feel it. "We back to not talkin'?"

Tonya cleared her throat. "Just trying to focus."

"Mm."

Haley slid her arms around her.

Tonya's whole world tilted on its axis and everyone else fell away.

Her heart rammed against her chest, and breathing? She wasn't sure what that was. Surely, Haley could tell.

Haley positioned her hands. "Hold the cue like this." Her voice was deeper, scratchier than it had been a second ago. "Now, lean forward."

Tonya was on automatic pilot. She followed Haley's voice and her body. Their hips lined up perfectly.

That was when she felt it. There was a little something extra between Haley's legs. Tonya's stomach dropped to the floor and there was nothing she could do to hide or stop the shiver that shot through her. Leaning back against Haley, Tonya reached for her arm and gripped it hard. She needed something to hold on to, to steady her.

Haley's hands fell to Tonya's hips.

Then Tonya heard it, felt it, the catch in Haley's breathing.

"Let's try this again." Haley's tone was soft and a little breathless. "Do you think you're up for it?"

Yes, dear God, yes. Her body was screaming at her. "Yes."

"Good girl."

The words heated her from within, sending out sparks. They were too close to the ones in her dream. She reveled in all the feelings bombarding her. It was an incredible rush. She was surprised, however, by the sound of her own laughter.

"Not the reaction I was hopin' for."

Haley was smiling again. Tonya could hear it in her voice.

"Me either."

"I'll take it either way."

Tonya glanced up and around her then. Stephanie was staring at her like she'd lost her head, and Haley's friends looked at them blankly. "I don't think your friends like me very much."

"I don't give a good goddamn."

Tonya learned how to hold the cue and break the balls despite the arousal whisking through her body. They talked and laughed. Haley was never more than an arm's length away, and somehow, she was always touching her. Time seemed to fly by, and soon Tonya was starting to get sleepy. She turned to Stephanie. "I'm going to the bathroom. You coming?"

"Yes, since women have to travel in pairs."

Tonya chuckled.

Once they were around the corner, Stephanie pounced. "Holy crap! I've never seen you like that before. Not that I ever had the chance, but holy shit, Tonya, you need to jump on this train. I think it's coming for you whether you want it to or not."

She could be right, and at that moment, Tonya couldn't remember the reasons she was against it in the first place. She nodded, "Yes, I—"

Stephanie grabbed her arm in a viselike grip and squealed.

"No...don't. Please don't do that."

"I can't help it!"

"Try." Tonya smiled.

"Oh, so you're only excited when Haley's around?" Stephanie teased.

"Did you just regress into a teenager or something?"

"Don't know. Possibly? I'll stop. Promise."

"Good, but I think I'm done for tonight."

The line for the bathroom moved slowly. Tonya was tempted to give up altogether, but she really had to go. When they finally came back out, Haley was in the hallway.

Stephanie nudged her. "I'll see you up front."

"I'll walk her out," Haley said.

"Oh, well, I guess I'll see you at the car, then." Stephanie grinned and walked away.

Haley moved slowly down the hallway, and Tonya inched along with her. Haley had her hands stuffed in the pockets of her cargo pants. Their elbows and shoulders touched.

"So it's time for you to go, huh?"

"Yes, it's been a long day. Most of it was good."

Haley flashed a smile. "Glad to hear that."

"You should be. You had a hand in it."

"That's even better."

They stopped as they got closer to the restaurant area, and before Tonya could say more, she was in Haley's arms again. This hug was different. Haley's hand slid down her back. The caress left a trail of fire that made Tonya's insides tremble. Reluctantly, Tonya stepped back. Before moving away completely, she pressed her lips against Haley's cheek. She wanted to do more, but for some reason, she didn't.

Haley pulled her close again.

"Friends do that. I don't wanna be your friend."

When Haley's lips brushed against hers, Tonya gasped at the softness of the kiss. Trickles of heat filled her. She whimpered and clutched at Haley's shoulders.

The world fell away again.

The kiss ended, but Haley's mouth ghosted over Tonya's cheek. Haley's chest heaved and her breathing was loud, ragged.

"Go out with me," Haley whispered.

Tonya could almost taste her words and the need they were wrapped in. "Okay."

This time when their lips met, Haley moaned. She tilted her head to the side and teased Tonya's lips open.

It didn't take much.

Tonya was spinning. She felt drunk. The need to take in air burned her lungs, but breathing was something she could do any day. There was a different fire in her that took precedence. Haley's hand tangled in her hair, and Tonya accepted that she was going to be consumed.

It took someone bumping into them to tear them apart.

The man slurred, "Excuse me," then wobbled his way down the hall.

Haley stared at her, but Tonya couldn't read her expression. A slow smile spread across Haley's face, and she became an open book again. "You said yes."

"I did."

"Yay!" Haley looked like she had won something big.

Tonya laughed. She couldn't remember ever feeling this alive.

Haley grabbed her hand and pulled her out of the hallway. "So call me when you get home."

Tonya was surprised. "It's already after one."

"Don't care. Just for a minute. We can set a date and make plans when I talk to you later this mornin'."

"Yes, okay." Tonya tugged on Haley's hand, and when she turned, she wiped at Haley's mouth. "Lipstick."

"Mmm, thanks. Do you remember where y'all parked?" Haley pushed the door open, and Tonya immediately missed the air conditioning. The humidity was stifling.

"I think so." Tonya pointed with her free hand.

They walked for several seconds. Haley never let go of her hand. Not that Tonya wanted her to. "There it is." They were parked near a streetlight.

Stephanie helped by honking the horn and waving.

Haley bent forward as Stephanie let down the passenger-side window. "Here she is, safe and sound."

"Well aren't you a gentleman," Stephanie said.

"Occasionally."

She stood up, winked at Tonya, and opened the car door.

"Don't forget to call me. I have my phone in my pocket. I'll step out to answer."

"I won't," Tonya promised.

Haley gazed at her. She reached and played with the ends of Tonya's hair, looking at her like she saw something incredible. It drew Tonya closer, and before she knew it, they were kissing again with enough hunger to make her weak.

When Haley stepped back, Tonya was breathless.

"Jesus," Haley whispered.

Tonya laughed as the dream from this morning flashed before her. She had said the exact same thing, but the reality was a hundred times better.

"There you go, laughin' at me." Somehow Haley looked put out and amused simultaneously.

"No." Tonya got in one last chuckle. "It's not you. Well, it is kind of. I had this dream. I'll explain later."

"Okay. I better get back."

Tonya nodded and got into the car. Haley waved and walked away. Tonya watched until she was back inside. It was only then that she turned to Stephanie.

Her friend's smile was so big, it probably hurt her face.

Tonya sighed but smiled back.

Chapter 17

Haley added an insane amount of sugar and cream to her coffee, so much so that it was lukewarm when she sipped it. She smiled and smacked her lips. The chocolate-and-caramel creamer really hit the spot.

The leather of the sofa stuck to her bare legs, but at least it was warmed now by her body heat. Haley yawned so hard her toes curled. Propped up slightly, she leaned her head back against a cushion and sucked in a deep breath. She was a morning person but didn't necessarily like that about herself. Still, mornings had become more interesting. So she was learning to appreciate them in spades.

The past few weeks had been unbelievable, but now things were different. Now she knew how Tonya tasted, how she felt, and the way she sounded. The phone calls brought all that back full force like some sort of virtual reality. Haley loved every minute of it. She'd always enjoyed the chase, but it was usually a short one where soon she lost interest.

Haley was still trying to figure out what it was about Tonya. She was smart as hell, funny, and she knew her own mind. And she was hot. Her hair, those curls, they always looked tamed and mussed at the same time. There was the way she smiled. She didn't do it often, but when it happened, it was always something to see. She was almost as tall as Haley, which pretty much ensured that she would have every curve pressed against her when they were close. Yeah, that was definitely a bonus. Haley took a sip of coffee. Her mouth was getting dry.

Haley's thoughts came back around to the kiss. Jesus Christ she hadn't expected it to feel like it did, like she was in the middle of a flash fire that started from the inside and swallowed her whole. She wanted more. Maybe Nate was on to something with that whole nuclear-winter thing.

Just thinking about their upcoming date this weekend made the butterflies in her stomach play tennis. She had no idea where to take her. Tonya had money but she didn't seem to like to flaunt it. Haley got the feeling that something overly fancy would be the wrong move. It was Thursday, so she still had two days to figure it out. Nate and Jen had a ton of suggestions.

Haley smiled and tossed back the last of her now-cold coffee. They were cute. Nate and Jen seemed like they were almost as invested in this "relationship" as she was.

Her cell phone started vibrating, dancing around on the coffee table. Haley picked it up quickly.

"Mornin'."

"Good morning."

"Dream about me last night?" Haley asked. She was grinning the whole time.

"As a matter of fact…"

"Really?" Haley sat up. "Do tell."

"You were showing me how to fire a gun."

"Aww that's all? I was hopin' for somethin' a li'l more sexy."

"Well, you were in uniform." Tonya was breathless.

Haley perked up even more. "And you like me in uniform?"

"Yes."

Haley's stomach knotted. "Mm, at least you got somethin' out of it." Speaking of her uniform, she should probably get up and start getting dressed for work.

"Maybe."

Haley tilted her head to hold the phone between her shoulder and neck while she put on her pants.

"You're not still in bed, are you? I hear rustling."

"No, just gettin' dressed. I got a little distracted. I guess it's too bad we can't video chat since I have an Android. Coulda been a nice show."

"I'm driving," Tonya said, but there was amusement in her tone.

"And? I shouldn't be the only one sufferin'."

Tonya didn't say anything for a few seconds.

"I was your distraction?"

"Mm, and I don't mind it at all. Relivin' the other night, I can't complain."

"Haley."

She loved it when Tonya said her name, like she was aching. This was new, and Haley was totally into it.

Haley hummed in response.

"I'm driving," Tonya repeated.

"What if you weren't?" Haley was now on a mission to rattle Tonya.

"Then I'd be walking into a cold shower right now."

Haley wasn't disappointed. "Does that help you? 'Cause it doesn't do a damn thing for me."

Tonya sucked in a breath. "You're doing this on purpose." It wasn't a question.

But Haley answered it like it was. "Yeah, I am."

"Congrats. You won."

"Wasn't a game."

"What would you like to call it, then?"

"I just like the way you make me feel, and I don't mind showin' it. Too bad I won't get to see you in person 'till Saturday, but I know you like things a certain way. I'm cool with that. Doesn't keep me from tryin' to tempt you, though. You could just come over for dinner tonight, but I should tell you about the no pants rule."

"Your friends are okay with that?"

"It's somethin' I just started for special guests. 'Course it wouldn't be just you. I do it all the time. Just want you to be comfortable."

Tonya laughed. "Oh, is that all?"

The laughter broke down some of the growing tension. Haley was okay with that. "Mm-hm."

"If you're like this now, I bet you were a handful as a kid."

"'Course I was. I spoke my mind, and if there was somethin' I didn't wanna do, I found a way out of it. Used to drive my mom crazy. When I was little, I didn't like wearin' dresses. Didn't feel right. There was some Fourth of July community thing going on and my mom bought me this sundress. It was some weird peach color. She thought it would appease me to let me wear Wonder Woman underoos with it. Once we got there and her and my stepdad's backs were turned, I came up outta that dress. I think I was able to run around for a full ten minutes in my underoos, white bobby socks, and patent leather shoes before they caught me." Haley pulled on her shirt and stared buttoning it.

"Oh. My. God." Tonya's laughter was loud and long. The sound brought a smile to Haley's face. She waited for Tonya to calm down before continuing.

"If we were doin' somethin' I really enjoyed, like skatin', I could be a perfect li'l angel. Didn't wanna mess that up. It was one of my favorite things to do."

"Really, that was your favorite?"

"Yeah, that and playin' house with the neighbor's Barbie dolls, but only when she let me play house with her too."

"You're making this all up!" Tonya was laughing again.

"I am not!" Haley paused. "I'm not tryin' to dampen the mood or anythin', but I know you didn't have the chance to do a lot of kid stuff growin' up."

"No, you're right. I didn't." Tonya sounded wistful.

"I tell you what. I like havin' fun, so maybe you can consider hangin' with me kinda like your second childhood. Maybe we'll play house too." Haley put on her shoes and gathered the rest of her things before heading back toward the living room.

"You make it sound *so* appealing."

"It'll be an adventure for both of us. I haven't really dated anyone since freshman year in college, and that crashed and burned because I got tired of being sucked into lesbian drama. Everyone knew way too much of my business. She made sure of that."

"Sounds like something a little girl would do. I don't think you have to worry about that with me. I grew up a long time ago."

Haley liked the sound of that, especially that last part. "I know. I like that about you." She paused. "You said 'with me'. Are you?"

"I have my fair share of drama," Tonya said.

"I know that, but it was there already. I'm only a part of it because I wanna be."

"Why?"

"I got this feelin' it'll be worth it."

"How would you know? We haven't known each other long." Tonya didn't sound upset.

"We've done nothin' but talk, and I think it was the best thing for us. I probably know more about you now than I woulda learned in ten dates. I *know* you, Tonya. I'd like to think you know me too, and you didn't answer my question."

"Yes, I'm with you."

Something bubbled up in Haley's chest. She silently pumped her fist in the air like she was in some corny '80s sitcom. It was a little embarrassing, and she was glad that she was alone.

"Haley?"

She closed her eyes. There it was again. That sound. "Yeah?"

"I like the way you make me feel too."

Haley sat down. If Tonya was in front of her right now, they'd probably be setting the whole room on fire. "Okay."

"Okay," Tonya repeated softly.

Haley was suddenly struck with an idea. "Don't worry about Saturday. I got it covered." She couldn't keep the enthusiasm out of her voice.

"Should I be scared? You sound like you did when you were telling the underoos story."

Haley chuckled. "Well, you're either gonna love it or think I'm crazy as hell. I'll pick you up at six o'clock. Don't wear anythin' fancy."

"That's...well, okay."

Haley locked her front door and headed for her truck. "It'll be memorable?"

"I have no doubt."

Haley shook her head as she stared at Tang. He looked like somebody had run him through the washer a few times, and it wasn't the gentle cycle. He was kind of clammy and a lot paler than usual.

"You look like petrified shit and it's gettin' harder every day."

Tang glanced at her as he started the car. "Well, fuck you very much."

"You're welcome, but seriously? That's all you gotta say?"

"What in the blue fuck do ya want me to say? You know the deal. So get off my goddamn back."

"No, you're my partner. I'm doin' what I have to do."

"Well, I got enough shit to carry; I don't need your useless ass on me too."

"Insultin' me isn't gonna change anythin'. Are you supposed to be scary? Or just hurt me? You gotta know by now I don't break all that easy."

Tang grumbled.

"What?"

"Nothin'!"

"That's what I thought. Listen, just take a day or two off and catch up on sleep. It's paid, and it makes sense. Hell, even do some sick days until you get over the hump."

"Yeah, I'll think about it. That's actually not a bad idea." He took a long sip from an energy drink.

Haley noticed that there was a brand new can of that crap in the cup holder. "And stop drinkin' this shit too! It just fucks with your brain."

To tell the truth, Haley was worried and she was fast becoming a little disgusted with him as well, but showing that wouldn't help matters any. "I get it. I do. You're not concerned about yourself right now. It's all about your uncle, but what about me? The less sleep you get, the worse your reaction time will be. I'm tryin' to have your back here, but I need to make sure you're able to cover mine too. This isn't small-town USA. Shit really goes down here."

As he stopped at a red light, Tang sighed and let down the window to pour out the drink, the opened one anyway. It was a start. She stared at him. His face was flushed red. She wasn't sure if that was due to lack of sleep, embarrassment, or anger. Could be a combination of all three.

"You're right. I know all this shit, but I guess I've been so blindsided." Tang glanced at her and then looked away. Haley kept studying him, looking for other clues that he was falling apart. His grip was white-knuckled on the steering wheel. His throat bobbed as he swallowed.

In the periphery, she saw that the light had turned green. The car didn't move. Instead of blowing their horns, people just drove around them.

"They're not gonna let you ride by yourself. You're still too green."

Haley figured that.

"I'm not…I'm not gonna come back the next day and find out you put in for a partner change, am I?"

She was surprised by the question. He barely looked at her, clearly bracing himself.

"What? No! If I was gonna do that, I would've the first two weeks. Trust me when I say I was tempted as hell."

It was kind of an emotional moment, and Tang tried to cover it up by snorting. "You and me both, Rook." The light was green again. Tang drove forward.

Haley rolled her eyes. "Whatever." She didn't speak for a couple of minutes. "I'm not goin' anywhere. We'd really have to be a fuckin' mess together for that to happen, anyway."

Tang grunted. "So what's goin' on with the new panties? Y'all settled on that date yet?"

"I bet women just throw themselves at you. Don't they?" She went with the subject change; riding him about this whole thing wasn't going to fix it.

He grinned. "I don't got that name for nothin'. You gonna answer the question or not?"

Haley smiled. "Yeah, I figured it out. It'll either sink or swim. No in-between."

"You sure you know what you're doin'?"

She scoffed. "Hell no. I just know I can't do the same shit I usually do. She's different."

Tang laughed. "I remember that feelin'. I mean, I hate her guts now, but when me and my ex-wife first met, let's say she's the only woman that made me tongue-tied."

Haley shook her head. "Would you look at that? Mr. Poontang has a heart, and it might be a romantic one."

"I don't. Shut the fuck up."

Haley laughed.

Tonya was soaring toward an unfamiliar high. With everything that was going on with her family, she should have been contemplative, angry, even fearful. Tonya was indeed all those things, but today, right now, those emotions were background noise. At the moment, she was teetering toward happiness. She'd flirted with contentment before: when her mother was alive and close to being the woman she remembered; spending time with Stephanie; and even her job during a time of breakthrough or understanding. However, the feeling was never as palpable as it was now. Tonya could almost reach out and touch it.

It was hard not to trust something that brought so much warmth with it. Wasn't it time? Wasn't it her turn? Tonya wallowed in all the good stuff coming her way. She leaned back in her chair to enjoy it.

A knock at her office door brought her thoughts to a screeching halt. Tonya glanced at the time. Fifteen minutes had passed without her even being aware of it. She looked toward the window and waved the tech inside.

Tonya smiled when he entered with a patient in tow. She extended her expression to encompass them both. "Thank you, Marcus."

The tech dipped his head slightly before leaving. Tonya gave her attention to the man still standing. He was tall and several shades darker than her own creamy complexion. His head was bald, but his eyebrows, mustache, and stubble were white. He looked to be a man who used to take care of his body. His forearms were corded with muscle that extended underneath his T-shirt, but his stomach protruded over his pants.

"Have a seat, Mr. Ives."

He didn't look at her or even acknowledge that she'd spoken. Tonya gave him a few seconds to comply.

He remained standing.

It was a little strange that Mr. Ives chose to be obstinate about such a small request. "Do you want me to stand up too, or are you okay with me sitting down?"

He looked at her then. "That's up to you. I don't have control over what you do."

"That's true. Would you be willing to answer some questions, Mr. Ives?"

He shrugged. "That depends on what they are."

"Some of them are personal and could be difficult."

"What'll happen if I don't answer those?"

"Not a thing."

He stared at her. Then his eyes narrowed. "No tricks and no special medicine to put me in a…easier mood?"

"We don't do that here."

Mr. Ives grunted.

"Why do you think you're here, Mr. Ives?"

He just stared at her.

"You're in an adult mental health ward. Do you think that's where you need to be?"

He still didn't respond.

Tonya studied him. "Do you plan on answering any question I ask you?"

Mr. Ives blinked.

Inexplicably, Tonya was agitated. She picked up the assessment paperwork and stood.

She walked toward him slowly. "How about this? You look over this form and mark the questions you're willing to answer or just go ahead and write down what you want to say." She wasn't above meeting him halfway. Whatever helped the most.

Tonya held out the paper. Mr. Ives glanced at her and took the form. He folded it and put it behind his back.

Tonya tried really hard not to sigh out loud. It wouldn't help for him to know he was getting to her. Frankly, she was stunned by her reaction, especially given her recent good mood.

"I'm here to help, Mr. Ives. I don't want to take anything from you or force you to accept something you don't want. I want to work with you, not against you."

Mr. Ives brought the paper to his chest and started tearing it to pieces. He stared at her, defiant. Tonya looked at him and analyzed her growing irritation. His attitude, passive-aggressive behavior, and obvious need for control reminded Tonya of her father. She wasn't the right person to help this man.

She walked around and behind him to open the door. Mr. Ives turned, and Tonya did her best to smile.

Mr. Ives looked confused. His face hardened and then went blank as he walked out the door. Tonya motioned for a tech to follow. She glanced toward the main desk. Stephanie was staring at her. She must have seen something in Tonya's face, her eyes. Stephanie began to move toward her.

With a shake of her head, Tonya silently stopped her. Stephanie nodded but still looked worried. Tonya tried to smile, but it wasn't easy.

Tonya turned and reentered her office. Her anger shifted from the background to the forefront. She was upset with herself, but most of all, she was upset with her father. Tonya couldn't allow their deteriorating relationship to seep into her professional life. It wasn't healthy for her or her patients. She had to find some way to deal with it. She looked at the time and pulled her cell phone from her purse.

She dialed without hesitation.

"Hey! Pretty good timing. I still have twenty minutes to my next class," Tracy said.

"I think there's a possibility that you can help me with Daddy."

Tracy was quiet, but Tonya could practically hear her thinking. Maybe she was trying to come up with ways to let her down easy. Why would she want to damage her relationship with their father? It was damn near perfect as far as Tonya could see.

"Okay, but I can't come until after work Saturday night. I got another part-time job so I could start saving money now, but I could be home by eleven thirty or so."

Tonya blinked. She opened her mouth to speak, but she had no words.

"You're my sister, my family. I want things to be right between all of us."

Tonya cleared her throat, but the lump was still there. "I do too."

"You know, I'm really ashamed of it now, but there were times when I was so jealous of you. I knew Daddy treated me differently, better, and I played that up just to hurt you. The last time wasn't that long ago either."

Tonya's grip on her phone tightened, and she dug her fingers deep into the leather on the arm of her chair. For a few seconds, she felt hollow. They had been hiding from each other for so long. After the moment passed, confusion set in. "Why would you be jealous of me?"

"You're kidding, right? You're successful, beautiful, and strong. You knew exactly what you wanted, and you worked your ass off to get it. You take care of us. If the shoe was on the other foot, I don't think I could've handled even half of what you have."

"I disagree." Tonya was completely taken aback.

"It doesn't matter if you agree or not."

"I don't even know what to say."

"Yell at me. Tell me how terrible I am."

"You have all the freedom I didn't. You get to live your life, and he looks at you like you're his entire universe."

"Tonya, I—"

"No, I need to say this. Sometimes it was hard being in the same room with you. I thought as we got older that it would get easier. There were times when it was, but a majority of it wasn't. I felt so petty, and I didn't like who I was when that happened. I was…am jealous of you."

Tracy sucked in a deep, shuddering breath. Tonya's grip on her phone and chair eased. Instead of feeling apprehensive, she felt a bit lighter.

"We're something else, aren't we?" Tracy asked. "Can you imagine how different things could have been?"

"Yes. I used to wonder about that."

"What we did to each other…" Tracy's voice thickened, and then she sobbed. "We're…sisters."

Tonya couldn't breathe through the band of emotion tightening around her chest.

Tracy sniffed. "How can I help with Daddy? I'll do whatever you need me to."

Tonya was touched deeply. "Just tell him the truth, and I think it might help a little to know that you accept my sexuality."

"You think?"

"I don't know, but anything has to be better than it is right now."

"Yeah, I don't think he can ignore all this forever," Tracy agreed.

Tonya's stomach rumbled. She glanced at the time at the bottom of her computer screen and decided to finish one more progress note before taking a lunch. A few minutes later, her phone vibrated. She'd forgotten to put it back in her bag. Tonya peered at the words flashing across the screen and snatched it up immediately when she realized who the text was from. Haley.

> *I'm sorry 2 bother u durin the work day…*
> *well kinda but I hav a very good reason.*

Really? What's that?

Tonya smiled and something inside her lit up. Maybe this was just the boost she needed.

> *Shrimp poboy from Danny and Clyde's.*

??

Tonya's stomach growled again.

> *Lettuce, tomato, extra pickle, hot sauce,*
> *extra mayo and no onion.*

Is that what ur eating? You like no pickles
extra tomatoes.

> *Glad u remembered. No it's not mine. I'm*
> *close 2 the hospital. I could get it 4 u if u*
> *let me come c u.*

Tonya was thrown by the request. Like she sensed her hesitancy, Haley sent another text.

> *Saturday is 2 far away. I wanna c u*
> *jus for a min. I kno ur busy.*

We talk every day.

> *Not enough anymore.*

Haley was right. It really wasn't enough. There had been many times this week when Tonya wished she could crawl through the phone. Besides, seeing her would probably improve Tonya's mood.

I'm in uniform and I'll let u hold my gun.

Tonya chuckled. This impulse was too powerful, too good to pass up.

*Meet me on the first floor of the parking
garage near the elevator.*

Unless it was in an official capacity, Haley wasn't allowed on her floor, and it didn't make sense to meet her in the cafeteria or waiting areas where they'd have to deal with crowds of people.

For several seconds, there was nothing.

Really?! I'll be there in 15. Cold drink?

Sweet tea.

Got it.

Tonya stared at her phone. Yes, it was out of character to disrupt her day like this, but the incident earlier had left her vulnerable. She was less concerned about propriety than just feeling good again. She stood and went into the bathroom to check her appearance. Once satisfied, she left her office and nearly ran into Stephanie.

"Perfect, I was just coming—"

"I'll be back."

Stephanie gave her a strange look. "Is everything okay? Family emergency?"

"No, I'm meeting Hal—"

"Ohhh." Stephanie grinned. "She's coming here? To the hospital where you work? I'm sure that's probably against some rule of yours."

Stephanie was right, but for the moment, Tonya didn't care. "Well, if they're my rules, I can make an exception."

"Uh-huh, tell her hello for me. You know, if you actually get the chance to speak."

Before Tonya could respond to the playful snark, Stephanie turned and walked away.

When Tonya stepped out of the elevator, there was more than one police car in the parking garage, but apparently Haley spotted her. The doors to the cruiser closest to her opened. Haley and her partner emerged. Tonya didn't pay much attention to the man at Haley's side or the bag she was carrying. Haley moved with her typical confident swagger, but to Tonya it seemed more pronounced. When Haley grinned, Tonya's heart stuttered before correcting itself.

Haley's grin turned into a full-blown smile as she stopped in front of Tonya. Her eyes narrowed and she stared like she was trying to figure out a puzzle.

Her partner sighed and stepped forward. "I guess she left her manners in the car. I'm Tim. We didn't really get the chance to meet first time I saw you." He held out his hand and Tonya shook it.

"I'm Tonya."

"Sorry. Got a little distracted," Haley said sheepishly as a blush spread over her face.

Tim snorted. "I bet."

Tonya gave her complete attention to Haley. Before she knew what was happening, she'd stepped forward. Her stomach dropped. Haley's eyes darkened.

"Uh, I'm just gonna go wait in the car," Tim said.

"Yeah, okay." Haley didn't acknowledge him any further.

They moved back toward the elevator as a couple of cars came around the corner.

"What's wrong?"

Tonya was surprised by the question, pleasantly so. "What makes you think—"

"Because I'm pretty sure you wouldn't normally do somethin' like this."

Haley really did know her. Or, at least, she was starting to. "Rough morning." People walked around them to get to the elevator.

"Your dad?"

Tonya nodded.

"Sorry." Concern creased Haley's forehead. The expression made Tonya want to touch her.

"Thank you."

"Sure you don't wanna play with my gun? Safety's on."

Tonya laughed, and it felt incredible.

Haley smiled.

"No, but can I?" Tonya stepped closer until they were almost touching. Feeling bold, she slid her arms around Haley's waist as though it was something that occurred regularly.

"Anytime you want."

Tonya wrapped herself around Haley. *This* she was starting to crave. Tonya pressed her face into Haley's neck, making her shiver. Even though her hands were full, Haley found a way to return the embrace. Tonya felt comfortable, safe, and wanted.

"You could pencil me in. I'd be willin' to come do this every day."

Tonya chuckled, but there was no denying the warmth caused by Haley's words. More cars drove by. Tonya moved back slightly and glanced up at Haley.

"Wasn't kiddin'." Haley's eyes were dark again, filled with heat and sincerity in equal measure. Haley glanced from Tonya's eyes to her lips and back again. "I really wanna kiss you right now."

More people milled about, waiting in front of the elevator, but Tonya didn't care. She wanted this, and she had finally learned that it was okay to want. When their lips touched, everyone else ceased to exist anyway. Haley's kiss was soft, teasing. She brushed against Tonya's open mouth until she could barely stand it. She balled a section of Haley's shirt into her fist and held on. As if her actions were some sort of cue, Haley's tongue swiped across her lips before dipping inside.

Tonya whimpered as a sudden flare of arousal tightened her stomach.

There was a loud crackle, but it didn't hold Tonya's attention.

"Rook, we need to go. Fuckin' Zoo."

Haley groaned and ended the kiss, but she didn't pull away completely. Now holding the bag of food and the drink in the same hand, Haley reached up and fiddled with the radio attached by a flap on her shirt. "Yeah, okay." Her voice was husky and her breathing was shallow. She pressed her lips against Tonya's forehead. "Call me later."

Tonya nodded as she smoothed out the wrinkled part of Haley's shirt. Haley handed her the food. "It's probably cold."

"I don't care." There it was again, that smile. Tonya was starting to think it was just for her.

"Later." Haley turned and jogged toward the car.

"Text me. Let me know you're okay!" Tonya called out as she remembered where they were going. It was one of the most dangerous parts of the city.

"Okay!"

Tonya watched until they drove away. Her heart was in her throat and her stomach was on the concrete. She was glad that she'd broken the rules.

Tonya was exhausted when she walked into Dr. Finn's office, but there was a heavy buzz right under her skin that made her feel as if her entire being was humming. It was a unique experience, and she was pretty sure it wouldn't be the last time she felt this way.

She sat down, and Dr. Finn studied her silently for several seconds.

"I apologize again for moving our appointment to later than usual."

Tonya waved it away. "There's nothing to worry about." She paused and met Dr. Finn's unwavering gaze. "A lot's happened."

"Somehow, I knew you were going to say that. Start wherever you want."

She began with her father and sister and ended with Haley. Once she started talking, it was difficult to stop. There was so much to release, pick apart, and celebrate.

Dr. Finn had started to smile halfway through and she hadn't stopped since. "The idea to include your sister is a creative change of pace. Well done, and it sounds like you and Tracy have taken several steps closer to each other. As for Haley—"

"I just feel so…" Tonya looked down at her hands, trying to find the words. "Selfish, but it's my turn to do what I want. I don't want it to stop, and it's all happening so fast I have to use both hands to hold on. I want a life. I want my family and Haley too. I want everything." She glanced back up at Dr. Finn. "Is it too much?"

She was still smiling. "Does it feel like it?"

"Sometimes, but just when I think it is…" Tonya thought back to earlier that day and Haley's appearance at the hospital. "She, Haley, balances it out. I'm not sure how."

"Because you let her. Remember, it's nice to have something positive when there is negativity surrounding you. It's good to see you finally taking a chance and letting people in."

"Multiplies my chances of getting hurt." Tonya wasn't being cynical. She was trying to be realistic. The thought sobered her a bit.

"That's part of the risk, yes, but you are getting to see rewards too."

"True." There had been times when she actually wanted to thank the idiots from the gas station. They had provided her with an eye-opening experience in more ways than one.

"No more nightmares or dreams we need to discuss?"

"No. They're evening out for now. Nothing new or troubling."

"Good. I am so proud of you. I want you to know that."

Tonya smiled. "I think that I'm proud of me too."

CHAPTER 18

Haley just stared, her mouth hanging wide open. She'd put pants on for this. "Look, I know I probably asked for advice when she first agreed to go out with me, but I figured it out. Not changin' things now."

It was barely 9:00 a.m. on a Saturday, and Nate and Jen were lounging around in her living room before heading to the restaurant. This was supposed to be her Saturday to work as well, but she'd been able to work some magic since Tang had taken off too.

Jen threw up her hands and sighed. The demented pixie look was back, but Haley found it more comical than anything. "You said she was older. Do you really think she's gonna enjoy somethin' like that?"

"I'm with Jen on this one, Haley. Maybe you're rusty or somethin', since you haven't done the datin' thing in a while."

"Whatever." Haley got up off the couch and headed into the kitchen to refill her coffee cup. "I'm nervous enough as it is without you guys goin' all mama bear on me!"

A couple minutes later, Haley sat down between them and sipped on her full cup of coffee. She didn't offer Jen and Nate any. They knew where the damn kitchen was.

"Okay, since I've known you, there's only been a handful of times I've seen you nervous about anythin' and the most recent has been about this woman."

Haley didn't hear a question in there anywhere, but Nate kept on talking anyway.

"Fucked anyone lately?"

"Yes, a few weeks ago, but what the hell does that have to do with anythin'?" Just thinking about it made Haley feel a little guilty, which, in turn, brought out some defensiveness. It really wasn't a big deal. She and Tonya hadn't been defined at the time. At least, that's what she told herself.

"Did you enjoy it? Or did you do it out of habit?" Nate wouldn't let up.

Haley shrugged. "I guess more of the second thing you said." That was easy enough to admit.

"No one since?" Jen asked. She was looking normal again.

"Nooo. Can we move on?"

Nate laughed. "I can't wait to meet Tonya. I'm impressed by what she's done in such a short amount of time."

"You act like I just met her yesterday. I'm pretty sure this whole thing started right after the shootin'. I was bumblin' around like some idiot tryin' to talk to her even then."

"Well you left that tasty bit out." Jen raised a brow.

Haley shrugged again.

"You'll be gettin' rid of the video games soon and probably end up wearin' collared shirts." Nate had a big-ass smile on his face.

Haley glared. "I plan on teachin' her how to play." She paused. "And I don't mind wearin' a polo or whatever every now and then. Can we get back on topic?"

"I thought we were." Nate just kept on grinning.

Haley growled. "I'm not changin' it. You guys don't know her. I was shaky about it at first, but now I know the idea is perfect. She needs some fun right now."

Jen pinched her arm. "Why didn't you say all that in the first place? Ass."

"Ow! Really?" Haley rubbed at the sore spot on her bicep. "I didn't think I had to. I thought you guys, of all people, would believe that I had this."

Jen deflated a bit. "Okay, maybe I'm a little nervous about all this too. I so want this to work out. I've never seen you like this."

"Yeah, I know. What I don't get is why I'm not runnin' or scared shitless. Maybe I'm savin' it all up for later. I don't wanna hurt her. She's been through enough. But I don't wanna stop either. I don't think I can."

Jen leaned against Haley's shoulder. "Relationships don't have to be all melodramatic. We're all adults, and sometimes things are just easy. I'd say hold on to that."

"Yeah, remember when we first met?" Nate smirked at his wife.

Jen rolled her eyes. "I'm gonna take that as a rhetorical question."

"When things got hard, I think knowin' that it used to be just the opposite helped."

"Yeah, I agree. And since we're goin' down memory lane, how about when you first introduced me to Haley?"

Haley groaned.

Nate and Jen laughed.

"You mean the fact that she was drunk, tried to hit on you, and then threw up on you?"

"Yes, that!" Jen agreed.

"Well, I've been waitin' forever to get revenge, so just wait till I meet Tonya."

Haley waved him off but grinned. "Go 'head. I bet she'll cut you off at the knees. I'll be right here laughin' my ass off. I still say if I'd been sober and Jen wasn't yours, she woulda been leavin' with me in fifteen minutes, tops."

"Bullshit!" Nate's face turned red, as it always did when they talked about this. It was epic, poking fun at him this way.

"She's sittin' right here. We could just ask, and maybe she'll be honest this time and actually give us an answer."

They both looked to Jen. There was a little smile on her lips and a look in her eyes. She was obviously amused. "No, this is a stupid conversation, and I refuse to lower myself to y'all's level."

Haley snickered. She'd expected that answer. It really was a stupid conversation.

Nate stood. His face wasn't red anymore. "I'm gettin' cereal. Anybody want?"

Haley shook her head and downed the rest of her coffee.

"No, I prefer not to be hopped up on sugar to start my day," Jen answered.

Nate made his way to the kitchen.

"Don't touch my Cap'n Crunch!" Haley yelled a minute later.

"Too late!"

Haley sighed irritably, and Jen patted her on the knee.

"You pick out a T-shirt and shoes yet?"

Haley looked away, feeling a little embarrassed. "Kinda. Two days ago."

Jen just smiled and waited.

"It's between Superman and Flash."

Jen laughed. "From what you've told me about her, I get the feelin' that she wouldn't care what you wore. Go with Superman."

Less than an hour later, Haley was alone. She was tempted to call Tonya, but they had already talked earlier. Haley was sure she would answer, unless she was still working out, but that was beside the point. She didn't want to overload Tonya on, well, her. They talked at least twice a day, and at night, sometimes it extended well past midnight. It was a wonder that she didn't go to work worn out. Somehow, she always had energy for more.

Haley sighed and got comfortable on the couch.

The whole thing had snuck up on her. It wasn't as if she walked around in fortified armor specially designed to repel women. Haley just liked things to be as uncomplicated as possible. So after that mess in college, combined with the revolving door of her mother's love life and the ups and downs with Nate and Jen, she figured there was no such thing as a smooth ride, especially where relationships were concerned.

In direct contrast, she'd chosen what could be a dangerous and demanding career. So what the hell was up with that? She'd been shot at, cursed at, and seen enough dead bodies to start her own mortuary. Haley had taken it all on the chin as part of the job. Was she affected? Hell yes, but she did her best to maintain some perspective, and having a support system helped things stay together. Haley was willing to put her body through hell to make it stronger. She had never wanted to do the same with her heart, but that tune was changing.

Haley refused to sit there and analyze anymore. She got up and headed into the kitchen for another bowl of Cap'n Crunch. If there wasn't at least half a bowl left, she was going to kill Nate.

With a glass of sweet tea in her hand, Tonya sat on her front porch to watch the late part of the day roll by. It had been ages since she'd done this. Lack of desire, and the heat, usually kept her indoors, but this afternoon the temperature was in the mid-80s. So with the ceiling fan on high and blowing directly on her, it was tolerable. As for desire, she had recently found the drive to do all sorts of things.

She waved at neighbors going into their homes, and even watched a group of teenage boys playing a very physical game of basketball. She didn't understand what she was seeing, but they seemed to be having a good time. Tonya shook her head and rolled her eyes when they argued about something called a flagrant foul. She stood, and the movement caught their attention.

They were all shirtless and sweaty, but a majority of them jogged across the street toward her anyway. The biggest one, the one who had been flat on his back on the concrete, stepped forward. His head was bald, and his chest was hairless and chiseled. He was a good-looking black man, definitely not a teenager. In fact, several of them looked a bit older.

"You saw, right?" He smiled, tone light and teasing. His gaze was direct.

Somebody groaned. "Brah, stop trying to flirt and let's get on with it."

"Yeah, it's a pickup game, and ya'll are losing. Free throws aren't gonna help."

Tonya was amused. "I saw you on the ground. I can testify to that."

More than one young man laughed.

"Well, I'm guessing you were watching me pretty closely. You had to see him practically clothesline me." He pointed toward one of the men in the back. "I'm Nick, by the way."

Tonya smiled. "Thank you, but telling me your name isn't going to improve my understanding of basketball."

Just then, the front door opened and her father stepped out. "It was all ball. Saw the whole thing."

"Told you! Can we stop wasting time? I gotta go to work in an hour."

Tonya glanced at her father. She turned back to Nick and said, "Hope that helps."

Nick smirked. "I could teach you the fundamentals. That way, next time you're out here, it'll make sense."

Tonya was flattered by his interest and repulsed by his sloppiness at the same time. "That's okay. I'll survive." She swirled her glass, circulating the ice cubes to make sure the last little bit of her drink was as cold as possible.

Robert stepped forward then and introduced himself. When she heard him say, "This is my daughter, Tonya," she snapped to attention, but it was his next words that made her stomach sink.

"You look like you need a cold drink, or we got sweet tea. Tonya made it, and it's good."

Was he presenting her like some sort of prized pig? Her father was standing right in front of her, but never had he seemed so far away. More sad than angry, there were so many things she could have said in that moment, but they were things he already knew yet refused to acknowledge. Instead of making a scene, Tonya walked into the house, leaving her empty glass behind.

Later, she wasn't surprised to hear from Stephanie. She'd been a ball of excitement ever since Tonya'd told her about the upcoming date.

"You want me to come over?"

"I've been on a date before. You know that, right?"

"I know that! But not since I've…how long has it been, anyway?"

Tonya sighed. "About a year."

"Jesus, your last date was that boring to you—"

"Yes, I didn't see a point. I just wasn't very interested in the whole thing anymore."

"Haley is different," Stephanie said.

"I agree. She is."

"That's not even the half of it. The two of you together almost burned my eyebrows off." Stephanie's voice was full of amusement.

Tonya smiled. She agreed with that too.

"You nervous?"

"You've already asked me that, what, every day this week?"

"And you haven't really answered me."

Tonya tried to think back, but she couldn't remember with any accuracy. "Yes and no. I'm looking forward to it." She paused. This was Stephanie. It was okay to be open. "I need this."

Stephanie was quiet for several seconds. "Is it getting easier? To talk to me, I mean?"

"I just don't see the point in holding things in anymore. It hasn't gotten me anywhere."

"You're right. Mercury must be in retrograde or something. Look at what you've got going on. We're closer than ever. There's Haley, and the thing with your sister. Has your dad—"

"No, he hasn't come around, if that's what you were going to ask. In fact…" Tonya told her about what had happened on the porch.

"You're fucking kidding?" Stephanie was outraged. Tonya didn't need the validation, but it was still good to hear.

"I wish I was." Before her morose thoughts struck again, Tonya interjected a moment of levity. "Nick would be perfect for you."

"Oh really? What does he look like?"

"Mm, think Tyrese Gibson."

"Oh God, I need to come hang out at your house more often. Maybe wear a bikini and stand on the curb with a pitcher of lemonade."

Tonya laughed. "That's quite an image."

"It would certainly be memorable."

"Yes, indeed it would. Now enough about me and my fantasies. It's almost four thirty. Go get ready."

Tonya couldn't argue with that.

Sometime later, Tonya looked at herself in the full-length mirror in her bedroom. She'd used a little more makeup than usual, making her appear smoky and sultry despite the casual attire. She glanced down at her pale blue shirt, done up to the last button, and loosened a couple of them, revealing a hint of cleavage. The silver chain with the dangling heart charm called even more attention to it. Tonight, she wore jeans instead of her normal pants. They hugged the curve of her hips and ass perfectly and drew attention to the length of her legs. She ran a quick hand through her hair to adjust a few errant curls, which only added to the tousled look she knew worked well for her.

Tonya took a deep breath and smiled. She had no idea where they were going, but Tonya had made her peace with that. Surprises were not a bad thing. She'd had a few of them lately that had ended up being very pleasant. Besides, it was Haley, who made her laugh, and ache.

Her phone chirped. Tonya grabbed it off the bed. It was Haley.

On my way, will call if I get lost.

Tonya pressed a hand to her stomach as heat curled through her. Still, she smiled as she typed.

I'm easy 2 find. Shouldn't b a problem.

See u soon.

Tonya put the phone down and turned back to the mirror, studying herself. There were no physical changes, but she knew she was different. Finally, she went downstairs. Instead of going into the living room to wait, she went to the kitchen to get a bottle of water. Her father was there, reheating something in the microwave. Tonya watched silently as he went from the microwave back to the refrigerator.

He paused for a second but didn't say anything. Tonya refused to let it affect her. Not tonight. They moved around each other as though they were dancers listening to completely different tunes. Tonya unscrewed the cap from her water and took a swig. She could always reapply her lipstick in the downstairs bathroom before she left.

Just as she raised the bottle to her lips again, the doorbell rang, and Tonya nearly poured water down her shirt. She looked at her watch. It was 6:01. Tonya had expected a phone call or a text when Haley arrived. This was a little old fashioned, as well as totally charming. Her father looked at her then, and Tonya smiled. She left him with his reheated food and walked to the front door.

She opened it, and Haley stood there.

Tonya blinked. She took in the Superman T-shirt and matching blue sneakers. It fit her well, and for some reason, Tonya was charmed even more. She chuckled. "So we're feeling super tonight?"

Haley's smile was huge, bright. "Yeah, we are." She stepped forward and pulled Tonya into a hug. Tonya held on tight and sank into the welcoming warmth.

Easing back a little, Haley whispered, "You look good." Then she kissed her. It was soft and quick, but Tonya felt it all the way down to her toes. "You ready to go?"

Tonya nodded and turned back to close and lock the door. She stopped when she saw her father standing in the dining room, watching them. His face registered anger, disbelief, and disappointment.

Before she could be bombarded with her own feelings, Haley wrapped an arm around her. "It's okay," she whispered right into her ear before pressing a kiss against it. Tonya glanced up; Haley looked like she believed what she'd said. So Tonya did too.

She closed the door.

As Haley pulled away from the curb, she glanced at Tonya. "You wanna talk about it?"

Tonya shook her head. "No. This isn't about him right now. This is about us. This is about feeling good." She meant every word. Nothing was going to ruin this.

"I'm all for that."

"Good. Will you tell me where we're going now?"

"Not a chance, but I'm damn sure you'll get a kick out of it. I really can't believe this is our first official date. Feels like we've been doin' this for a while."

"True. Is that your way of saying we're behind and you should've been in my pants already?" Tonya teased, smiling.

Haley laughed loudly. "No, but if you wanna get technical, you do dream about me. I bet I get plenty."

"I never said that!"

"Give me time."

"I don't know how you walk around with a head big enough to have its own zip code."

"I'm lookin' forward to you takin' me down a peg or two."

Tonya huffed. "I don't think it's possible."

"Well, if it helps, you could do anythin' you wanted. I don't think I'd mind."

Something burst inside Tonya's chest and spilled all over the place. She was hot and cold at the same time. For a moment, there wasn't room for anything else. "You say that now—"

"I gotta feelin' it'll be the same tomorrow too."

Tonya just stared. Haley paused the truck at the tollbooth and handed the lady a five-dollar bill. While she waited for change, she glanced at Tonya and gave her a dazzling smile. It was enough to kick-start Tonya's ability to form words again.

They talked on various subjects for some time, and finally Tonya realized they had been driving for a while. She looked out the window. "Are we in Metairie?"

"Yep."

"I wasn't paying attention, but since everything seems so clean, I figured."

Haley chuckled. "And no potholes. My shocks and struts are safer here, and so are we."

"I agree. I hate what Nagin said about New Orleans after Hurricane Katrina."

"Ah, yes, chocolate city."

"Exactly. The big leap in crime was blamed on all the black people coming back in, but most of them were the same people who lived there before. New Orleans was vulnerable, so it was easy for more criminals, whether they were black, white, or Hispanic, to slip in and take advantage."

"True. It was bad before, but nothing like it is now. I still love it here. Eventually, somethin' will break for the better and the city can move forward." Haley's words were naïve and idealistic, but she said them with conviction.

"That's—"

"I know how it sounds, but I'm gonna stay hopeful as long as I can."

Tonya smiled. It was good to be around such a positive person. She looked out the window again as Haley turned near a Taco Bell and then drove past it. "I got scared for a minute. I don't do Taco Bell. I was going to get out and walk home."

Haley laughed. "Some stuff on the menu is pretty good. I wish they had breakfast."

"I just lost all respect for you."

Haley didn't speak as she parked in a rather large lot. Tonya looked around, then up toward the sign reading *Airline Skate Center*. She was shocked, touched, and apprehensive. She didn't know the first thing about skating.

Haley glanced at her and reached out to rub the back of her neck. She looked eager and a little hesitant. "Well?"

"I think...I think this is the most unusual date I've been on. You have my attention, but you've had that since we met."

"Good on all counts. I thought you might like it. I haven't been skatin' in years. I'm probably more excited about it than I should be."

"Well, I guess I should probably tell you that I don't know how to skate." Tonya thought it was best to be up front.

"Don't worry about anythin'. I'll teach you the basics and be beside you the whole time."

After she paid the cashier, Haley opened the door. Once inside, the bass was deep enough to make Tonya's bones rattle. At first it was cacophonous, but her senses settled when Haley pressed her hand to the middle of her back and ushered her forward. The place smelled like leather, hot dogs, and nacho cheese. Picnic tables dotted the sitting area, and most of them were taken by people eating, resting, or changing into their skates. Tonya took it all in, and a bubble of excitement lodged in her chest.

A few minutes later, Tonya sat down, Haley beside her. She pushed her feet into her skates and tried not to think about the thousands of feet that had been in them before hers. In the middle of tying them, Haley kneeled down in front of her. She brushed Tonya's hands away and pulled roughly at the laces to make sure they were tight enough.

Haley said something Tonya couldn't hear over the music. She leaned forward. "What?"

"Feel good?"

Tonya smiled and nodded. Yes, all of this felt good.

Haley moved away to give Tonya room to stand, but when she tried, the world tilted and slid from underneath her. Tonya ended up right back where she'd started. At least it was the bench and not the floor.

"Sit tight. I'll be right back."

"Okay."

It wasn't long before she returned with some kind of contraption behind her back. "What is that?"

Haley went from smirking to grinning. There was a mischievous look in her eyes. With a flourish, she revealed her surprise. Tonya stared. The thing reminded her of a tiny walker. She scanned the sitting area. A lot of children had them as well. Tonya glared.

Haley laughed.

"You're an ass!"

"Oh c'mon! You know it's funny."

Tonya's lips twitched. "Maybe a little."

Haley reached out a hand, and Tonya took it. The world shifted again, but this time she was a little more steady while navigating it. Haley kept her eyes on her the whole time. Bending slightly, Haley whispered, "You ready?"

Tonya nodded. Haley kissed her ear. It was chaste and gentle, but Tonya still burned.

She was able to remain upright until they actually got on the rink. But when Tonya's feet slipped from under her, Haley was there to put things right again. She took Tonya's hand and held on tightly. People stared, but to Tonya their gazes meant nothing.

"Use the railin' if you need to slow down, not the stoppers on the skates."

"Okay!"

Tonya's heart raced as they went one complete turn around the rink. She was scared of falling, but at the same time, exhilarated by the music—something by Beyoncé. Haley was solid and warm against her. With each pass, they moved faster until it felt as if they were flying. It really was freeing. Haley glanced at her every few minutes. Tonya had initially been afraid to take her eyes away from the ground or the people in front of them. She wasn't anymore. She met Haley's gaze.

Haley smiled and started singing the song and bobbing her head. Tonya laughed and attempted to wiggle and sway to the beat. When she didn't quite pull it off, Tonya laughed even harder. Suddenly, she stumbled and the ground jumped up to meet her as if it had been waiting. Tonya yanked Haley down with her. Even then, she couldn't stop laughing. She wasn't hurt, and Haley was smiling so hard it had to be painful. But, her eyes…she looked at Tonya like she could swallow her whole. For a moment, Tonya lost the ability to breathe. People skated on around them while she reveled in the moment. Finally, Haley stood and pulled her up as well. She brought Tonya's hand to her lips and kissed her open palm before leading them around the rink once more.

When it was time to leave, Tonya was still flushed and soaring with excitement. She had no idea how to come down. Not even a blast of the hot, humid air from outside helped. Haley's hand was on her back. She would probably feel the imprint long after the night was over.

"You look happy."

"That's because I am."

"Winnin'." Haley grinned.

"Most definitely. So am I allowed to know about the rest of the date now?"

"I guess, but I'm sure we'll have to wait for a table since it's Saturday night, so let's stop for snoballs first. I'm thinking Deanie's Seafood for dinner?"

"Bucktown or the French Quarter?"

Haley stared. "Do I look like a tourist? The smell of urine and fried seafood just doesn't mix."

Tonya chuckled. "Bucktown it is." If this was what having complete autonomy over her life felt like, Tonya could never go back. In fact, she was sorry she hadn't done this a long time ago.

Haley sat down beside Tonya on one of the benches outside the snoball stand. Using her spoon, she mixed evaporated milk into her wedding cake snoball and watched as Tonya did the same with hers. So far, the night had gone way beyond her expectations. Haley wasn't sure if she could top the skating rink. Tonya had come alive. After seeing the dullness in her eyes when the date first started, her enjoyment was a beautiful thing to behold. Haley'd had no idea that she was capable of making someone that happy. It was a heady feeling that she could get addicted to really fast.

She studied Tonya's profile for a few minutes. She was still smiling slightly, making those dimples pop in the fading daylight.

"Stop. I can feel you looking at me." Tonya's words were so soft, Haley barely heard her.

"No." There was no reason to. When Tonya turned to look at her, the air thickened between them. "I don't want to." Haley reached out and brushed errant curls behind Tonya's ear. "I know you've had a lotta stuff goin' on in your life, but I just don't get how a woman like you is alone."

"Lately, it's been by choice. And what do you mean, a woman like me?" Tonya was a little breathless. Haley couldn't blame her; her own heart was threatening to beat its way out of her chest.

"You know? Beautiful, intelligent, strong…" Haley's voice trailed off. "How long has it been since you've done this?"

"Done what?"

"The whole 'datin' gettin' to know you' thing. I guess I never thought to ask. Not that it makes any difference."

"Almost a year, but it's never been quite like this. If you were aiming for the moon, you went way past it."

"I'll take that as a compliment."

"You should."

Haley shifted to straddle the bench. "I'm really glad you're havin' a good time." She swiped her thumb across Tonya's cheek.

Tonya shivered and moved into the caress, and Haley's stomach twisted. She wanted to kiss Tonya. More than that, she wanted to stretch out the tension and see how far they could go before one of them broke.

Haley had been right about the wait at the restaurant. It was near closing time when they walked back out into the parking lot. In one hand, Haley had a bag of leftover stuffed shrimp and crabmeat au gratin. She pressed the other against Tonya's back, guiding her toward the truck.

Tonya chuckled, rambling about the amount of fish paraphernalia that covered the walls, but she went quiet when she got in the truck.

"You okay? Dreadin' home?"

"No, I think I'm prepared for that. I just realized that I don't want this to be over."

Haley loved her honesty. "I know the feelin'."

Tonya looked at her with an intensity that sucked the air out of the truck.

"What is it?" Haley asked.

"You don't think, this, us is a little bit too perfect? I'm pretty sure it's not supposed to be this easy."

Haley chuckled. "I remember sayin' the exact same thing, but I've been told that this is what happens when semi-healthy adults like each other."

Tonya continued to gaze at her, heat and desire filling her eyes. Haley's whole body tingled.

"Are you even real?" Tonya whispered.

Haley searched for the right words. After finding them, she took Tonya's hand, brought it to her face, and pressed it against her cheek. "Do I feel real?"

Something finally broke between them. Haley wasn't sure who moved first, and she didn't give a damn as she crushed her lips to Tonya's.

Tonya whimpered, and the sound burned through Haley like fire on paper, leaving her insides scorched. The kiss was openmouthed, sloppy, and when she dipped her tongue inside, Haley moaned at the feel of her. One of Tonya's hands scraped across the back of Haley's neck before tunneling into her hair.

Haley shivered.

The next few seconds passed in a blur, but they ended with Tonya in her lap, straddling her. Fumbling with the seat controls, Haley found the right button and eased them back. Her mouth raked over Tonya's neck. Tonya arched her back and tilted her head to the side. Her breathing was hot, ragged.

Haley couldn't breathe at all, but this was so much more important. When their lips met again, Haley lost herself. Need clawed at her stomach and spread through her body.

Tonya's arms were around her neck and against her ears, blocking out sound. But Haley felt the moans rumbling through Tonya's chest and she wanted more. She smoothed her hands down Tonya's back and under her shirt in search of skin.

Tonya was soft, smooth, and blazing hot. Haley scratched down her back. Tonya's strangled cry left Haley dizzy and completely turned on. So Haley did it again, harder, and the needy grind of Tonya's hips blew her away. She slid her hands over Tonya's ass and got a firm grip.

The sound of a very close car alarm ripped through Haley's senses and reminded her where they were. It didn't matter that her windows were tinted. This just wasn't the right place.

Haley sucked in a shaky breath and leaned back.

Tonya groaned and loosened her embrace. She leaned forward slightly until their foreheads touched. "Yes. You feel real."

Damn right she did. Those words did something to her heart, her body, and it took every ounce of willpower for Haley to keep from revving things up again. They sat there for a few more minutes, pressed against each other. Breathing returned to normal although she was still aroused, but there was also a wave of comfort. Haley wanted to bask in it a little while longer. Was Tonya feeling the same?

Tonya brushed her lips against Haley's forehead, and that was all the answer she needed.

Over an hour later, Haley walked Tonya to her front door. They were holding hands. Both were quiet. They had already said so much. Haley pulled her close when they reached the porch. This time, she made sure her kisses were gentle. Tonya clung to her. Or was it the other way around? God, it didn't matter.

The front door opened, and a woman leaned against it. "Do I need to get the hose?"

Haley smiled while Tonya glared.

"You must be Tracy. Nice to meet you."

Tracy's smile was slow and wicked. "Nice to see you again. I can tell it won't be the last time."

Tonya sighed and held up a hand in front of her sister's face. "I'd better go. Text me when you get home."

"I will. Later."

"Later." Tonya's smile was blinding.

After Haley got through the toll, she called Nate. She had a feeling he would understand.

He answered on the second ring. "So how did it go?"

"I don't...I don't even know how to explain it."

Nate whistled. "You, my friend, are a goner."

He was probably right. Maybe she was.

CHAPTER 19

Tonya thrust her hand out in search of her ringing cell phone. When she found it, she pulled it back under the duvet and looked blearily at the name flashing across. She yawned and smiled sleepily before answering.

"Lo?"

There was a slight pause. "You were sleepin'?"

"Mmm."

"You want me to call back later?"

"S'okay."

"Is it wrong that I find the way you sound right now sexy as hell?" Haley asked.

Tonya smiled and groaned as she stretched.

"Jesus. Stop."

Tonya's drowsiness cleared. "Should I apologize?" Her words were teasing.

"Hell, no. I guess I'm more on edge than I thought after last night."

Tonya basked in the zing of electricity that shot through her body in remembrance. She couldn't recall things being that powerful on a first date, or a second, or a third. "Thanks for reminding me."

"You're welcome. I don't like to be alone in my sufferin'."

A slow fire started to burn in Tonya's stomach and drifted lower. She pressed her thighs together. It didn't help at all.

"Whatcha doin' right now?"

Tonya laughed. "Nothing."

"Liar. Wanna know what I'm doin'?"

Even though Haley sounded perfectly coherent, Tonya's mind filled with erotic images of muscles tensed and elongated, sweaty skin, and Haley moaning. "Haley." She didn't mean to sound so breathless.

"I win."

Tonya silently agreed with her. "You called me at seven o'clock on a Sunday morning to torture me?"

"Yes and no. I just wanted to make sure you were all right after what happened with your dad, and to see if he—"

Tonya melted for a whole different reason. "He was in bed when I got in. So this morning is sure to be interesting. Thank you for checking up on me."

"No problem. You goin' back to sleep?"

"Really?"

Haley chuckled.

There was a knock at Tonya's door. She pulled the covers off her head.

"You can dream about me. Wait, did you already do that?"

"Come in!"

Haley groaned. "You can't go until you answer my question."

Tonya smiled into the phone.

Tracy poked her head in. She opened her mouth to speak but stopped and stared instead.

"I win."

Haley gasped. "You play dirty."

Tonya laughed. "Later?"

"Yeah, call me if you need me."

"I will."

Tonya put her cell phone back on the nightstand and waved her sister in.

"Well, that sounded interesting."

"Mmm."

"And you're still smiling."

Tonya didn't even try to stop.

Tracy glanced at the empty side of the bed. "You mind?"

"Not today, no."

"Damn. There's this new car I want—"

"No."

Tracy grinned. "I was kidding anyway." She sat down and scooted up to the headboard. "I'm loving this mood you're in."

The truth was that Tonya did too. She felt fortified against what was to come. "Thank you."

"Sooo, still high on last night?"

"That sounds like a Stephanie question. I'm sure she's going to call soon and ask me the same thing."

"Well, I'm asking you now. Are you gonna answer?"

"Yes, I am, especially after that phone call," Tonya said in a rush.

Tracy stared at her again. "Whoa, I'm really surprised that you shared that with me."

Tonya blinked. "Me too, but we can't improve communication if we don't communicate. It's easier to talk to you the more I do it."

"Ditto. I can tell you really like her. It looked like your face was gonna split in two."

Tonya lips twitched. She glanced at her sister. They were sitting side by side, shoulders touching. She was really starting to enjoy this new dynamic between them.

Tracy exhaled loudly. "But you don't think it's too soon for you to be that into her? Trust me, I know I'm not one to talk."

Tonya wasn't upset by the question. It came from a place of concern, and she had an inkling that this was how things were supposed to be between sisters. "I thought that at first…too fast and too easy, but I realized last night that this whole thing just feels natural and it's moving along at its own pace."

Her sister smiled. "You're different, but it's good. It's a big chance you're taking, and I like how you're doing the same for me and Daddy."

"I'm really trying, but he…" Tonya shook her head and told Tracy about their father's behavior the night before. When Tonya was done, Tracy's lips were a thin line and her face was scrunched up in disgust.

"I don't know if I've said it already, but I'm sorry I never told you I didn't give a damn about your sexuality. Just in case Daddy doesn't come around, on his behalf, I apologize for everything." She put her head on Tonya's shoulder.

The gesture made Tonya feel warm, wanted, and understood. She leaned into Tracy. "He's making this about him. It's selfish, in a way, that he can't see it affects me and our relationship."

"I'm certainly willing to tell him all that. It might have a bigger impact coming from me, since it's not something we've talked about. He probably thinks I still have my head in the sand like he does."

"You know, this may put you in the same predicament with him that I'm in."

"I know," Tracy said softly. "But if he pushes us both away, he'll be on his own. Doesn't seem like a good place to be. I'm sure you know what that's like. Not that any of it was your fault."

Tonya didn't have to respond. Tracy had filled in the blanks herself.

"It must feel good to finally live your life the way you want to."

"It does, and I don't think… No, I *know* that I can't go back now."

"I wonder what Mama would've said about the way he's acting."

"I'm pretty sure Daddy never brought it up with her. It could be a good thing. Even during that stretch of time where she was lucid, she was still fragile. I was scared to tell her. I wanted to keep things as normal as possible. Besides, Daddy was already disappointed with me. I didn't want her to be that way too. I know it was probably because we'd lost so much time, but she made me feel like a superhero during college, medical school, and after."

"Yeah, I remember. She really was proud of you. Do you—" Tracy cleared her throat. "Do you think she'd be proud of me of what I'm becoming?"

"No doubt. I am too."

"Thank you. I can't tell you what that means. I miss her so much sometimes. A little over ten years wasn't enough time to really get to know her, to love her after not really knowing her at all." Tracy sniffled and wiped at her face.

Tears stung Tonya's eyes too. "I know the feeling."

Tracy sighed. "Okay, it's probably not a good idea to get bogged down with this, especially with the huge hurdle in front of us."

"You're right."

"You sound surprised. We younger folk, as you well know, have our moments."

Tonya grinned. "I suppose."

"Good, now let's go fix this thing with Daddy before we have even more regrets. He's probably on his second cup of coffee by now."

"Go on down. I need to shower first."

Tracy got out of the bed. "All right."

They gazed at each other briefly. Tonya smiled. It was good to have family in her corner. The feeling bolstered her.

Tracy grinned back.

Fifteen minutes later, Tonya was in the process of getting dressed when her phone rang again. This time it was Stephanie.

"I'm offended that you didn't call me last night."

"It was late."

"Ohhhh, and so what?"

"Everything was great."

"Your vocabulary is much bigger and more descriptive than that."

Tonya chuckled. "It is, but I have to cut this short for now. Tracy's home, and I'm going to try to talk to Daddy again."

"Oh, sweetie, okay. I'm here and on your side. You know that, right?"

"I do. Thank you."

A few seconds later, Tonya hung up. Right now, she felt like she could take on anything or anyone.

Tonya walked briskly down the stairs. She wanted to get this over with. When she entered the kitchen, Tracy and their father were seated at the island. Even though they had a perfectly serviceable dining room, the kitchen was the hub of family activity. The smell of cinnamon and coffee wafted through the room. As Tonya sat down on a stool across from them, Tracy stood and pulled a third mug from the cabinet. She filled it with coffee, then emptied a couple of packets of Splenda into it before adding cream.

"This one's yours." Tracy peered over her shoulder in Tonya's direction.

Tonya flashed a smile. As Tracy turned, toast popped up out of the toaster. Surprisingly, her sister buttered both slices before putting them on a saucer. Tracy set Tonya's breakfast in front of her before going back to her seat next to their father.

"Thanks."

"You're very welcome."

Tonya broke a slice of cinnamon raisin toast in half and dunked it in her coffee. As she ate, they all sat quietly, but her father stared at the same spot on the same page of *Gambit Weekly* the whole time. Meaning, he was watching them. She glanced up at her sister. Tracy met her gaze head-on and nodded.

Now was as good a time as any.

"Daddy?"

Just like Tonya expected, Robert turned to his youngest daughter and smiled. "What's up, baby girl?"

"I'm not the only one sitting here."

"You're the only one I care to talk to."

Tonya almost scoffed. His words weren't a surprise, but it still stung to hear him talk like that.

"Whoa, so do you really think hurting her is gonna change anything?" Tracy's voice was calm and even, but she narrowed her eyes and set her jaw.

"I'm not hurting anybody."

The fact that he could say it so nonchalantly floored Tonya. It must have shown on her face. Tracy was staring. Her eyes held a flash of empathy before the anger bled through. Abruptly, Tracy stood.

Their father turned to her then as if really seeing her for the first time. "What's wrong with you?"

"So using your own daughter as a nurse and pretty much denying her the right to live her own life isn't hurtful?" Tracy kept her voice steady. She crossed her arms over her chest, looked their father dead in the eye, and waited.

His mouth literally dropped open. The stunned expression only lasted a few seconds before fury set in. "You don't talk to me like that."

"Like what? So I shouldn't tell the truth? Out loud anyway. I haven't raised my voice, called you names, or disrespected you at all. It's all true, whether you want to admit it or not, and the fact is, you're still trying to keep her from being who she is."

He sputtered like he was about to say something but couldn't get it out.

Tonya was proud of Tracy, and she had never felt closer to her than in that moment. Hope snaked its way into her chest and lodged there.

"I'm an ass for not saying something sooner. I've never seen you hug her or be nearly as affectionate with her as you are to me. You don't think that hurt her then and now? What was she doing when I was cheerleading and hanging out with my friends? Why didn't she get to do the things I did? I'm not blind, Daddy. At least not anymore."

"We all had to make sacrifices for the family." He stood then, chest puffed out and head held high.

"For a long time, Mama didn't have a say in the matter. I don't remember you giving up anything that I saw. Tonya nearly sacrificed her whole childhood, and you wanted her to do the same with her sexuality. Obviously, you still do after that stunt you pulled yesterday."

He clenched his hands into fists and his whole body stiffened.

"She's filling your head full of bullshit. I…none of it happened that way."

It was her turn to speak. Tonya had so much to say, but she condensed it down to one question. "What's your perspective then, Daddy?" There was no malice in her voice

He whirled around and looked at her in surprise. Had he forgotten she was even there? He started to glare and back away, moving quickly. This was when he usually ran, when things got too heated or when the truth was too big. Could she keep doing this? She caught Tracy's gaze, and again her sister clearly read everything on her face

"Sit down, Daddy." She pointed at his chair. "If you don't, you'll be lucky to get more than a text from me for a very long time." Tracy's tone was firm, expression shuttered.

Tonya relaxed minutely. She was impressed with her sister's strength and will.

"I know none of this can be fixed in a day, but you can at least try for all our sakes. We're all the family we have."

Slowly but surely, Robert sat back down. Several emotions flitted across his face, and for once, he was easy to decipher. He was shocked, confused, upset, even sad. He reached for his coffee cup and brought it to his lips. His hands were shaking. Hours seemed to pass, but still he said nothing.

Tracy caught Tonya's gaze. Tonya saw optimism in her sister's eyes. Feeling another gaze, she glanced over to see her father staring.

He looked away quickly.

"Daddy?" Tonya was too tentative to say more.

"You were the oldest. I remember how you wanted to help." His voice was scratchy, thick. "I didn't mean to let it go that far. It was just…easier." He didn't look at her. He didn't get up.

Still, relief uncurled in Tonya's chest, splashing warmth through the rest of her body. She'd gotten validation from Dr. Finn, from her sister, from Haley, but there was no equivalent to receiving it from her father. He'd only said couple of sentences, but Tonya considered it a solid first step forward.

Tonya swelled with emotions. She couldn't decipher them all. She was overwhelmed, and her eyes started to burn. Someone touched her hand. She glanced up to see Tracy smiling. Before she could pull away, Tonya slid her hand into her sister's.

"Thank you."

Tracy's eyes were glassy. "It's the least I could do."

Haley was wound so tight it was hard to concentrate. Her body was humming, and it was all Tonya's fault. Yeah, not that she minded. Only a complete idiot would be bothered by something like that.

She finished her Cap'n Crunch and drank the remaining milk. Her spoon clattered as it hit the side of the bowl. Haley stood and moved toward the kitchen. Maybe a good workout would give her some perspective and tap into a whole different set of endorphins, sort of. Then, when she got home, blowing shit up on her Xbox would hit the spot. Within minutes, she was out the door.

An hour and a half later, she stepped into her own shower. Her entire upper body felt like jelly, and parts of her still burned. It was a beautiful thing, but the whole workout plan had done absolutely nothing to clear her head. If anything, she was more focused on Tonya than before. Her palms actually itched. All she wanted to do was pick up the phone and call her just to hear her voice, her laugh, and her sarcasm. Haley groaned and tilted her head back, letting water pelt her face. Jesus Christ, this was getting out of hand in the best way possible.

Haley grabbed her phone as she reentered the living room and made a call.

"Hey, honey." Her mother sounded chipper, just like she always did. Haley smiled.

"Hey, Mom."

"I was just thinkin' about you."

"Jethro singin' my praises again?"

Her mother chuckled. "You know better, but I got him handled; nothin' to worry about."

"I don't even wanna know what that means."

Cathy hummed cryptically. "So how's your week been?"

"Same old. Tang is still goin' through some stuff. I'm doin' my best to snap him out of it. The field isn't a place to get distracted."

"You're right about that. Maybe…maybe you should think about movin' on to a partner who can separate the personal from the professional and pull his weight."

"Mom, no! I can't just leave him, and it doesn't work like that. I had to work my ass off to get where I am with him now. You know things were rocky at the beginnin'. He knows he's in a bad way and that it's affectin' me. He's actually scared I'll try to leave 'im."

"This is your life we're talkin' about. I know loyalty is a big thing for you, but you breathin' is more important to me."

"Mom—"

"Dammit, I'm naggin' and I always said I wouldn't do that. You know I worry, but I don't wanna bog you down with it."

Haley smiled despite the heaviness of the conversation. "I worry too. I have to. I know I haven't been doin' this long, but I think if I didn't feel anythin' that would be really bad." She sobered. "I know I put you, Nate, and Jen on pins and needles, and it's the nature of the job. Anythin' can happen out there, no matter who my partner is. I don't take any of it for granted, believe me." Haley took a deep breath and made the decision to put everything out there on the table. The thing with Tonya wasn't abstract anymore. It was developing lines that were coming in clearer every day.

"Good. I know why you do this, and I don't wanna change you. I never have."

"I know, Mom." Haley paused and then let her feelings take over. "Tonya gets worried too."

"Who's Tonya?"

"I met somebody. It's kind of an interestin' story if you wanna hear."

"Well, it's just stupid to even tease me like that. Of course I wanna hear. What's wrong with you?"

Haley laughed and told her how they'd met.

"Holy shit." Her mother's words were full of surprised wonder.

"Mom!"

"What? Like you've never heard that come outta my mouth before."

"I have, but still."

"Whatever. That's a beginnin' with bang."

"I totally agree." Haley smiled and leaned back on the couch.

"Things like that happen for a reason."

Haley had never thought about it like that. "Maybe."

"I haven't heard you talk about a woman since what? College? And it wasn't like I got to meet that one. I haven't met any of your girlfriends, except for the neighbor's kid you were foolin' around with in middle and high school."

Haley laughed. "You knew about that?"

"I'm your mother. I suspected. I knew you didn't go over there to play with her dolls when you guys were younger, and I don't remember being that happy when I was a teenager after a sleepover."

"I'm not even sure how to respond to all that."

Her mother scoffed. "It's not like you could've gotten her pregnant."

Haley laughed even harder. "Stop!"

"Let me guess, you were the daddy when ya'll played house?"

Haley couldn't breathe. Her mother was having way too much fun with this.

"Okay, okay, what were we talkin' about?" Cathy chuckled. "Your girlfriends?"

It took a few more minutes, but Haley was able to calm down. "All right, well, you haven't met anyone because there really hasn't been anyone except for that mess in college. She turned out to be someone I definitely wouldn't bring home."

"Oh, I see. So do I need to prepare myself to meet this Tonya soon?"

Even though nobody else could see her, Haley smiled so hard that she was damn close to giving herself a headache. "Maybe. Yeah, probably."

"Well, if we subject her to Jethro, that might scare her away."

Haley snorted.

"And she's okay with the whole cop thing?"

"We have an understandin'. She gets it. I think she gets me."

"What do Nate and Jen think of her?"

"They haven't met her yet, but they've been helpin' me navigate the waters, so to speak."

"I don't get it. If she's that special and they are right there, why haven't they met yet?"

Haley didn't hesitate. "I'm not ready to share her."

Her mom was quiet for a few seconds.

"Ohhh, sweetie."

Heat flooded Haley's face. She wasn't embarrassed. It was more like a rush of emotions, reminding her of all the good things that had been happening. "Yeah, I know. It's only been a little over two months since we officially met, but—"

"That doesn't matter."

Maybe it didn't. "Mom?"

"Hmm?"

"Have you really been in love that many times?"

Cathy burst out laughing. "No!" She lapsed into a chuckle. "Not all the time, but I don't like bein' alone. If someone fits me comfortably, that's usually enough for me."

"So Jethro is like an old pair of shoes?"

"Pretty much." There was amusement in her mother's voice.

Haley heard something in the background. Speak of the devil. "Did we conjure him up?"

"Stop," her mother whispered, trying unsuccessfully to smother her laughter. "Seriously, though. I know he hasn't always been respectful, but that's gonna change. I shoulda nipped it in the bud a long time ago."

Yeah, she probably should have. "Okay."

"I'm gonna go. Call me if you need me."

"Okay, Mom."

It was easy to understand where her mother was coming from, but Haley didn't want comfortable. Somewhere along the way, she'd figured out that she wanted the bells, whistles, and sparks, and that was just the beginning. Shit, to be honest, she wanted the whole roller-coaster ride if it made her feel anything like she did when she was with Tonya. If drama was part of the package, Haley was willing to take that too.

Haley didn't realize that she'd fallen asleep until she was jerked awake by somebody pounding on her door. She sat up quickly and rubbed her eyes, trying to wipe away the cobwebs. The banging kept going.

"Hold on!"

She reached for her cell phone on the table. It was almost one o'clock, and she had two missed calls from Tang.

Haley parted the curtains, and sure enough, he was standing there. He caught her looking, and good God, he was even worse off than when she'd seen him last. That shouldn't have been possible. Tang didn't smile as he gazed back at her. His eyes were bloodshot, haggard, and maybe a little puffy. Had he been crying? Whatever brought him here must have been over-the-top bad. She unlocked the door and pulled it open.

Tang stumbled inside. Was he drunk? He didn't smell like it. He must have been exhausted as all get-out. After the conversation she'd had about him with her mother, seeing him like this made Haley livid.

"What the actual fuck, Tang? Why didn't you just ring the bell? You worked a double, didn't you? You told me you were gonna—"

"Get off my fuckin' back! I can get all the rest you fuckin' want me to get now. Those sons of bitches fired me. How goddamned pathetic is that? I'm a cop, and I got fired from a shitty security job."

Haley's heart dropped as she stared at him. She reached out and touched his shoulder. He flinched slightly, and then she noticed that he was shaking. "C'mon." She led him to the couch and made him sit. "What happened?" She sat down beside him.

"I fell asleep. It was my third warnin'."

Haley didn't say anything.

Tang leaned forward and buried his face in his hands. "What am I gonna do?" His words were muffled.

"Get another job. Maybe you can find somethin' downtown or at the casino."

He glanced up at her, and he looked so lost. "Honestly, with everythin' I gotta take care of, I only had about a fourth of the money. I probably wouldn't have made the deadline anyway. It's not easy gettin' on at the casino, and I worked for Ochsner. They own just about every hospital in Orleans Parish. There's no way they'll let me back in."

"Shit. Well, maybe Crest Manor will accept what you have and give you time."

"They won't. They were pretty clear. I let 'im down. He never did that to me, but I let 'im down. He's gonna have to come home. Medicare isn't gonna pay for around-the-clock care. I can't put him in some shithole. That's the only thing they'll pay for. He deserves better than that."

Haley wished she had the money to give him, but the couple hundred in her bank account wasn't enough. Haley sat there and listened while he came up with some tentative ideas and dismissed them. She even offered to see if she could borrow the money from Nate and Jen. Eventually, Tang could barely keep his eyes open. Haley stood and pushed him back on the couch.

"I should… I should get home."

"No, you're crashin' here. You don't need to be alone. The couch lets out into a bed, but it's just as comfortable like it is."

Tang gave in without a fight. She helped him take off his shoes, then went to find a spare blanket and pillow. When she got back, he was already snoring, so Haley covered him up. She stared at him for a few minutes, wondering how much more it was going to take for him to go off the deep end.

Chapter 20

Haley smiled, then covered a yawn as she watched Tonya dip part of a scone into her coffee. It was certainly a unique way to eat carbs in the morning. CC's Coffeehouse had a few stragglers, but they were the only people sitting down. The place had barely been open an hour, so everything was spotless. Haley kind of hated these café-style places. Even though the dark wood of the countertops and tables was eye-catching, she disliked the tiny tables and chairs. They were uncomfortable as hell.

It was early to be up and out, but Haley would get up at the ass crack of morning every single day if it meant she got to see Tonya. It was Thursday, and the second time this week they'd met for coffee. Haley was proud as hell that she'd suggested it. There was no way on earth that she could wait until the weekend. No way. Seeing Tonya was like starting the day on a really special high. Not the drug- or alcohol-induced kind either. This feeling had a purity to it. Haley sipped at her own coffee. It was getting cold, but she didn't care.

Tonya looked completely put together for so early in the morning. Her outfit was simple: cream-colored blouse that flashed a tiny amount of cleavage and offered just a peek at defined collarbones along with gray slacks that looked soft as butter. Her legs went on forever, and the material clung to her curves in a way that made Haley want to reach out and follow the lines. Her makeup was flawless and barely there, but somehow it made those big brown eyes even bigger. Then there were the dimples that flashed every time Tonya smiled, which was a lot. Tonya was at a face-melting level of hot, and here Haley was in a pair of drawstring shorts and a T-shirt with no graphics to at least make it interesting.

"Has Tim perked up at all?"

Haley almost missed the question. She was happy to just sit there and stare. That wasn't weird. Was it? She grimaced. "No, not really."

"The symptoms of situational depression can get pretty severe. You're a good friend trying to help him through it, but if you feel like it's affecting his job, encourage him to get help. It can just be between the two of you. I'm not saying this just for him. He's your partner, and he's the only one there to watch your back. It's…worrisome."

"I can understand that, but I was more worried about that when he was working his ass off than I am now. Still, I'm keepin' my eye on him just in case."

Tonya gazed at her. Haley knew her reassurances weren't really enough, but they were all she had. She reached over to snatch a piece of Tonya's scone, but Tonya smacked her hand away.

"I'd be more than happy to get you a cruller."

Haley smirked but kept her hand close to Tonya's. "Ah yes, cops and donuts. That's an awful stereotype."

"I know nothing about those." Tonya's eyes glittered with amusement.

"Ha-ha."

"Mm."

Haley pushed her coffee away. She was done playing with it. "So you know, speakin' of friends, and I use that term really loosely with these ladies."

"You mean your fanclub?"

"I wouldn't call them that."

"I would because that's exactly what they are." Tonya smirked and leaned forward, propped up on her elbow to listen.

"Okay, okay, I see your point, but that sounds so—"

"Arrogant?"

"Yes! That."

"And that's not you at all?"

Haley glared, but she smiled too. "Shut up."

Tonya chuckled. "Go on."

"Why, thank you. I was gonna say they're pissed at me because I'm datin' someone."

"Really?" Tonya asked.

"Yeah, that's not juvenile at all."

"Well, it is, but it's to be expected. I think. They don't know you any other way."

"I guess, but still."

"Is it strange for you to be dating only one person?"

Haley held Tonya's gaze. She looked for apprehension and hesitation and found both; it made her stomach slither. Regardless, Haley pushed on. It wouldn't be good to hedge about the issue. "You know that's not what I was doin' with them, but it *is* what I'm doin' with you."

Tonya smiled softly. "That's sweet." She paused. "You don't miss living like that?"

Haley wasn't surprised by the question. "No, I thought it was gonna be hard, to walk away from all that since I'd been doin' it for so long. But that lifestyle was getting old. For a while, it was good stress relief, a diversion, I guess. But here recently, I was getting more outta talkin' to Nate, Jen, and my mom. I'd rather spend my free time with you anyway." Haley paused, but Tonya didn't comment. That was good, because Haley had more to say.

"I think I was tired of splittin' myself into fifty pieces. There was party Haley, cop Haley, and best friend Haley. I mean, I know I have to keep work separate from my personal life, but with everythin' else, some of those pieces weren't worth keepin'. I'm more myself around the people I care about, and that means you too."

"Maybe that was the point. You needed to be somebody else. I think I can understand that."

"Well, I don't want it that way anymore. So, speakin' of people I actually *care* about. Is it too early for you to meet Nate and Jen, you think?"

Tonya's eyebrows rose. "You're asking me? I'm no expert. This relationship seems to have a mind of its own."

Haley stared at her and smiled. "I kinda knew that already, but that's what this is. Isn't it?"

"Yes." Tonya grinned as well.

"Okay."

Haley brushed her fingertips against Tonya's. She opened her hand, palm out, and Haley traced each line before threading their fingers together.

"Okay," Tonya whispered. "So where are we going on our next date?"

"I don't know. Isn't it your turn to pick?"

Tonya squeezed Haley's hand, and her gaze darkened. "I thought you liked being in charge."

Lordy. Was it just her or did the air around them really just catch fire? She couldn't feel her face anymore, but it didn't seem to matter. Haley decided to draw things out a little. She wanted to know what else Tonya was going to say. "Maybe."

"I'm okay with that. Sometimes. I'm no pillow princess."

Images flashed through Haley's mind. She could practically feel Tonya's hands sliding up the inside of her thighs as she knelt between them. Surprisingly, she was so okay with that. She trusted Tonya enough to give her at least that much. Haley's stomach dropped to her knees. It didn't matter that she was sitting.

"Where did you just go?" Tonya's voice was kind of breathy.

Had it been that long? "Someplace dirty but really nice."

Tonya laughed, but when she lifted the cup of coffee that had to be ice-cold by now, her hand was shaking. She put her drink back on the table and licked her lips. "Behave."

"You started it." It would probably be completely inappropriate to tackle Tonya to the floor, no matter how much Haley wanted to.

"Mm."

"You could meet Nate and Jen at my place. I'll cook dinner. Or we could hang out somewhere neutral."

Tonya stared at her for a few seconds. That intensity was still there, but her lips quirked into a smile. "Well then, it would be only fair to formally introduce you to my sister and Stephanie uncut soon."

"My mom, when we get around to that, will probably like you too."

"You're lucky to have that kind of support."

"I know. At least you and your father are talkin' now. That's somethin'."

"True. I still have to pull everything out of him, but it's better than nothing. Progress is progress."

"Yeah, it is." Haley glanced at the clock on the far wall. She groaned. "I need to get home. I still have to get showered and changed."

"I'm not important enough to shower for?"

"Not this mornin', but I brushed my teeth for you."

Tonya stood. "I guess that will have to do."

After tossing their trash, Haley met Tonya at the door. She walked Tonya to her car, shoulders touching. Instead of getting in, Tonya leaned against the driver's side door. She reached out and tugged on the string of Haley's shorts, pulling her close.

Haley wasn't surprised by the stab of arousal. She was in a constant state of simmer around Tonya. Something in her expression must have given her away. Tonya's breathing hitched. Haley was painfully aware that it was broad daylight. People were milling about in the parking lot, and traffic had increased. There couldn't…wouldn't be a repeat of last Saturday night. Haley dipped her head anyway and curved her arm around Tonya. She brushed her mouth teasingly against Tonya's soft, full lips and ended the kiss with a swipe of her tongue. Tonya's grip on Haley's shorts tightened and so did Haley's stomach.

It was a miracle Haley was able step away, but Tonya wouldn't let go. She slid her free hand over Haley's cheek, behind her neck, and into her hair.

Haley groaned. "Stop."

Tonya sucked in a shaky breath, and her eyes were all fire. "You make it hard."

She just bet it was. Jesus, her mind was so wallowing in the gutter.

A second later, Tonya laughed. "That's not what I meant."

Talk about written all over her face.

"I know. Obviously, you've turned me into a teenage boy."

"I'm not complaining. So, later?"

Haley nodded. "Yeah, later." She backed away completely, and this time, Tonya let her go. Haley watched Tonya until she drove away.

As Tang drove them through Hollygrove, Haley hung on to the passenger-assist handle. The car was bucking like a bronco thanks to the potholes. Some of the roads were so fucked up that orange caution cones were placed there in warning. Dead power lines swayed in the wind, and the poles they hung from looked like they could topple over if someone blew on them. Regardless, a lot of the residents took pride in their area. It was usually the criminals who didn't give a damn. Their lawns were overgrown, and trash was everywhere. There were mattresses, tires, even clothing peppering the yards. These were the people who gathered on the corners blaring loud music and smoking their own shit while they sold the rest. Daytime was a bit different, but sometimes the sun just made things starker.

Haley was always on a razor's edge when they came through here, but that point wasn't sharp enough to make her trigger-happy. Almost all her arrests and shootings had been here, but she did her best to treat everyone she came across with respect. It probably would have been a lot easier to use the power behind the uniform. It could be intoxicating to see fear or even hate in people's eyes, but she refused to let herself get drunk or even buzzed on that kind of power.

Tang drove over a particularly deep pothole, and Haley nearly slammed her head on the roof of the car.

The more marginalized the people, the worse the area seemed, at least in greater New Orleans. Haley wished she could wave a magic wand, but this was real life, and patterns of behavior were ingrained deep in the infrastructure.

None of that was going to keep her from trying.

Haley rolled down the window as they passed a group of young kids. They still had their school uniforms on. She smiled and waved. A couple of them returned the gesture, but the rest just stared. She didn't blame them. Once upon a time, the NOPD was the most corrupt police department in the country. Then there was that shit that happened after Katrina. The police had a long, long way to go to earn trust or even have people believe in them. There was a huge chance that that gap was insurmountable.

Haley felt Tang's gaze on her and she turned to glance at him. His expression was flat and watchful. He didn't say a word. There was a shitton for him to be miserable about, but at least the black smudges under his eyes were gone. Haley missed his jokes. Tang still talked, but he wasn't himself. Haley had even tried to gross him out. It hadn't worked all that well. Nothing really had.

On the mornings they didn't have coffee, she and Tonya still talked. At night, it was getting harder and harder to hang up. There had been several times this week where they would stay on the line until one of them fell asleep.

Haley wasn't ashamed to admit that she lay in bed listening to Tonya breathe more than once. She made these cute little noises in her sleep. Haley's insides knotted. This was getting ridiculous. Everything about Tonya seemed to turn her on in some way.

Haley heard music and then felt the bass before the SUV turned in front of them. It was enough to pull her from her thoughts. She glanced at Tang just as he was flipping the switch to activate the lights.

Haley swallowed as dread filled her stomach and spilled out everywhere. Thank God he didn't turn on the siren.

"What the hell are you doin'?"

"What does it look like?" Tang glared at her. His eyes were hard, voice gravely.

"There's no reason to pull them over." She couldn't see through the tinted windows, but she didn't need to. The SUV veered to the side. Tang eased behind it.

"Plates look expired. No sticker."

"Then run them first to check." Haley reached over and turned off the lights. "Don't be such a fuckin' cliché. Look where we are. Harassin' somebody and stirrin' shit up isn't gonna fix anythin', and it's sure as hell not gonna make you feel better."

"Who gives a purple fuck?"

"I do, and if you turn those lights on again, I'll report you for misconduct my damn self."

Tang froze and his lips thinned. "We're partners. You'd rat me out just like that?"

Haley held his gaze. She wasn't going to let him keep spiraling downward. Not if she could help it. Why couldn't he see that? "Bet your ass I would."

Tang looked away and kept one hand on the steering wheel while the other fisted. "Good to know," he mumbled under his breath.

He drove around the SUV and back onto the street. It suddenly felt like they were in the Arctic. Haley couldn't remember it ever being this cold between them, even at the beginning. This wasn't the way to reach him, but Haley was glad she'd kept him from doing something stupid. "Look, you don't need to do shit like that. Talk to me. I know I can't fix it, but it's gotta be better than keepin' things bottled in."

He was quiet for a long time.

"What else is there to say about it?"

"Hell if I know."

Tang sighed. "My life is so far down the shit hole I can't even smell fresh air anymore."

"Yeah, it must feel like that right now." Haley glanced at him. He looked back and started talking.

Haley felt a very small sliver of relief.

Tonya was in the process of powering down her laptop when her office door opened. She smiled as Stephanie walked in and sat down.

"I'm a little wired."

"Why?" Tonya asked.

"It's been a slow day, very quiet. We haven't had that in a while."

"True, but you should probably look at it as a good thing after what we went through last month during the anniversary of Katrina."

Stephanie shrugged. "Yeah, you're right."

They both went quiet as Tonya continued to gather her things, but she could feel Stephanie's eyes on her.

"You're burning a hole in my head, and I can practically hear your wheels creaking."

Stephanie laughed. "Sorry. I was just thinking."

"Careful. You might hurt yourself after such a light day."

"Funny. No, but really, can I be you when I grow up?"

Tonya sat her purse on the desk and stared. What was going on in her head? "What are you talking about?"

"I'm talking about you. After everything you've been through, things are finally working for you."

Tonya leaned back in her chair and sighed. "I hope so, but I don't want to jinx it."

Stephanie snorted. "I don't think it works that way."

"Maybe." Since they were on the subject, somewhat, Tonya decided to add, "Haley wants me to meet her friends soon. I was thinking I should do the same."

Stephanie's smile was big enough to fill the whole office. "We've already met. Maybe you just forgot I was there since you were staring at each other the whole time."

"That didn't really count for you."

"Okay. I'll try not to scare her away. Anything else you want to tell me?" Stephanie gave her a pointed look, and her grin turned lascivious.

"No, nothing that I want to."

"Aww, c'mon. If I can't live vicariously through you—"

"You have other friends."

"Not like you."

Tonya was touched and amused at the same time. She smiled. "Uh-huh."

Stephanie rolled her eyes and threw her hands up in the air. "Ugh, fine. Be that way."

"Thank you, I will."

"Bitch."

Tonya chuckled.

"Anyway, my mom's on my case again about finding Mr. Right."

Tonya cringed. "Oh, sorry."

"Yeah, I'm tired of trying to explain to her that it's the twenty-first century and Mr. Right Now is where it's at. Not that I've had a decent date in months. Maybe I should have given the guy with the dick pics a chance. He was impressive."

"You probably would have ended up on video, splashed all over those free amateur porn sites."

Stephanie gave her a strange look. "How do you know about those?"

Tonya shrugged. "Doesn't everybody?"

"You're probably right. You sure Haley doesn't have a brother or a single male friend hiding somewhere? Because whatever magic she's got has to run in the family."

Tonya laughed. "No, and stop. You're making it sound like you're desperate."

Stephanie shook her head. "No, I'm not there yet. Just lonely. Don't get me wrong. I'm happy, and I have a great life with lots of love in it."

"I'm not going anywhere."

Stephanie's lips curled slightly. "I know that now, but a couple months ago, I wasn't so sure. I love how the dynamic between us has changed. I feel like we're equals now. Plus, I know you couldn't go a day without me and my sunshine."

"Whatever. I'm glad I got my head out of my ass."

"It wasn't *up* there. It was just ass-adjacent."

Tonya glared. The things that came out of that woman's mouth sometimes were very strange. "Is that even possible?"

Stephanie shrugged. "Don't know. It's your head and your ass. You tell me."

Tonya sighed and stood. She glanced at her watch. If she didn't leave now, she was going to be late. "I'm going to leave that up to the universe to decide. Walk me to my car?"

As the elevator opened on the fifth floor, Tonya admitted to herself that she felt a little guilty about keeping her psychotherapy appointments a secret, especially after everything else she'd divulged. She walked down the hall toward Dr. Finn's office and shook the feeling off. These sessions weren't for her family. They weren't for Stephanie or Haley. They were for her, and when she was ready—if she ever was—Tonya would let them know.

No sooner had she entered the waiting area than Dr. Finn was opening her office door. She nodded at Tonya.

"Restroom break. I'll be right back."

"Take your time."

Dr. Finn smiled slightly as she breezed past.

A few minutes later, Tonya was taking a seat inside the office.

"Well, I have to say, you look more relaxed than I've ever seen you."

Tonya smiled. "I was just telling Stephanie not too long ago that I didn't want to jinx it, but yes, it feels like all the little pieces are starting to come together. Daddy is reluctant to talk about me being a lesbian, but he's taking baby steps toward talking about Mama. That's more important to me right now. As far as Tracy is concerned, given how things were, I never thought she'd be a person I could count on, but now I'm learning what it is to have a sister."

"Excellent, and what about Haley?"

Taking her time to answer, Tonya chose her words carefully. "I used to feel invisible. I know part of that was my fault for not reaching out to people, and the rest is, well…my childhood. I don't feel that way anymore. I mean, Haley sees through me, inside me, but it's because I let her. It's because she wants to."

"I think it's fair to say most areas of your life are in transition."

"Yes, I agree. It's a very different kind of snowball effect."

"Do you feel like you're using positive coping skills to keep from being overwhelmed?"

"At first, I was being fatalistic, waiting for things to just fall apart around me. Now I'd like to think I'm more open to going with the flow, especially since it's moving forward."

Dr. Finn gave Tonya one of her smiles. She'd seen them a lot the last few weeks.

An hour and a half later, Tonya walked through the house in bare feet after taking a long, hot shower. She traded her contacts for glasses and her work clothes for shorts with a matching lacy tank top. She even tamed her curls back into a ponytail.

Tonya leaned against the counter as she poured a glass of wine. She was alone, and the house was quiet. She raised the glass to her lips in celebration of that fact. Just as she finished the first glass of wine and poured another, her phone rang. Tonya smiled as she answered.

"Hey," Haley said

"Hello," Tonya answered. There was something about Haley's tone that raised a red flag. "What's wrong? Bad day?"

Haley chuckled. "Yeah, but can I tell you that it's sexy as all get-out that you know me like that?"

"Yes, you can."

"It really, really is, and all it does is make me want you more." Haley sighed. "Yeah, it was a bad day."

Despite the pleasant buzz of Haley's compliment, Tonya forced herself to focus on more pressing matters. "Tim?"

"Yeah," Haley confirmed. "Even when things evened out, it was a shitty day. I know how you feel about us goin' out on a weeknight, but I don't want my night to end wrapped up in the clusterfuck it might have been. Can I come over?"

She was tempted. The buzz became a heavy vibration that left her entire body humming. It was odd and refreshing, but she wasn't going to make it easy, regardless of the situation. "That's just semantics."

Haley chuckled. "I knew you were gonna say that. Tonya, c'mon, please?"

Tonya brought a hand to her chest. It actually felt like somebody had reached inside and squeezed her heart. The need in Haley's voice trumped everything else.

"I thought about hangin' out at Nate's until they got home. They always know what to say to make me feel better. But they're not you. I like the way you make me feel more."

Haley left her breathless.

"You should've led with that."

"If that's a yes, I promise that I'll remember it for next time."

"It was a yes." Tonya didn't mean for her words to come out whisper-soft, but where Haley was concerned, she'd learned that her body did what it wanted. "Luckily, my father isn't here, but he left what's probably really good jambalaya in the fridge if you're hungry."

"I am, actually. I have to tell you, though, I don't care if he's there or not. I still wanna see you. Would it have mattered to you?"

"No." Tonya's answer was automatic and sincere. This was her home. This was her life.

"I'm not far. I'll be there in fifteen minutes."

Give or take fifteen minutes later, Tonya opened her door, smiled, and gave Haley the once-over. Her black T-shirt was embroidered with the words *I'm a Fringe event* and complemented by a pair of khaki cargo shorts. There was definite strain around Haley's eyes and a stiffness to her posture. She looked exhausted. Haley had barely stepped inside when she pulled Tonya close.

They kissed softly, and Haley relaxed against her. Knowing she had that kind of power over Haley was heady indeed.

"Mmm, I needed that." Haley grinned.

Tonya tightened her hold around Haley's neck. "Maybe I did too."

Haley's grin widened. "Good to know." She reached out and touched the rim of Tonya's glasses. Haley's expression morphed into something heated. "Jesus, I knew you'd be hot in those, but *goddamn*."

Tonya melted, and a jolt of electricity started in her chest, only to spread to her toes and back. All Tonya could do was stare. Haley's eyes were so blue, and her expression was so open that Tonya could see truth in every word.

"I really like the look on your face right now."

It was only fair, because Tonya really liked the way Haley was making her feel right now. "I don't know…" she cleared her throat, "how to respond to that."

"You don't have to. You already did." Haley's thumb traced over Tonya's bottom lip. Heat pooled in Tonya's stomach, and her heart rammed against her chest.

Haley sucked in a breath and shook her head. It took an eternity for her to step away. "Uh, you said somethin' about food?"

Tonya blinked. She did? Their gazes remained locked for a few more smoldering seconds before becoming a simmer.

"I did." Tonya led Haley into the kitchen. She pointed toward the stools and opened the refrigerator. "Help yourself to a glass of wine if you want."

"I think I will. I'm not usually a wine person, but it tastes pretty good."

Tonya stopped what she was doing and glanced over her shoulder. Maybe *simmer* wasn't the right word. There were way too many flames blazing around them for it to ever be something so benign.

Haley looked at her innocently, but her grin gave it all away.

She smiled in response.

A few minutes later, they were talking as they ate.

Haley moaned. "This is really good."

"I told you."

"You know what brand of sausage he uses?"

"No idea. I just know its andouille."

"Some help you are."

"I try." Tonya paused. "What happened today?"

Haley kept eating. It was several minutes before she relayed the whole story.

"I'm just thankful to whoever was listenin' that I have some influence over him."

"Me too. There's an obvious imbalance in your partnership right now. It sounds like you both realize that and are trying to compensate for it. So far, it's been successful."

"You think it'll stay that way?" Haley looked so hopeful. "I'll toe the line for as long as I have to, as long as he's open to it."

Tonya wanted to tell her yes, but she wasn't going to lie. "I don't know. You know him. What do you think?"

Haley shook her head. "You should have seen us when we first started workin' together. I couldn't stand him. Hell, we couldn't stand each other. Then, things changed, and here we are. He needs me. I'm his partner, and I'm willin' to do whatever I can to help."

"Relationships evolve, especially if everyone involved is willing to change, but what you're doing with Tang takes a special amount of patience. It's... You're very impressive."

Haley stared at her, and she blushed. It was charming. "Thank you?"

Tonya smiled. "You're welcome."

Soon, they moved to the living room.

"Dear God, I'm so bringin' my Xbox over here. Plugged into that TV, everythin' would be epic. I guess I wasn't payin' attention when I first came in. What is that, fifty-five inches?"

"Sixty," Tonya answered as she sat on the couch.

"That's disgustin'. I love it."

Tonya laughed. "Do what you want with it. I'm barely in here. I'm not a big TV watcher."

"Oh, I know, and that's so gonna change. I have *so* much work to do." Haley grabbed the remote and eased down next to Tonya. "We'll start with *Buffy* and work our way to *Firefly*, and before you know it you'll be drooling over *Game of Thrones*."

"If you say so."

"I do. I really, really do. I like a challenge."

"Yes, I'm aware." Tonya chuckled and shook her head.

"It's good that you're prepared." Haley clicked on the guide.

"What are you looking for?"

"*The Big Bang Theory* reruns."

"The what?"

"Shhh, just watch, and consider this a preliminary introduction."

Tonya rolled her eyes, but Haley was adorable in her geekiness. "Uh-huh."

Haley shushed her again. "Here we go."

One episode bled into another. Tonya laughed uproariously. She couldn't remember ever doing that over a TV show. She was surrounded by laughter and Haley's warmth. Tonya's chest flooded with a realization, leaving her momentarily breathless. This was just another level of happiness. Feeling Haley's burning gaze, Tonya glanced at her.

Haley's eyes were dazzling. Her expression was hungry. "Christ, look at you. How am I supposed to keep my hands to myself?"

"I never said you had to."

Tonya moved first. She was sure of it. She surged forward, and they crashed together. Tonya whimpered before their lips even touched, and when they did, the world started to spin. She raked her hands through Haley's hair, holding on to her and pulling her forward at the same time. Tonya couldn't get close enough. The kiss was sloppy, uneven, and utterly arousing. Tonya's nipples hardened as bona-fide evidence.

Haley moaned, and before Tonya had time to savor it, she was being pulled onto Haley's lap. Tonya broke away momentarily and admired the view. Haley's lips were swollen. Her breathing was ragged, broken, and her eyes were nearly black.

"Jesus," Haley whispered.

Then they were kissing again. Haley's tongue teased the roof of Tonya's mouth before licking against her teeth. Her hands inched under the back of Tonya's shirt and she arched forward as if hit by a live current. Haley didn't stop there, not until she was cupping Tonya's breasts.

Tonya wrenched her mouth away and cried out.

Haley didn't waste any time. As her thumb brushed against Tonya's nipples, her teeth scraped against Tonya's neck. In tandem, Haley's fingertips and mouth went from whisper-soft to a firmness bordering on pain. Tonya pulled at Haley's hair and moaned as pleasure arced through her. Her arousal pooled heavily between her legs, and as a result, Tonya's hips began to thrust in search of friction. There was very little to speak of, but it just made Tonya work harder and want even more.

Haley groaned as her hips shifted forward, rolling into Tonya's. She nipped at Tonya's ear. "You're not the only one who has dreams," Haley whispered raggedly. Her hips stilled as she slid a hand between their bodies. Tonya felt the brush of fingers between her legs, but there was barely any pressure. Then it was gone.

Haley grabbed Tonya's ass and yanked her forward…hard.

Tonya gasped and whimpered. The sudden thickness pressed against her center sent a bolt of heat through her body so intense she couldn't breathe.

"You feel it." Each word was spoken directly into Tonya's ear.

It wasn't a question.

"I've been waitin' for a good time…" Haley tightened her hold on Tonya and lifted her own hips, grinding into her leisurely.

Tonya didn't recognize the sound that exited her throat. It was raw, wanton.

"I think this is it," Haley moaned. "It was just like this."

She loosened her grip, and Tonya met her thrust for thrust. This time the friction was maddening and in all the right places. Tonya made that sound again.

"Yesss," Haley encouraged.

Haley's voice, her words sent tingles through Tonya's body, increasing her fervor.

"You were ridin' me, and I was so deep inside you—"

"Oh God." Tonya's pace quickened. Her senses were fast becoming overwhelmed. All she could feel was Haley. All Tonya could see were the images her words evoked. Haley was everywhere.

"That I couldn't see straight. I didn't wanna stop." Haley's lips trailed from Tonya's ear to her mouth. Her kiss was soft, almost chaste considering what they were doing. Haley took control once more, moving Tonya's hips in deep, slow circles and then with bruising intensity.

Tonya felt a burning pressure building at the bottom of her spine. Cloying heat seeped through her. Every breath ended in a whimper.

"No matter how much you came. No matter how h-hard." Haley's voice was strained, unsteady. She was just as affected. She was just as invested.

Something flashed behind Tonya's eyes, from red to a blinding white.

"No matter how hard *I* did." Haley whispered the words hotly.

Tonya cried out once more and flew apart as an orgasm sloshed through her. Her hips bucked helplessly. Sensation after sensation bombarded her, wringing every ounce of pleasure from her and leaving her quivering. She slumped forward weakly.

When the world righted itself, Tonya felt her damp curls being pushed back behind her ears. She couldn't even remember when the hair tie had been removed. She opened her eyes, and Haley looked at her with such wonder, with such need. Tonya's stomach contracted in response.

When Haley touched her face, her hands were shaking. Tonya leaned into the caress and grasped Haley's hand, bringing it to her mouth. Tonya kissed her palm.

Haley whispered, "Holy Christ."

"Yes." Tonya dipped her head. This time when they kissed, it was slower, more controlled, but no less heated, as if what happened previously was practice and *this* was the real event. Haley moaned into her mouth. The television flashed behind them, the audience laughing in the background. Tonya blocked it out and reached down, intent on pulling her shirt over her head.

A throat cleared loudly.

Startled by the sound, Tonya glanced up. Her stomach dropped for a very different reason. Tonya met her father's gaze. His eyes were wide, and his face was pinched in shock and disgust. She'd seen that look on his face enough to know it.

Haley's body shifted and she turned as well. "Ah, shit."

Indeed.

As if moving through mud, Tonya stood slowly. "Daddy?"

He was frozen, and his expression was as well. After a few more seconds, he turned and walked away.

"Tonya?" Haley grabbed her hand.

Tonya held on to it tightly. Anger clawed at her, but it quickly changed to fear. She and her father had taken a step forward. Had they just jumped fifty back?

Haley got up off the couch and pulled her close. "What do you need me to do right now?"

Tonya found it in herself to smile. Haley's words touched her, and if she hadn't already tunneled herself into Tonya's heart, she would have done so at that moment. She brushed her lips against Haley's. "Go home. I'll be okay."

Haley sighed, her expression pleading. Despite that, she nodded. "I really don't want to leave you alone—"

"I can handle it. Don't worry."

"You call me. I'm not kiddin'. I'll come right back if—" Haley's voice was stern as she hugged Tonya tight.

"I know. I will." Tonya kissed her again and returned the embrace. Then she walked Haley to the front door. She watched, waving as Haley drove away. To say the last few minutes between them had been rushed did not do it justice. Tonya closed the door and walked quickly from the living room into the kitchen.

The area was empty, but she wasn't all that surprised. It had been a long shot. She peeked out the kitchen window to make sure his truck was still parked in the driveway. It was. Tonya went from the kitchen to the hallway. The bathroom was dark but there was light spilling from under her father's bedroom door. Not wanting to overthink the situation, Tonya took a deep breath and knocked. It was better to deal with this head-on.

There was no response.

Tonya wasn't deterred. She knocked harder. Her father yanked the door open and stood there, tall and rigid. His face was like granite. They stared at each other.

"Say something."

He looked away. "What do you want me to say?"

"Did we just move back to square one?"

Robert said nothing.

"This wasn't a secret."

He glanced at her. "No, suppose not."

Tonya was not in the mood to dance around the issue. "You didn't answer my question."

"I'm trying, but this here mess, I don't know how to deal with. I'm not ready for it to be in my face like that."

There was a tiny voice in her head, reminding her that there was a way to simplify all of this. All Tonya had to do was pretend for him, just as she had before. Behind his back, she could have Haley, and then, she could have a relationship with her father. Tonya could have it all. The thought of that level of regression nauseated her.

"Haley is welcome here anytime she wants. I'm not going to sugarcoat my relationships for you anymore, Daddy." Her tone was as sincere and respectful as she could make it. "Maybe it's best if you prepare yourself."

His mouth opened, but no words followed. For a second, he looked hurt, and then his eyes hardened. He stepped back and slammed the door in her face, and the wind it created ruffled Tonya's hair.

She barely jumped. She should have felt saddened by her father's display, but his response wasn't unexpected. He was a man stuck in his ways. Tonya refused to let the glue that had held him captive for all these years hold her back.

Tonya knew what she wanted.

She knew who she was, and Haley was her chance to finally just be.

Suddenly, it seemed paramount to finish what she and Haley had started tonight. It was a big step forward, and Tonya was all about progress and momentum. For her own personal growth, and for them, as a couple, she needed to capitalize on this. They needed to solidify what they had. Before Tonya even realized that she'd moved, she was already in the kitchen. She ran up the stairs toward her room. Tonya's breathing was irregular when she opened her closet door and entered, but it had nothing to do with exertion. Wooden hangers banged and rattled as she yanked her work clothes to the side in search for an outfit for tomorrow. Was she being presumptuous? Yes, she was, but Tonya was willing to take that chance. Somehow, she knew that Haley wouldn't let her down.

She found a suitable bag and filled it with clothing, shoes, and toiletries. As she passed her mirror for the umpteenth time in five minutes, Tonya stopped to look at herself. Her hair was literally all over the place, but it was the expression in her eyes that gave her pause. There was fire and fight in them. That brought a smile to her face. Tonya was also reminded that she was pretty much in pajamas, which probably wasn't the most appropriate thing to drive around in at night. She took another ten minutes trying to find the right underwear and jeans.

When Tonya opened the door to the garage, she was practically pulsating with excitement, anticipation, and achievement. She held on to that combination of feelings tightly as she pulled out of the driveway and into the street.

CHAPTER 21

Haley was far from impressed that she had gotten to level nine all on her own in *Call of Duty: Black Ops*. She had ended over a hundred zombies plus those irritating dogs, but she couldn't keep her mind off the obvious. She was worried about Tonya. Dammit, she should have found a way to stay. She knew not to press Tonya, especially concerning her father, but Haley hated that she was alone with that man.

"Ow!" Her hand cramped. She was holding on to the controller way too tight. Haley needed to relax. Tonya could take care of herself. She didn't need a hero. Not that Haley was one anyway. *Just relax*, Haley told herself over and over, but that was almost impossible to do. Her mind was in a whirl, and her body was screaming at her about unfinished business. At least Tonya had...

Haley's thighs clenched, and her stomach, which was already in knots, pulled even tighter as she replayed the way Tonya sounded; the way she looked; and the way she clung to her like she had no intention of ever letting go. Haley turned her Xbox off, set the controller down, and ran a hand over her face. She hadn't gone over for sex, but my God what she got was something hot enough to melt her face off. It had been a while since she'd been that turned on. Hell, she couldn't remember ever wanting someone this way. Maybe a shower would help, but Haley shot that down. Even if she brought her cell into the bathroom, what if she somehow missed Tonya's call? What if she was actually needed?

She scoffed. That was just dumb. Tonya was making her stupid. She might as well accept it. Haley picked her phone up off the table and looked at the time. An hour and a half had passed. Wasn't that enough time for a person to argue with her father? She sat her cell back down, and nearly came out of her skin when it rang. No, she wasn't tense at *all*. Nate's name flashed across the screen, along with a goofy picture of him and Jen.

After another ring, she sat down and answered it. "Jesus, don't do that!"

"Don't do…what?" Nate asked.

"Call me like that."

"Well, my tin can and string are in the shop. What the hell is wrong with you?"

"I'd be fine if you hadn't scared the shit outta me or if you were someone else entirely."

Nate was quiet for a moment. "I'm so confused, and I know not to ask you for help. I can't even—" He stopped abruptly, and Haley heard voices in the background.

"I'm handin' her over to you. Maybe you can translate."

Jen laughed. The sound got louder. "I think you broke him. What's up with you?"

Haley'd had more than enough time to gather her wits. She sighed. "I was waitin' for Tonya to call. I guess I was so fixated that when the phone rang—"

"Ah, gotcha. Why don't you just call her?"

"Because I don't wanna interrupt. I was over there and her father kinda walked in on a, um, delicate moment. He looked pissed, and I'm sure they were about to have a nice little discussion after I left."

"Wait. Isn't she a grown-ass woman?"

"That she is."

"And it's her house, right?"

"Yup."

"What right does he—"

"It's a long-ass story, and it's not mine to tell."

"I see. Well, on a lighter note, you guys sealed the deal."

"Uh, well—"

Haley's doorbell rang. The chime was followed by a very brisk knock. Somebody was impatient, and she hoped to God it wasn't Tang. She was all Tanged out for today.

"Somebody's at the door."

"Who?"

"Obviously, I have no idea." Haley got up off the couch and went to peek out the window. She gasped. Her mouth went dry, and the ability to breathe disappeared too.

"What? What's wrong?"

"Nothing, nothing's wrong. Tonya's outside. I gotta go."

"Oh, okay. C—"

Haley didn't let her finish. She hung up and opened the door. Haley gazed at Tonya greedily. She was in one piece, at least physically. It took her a second, and then she wasn't sure how she'd missed the bag slung over Tonya's shoulder.

Instead of being floored by the implication, Haley's insides turned molten. They stood there, staring at each other. The way Tonya looked at her made Haley breathe heavily. There was something primal about it.

The next minute happened in slow motion. Haley stepped back. Tonya moved forward, and the bag over her shoulder thudded when it hit the floor. Haley closed the door.

Then Tonya was in her arms and they were in the real world again.

Tonya moaned when their lips met, and Haley's own need flared to life a shitload stronger than it had been before. Tonya's nails raked over Haley's scalp, making her shiver. When Tonya pulled at her hair, Haley growled. Tonya's kiss was equal parts desperate, powerful, and erotic. She plundered Haley's mouth like she owned it, and right then, Haley was willing to let her take whatever she wanted if she promised not to stop. Haley walked Tonya backward until she was pressed against the front door.

Needing to breathe, Haley wrenched her mouth away.

Tonya whimpered in protest, but thank God she was willing to put that mouth somewhere else. She nipped at Haley's chin before trailing her lips to her neck. Every kiss, every suck, and every flick of her tongue led to a tiny eruption between Haley's legs, reminding her that she'd been far from satisfied earlier. It certainly didn't help matters when Tonya started grinding against her thigh.

Haley's brain began to misfire. Words fell from her lips, but she had no idea what she was saying. She was nowhere near as suave as she'd been before.

"Just…hurry," Tonya whispered urgently into Haley's mouth before gliding her tongue inside.

Haley moaned loudly. She yanked at Tonya's shirt, pulling it over her head and throwing it on the floor. A minute later, Tonya was standing there in matching lacy red underwear.

Good God. She was starting to feel light-headed.

Haley barely got a second to enjoy the view before Tonya was clawing at her shorts. Her belt jangled as Tonya pulled it free. When she unzipped her shorts, the metallic sound was sensual background noise.

Her shorts fell away and her shirt was soon to follow.

Haley closed the distance between them and groaned when skin met skin. This time when Tonya thrust against her, she was all damp heat. Haley flexed her thigh and increased the pressure. "God, you feel…"

Tonya whimpered and bucked against her.

Haley had no doubt that Tonya was turned on enough to come just like this, but they had been there. They had done that. Haley belonged inside her, and that's where she was going to be.

Haley brought their mouths together again, muffling Tonya's cries and taking them as her own. Tonya traced her hand over Haley's stomach and hip until her fingers closed over the thick shaft of the toy still inside Haley's boi shorts.

She tore herself away from Tonya's mouth and met her gaze. The intensity of it was gut-wrenching. It took a minute for Haley to drag herself away and look toward the heated space between them. Haley's breath stuttered in her chest as she watched Tonya trace the length of her. Her arousal jumped to world-ending levels, but this wasn't going to happen against her front door. Tonya deserved better than that. She wasn't some fuck du jour, and Haley wasn't going to treat her like one.

"Not like this."

Haley stepped back, took Tonya's hand, and pulled her past the open French doors into her bedroom. It was only a few feet, but it took entirely too long. Tonya refused to keep her hands to herself. She pressed into Haley's body from behind, and she could feel every delicious curve. Tonya's fingertips plucked at her nipples. They were a direct link to her clit. And when Tonya's hands slid over Haley's stomach, her muscles jumped and danced like her body had fallen on a live wire.

Despite everything she was feeling, her head screamed for her to take charge. Haley spun around and instead of moving forward, she was falling.

Her back hit the bed. Tonya had pushed her. A few seconds later, she was climbing on top of Haley, and she was completely naked.

"Oh Jesus."

Tonya's breasts bounced as she moved, and when she straddled Haley's thigh, she could have sworn the room tilted. The fact that she could make this woman that aroused, that wet, made Haley feel as though she had touched the moon.

Tonya moaned thickly, grinding herself against Haley. Their gazes met, held and smoldered, but it wasn't long before Tonya closed her eyes and tilted her head back.

Haley couldn't just sit there. She reached for Tonya, intending to pull her closer. Tonya's eyes opened, and she continued to roll her hips and make those sounds. Still, she slapped Haley's hands away.

"What the—"

Tonya yanked Haley's boi shorts down, and the sleek, black toy sprang free.

Tonya wrapped her hand around the base of the shaft and moved upward until her thumb and forefinger wrapped around the head. She repeated the motion again and again, with just enough pressure to send sizzling jolts of pleasure between Haley's legs. The imagery was enough, and combined with everything else, Haley nearly lost her mind.

This wasn't how she thought it was going to go. Tonya was running things and, dear God, Haley was completely into it. She was back to mumbling, whimpering, and trying hard to get a hold of herself so she wouldn't go off like a rocket.

But Tonya was on the move again. She hovered over Haley's thighs. Her legs were splayed wide and everything in between them was open and exposed.

Haley died a little.

She reached for Tonya's hips, and this time she wasn't swatted away. With one hand still fisted around the toy and the other pressed against Haley's stomach, Tonya gasped and moaned as she lowered herself. The sounds cut through Haley, making her feel like her head was about to explode.

Her grip on Tonya tightened.

It took everything Haley had to keep from slamming into her. Instead, she watched herself disappear little by little. She couldn't decide where to look, Tonya's face, slick with sweat and shining with pleasure, or her sex slowly being filled to the hilt.

It was a draw.

Haley split her attention. Her vision grayed when their hips were finally flush. Tonya groaned hoarsely and started gyrating slowly. Haley cried out. Each movement was like an electric current against her clit. Haley arched upward, meeting Tonya in a slow grind. She dug her hands into the fleshy part of Tonya's ass to speed up and take control of Tonya's movements.

Tonya stopped altogether.

"No…don't. Shit," Haley pleaded.

Tonya stared at her and her gaze held a challenge. That look turned Haley on even more. Tonya leaned forward. She took Haley's hands off her ass and slid them up her torso until they were covering her breasts.

Haley didn't mind that at all. She had been a bit neglectful toward them.

She traced their softness. Her thumbs brushed over Tonya's hardened, brown nipples before tweaking them between her fingertips. Haley's mouth watered. Just as Tonya started rolling her hips again, Haley sat up, wrapped an arm around Tonya's back, and replaced one of her hands with her mouth. She flicked her tongue over Tonya's nipple before sucking it into her mouth, hard.

"Fuck!"

Haley almost came then and there.

Her ears were ringing, and Tonya began moving her hips in earnest, lifting them high before slamming them down again. Haley saw stars. She couldn't breathe. She couldn't think. Her body operated on pure instinct. Her hands were everywhere, grasping, scratching, and guiding. Her mouth went from one breast to the other, pulling at Tonya's nipples until she could taste them in the back of her throat.

One second, Tonya yanked at her hair like she wanted Haley to stop, and the next she held her tight like she couldn't get enough. Their lips met again, but Haley couldn't concentrate on kissing. She was too in awe of what she was feeling. Their lips just clung to each other, trading breaths and moans.

Where were Haley's words now? She'd had so many of them not too long ago, but this time, her body did the talking. Haley'd had many women in this position, but it had never been like this. It was like her insides were on fire, and each thrust of her hips brought her closer to explosion.

"So good," Tonya whimpered, and the words went straight to Haley's core. It was, incredibly so.

"Oh, God." Tonya picked up the tempo, moving her hips even faster. Her hair fell in her face.

Haley followed her lead. Knowing that Tonya was almost there pushed Haley closer. An almost unbearable wave of heat settled low in her stomach. Haley whimpered as it seeped into her limbs. It was too much, but Haley reached for it anyway. Her hips moved at a blistering pace. Her fingertips dug into Tonya's shoulders, but Haley needed to bring Tonya with her. She slid her hands down Tonya's sweaty back and over her buttocks. She grabbed hold for a third time, and if Tonya couldn't keep up, Haley was going to make her.

"OH GOD! FUCK!" Tonya shook wildly. She sank her teeth into Haley's shoulder, and that explosion she had been waiting for happened, ripping her apart.

Haley moaned. She couldn't stop and neither could her hips. Each movement brought pleasure sharp enough to cut. Again, her vision dimmed, but the rest of her was floating. When Haley fell back into her body, she shivered as Tonya's tongue brushed over the bite she'd inflicted. She wrapped her arms around Tonya and breathed her in.

Tonya grazed the area with her teeth. Haley hissed and her stomach twisted. A few seconds later, Tonya did a hell of a lot more, biting down harder than she had before.

Haley was instantly excited, as if she hadn't just had the best orgasm of her life. "Shiii…" She arched forward and so did her hips.

Tonya groaned as her lips brushed Haley's. She whispered hotly, "Don't stop."

She licked at the roof of Haley's mouth.

There was no chance of Haley stopping anytime soon.

Tonya hid a yawn behind her hand as she entered the kitchen. She was surprised to see her mother sipping on a cup of coffee.

"You're up early."

Nicole glanced over her shoulder and smiled. "Robert said you were home. You haven't been able to visit for a while. I didn't want to miss anything while you were here."

Tonya felt a flash of guilt. "School keeps me so busy."

Her mother waved her off. "That's the way it's supposed to be." She opened the cabinet above the coffeepot and pulled out another mug. "You want raisin or just cinnamon toast with your coffee?"

"A slice of each, please."

"Okay. I'm surprised you're up so early. You probably don't get much sleep these days."

"I don't, but the early-riser thing is a habit. I'm usually up by seven o'clock no matter what." Tonya added a bit of cream and two packets of Splenda to her coffee.

Her mother turned and gave her the once-over. "It must be because you're young, but you look good for somebody who doesn't sleep."

Tonya grinned easily. The fact that she could have a normal conversation with her mother made it so. "Thanks."

The toaster popped out her breakfast.

Tonya shooed her mother away as she buttered her own toast. "Where's Daddy? He's usually up by now." Not that he would pay much attention to her if he was.

"He left an hour or so ago to help some friend with something or other, and your sister is dead to the world."

"It's quiet without those two around."

"Isn't it?" Her mother's lips twitched. "They play way too much."

Tonya chuckled even though she didn't mean it. "That's what happens when you're Daddy's favorite."

She meant that, every word. Tonya took a sip of coffee and met her mother's gaze over the rim of the mug.

Nicole's eyes turned sad. "What happened to all of you? You were supposed to take care of each other now that I'm gone."

Emotion welled up in Tonya's chest. "So much, Mama. I've been trying so hard with him, but I'm tired."

"He loves you."

Tonya shook her head. "I'm nothing but a disappointment to him."

Her mother stepped forward and brushed her fingers against Tonya's cheek. "That's not possible. Look at you."

She did. Tonya was now dressed for work, giving her the appearance of someone confident and capable. She swallowed and wished that she actually felt that way.

"Mama, I want to tell you something, but I don't want to see that look on your face too."

"There's nothing you could say."

Tonya let the words fly. "I met someone. We've only known each other a couple months, but I've never laughed so much, felt so much. I didn't think I could."

"Who is he?"

"She," Tonya corrected. "Her name is Haley." She looked away then, steeling herself for a lecture, for tears and possible outrage.

The kitchen was quiet except for the hum of the refrigerator. Tonya was afraid to glance up. She gasped when her mother's hand wrapped around her own.

"Haley. I like that name."

Tonya woke up abruptly. She sucked in a deep breath and opened her eyes, savoring the last dregs of her dream even if the last part had no basis in reality. The smell of coffee and food cooking made her nose twitch. She couldn't stop the smile forming on her face and didn't want to. Tonya loved being in Haley's bed. It wasn't as comfortable as her own, but it smelled like Haley and the sex they'd spent all night having, so that was enough. As Tonya stretched, she looked around the bedroom expecting to see superhero posters, but there was only a collection of photos with Haley and two other people she assumed were Nate and Jen. She sat up to get a better look and chuckled in delight when she saw the Batsignal above Haley's bed.

"You had to be expectin' that."

Tonya jumped in surprise and whipped around. Haley was leaning against the couch in the living room watching her.

"And I wasn't disappointed."

Haley grinned. "There're lightsabers under my bed too."

"You and Nate play with those when he comes over?"

"Only if he comes alone." Haley's gaze went from her eyes to her lips and then to her chest. Where it stayed.

Tonya hadn't even noticed that the sheet had fallen away. Her nipples tingled and stiffened.

"You need to put those away. They have way too much power over me."

"Mm." Tonya's body heated. There had been a time during the night when Haley's mouth was on her breasts, sucking with such intensity that it led to an orgasm.

Haley moved toward the bed, smiling the whole time. She crawled over Tonya and drew her into a kiss. The caress was slow, unhurried, nothing like the frenzied pace between them the first part of the night. Tonya curled her arms around Haley's neck and tried to pull her down, but Haley groaned and wrenched away instead.

"Don't we need to talk…or somethin'?" Haley asked breathlessly.

Tonya sighed. "About what?"

"I don't know, about us, I guess? I mean, are you okay with all this?

Haley looked so concerned and so sincere. It was sweet. Something inside Tonya melted. "I'm more okay than I have been in a long time. That means we are too."

Haley's smile was so big that Tonya couldn't help but to smile back. "Was last night as good as that dream you were talking about?"

"Eh." Haley tilted her hand back and forth.

Tonya glared.

Haley dipped her head again, brushing Tonya's lips with her own. "Are you sore? If the answer is yes, that's all you need."

Tonya gasped. The answer *was* yes. She clenched her thighs together and felt her arousal go up a notch. Obviously, she wasn't that tender. She took stock of her entire body. There were some other muscle aches, but overall she felt boneless and well taken care of. Still, she wanted more.

"Don't look at me like that, or breakfast is gonna get cold and we're gonna be really fuckin' late."

Tonya didn't stop. She licked her lips and asked, "What time is it?"

"It's probably around six-thirty by now. I figured you had an alarm set on your phone, so I turned it off and let you sleep in since you're not drivin' in from Covington."

Tonya closed her eyes and sighed. She had to be good. "So you said something about breakfast?"

Haley grinned. "It's not much. I need to get groceries." She eased back from Tonya's embrace. Her grin widened when Tonya refused to let her go.

Haley had to make two trips. One was with a plate full of scrambled eggs topped off by four biscuits. The second was to bring coffee and a jar of strawberry preserves. They sat back against the headboard close enough for their shoulders to touch. Tonya ate her first forkful and hummed at the taste. "What did you put in these? It's really good."

"Half-and-half, dill, and cheese."

"Is that how you usually cook them?"

"No, I didn't have paprika, so—"

"How'd you know it was going to taste good?"

Haley shrugged. "It was either dill or tarragon. D comes first, and you usually can't go wrong with herbs."

"If I lived alone, I'd be surviving on salads."

Haley chuckled. "Well, you know, my mom taught me, but I like adding my spin to things. Most of the time it works."

"Well, it's definitely a hit this time." Tonya broke off a piece of biscuit and dipped it in her cup.

"Not that it matters, but I'm curious. How'd you get my address?"

"You gave it to me, remember? You wanted me to come over after that other big fight between me and my father."

"I forgot about that. With all that's goin' on, I'm surprised you remembered."

"I listen," Tonya said.

"That you do."

They finished eating in silence. As Tonya drank the last of her coffee, she looked up to see Haley staring. Her expression was thoughtful and intense. "What?"

"I like the way this feels. I thought I was gonna freak out at first because you spent the night. I don't let that happen."

"But you didn't freak out."

"I didn't."

"I'm glad."

"Me too," Haley agreed.

"So how *does* it feel?"

"Like I could do it over and over again." Haley reached out and curled a strand of Tonya's hair around her finger.

Tonya exhaled shakily. So could she. She covered Haley's hand with her own and entwined their fingers. A slow smile spread across her face.

Apparently, that was enough for Haley, who grinned right back and leaned over for a kiss.

CHAPTER 22

Haley stretched and yawned. She reached for her phone and pressed *one* on speed dial. She was grinning by the time Tonya picked up.

"Good mornin'."

"Hello again." There was laughter in Tonya's voice.

"You're always laughin' at me."

"Well, yes, I can't help it at the moment. I just saw you fifteen minutes ago."

"It's a record. The past couple days I barely waited ten minutes to call. I'm learnin'."

"There is that. I'm proud of you."

Haley chuckled. "Know what I'm proud of? That my bed still smells like you."

Tonya's sharp gasp was music to Haley's ears.

"Is that right?"

"Mmm-hmm, I can still smell you all over me too."

Haley could have sworn she heard a whimper.

"Are you trying to ruin me for the rest of the day?"

"It's only fair. Am I gonna see you tonight?"

"I've stayed over three nights in a row already. You're going to get tired of me."

"There's no way I'm gettin' tired of you. You can't do what you did to me and not expect me to want it all the time."

"Oh yeah? What did I do?" Tonya's tone was lower, breathier.

"What is it we young folks say these days? You turned me out."

Tonya laughed. "I don't think that's used anymore." She paused. "How do you do that?" Her voice was full of warmth and affection.

"Do what?"

"Get me so excited one minute and make me laugh the next."

Haley shrugged even though no one could see. "Talented, I guess, and if I didn't spend some time makin' you laugh, you'd never gotten outta this bed. There woulda been prunin' and chaffin'."

Tonya laughed even harder.

"Chaffin' or not. Wouldn't have made a difference. I still woulda kept on goin', and I still want you like crazy."

"God, Haley," Tonya whispered.

"Was that a yes?"

"It certainly was, but I'll have to come over later tonight. I've only been home once the past few days. I wanted to give Daddy some space. I think I've given him enough."

Haley shifted gears. "You think he'll talk to you?

"I don't know, but if he's home, I have an idea on how to break the ice."

"Good. I hope things work out. I know how much you want this. I guess we both have our own crosses to bear tonight. Tang texted me not too long ago. He needs my help tonight and it won't be pretty, I imagine."

"I don't want to pry, but be careful. I'll try to make it all better when I get there."

Haley chuckled. "Damn right you will."

"Turning you out wasn't all that hard."

Haley laughed. "You have no idea. Look, I almost forgot since I've been so distracted. I'm doin' Rock'n'bowl with Nate and Jen on Saturday. You wanna come? It'll be the perfect time to meet them."

"I'm not sorry, and I'd love to meet your friends. Although, Stephanie is probably going to be a little upset with me cancelling on her."

"Just tell her to come with."

"You sure?"

"Yes, I'm sure," Haley answered.

"I have to be honest with you. I'm a little nervous. I can't remember the last time I did the friends-and-family thing."

"Well, I've never done it, so it'll be like the blind leadin' the blind."

Tonya scoffed. "That's not all that comforting."

"A little alcohol and none of us will care."

"I'll keep that in mind. I just pulled into the doctors' garage. I'll see you later."

"Yeah, later."

Haley looked up at her ceiling. She was running late but just couldn't bring herself to get up. Rolling over, she pressed her face into the pillow Tonya used. Haley groaned as her body responded to the smell of her. Reluctantly, she turned her thoughts to the day ahead. Milt was moving back home today. Transporting him was going to be some serious shit. Tang wasn't going to be in a good mood. Did it make her selfish that all she wanted to do was come home and wrap herself around Tonya? The past few days had been…Jesus. He must be tired of her taking his name in vain so much, but Haley couldn't help it. Waking up with Tonya sprawled all over her? No one had invented words to describe that yet. She laid there for a few more minutes, then dragged herself out of bed to get ready for work.

Haley sighed. She'd been talking to Tang off and on for what seemed like forever, and all he did in response was grunt. His mood was foul as fuck. Haley should've given him a pass, but she refused. Tang was vibrating with tension. She had to do something about it. "Can you use the actual words when I'm talkin' to you instead of the language of backwoods Alabama?"

Tang glared at her. A minute later he sighed too. "I'm sorry. I know I've been shitty company."

"Well, don't sit and stew. Let's talk about somethin' neutral like the Saints to keep things goin'."

"I'm not neutral on 'em. They suck, and the fact that they lost the first two games of the season is compellin' evidence. People are gonna start wearin' their brown paper bags soon."

"I'm reservin' judgment. They've got a good chance to beat Kansas City," Haley said.

"Pffft, they lost almost every single game durin' preseason too. Nothin' to be hopeful about."

"Those don't count!"

"It's like precum, it fuckin' counts." He slammed his fist against the steering wheel.

Haley couldn't help but stare at him. That was probably one of the most disgusting things she'd heard him say. She laughed loud and hard. It was good to see a glimpse of his old self.

Tang glared again, but his eyes softened. He started to chuckle at first before going into full belly laughs. It took a while for them to settle down. Tang shook his head. "Thank you. I don't know how you did it, but I needed that."

"I'm glad I could help. It's probably not good for Milt to be around all that tension anyway. How is he today, so far?"

"Agitated and mean. The people who really care about him at Crest Manor are sad to see him go."

"I'll do my best to keep your mind off things."

"That's probably a good idea."

"I agree. Let's hit that wing place for lunch. My treat."

"Naw, Rook. I got it. Least I can do."

"You don't have anythin' to make up for. I'm just glad to get a rise outta you."

As discreetly as she could, Haley looked at Tang. They'd been parked in front of Crest Manor for the last ten minutes. The radio was off, the only sounds the blast of the air conditioner and their breathing.

"Don't say it."

She looked at him straight on. His throat bobbed as he swallowed. "I have to."

He clenched his jaw and sighed. "I know."

"You gotta do this."

Tang closed his eyes and opened them again a second later. "Yeah." He took a deep breath, turned off the ignition, and opened the car door. Haley followed close behind.

The same woman from before, Mary, escorted them back. "You know what he's like on days like this."

"Yeah, I know."

They stopped outside Milt's door.

"I hate that you have to do this," Mary said.

Tang smiled tightly at her. "Yeah, me too."

Haley put a hand on his shoulder and squeezed, and the nurse opened the door. Milt stood in the middle of the room. He stared at the two duffle bags on the floor near his bed, looking confused, scared.

"Uncle Milt?"

He turned toward them and blinked. "How you just gone barge in my room? What kind of goddamn place is this?" Milt pointed at the bags with his cane. "Is somebody movin' in here? Nobody asked me! Where the fuck he gone sleep?"

"Nobody's movin' in," Tang told him.

"Good. Now who the fuck are ya?"

Haley stood close enough to Tang for their shoulders to brush.

"I'm Tim."

Milt waved a hand around. "Bullshit, and who is this slut with ya?"

"We're just here to help, Milt," Tang said.

"Help me do what? I know I was supposed ta do somethin', but I can't…" Milt shook his head. His gaze was desperate and lost.

Haley glanced at Tang. So was his.

"We came to…" Tang cleared his throat. "To move you back to 'Bama."

"'Bout damn time! Let's go, then."

Haley thanked every god she could think of that Milt was going with them willingly. She was pretty sure Tang would break if things got ugly. She put Milt's bags in the trunk, and just as Tang was opening the car door, Milt started to sob.

She looked at Tang. There were tears in his eyes, but they didn't fall. He held his uncle's elbow firmly and helped him into the car. By the time they made it to Tang's house, Milt was screaming.

Haley had seen a lot the past few months, but there was only one other time she'd felt this shaken. Somehow, Tang managed to get him inside. Haley had forgotten for a minute that he'd probably dealt with this situation many times before.

Milton was back to sobbing when Haley brought his bags in. Maybe he'd recognized something and it brought him some comfort. Tang still had a hand on his elbow. They stood in the living room but started moving again when Haley closed the door.

"Follow me and just put the bags outside the bedroom door."

"Okay."

As they walked, Tang's hand moved from Milt's elbow to his back. He rubbed it with long, slow strokes. "Almost there."

"I missed 'Bama."

"I know you did."

Haley set the bags on the floor like she was told and walked back into the living room, not wanting to intrude or aggravate the situation. Her heart was in her throat when Tang came out a few minutes later.

He wiped a hand over his face. He looked so tired. His eyes were glassy, but there weren't going to be any tears.

"I can stay as long as you need me to," Haley said softly.

"No, I got it. I have to learn to deal with all this again. Might as well just throw myself into it."

Before she knew what was happening, Haley wrapped him in a tight hug. He didn't return it at first, and then, suddenly, she couldn't breathe he was squeezing so hard. "You're not by yourself. Call me if you need me."

"Okay." His voice was hoarse.

Haley pulled away. She gave him another long glance and left, her need to be near Tonya tripled.

Tonya's intentions were to finish her last two progress notes before leaving work. As she stared at the monitor, she suddenly realized that she was in the same spot she'd been in ten minutes ago. The cursor winked at her, making fun of her inactivity. Tonya rolled her eyes. "I see you."

Tonya looked up as her office door opened. Stephanie walked in. "I've been knocking and waving forever trying to get your attention."

"Sorry. I was distracted." Tonya smiled.

"No shit." Stephanie tilted her head to the side and stared like she was studying something under a microscope.

It made Tonya a little uncomfortable. "What?"

Stephanie shrugged. "I don't know yet. You've been…" She shrugged again. "Anyway, are we on for tonight?"

"Sorry, again. I have plans with Haley."

"No big. I'm not surprised. People lucky enough to be in relationships always have plans on Friday nights one way or another. Saturday?"

Tonya looked away and started touching everything on her desk. She was fidgeting, and there was absolutely no reason for it. She wished her body knew that.

"Hello?"

"Um…"

"Did you just um me? Don't do that. I really don't want to sit at home. That pint of ice cream I bought yesterday has been calling me. I'll eat the whole thing. Everyone else I know has plans—"

"Calm down. It's a good um."

"There are no good ones."

"This one is. I'm going out with Haley and her friends. I want you to come."

"Ohh."

Tonya grinned. "Was that a good oh?"

"Oh's are universally good since they can double for sex sounds." Stephanie's answering grin was wicked.

"So that means you're coming?"

Stephanie's smile widened. "I wish."

Tonya's thoughts took a dive into the gutter, reminding her that she'd come rather spectacularly this morning and for the last few days as well.

"Okay, your eyes just glazed over. Where did you go?"

Tonya waved her away. "I'm fine."

"All I said was…" Stephanie's mouth dropped open. "Oh. My. God. You've had sex with her." She lowered her voice to a whisper.

Tonya didn't say anything. She didn't really know how to describe what they'd been doing.

Stephanie rolled her eyes. She peered down at her watch and waited. "What are you doing?"

"There's two minutes until our shift officially ends."

"It wasn't—"

"Shhh."

"But we've been talking about her since you came in."

"Shhh." Stephanie held up her hand. "Okay, now I want details." She looked at Tonya hopefully.

Without meaning to, Tonya started laughing. She covered her mouth with her hands and stared at Stephanie.

Stephanie's eyes widened and she sat down. "It's that good?"

Tonya nodded. She chuckled for a few more seconds. "I don't even know how to explain it."

"You don't have to, because your face lit up like the superdome. I'll be more than happy to be a fifth wheel on Saturday."

"Thank you. It means a lot. You're important to me, and Haley is becoming more so every day. It's—"

"Important?" Stephanie smirked.

Tonya smiled. "Yes, it is."

When Tonya got home, she was surprised and glad that her father's truck was in the driveway. She was riding on a high and wanted to use that to get them back to step one. She entered through the kitchen, but Robert was nowhere to be seen. Tonya ran upstairs and retrieved the photo album she'd made a few years back when her mother was alive and the best she'd ever been. She pressed it to her chest like it was a precious thing.

This time when she entered the kitchen, he was there getting a cold drink, but Tonya harbored hope that he'd heard her and was waiting. "Can I have one too?"

He didn't say anything, but he did pour her a Sprite. He held it out for her, and Tonya took it. "Thank you."

Again, he was quiet.

"I have dreams about Mama. I've had them for a long time. Sometimes they're good and sometimes they're bad. It's my subconscious's way of sifting through the memories. I miss her, but she was suffering way too much. It was time for her to stop. She was so beautiful, and I'm proud that when I look in the mirror I see her all over again. When I came home from med school, I'd take pictures of her. There's not a lot of them. I figured there would be…time later." She choked up but breathed through it. "We can look at it together." Tonya continued to hold the album to her chest.

He looked at her for a long time. His gaze was blank, but finally it softened. He nodded. "Okay."

Tonya took her cold drink and the album and sat on one of the stools around the island. She expected her father to sit across from her, but she was shocked, pleasantly so, when he chose to sit beside her instead.

He sucked in a breath when she opened it.

Her father smiled. He reached out to touch one of the first pictures. "She was the most incredible-looking woman I've ever seen. I was glad…lucky to be hers."

Tonya was tempted to touch him, but she held back. As they continued to look through the pictures, they barely said three words between them. She was fine with that because somehow, this still felt like a form of communication.

Her father made various sounds as he turned the pages: chuckles, deep breaths, and noises of contentment.

He lingered on one picture in particular. Nicole's smile was blinding. Tonya recalled that day, and the way her mother had looked at her with such love and pride. It was the perfect time to test the waters. "I'm a product of both of you."

"What do you mean?"

She chose her words carefully. If she said too little, he would brush her off. If she said too much, he would shut down. "Despite everything that happened, you're both my parents. I can't undo that, and I wouldn't want to even if it were possible." Tonya took a deep breath. "You can't undo me either. You made me." She pointed at the picture of her mother smiling.

He looked at her. His gaze was heavy, and somehow Tonya could tell that he was really seeing her. "We did. If I could go back in time, I'd find a way to make sure she was here, and there's no way in hell I'd change having you."

Tonya's heart was so full, but she was light enough to float. She stared at the photo of her mother. "I think we're finally at a good starting point to try to fix us."

They got to the end, which was little more than halfway through; the rest of the pages were empty. When she closed the album, her father stood. He was unsteady on his feet and held on to the counter to right himself. "I think that's all I can handle for tonight."

Tonya let him go without protest. When she was alone, she took out her cell and texted Haley.

Be there soon.

A few seconds later, Tonya got a reply.

K.

There were no emojis, no jokes, and no sexual innuendo. Something was wrong. Tonya went back upstairs and packed enough clothes for the next couple days. As she drove past the toll booth, she was tempted to call Haley, but it wasn't enough. She wasn't going to be satisfied until she saw her face-to-face.

Tonya got to the 7th Ward in record time. She rang the doorbell. After several seconds passed, she did it again. Tonya leaned toward the door. The TV was loud with the sound of gunfire and explosions. Instead of trying the bell again, she tried the door knob. It turned easily and Tonya let herself in.

Haley was sitting on the couch. She grabbed the remote and lowered the volume on the television. When she turned to Tonya, she looked so sad and helpless.

"Sorry, I didn't get up—"

Tonya moved toward her quickly. Standing front and center, she looked down at Haley. There was an actual pain in her chest. She wanted to wipe that expression off Haley's face and replace it with the smirk or smile she was used to seeing. Haley opened her legs and wrapped her arms around Tonya, pulling her closer. She pressed her face into Tonya's stomach, and in return, Tonya sifted her hands through Haley's hair.

Haley glanced up. "Hey." Her voice was quiet and more reserved than Tonya had ever heard it.

"Hey back," she whispered and waited.

Haley cleared her throat. "I don't even know where to start."

"Let me sit down."

She made a noise in protest as Tonya tried to step back.

"Not going anywhere."

Haley finally let her go.

Tonya sat down, and when she got comfortable, she patted her lap. Haley smiled slightly and lay down, pillowing her head on Tonya's thighs. Finding it hard to keep her hands to herself, Tonya scratched at Haley's scalp.

Haley sighed. "Tang is havin' money problems…" Several minutes had passed by the time Haley was done.

"God, that's horrible. I knew it had to be something significant to affect him that way."

"Yeah, it is. I knew you of all people would understand after all you went through with your mom. I woulda told you about him sooner, but I was tryin' to keep at least some of his private life, private. I just couldn't hold it in anymore. It was too big for me."

Tonya didn't speak.

"You kept your promise. You made it better."

"I didn't do anything." Tonya was touched.

Haley reached up and wrapped a couple strands of Tonya's hair around her fingertips. "Yeah, you did."

Tonya tucked her hair behind her ear and bent down, brushing her lips against Haley's. Haley smiled into the kiss. She pulled back slowly, reluctantly, and that smile Tonya wanted to see was still there. The ache in her chest disappeared.

"How'd things go with your dad?"

"It went well. I think…we have a chance."

"Good." Haley's gaze turned dreamy. It almost looked like she was drunk.

"I've been seeing a psychotherapist weekly for the past two years." Tonya wasn't sure why she blurted that out like she did. Maybe she just wanted somebody close to her to know. Maybe it was just an attempt to share more of herself.

"Yeah?"

"Yeah."

"Don't blame you."

Tonya didn't know what she was expecting, but this reaction would certainly do.

"Does it help you?" Haley's tone was curious.

"I'm a very different person than I was two years, really two and a half months ago."

"When you met me?"

"Yes, when I met you," Tonya answered softly.

Haley went quiet and stared. Her gaze was intense, deep. It was hard not to turn away from it. Tonya felt emotionally naked, but she didn't, couldn't look anywhere else. "What is it?"

"You're…incredible. I don't know what I did, but when I find out, I'll do it every fuckin' day if I have to just to keep you."

Tonya thought her heart was full before, but now it was running over. There was no way to contain everything she was feeling: warmth, hope, need, and so much more. She leaned forward and kissed Haley again, pouring herself into the caress.

Haley made a sound somewhere between a whimper and a moan. She tangled her hand in Tonya's hair, holding her there. There was no need.

Tonya didn't want to escape.

CHAPTER 23

"You sure you don't want more coffee?" Haley asked.

"Yes, two cups is my max. By the way, I really like scrambled eggs with paprika now."

"Knew you would." The leather couch squeaked lightly as Haley got comfortable. She turned toward Tonya and held up the Xbox controller. "Okay, just shoot every zombie you see. Don't let them gang up on you. Press the right trigger to shoot; A to jump…" Haley didn't stop until Tonya nodded in understanding. "You sure you got it?"

"Positive."

"We're gonna be playin' split screen."

"What's that?" Tonya's face was all scrunched up. It was cute.

Haley smiled. "You'll see. Just keep your eyes open." She started *Black Ops* zombie mode. It only took a few seconds before the zombies came shuffling out of the woodwork. Haley rained hell down on them.

"I got one!" Tonya announced.

Haley glanced at Tonya's side of the screen. She was kind of just standing there and the zombies were coming straight for her. "Shit!" Haley retraced her steps and took them out. "Just stay with me."

"I was!"

"Uh-huh." Haley changed weapons to a shotgun and went to work.

"I got another one!"

Haley cut her eyes to Tonya's side. She laughed. "No! I got one. Keep your eyes on your own screen."

"I am!"

"Okay. Then what kind of gun do you have?"

"A big one."

Haley chuckled. "No, that's me again."

"Oh."

Somehow, they got to the next level.

There were even more zombies than before. Haley took care of almost all of them. "Get those two comin' for you."

"On it."

My God she was completely adorable. After taking care of the last two zombies, Haley took another quick glance at Tonya's screen. "Wait. Why are you jumpin' in the air?"

"I'm not. I just killed the last two." Tonya moved her whole body, twisting and turning as she hit the buttons.

Was she serious? Haley looked at Tonya's expression. Her face was scrunched up again. She *was* serious. Haley bit her lip, but there was really nothing she could do to keep from laughing.

Tonya glared.

Haley smirked and batted her eyelashes. She paused the game and held out her controller, compressing the right trigger. "This is how you shoot, remember?"

"I know. That's what I was doing."

Haley snorted. "Split screen. You're on the left."

"Okay."

She returned the game to live action.

"I stabbed one in the neck!"

Haley laughed so hard she was starting to wheeze. "No, baby. That's you crawlin' on the ground. You're dead."

"You're laughing at me."

"Yesss, I am." Haley couldn't breathe. She ended the game. There was no way they could continue playing. She was going to end up with a hernia.

"And you're still laughing."

Haley nodded. "I knooooow. You're too much. I can't wait to explain football."

Tonya glared at her again.

Haley leaned over and gave Tonya a peck on the cheek. "I was just kiddin'."

Tonya smiled, shoved Haley, and tried to get up off the couch. "I don't like you very much right now."

"I find that hard to believe. I'm irresistible." She yanked Tonya back down, and she ended up sprawled on top of Haley.

Tonya chuckled and straddled Haley's lap. "You are way too full of yourself."

Haley smirked. "What? *You'd* rather be full of me instead?"

"That's not what I said." Tonya laughed.

Grabbing the outside of Tonya's thighs, Haley pulled her closer and thrust upward. She nipped at Tonya's earlobe and whispered hotly, "I know that's what you want."

"Mmm, I always want that." Tonya rolled her hips. "But that's not all…" She whimpered. "I want your hands. I want your…mouth."

Tonya was breathless by the time their lips met.

Haley pulled the shower curtain aside. She smirked at Tonya. "Good, I was hopin' that blob I saw was you."

"It was." Tonya smiled slowly as her gaze crawled down Haley's body. She took her time drying off.

"You were singing."

"Huh?" Haley rubbed the towel over her head.

"In the shower. You were singing."

"Oh, I do that sometimes, especially when I'm in a good mood."

"Is that right?" Tonya pushed away from the door.

"Mm-hmm." Haley leaned back for a kiss.

Tonya smiled into the caress. "Good, I'm glad you're happy."

"We're comin' down to the wire here. You nervous about meetin' them?" Haley watched Tonya closely.

She brought her thumb and forefinger together. "Maybe just a tiny bit."

"Nothin' to worry about. They already think you're great for puttin' up with me." Haley glanced toward the mirror and put goop in her hair.

"You're not so bad." Tonya had that look in her eye again. That hungry one that usually led them right back to bed, the couch, or the shower. It heated her from the inside out.

"I know, but still." Haley wrapped her towel around her waist. Like it would make a difference. She almost snorted. "They're great people. I take my friendships seriously, and I don't have many of them. Nate and Jen are the best."

Tonya pressed into her from behind and pillowed her chin on Haley's shoulder. "I believe you, but I'm pretty sure it's normal to be a little nervous."

"Yeah, you're right." Haley put the finishing touches on her hair. She wasn't surprised when Tonya's hands covered her breasts. "Aren't you tired of playin' with those?"

"Not when they're like little knobs leading straight to…" Tonya tweaked one of her nipples, sending a flash of pleasure between Haley's legs.

Haley went breathless, but somehow she laughed anyway. "I'm rubbin' off on you. Sounds like somethin' I would say."

"Maybe."

Haley loved that they couldn't go more than a few hours without touching each other. She didn't think she would. It was damn near close to being clingy and smothery, but nothing between them felt invasive.

Tonya slowly slid her hands down Haley's torso. The muscles in her stomach jumped in excitement.

"Mmm, you like it when I touch you."

The butterflies that were always fluttering around in Haley's belly when Tonya was around went crazy. Christ. "Yeah." It wasn't something Haley allowed often, but with Tonya she couldn't seem to help it. "Sometimes I don't want you to stop."

Tonya pulled at the towel around Haley's hips. They'd just crawled out of bed a little over an hour ago. Was she willing to go back in? Hell yeah, but…

"They'll be here soon."

Tonya groaned and kissed Haley's shoulder. "Okay." She stepped back.

A few minutes later, Haley pulled on the T-shirt she'd picked out. Tonya was in the living room, giving them both some much-needed space, but the doors were open and Tonya's gaze was on her. Even though Haley was wearing her boi shorts and the T-shirt, she felt naked.

"I voted for Pedro." Tonya paused. "But my dreams didn't come true." She chuckled. "I know that one. The movie with the weird kid who could dance."

Haley smirked. "Yep." She pulled on a pair of cargo shorts. They were always loose and accommodating. She adjusted herself and slid her feet into a pair of white Vans lined in red to match her shirt. "Hey, is my belt in there?"

"I don't know. Let me…" Tonya ducked down, disappearing from view. A few seconds later, she stood and walked toward Haley with said belt dangling in her hand. "It was under the couch. I thought I saw something peeking from under there."

"Huh, not gonna even ask how it got there." Haley grinned.

"You probably shouldn't. Can *I* ask you something, though?"

Haley took the belt and slid it through the loops on her cargo shorts. She raised a brow. "Yeah, anything."

Tonya took a step closer. Her gaze dipped and stayed between Haley's legs.

Haley's stomach tightened. Jesus, weren't older women supposed to have more self-control? Haley sure as shit didn't. She could only take so much, and Tonya was looking at her like she wanted to eat her alive.

"Why is it black?" Tonya licked her lips.

For a moment, Haley didn't breathe. "You probably shouldn't ask *that*."

"Why?" Tonya smiled wickedly.

Was she trying to kill her? Haley's heart slammed against her rib cage and she had to fist her hands in order to keep them to herself. "Because Nate and Jen will be here in ten minutes."

Tonya reached out and hooked her finger into one of Haley's belt loops, which would have been fine if it wasn't an inch away from her crotch. "Then answer me, and I won't keep badgering you."

Haley swallowed and looked down. Tonya's idea of badgering was to slide her hand between Haley's legs and over her right thigh. She closed her hand around the dildo, making the outline visible even through Haley's clothes. "Why?"

She held Tonya's gaze and felt it in every cell of her body. "I like the way it looks wet."

Before she could take another breath, Tonya kissed her, whimpering at the same time. Haley tangled a hand in Tonya's hair and kissed her back like the fucking world was ending.

The doorbell rang.

Haley moaned in protest. Just a few more minutes, that's all she needed. She walked Tonya toward the back of the couch while Tonya worked frantically to unbuckle her belt and unzip her.

It rang again and again, as if someone had taped the fucker down. If she didn't answer soon, Nate was going to use his key.

If he did, she was going to kill him.

They broke apart. Tonya was breathing heavily. Her eyes were unfocused and her lips swollen. Dear God, Haley was going to kill Jen too.

"You okay?" Haley asked as she sucked in a ragged breath.

Tonya closed her eyes and nodded.

Haley stepped away completely and headed toward the door. When she got there, she glanced at Tonya, giving her a few more seconds. "Hold on!" While she zipped and buckled up, she counted to twenty in her head and then opened the door.

Nate pushed his way through and stared at Haley. "Damn, did you forget the way to the door?"

Jen rolled her eyes and came in after him.

"I mean, really, what were you doin'?"

Jen smiled at Haley and turned her gaze toward Tonya. She paused for a second and looked back and forth between them.

"We were out there for—"

Jen moved quickly to grab her husband's arm. "Shut up," she growled.

Haley gave them both a glare before moving back toward Tonya.

"Why are you growlin' at me?" Nate looked up and around. "Ohhhh, we interrupted somethin'." He paused. "Oops?"

Kill him to death.

"At least we'll be memorable now."

Jen shoved him. "Will you shut it! God."

Haley laughed and glanced at Tonya. She was smiling as well.

"I've only seen him for two minutes, and I can already tell he should've been your brother," Tonya whispered.

"I know, right?"

Jen stepped forward and held out a hand. "Hi, Tonya. I'm Jennifer. You can call me Jen or Jenny. Doesn't matter."

Haley put her hand at the small of Tonya's back for support, for emphasis, or maybe she just wanted to keep on touching her.

Tonya's smile was huge, dimples and all. "Nice to meet you."

"If you say so after all that. We're not the comic relief, I promise." Jen cut her eyes at Nate. "That one is my husband, Nate."

He waved.

"He's an adult most of the time, but when these two get together…"

"I can imagine." Tonya leaned forward and whispered, "There are lightsabers under the bed."

Jen's eyes twinkled. "I know."

Haley groaned. "Can you two wait at least until I turn my back to make fun of me?"

"No." Jen laughed.

Nate wrapped his arm around Jen's waist. "Sorry about all that." He grinned at Tonya and reached out a hand.

"The hell you are," Haley said.

"Well, no, but it sounded nice." Nate smiled.

"Ass."

Tonya chuckled as she shook his hand.

Haley watched the whole thing and exhaled shakily. Maybe she had been nervous too, but this was a bang-up beginning. "So we ready to bowl? Tonya's friend Stephanie is going to meet us there."

"I'm ready. Let's do girls versus boys," Nate chimed in.

Haley glanced at Tonya. "You okay with that?"

Tonya grinned. Her gaze dropped for a second. Haley knew exactly where it went. "That's fine."

Even Haley's toes tingled. "It's on. Let me get my keys—"

"Just ride with us. Plenty of room," Jen said.

"Okay." Haley shrugged.

Tonya and Jen started talking again on their way out the door. Nate bumped Haley with his shoulder. She glanced at him.

"So? Nuclear winter?"

Haley searched for the right words. "More like an extinction-level event."

Nate blinked. "Damn."

"Yep."

Nate touched her elbow. "The way you look right now, it's not about the sex, is it?"

Haley smiled softly. "No, no, it's not."

Classic rock music played in the background, but it wasn't overly loud. Tonya watched as Haley and Nate tested the weight of the bowling balls. Haley threw her head back and laughed at something Nate said.

"I really am sorry. That's not the impression I wanted us to make on you."

Tonya glanced at Jen. She was smiling sheepishly.

"But I bought you a glass of Pinot Grigio to help ease any nerves you might have left over."

"Thanks, but you didn't have to, and it's okay."

Jen just stared at her.

Tonya laughed and took the wine. She liked Jen; she was very direct. "Okay, it could have gone better, but I'm over it, and Haley seems to be too. Any nerves I had are gone as well." Her gaze swung back Haley's way as she sipped from the plastic cup.

"Well, she doesn't let much bother her."

"True."

"And it's nice to finally put a face with the name we've heard about a million times now."

She felt warm all over. Tonya met Jen's gaze. "That many?"

"I may be exaggeratin' by about a hundred. Haley is nowhere near the stereotype of the aloof butch."

That was true too. "I'm—"

"Don't even say you're surprised, since you're sufferin' from the same affliction," Jen interrupted.

"Affliction? What?"

Jen smiled slowly. "You can't keep your eyes off her."

Extremely direct.

Tonya took the opportunity to look in Haley's direction again. "You're right."

Jen laughed. "I usually am." Then she sighed. "Okay, now that we got that all outta the way. I should probably tell you that I already like you. Hard not to after what Haley's said about you, and I know everythin' is true because it's, well, Haley."

Tonya smiled. "You totally just made up for the first impression."

Jen brought her own cup to her lips and took a brief drink. "Glad to hear it. I was willin' to put in the extra work. My husband, on the other hand, is the male version of Haley, so he's pretty much irresistible. I'm sure you've already forgotten he started this mess."

Tonya laughed. "Irresistible, huh? Don't tell her that. She's—"

"Already aware. I know."

"I've already told her that her ego should have its own registered zip code. Unfortunately, it just made the situation worse."

Jen groaned. "So it's your fault, then?"

"Pretty much."

"I want my wine back."

Tonya finished her remaining drink with a flourish.

Jen laughed. "She was right about you. You're hot, smart, and funny. Poor thing never stood a chance."

Tonya smiled. Maybe she hadn't either. Her heart expanded, making room for the past, present, and future. The result was a hammering rhythm that robbed her of breath. Once again her gaze fell on Haley. Everything within her stopped and started again when Haley smiled at her.

She was like a runaway train. Her impact on Tonya's life was inevitable.

"I joke, but that night she called to ask you out the first time, I was there. I told her not to stop tryin'. I'm glad you gave in." Jen said softly.

Tearing her gaze away from Haley, Tonya gave Jen her full attention. "Thank you," she whispered.

"No, thank *you*. She cares about you, and it looks good on her. I can tell you feel the same." Jen sounded relieved.

Yes, she cared. More than she'd ever thought was possible. Tonya didn't say anything out loud; she figured that she didn't have to. Nate and Haley were walking toward them. She looked so happy. It was written on her face and in her every movement.

Seconds later, Tonya was in Haley's arms, and before she could utter a word, Haley kissed her. Tonya wrapped her arms around Haley's neck and reveled in their connection, smiling as Haley nipped at her bottom lip. When she pulled away, Tonya used her thumb to wipe away lipstick at the corner of Haley's mouth.

"What was that fo—"

"You, and the way you were lookin' at me."

Tonya's insides puddled at her feet. As if they didn't have an audience, she stepped farther into Haley's embrace to smell her, feel her, and solidify her place inside.

There was a flash of light. Tonya turned toward it. Nate was holding up his phone. He had a goofy smile on his face, but it was filled with so much emotion.

"Sorry, I just couldn't help it," he said.

Jen sighed. "He means well."

Tonya grinned. "I know he does. I can tell."

"Send me a copy," Haley told him.

"Already did."

Nate cleared his throat and clapped his hands together. "Okay, everyone's on the scoreboard. We're just waitin' for Stephanie, right?"

"Yes, she's caught in traffic. There was a wreck."

"No problem. I'll go get drinks. Anybody else want?"

Everyone gave Nate their drink order, and a moment later, Stephanie showed up, a little out of breath.

"Okay, I'm here. Sorry." She smiled and thrust out a hand toward Jen. "Hey, I'm Stephanie. You must be Jen?"

Jen nodded. "That's me. Nice to meet you. Do you want somethin' to drink? My husband's at the bar."

"Sure. Spiced rum and Coke."

"Got it. Be right back. I'm sure he's gonna need help carryin' all that."

Stephanie sat down on one of the benches and took her shoes off. "I didn't mean to hold things up."

"Stop it. It's not a big deal," Tonya said.

"She's right," Haley chimed in.

"Thanks." Stephanie flashed a smile. "Look at you two all hugged up."

Tonya rolled her eyes.

"Keep those eyes in your head," Stephanie said.

"It's hard to do with you around."

Haley chuckled. "Good to see you again, Stephanie."

"You too, Miss Biceps."

"I'm much more than that, thank you." Haley grinned.

"I have no doubt. So what did I miss so far?"

So very much. Tonya smiled.

Stephanie narrowed her eyes, but she didn't say anything.

"You know what? I guess I shoulda asked." Haley looked down at Tonya. "Do you know how to bowl?"

"Well, no, but how hard can it be?" Tonya split her gaze between Haley and Stephanie.

Haley grinned slowly. "I'll teach you."

Stephanie groaned, but her expression was playful. "You guys are like a walking cliché. Any excuse to put your hands on each other."

"That's not true at all." Haley's smile was huge.

Tonya gave her a light shove.

Stephanie laughed. "Uh-huh."

"Okay!" Nate smiled as he and Jen joined them. "I have a white wine for you." He angled himself toward Tonya.

"Thanks."

Nate winked.

"Blue Moon for you." He handed it to Haley. "And a spiced rum and Coke for you." He gave the final drink to Stephanie. "Nice to meet you. I'm Nate."

Stephanie smiled, but it faltered a bit as she looked from Nate to Haley and back again. "Holy shit."

Haley laughed.

"If it wasn't for the eyes…" Stephanie's voice trailed off.

"And the breasts," Nate chimed in.

Tonya took a sip of her wine and joined in on the laughter, soaking it all in, letting it warm her from the inside out. She was pretty sure this night couldn't get any better.

"Okay, now that everybody's here. Let's bowl. Ladies first," Nate announced.

Jen pulled Tonya and Stephanie to the side. "Okay, since you just got here, you need to know that it's us against them." She glanced at Stephanie. "Nate sucks, but Haley's good."

Stephanie snorted. "Figures. I'm okay, but it's been a while."

"I'm—" Tonya started to say.

"Bait," Jen interrupted and grinned. "We can totally use her to distract Haley."

Tonya scowled.

Stephanie grinned. "Sounds like a plan."

Clearly, Stephanie and Jen were going to make great friends.

Jen bowled first and ended up with a spare. She threw her hands up and hooted as she walked back to the group. Stephanie clapped, and so did Tonya, albeit not enthusiastically. Jen scoffed at her.

"Oh come on, perk up. It's a win-win situation. You get what you want, and maybe we get what we want."

"I don't follow."

"You get to be near Haley, and we get a chance to win." Jen smiled.

"You're pimping me out."

Jen stared at her for a second before nodding. "Yep, I am."

Tonya laughed, short and loud. She really, really liked her.

Stephanie rolled her eyes.

"You have like a superpower or somethin'. It'd be a shame not to use it."

Tonya sighed and waved them both away. "Fine."

Haley chose that time to approach. "You're up." She looked at Tonya. "I'll walk you through it. Let's find you a ball first." She reached out her hand.

Tonya stepped forward and took it.

"Let's start with something that's medium in weight." Haley paused and leaned in. "So what is Jen cookin' up over there? Nate is awful, so I'm gonna have to win this on my own."

Tonya glanced at Haley and laughed uproariously.

"You're scarin' me." Haley smirked.

"Me." Tonya smiled. "I'm the plan."

Haley blinked. "She's an evil genius."

"I know. I'm enjoying it."

"So what are you gonna do to distract me?" Haley continued to fiddle with the balls. She grouped three of them together. "This one is perfect, I think." She eased up behind Tonya. "I put them in order from lightest to heaviest. Give it a try."

Sweet. She really was so sweet. Tonya picked up the first ball.

Haley wrapped an arm around her. Tonya arched into the embrace. "Well?" she whispered into Tonya's ear.

Tonya shivered. "I like this one. I think."

"Mmm, I like this one." She squeezed Tonya slightly.

"Corny." Regardless, Tonya was warmed by Haley's words.

"And? You didn't answer my question." She pushed Tonya's hair out of the way and kissed her ear.

"Nothing. I'm not going to do anything." Tonya glanced up at Haley. She looked so confused. Tonya smiled. "Let's get started. We're holding things up."

"The clock is tickin', lovebirds," Nate called out.

Tonya didn't respond to him, and neither did Haley.

"Okay, this part is obvious." Haley cupped Tonya's hand. "You put these three fingers in the holes." She traced the digits in question.

It was hard for Tonya to ignore the tingle that shot up her arm, but she did what she was told. Haley guided her toward the alley. She pointed at the floor. "The space between where the wood starts and that line is your startin' point. Don't ever cross that line." She pointed at where the alley began. "You'll probably end up fallin' on your ass, and even though it's a very nice ass. I'd hate to see it hurt." Haley grinned.

Tonya rolled her eyes.

"Okay, you're a beginner. So take as many steps as you need to get you a couple inches from that line because that's where the real technique comes in. You ready?"

She nodded.

"Go ahead. Take your steps."

Tonya walked three steps forward. Then, Haley was right behind her, pressing into her. "Good girl."

She shivered again. "You say that like I'm not always one."

Haley chuckled. "No comment. Now follow my body. I'll guide you." She slid a hand over Tonya's hip, bringing her closer.

Tonya gasped sharply.

Haley cleared her throat. "She really is a genius." She paused. Her voice was still low, scratchy. "And you're right. You don't have to do a damn thing except stand there and look like you do, smell like you do."

In one wet whoosh, arousal flooded Tonya, as if it had been waiting for the dam they'd created earlier to break open. It truly was amazing what Haley could do to her.

"Feel like you do." Haley's grip on her tightened.

Tonya felt the minute shift of Haley's hips as she pressed and rubbed against her. "Haley."

Haley exhaled shakily. "Bowlin', yeah. Just stay in the position you're in but bend forward. Aim and swing your arm back, then forward, and release the ball on the follow-through." She stepped away.

Tonya took a deep breath and let it fly. The ball went straight into the gutter. She stepped back toward the bin and waited for it to return. Haley's eyes were on her. She glanced over her shoulder and sure enough.

Haley stepped forward.

Tonya's heart slammed against her chest and her breathing grew shallow. "I think...I got it."

Haley licked her lips and nodded.

Her body refused to calm down, but when she took her second turn, Tonya knocked down two pins. She walked back toward Stephanie and Jen and refused to look at Haley. She couldn't.

Stephanie and Jen scooted over, making room in the middle for Tonya. They didn't say anything. Jen retrieved Tonya's wine and handed it to her.

Tonya was definitely thirsty.

She wasn't sure what Jen and Stephanie bowled. It was hard to pay attention, but when it was Haley's turn, Tonya couldn't turn away. She watched as Haley's muscles, especially her arms, pulled and contracted with her movements. It was truly a thing of beauty.

Jen whooped as Haley only got four pins on the first pass and two on the second. Nate threw his hands up as Haley walked back toward their bench. She sat down, and her gaze zeroed in on Tonya, who meant to look away.

They stared at each other, scorching the air around them.

Jen cheered and laughed, but Tonya wasn't sure what about. Right now, she didn't much care. The initial hour they paid for was up in no time. Haley managed to win, but it wasn't by much. She needed to breathe. She needed to cool off, because watching Haley and not being able to touch her was torture. Her heartbeat refused to slow and her level of awareness and arousal vacillated between a hum and raging. If they'd had a chance to finish what they started earlier…

When? When had she become this person? She'd always thought herself to be a controlled individual. But bit by bit she found herself bending for Haley, and the results had been spectacular. So she shouldn't be that surprised that her control was waning. Maybe if Haley hadn't looked at her the past hour like she wanted to tear her clothes off. Maybe if Tonya hadn't done the same thing. Tonya stood. An ice-cold bottle of water would probably help a little.

"Go ahead and start without me. I'll be right back."

Jen and Stephanie nodded and turned back to their conversation. Tonya didn't even look Haley's way. As she made her way toward the bathroom, the door opened and three women walked out. Tonya returned their good evening with courtesies of her own. She didn't really have to go, but she needed a moment to herself. Her nerves were frayed, too sensitive and attuned to Haley.

The same classic rock music from outside was piped into speakers in the bathroom. The two stalls stood open, empty. She went directly to the sink and glanced at herself briefly in the mirror. She was a little flushed, and the pulse in her neck was fluttering like it had wings. "God, what is she doing to me?" She closed her eyes and inhaled deeply, then let it out slowly. When she opened her eyes, the bathroom door opened too.

Haley walked in.

Their gazes met in the mirror and everything between them sizzled.

Instantly, Tonya's breathing hitched.

Haley locked the door.

In just a few steps, Haley was behind her, pressing her against the sink and pulling her against her body at the same time. Tonya whimpered. Haley's breath was hot and ragged against Tonya's ear. Then her hands were everywhere. Tonya arched and strained to meet each caress. She watched, wide-eyed, as Haley's hands trailed up her torso toward her breasts. Her nipples were hard. The evidence was there for both of them to see.

Tonya moaned thickly when Haley cupped her breasts and brushed her thumbs over the aroused flesh. Haley nipped at her ear and neck. Before Tonya could enjoy it and settle into all the other sensations, Haley tugged frantically at the button on Tonya's jeans. Tonya shook with anticipation. The woman in the mirror staring back at her was not anyone she recognized, but she liked her all the same. This was what need looked like: raw and vulnerable.

"Look," Tonya said in a rough whisper.

Haley did just that as she slid her hand inside Tonya's loose jeans.

Tonya cried out as Haley took the direct route, straight to her clit.

Haley dipped her fingertips lower. She groaned. Yes, Tonya was that wet.

She turned her head and met Haley's lips in a kiss that ripped her wide open.

Haley rubbed her clit in tight circles, and Tonya could already feel the burn of orgasm at the base of her spine. "I need…" she whispered into Haley's open mouth.

Before she could finish that statement, she was already filled. "God!" She was sore, but it didn't matter.

Haley moaned.

Tonya was barely hanging on, but she had to. She had to. She searched for a way to get her desires across with the least amount of wording. "I want you… to see. I want—"

"Oh fuck yes!" Haley yanked Tonya's jeans down her legs and immediately started fiddling with her own belt.

She wanted Haley deep inside her. She wanted to feel her hands, grasping, guiding, and controlling. She wanted Haley everywhere.

Tonya got her wish. She held on to the sink as Haley pulled the rest of her body taut. She stood behind her, tall, powerful, flushed, and ready.

All Tonya knew was that one moment she was empty and in the next she was filled.

She bit her lip hard to clamp down on a scream.

Haley's first few thrusts were slow, decadent.

"Yesss," Haley groaned. Within seconds, her pace shifted, becoming relentless. Her grip was bruising.

Tonya whimpered brokenly with every undulation as her pleasure increased. Haley wrapped her arms around Tonya, pulling her closer.

"I do this to you," Haley whispered in Tonya's ear.

Tonya imploded. For a few seconds, everything went black before flashing brightly again. She couldn't breathe. Pleasure gushed through her, leaving room for nothing else. She was dimly aware of Haley calling out her name as she slumped against Tonya, still holding her tight. It was a good thing; Tonya wasn't sure she could stand. Haley's hips continued to roll, and the aftershocks made Tonya moan as her body bucked in response.

That's when she heard pounding at the bathroom door.

Haley squeezed tighter before stepping away. She groaned. "Shit."

Tonya moved a little slower. Haley's faculties were quicker to return.

"Go in one of the stalls. Don't freak out. I'll take care of it."

Her growing mortification must have shown on her face. Regardless, Tonya nodded. When she got inside, she leaned against the side of the stall. Wanting someone had never been this urgent. It should have been scary, but Tonya smiled. Another door had opened, giving her a bigger picture of who she was, who she should have been, and who she could be.

"I'm a cop. A group of women just left the bathroom, and they looked high. I was just havin' a look around."

The people on the other side mumbled something, but Tonya couldn't hear clearly.

"No, no need to panic or get the manager. I didn't find anythin'. I guess they were just drunk. Give me a minute to clean up, and it's all yours."

Tonya chuckled. Then she heard water running. A few seconds later, the stall door opened.

"Laughin' at me already? Really?" Haley was smiling. She moved closer to Tonya, leaning against her and wrapping her arms around her. "You okay?"

Tonya nodded.

"Not mad at me for all this? I just couldn't—"

Tonya pressed her hand against Haley's cheek and kissed her, getting lost in their embrace. Having Haley in her arms grounded Tonya and made her feel like she could fly simultaneously.

"Mmm, so you know, *they* are gonna know what we were doin' in here. We've barely been gone ten minutes, but still. You ready for that?"

Tonya sighed. She wanted to revel a little while longer, but she was ready. "I'm surprised Stephanie wasn't the one beating down the door."

"Ah, she speaks."

"Shut up."

Haley laughed. "Uh-huh." She kissed Tonya again. "Let's go."

Tonya grabbed Haley's hand. "How'd you convince those women you were a cop?"

"Badge."

"You carry it around with you?"

"Yeah, it's kinda like a business card."

When Haley opened the stall door, there were two women standing at the sinks. They stared. Tonya ignored them. She stopped at the mirror. She fluffed her hair. Her lips were bare, but there was nothing she could do about lipstick until she got back to her purse.

After releasing Haley's hand, Tonya sat down near Stephanie while Haley joined Jen and Nate. She reached for her purse and reapplied lipstick.

With a raised brow, Stephanie watched her silently.

Tonya put the lipstick back where it belonged and turned to her.

Stephanie's eyes widened, and it looked like she was fighting hard not to smile.

Tonya did it for her and Stephanie joined in. "I love the effect she has on you."

"Me too."

Jen came over a few minutes later. Tonya looked up at her as she sat down.

Jen grinned, and there was a knowing glint in her eyes. "I sent Nate for drinks. I assumed everyone wanted the same as before."

Maybe another wine wouldn't hurt.

"We'll start another game then." Jen got back up. "I'll go—"

"No, I'll help. This round is on me." Tonya got out her credit card and stood.

"Oh, in that case, I wonder if they have champagne?" Jen smiled teasingly.

Tonya gave her a mock glare. Haley walked toward them. Their gazes met. Haley's smile was crooked, but her eyes gleamed. Tonya's insides heated.

She got to the bar just as the bartender was setting the first pair of drinks in front of Nate. "Close out the old ticket and open one on this card."

The bartender nodded and took it.

"Oh, hey, you didn't have to do that," Nate said.

"It's my turn. You guys got the others. I can help carry them back too."

"Good. I don't think you'd want your wine anymore if your cup was danglin' from my mouth."

Tonya chuckled. "No, probably not."

The bartender returned her card and went to work on the remaining drinks.

"I'm sorry. We haven't really had a chance to talk."

"I'm sure my wife had a lot of interestin' stuff to say in the meantime."

"Very interesting."

Nate grinned.

"You and Haley really do look a lot alike."

"I always take that as a compliment." He paused but he kept his gaze on Tonya. "I really like who she is nowadays, but she hasn't figured out what's goin' on yet."

Curious, Tonya asked, "Hasn't figured out what?"

Nate smiled, straightforward and sincere. "That she's fallin' in love with you."

Tonya's vision narrowed and everything inside her stopped. Seconds later the world opened up again and it was full of warmth.

Nate laughed. "Yeah, that look right there."

She stared at him.

"You didn't know either." Even though he barely knew her, Nate covered her hand with his own. He squeezed lightly before letting go. "I like seein' her like this," he repeated.

No, she hadn't known, but she didn't mind. She didn't mind at all. Tonya swallowed. Fireworks exploded inside her.

CHAPTER 24

"Oh God. We should never leave this bed, and the sheets. We should never leave these sheets," Haley said sleepily.

Tonya chuckled as she signed off on the last of her staff's progress notes. She glanced to the side and over the rim of her glasses to see Haley hunkered down like an animal in its den. The tribal tattoo across her shoulders, similar to the one on her arm, was the only thing visible besides her head. Tonya closed her laptop, took off her glasses, and adjusted the scarf holding her curls in place.

They had spent almost every night together since the bowling alley. The whole thing was highly domestic, and Tonya found that she was settling into it. Perhaps *settle* wasn't the right word. Embracing was better. However, this was the first time she'd done all this embracing in her own home. Fallout be damned. She had to see this through.

Haley was facing away from her. Tonya reached out and ghosted her fingertips over the tattoo. Goose bumps erupted where she touched. Tonya smiled at the response. "Did it hurt?"

"Hmm?" Haley lifted her head and turned toward Tonya. Her hair was all over the place, some of it partially obscuring her eyes. She brushed it out of the way.

"The tattoos. The people I've asked always tell me that they didn't hurt."

Haley's eyes cleared. "Hell yes, it hurt. I got them both the same day." She yawned. "Had to take like twenty breaks, and I still almost cried like a baby. Two was enough. I won't be gettin' any more."

"Aww, so brave."

"Uh-huh. Nate was with me too. He has a matchin' one on his arm, but it doesn't go all the way around. He couldn't take any more."

"I won't tell him that you told me that."

"Mmm, 'preciate that." Haley stretched, lifting her arms over her head and elongating her entire body. She groaned when she finished. "Now we gonna talk about the elephant in the room? Or do you wanna wait a little while longer?"

Tonya made a show of looking around. "I don't see anything."

"I'm being serious."

She sighed, "I know. I like that you know me so well."

"Well, you have a tell."

"I do?"

"Uh-huh, when somethin's up with you, I usually end up talkin' my fool head off. You listen, smile, and when you're ready, you open up. I just thought I'd speed things up a little tonight."

"We didn't do a lot of talking tonight," Tonya reminded her.

Haley grinned. "Oh, I know. I was there, but when we did. Well…"

"Since I bought this house, you're the first woman to stay the night here. In fact, you're the first woman I've been involved with to be in this room." Tonya paused. "I was going to tell you."

"I know you were, but whoa, why me?" Her eyes were wide. She looked surprised but not displeased.

"Because I wanted to, and since we're together, we should be *together* everywhere, even here."

Haley pulled her close and slid a hand underneath the T-shirt Tonya had stolen from her. "I like the sound of that."

She trailed her hand up Tonya's torso, between her breasts and back down again. "Your dad is gonna shit a brick when he sees me. I guess it's a good thing he was hidin' in his room when I got here."

"I know, but it is my house. I won't censor myself anymore in my own home. I hope he can learn to accept it."

"For your sake, I hope he does too."

Tonya's cell phone rang. It was after ten. She reached for it and squinted. It was Tracy. She held up a finger to Haley, halting their conversation, and answered the phone.

"Everything okay?"

"Oh yeah, sorry. I just got off work. I haven't heard from you in a few days. I just wanted to check in."

Tonya smiled. "It's been busy. I was going to call you this weekend."

"Well, I beat you to it."

"Yes, you did."

"How's things with Daddy?"

"We're talking. We're actually talking, and he's listening. I think he's learning his perception of things is vastly different from my experience. He actually told me he was ashamed of what happened."

"That's huge."

"I agree. It is, but we have a long way to go. He asked me if my childhood pushed me toward women since he wasn't there to protect me like he should've been."

"That doesn't make a lot of sense."

"No, it doesn't. But I'm glad he was able to bring it up." Tonya glanced at Haley. She lay beside her with her elbow propped up on a pillow, watching. She smiled. Tonya pushed a hand through Haley's tousled hair and smiled back. "Speaking of, I think, when you come home, it's time for you and Haley to meet. Too bad you weren't available last week; you could have come bowling with us. Stephanie was there, and Haley's friends." Tonya's body heated with memories. She met Haley's gaze again, grinning as if she had a dirty little secret.

Tonya watched as one of Haley's hands disappeared under the covers. She wasn't that surprised to feel it on her thigh, but she still gasped. She pushed Haley away and glared at her. Haley blinked back innocently. Tonya pointed at her and mouthed, "Stop it."

Haley nodded.

"Oh really?" Tracy said. "Will this be an 'I have to be on my best behavior' type thing or 'I can just be myself' type thing?"

"Be yourself. I'd never ask otherwise."

"You really do like her."

Tonya smiled and stared at Haley. "Mmm."

Haley grinned. She was taking in every word.

"I'm taking that as a yes, especially since you already told me."

Haley pulled the duvet over her head and started wriggling around underneath.

"Hold on." Tonya pulled away from the phone and muted it. "What are you doing?"

"Nothin', promise. Carry on." Haley's voice was muffled.

Tonya stared at the lump for a few more seconds, but it didn't move. Satisfied, she unmuted the call. "Sorry, I'm back."

"What was all that about?"

"Nothing. I was just—" Haley's fingertips brushed over the back of her knee. Tonya sucked in a shocked breath.

Haley did it again.

Tonya tried to back away.

Haley followed and tickled her some more.

Tonya sputtered with laughter. "Stop it!" Haley didn't stop, and soon Tonya was laughing so hard she couldn't breathe. She squirmed, swatted, and kicked the covers away, losing her iPhone in the process.

"Uh, hello?"

Somehow, the phone was now on speaker.

Haley's eyes were wide and innocent—as if she could play that card again. She rolled away and got out of the bed. She stood there, blissfully naked.

"Don't give me that look."

Haley smirked.

"Tonya! What the hell is going on? Do you have somebody...?" Tracy paused. "Hello, Haley." She sounded amused.

"Hello, Tonya's sister Tracy."

Tonya glared and reached for her phone. It was still on the bed.

Tracy laughed.

"I thought you'd be at home in bed. It didn't even occur to me you'd be out. Why'd you answer the phone?"

"Because it's you and I'm not out. I'm at home."

"Ohhh, Daddy's gonna freak. But you're not twelve, and it's your house. Look at you taking your power back. I'm scared of you." Tracy chuckled.

Tonya rolled her eyes.

Haley wrapped the duvet around herself and crawled back into bed.

"I won't be home until next weekend. We'll make plans then. Get off the damn phone with me. You have company. Don't be rude."

Tonya grinned as Haley inched up beside her. "Fine."

She barely had time to hang up before Haley covered her with the duvet. Tonya laughed, "You're so bad."

Haley sat up and leaned over her. Tonya parted her legs to be more accommodating. "I don't wanna talk about your father or sister anymore." She traced her fingers from Tonya's foot all the way to her knee, but there was nothing ticklish about this touch. Haley pulled Tonya's thighs farther apart. Her eyes dipped from Tonya's face to between her legs, and she dragged her tongue over her bottom lip.

"I thought you were going to sleep." Tonya's body sang with anticipation.

"Not yet."

Haley awakened slowly. It was barely light out, but the sun was high enough to shoot some rays through the curtains. Haley inhaled deeply, blinked, and opened her eyes completely to look around the bedroom, Tonya's bedroom. She moaned in contentment; that had to be one of the best nights' sleep she'd had in forever. Tonya whimpered softly and tightened her embrace. She whispered, "Mama," and Haley assumed she was in the middle of one of her good dreams.

She tilted her head to look down at the woman sprawled over her chest. Haley grinned and rubbed a hand over Tonya's naked back.

This was the shit.

Tonya whimpered again.

The sound did something to her stomach and made her heart beat just a little faster. That...that feeling would never get boring, and it seemed to be getting bigger. If her mom felt this for her father, Haley understood the need to seek it out and try to replicate it. She understood Nate's tears when he thought he'd lost it.

"Mmm, did the alarm go off and I didn't hear?" Tonya's voice was soft and slurred.

Haley stared at her. Tonya looked so sleepy. Her face was free of makeup, and she was still the hottest woman ever. Haley smiled, and it was huge enough and hard enough to make her face ache.

Tonya covered Haley's face with her hand. "You're blurry, but I can still see that grin. Turn it down. It's too bright."

Haley snorted. She kissed Tonya's palm before she moved it away. "Good mornin' to you too, and no, the alarm didn't go off yet."

"Then, why are you up?"

"Don't know. I just am. Enjoyin' myself, I guess."

Tonya hummed.

"You can go back to sleep."

"Maybe. What time is it?"

Haley reached out to the nightstand to get her phone. "Half past five…"

Tonya groaned. "Well, I'd say it's moot at this point."

"Surprised you didn't set it for earlier. Not gonna go work out?"

"No. Are you?"

Haley chuckled. "We're turnin' into slackers."

"Hardly. I'd say we've been working out plenty."

"Very true."

Tonya scooted up, and their lips met in a lazy kiss. Haley traced her hands over Tonya's back once more and didn't stop until they slid over her ass. They stayed in that same position, bodies flushed and kissing softly until the alarm rang.

Tonya moaned softly as she pulled away. She grabbed her phone to silence it and got her glasses as well. "Now you're not so blurry."

"Mmm, good thing you know where my mouth is."

"Yes, good thing." Tonya brushed her fingertips over Haley's bottom lip. "I really like this…us."

Haley smiled. "Me too."

"Shouldn't it be scary? I mean, I've never—"

"Me either, and I'm not scared. I was at the beginnin', but not anymore."

Tonya smiled and leaned down for another kiss. "Neither am I."

They got lost in each other for a few more minutes before Tonya pulled away reluctantly.

"I need coffee."

"I'll go get it. You get in the shower. I'm not gonna even ask to join you. We'd never get outta here."

"You're probably right, but my father might be down there."

Haley shrugged. "If you can handle him, I can too."

"You shouldn't have to."

"Ah, don't even go there. It's part of the package."

Tonya sighed. "Okay, but you might want to put some clothes on first."

"But I like makin' an entrance."

Tonya glared.

Haley laughed. "Okay, I know, duh."

A few minutes later, Haley took a deep breath as she went down the stairs. She could smell coffee, but when she got in the kitchen, no one was there. There was an open paper sitting on the island. Haley was relieved. She didn't want to start the morning with saying the wrong thing. She opened the cabinets until she found the coffee mugs and went to the refrigerator to see what kind of creamer Tonya had on hand. Café Mocha would do just fine. After filling her own cup with way too much of the stuff, she added coffee and took a long sip.

Haley heard footsteps and stiffened. She glanced over her shoulder to see Tonya's father entering the kitchen.

He stopped and stared.

She stared right back. "Coffee?"

He blinked, then storm clouds took over his face, but he didn't say a word. He sat on his stool in front of his paper.

Okay, then.

Haley turned back to the empty mug and prepared it for Tonya, adding a dollop of creamer and two packets of Splenda. She felt his gaze but brushed it aside.

"That's not how she takes her coffee." His tone was really close to being pouty.

She didn't look at him. Haley opened the cabinet and reached for a third mug. "Yeah, it is." She kept her tone soft, respectful. "How do you take yours?"

He grunted and flipped through the paper hard enough to rip the pages. Haley filled the mug and set it in front of him. "Black, then."

She went back to the counter and untied the cinnamon-raisin bread, putting two pieces in the toaster. It was time for Haley to buy Tonya a new loaf for her place. There was only one slice left. Haley glanced in his direction. He was staring at her. "Want some?" She held up the bread.

Robert grunted again.

Haley's attention went to the stairs as Tonya came down. The dark slacks only hinted at her curves, and the beige shirt didn't show a speck of cleavage. It was a minor shame, but she was still sexy and elegant. Haley grinned, not just because of Tonya, but because of Robert staring at her while she stared at his daughter. She wondered what he saw.

Tonya returned the smile tentatively. Then her gaze landed on her father. "Good morning, Daddy."

"Morning," he grumbled and went back to his paper.

Tonya looked at Haley and mouthed, "Okay?"

Haley nodded. "I made your toast."

"Thank you." Tonya patted her stomach as she walked around Haley and finished preparing her breakfast. "You should've made eggs."

"Yeah, maybe." Haley smirked. Tonya did like her eggs. She glanced at the time on the microwave. "I better go. I still need to go home."

"I don't know why you didn't bring your uniform. Do it next time. Things will be easier." Tonya smiled and dipped a piece of toast in her coffee.

Next time. She so liked the sound of that. "I'll keep that in mind." Haley was tempted to pull Tonya close but decided against it. She moved toward the stairs instead.

"What does she do? Work for UPS?"

Haley stopped and listened.

"No, Daddy. She's a police officer with the NOPD." Tonya's tone was irritated.

He grunted.

Haley shook her head and started walking again. She was sure he had more to say, but she didn't want to hear it.

Tang winced for the umpteenth time when he leaned back in his seat. Haley studied him. He looked a little tired but otherwise all right.

"You hurt your back or somethin'?"

He stilled. "What?"

Haley stared at him, but he wouldn't look at her. "Your back? You keep making this face like you're in pain."

Tang glanced at her. "You're seein' things."

Interesting.

"Uh, no, I'm not. I'm a cop; that makes me observant."

"No, it doesn't," he sputtered.

"Tang."

"What?" He practically screamed.

"What the fuck? For real? You just yelled at me because I expressed concern." She continued to stare at his profile.

He pressed his lips into a thin line. "You know I have a lot—"

"Goin' on. Yeah, I know that, but what does it have to do with you bein' hurt? You have two bedrooms. I know you're not sleepin' on the couch." She couldn't let it go. Haley wasn't sure why yet, but she couldn't.

"It's fine."

"What's *fine*?"

"That woman of yours."

"Tang."

He stopped at a red light and glanced at her. There was a haunted look in his eyes that hadn't been there before. "We had an accident."

"We? You mean you and Milt?"

"Yeah."

He went quiet, and after five minutes, Haley'd had enough. "That's all you're gonna say."

"Rook…Haley, just leave it. Nothin' you can do about it, and there's sure as fuck nothin' I can do either."

Something cold slithered at the bottom of Haley's stomach. That feeling in her gut gave her an idea of what it was. As he turned the car, Haley reached out and swiped her hand down his back.

"Shit!" Tang's face reddened.

"Pull over. Let me see."

"Hay—"

"Just…please pull over."

He looked at her. His expression was unreadable, but he did as she asked and turned into the Dollar General parking lot.

They sat there for several minutes.

"Show me," Haley said softly.

Tang exhaled noisily. He turned and pulled his shirt out of his pants.

Haley didn't say a word. There were deep scratches on his back, from his shoulder to the middle. A bandage covered just the ends of it. The rest was angry and red.

"Milt did this?"

"Yeah, he didn't mean to. He…was havin' a bad night." He paused. "I was tryin' to patch myself up. Couldn't reach all of it."

Her heart broke a little. "I'm gonna go in the store and get some supplies. I'll take care of it."

He glanced over his shoulder. His face was flushed, and his eyes were unreadable again. "I hate my life."

Haley got out of the car. She paused when she entered the store and pulled her phone out of her pocket. She pressed number One on her speed dial and scanned the store for the first aid products.

Tonya picked up right away.

"Hey, I know you're busy. I hate to cut into your day."

"I have a minute. What's wrong?"

Haley swallowed. "I just needed to hear your voice. I needed to hear somethin' good."

Tonya made a soft sound. "Bad day?"

"A little bit, yeah."

"I miss you."

Haley's breath caught. They'd just parted ways less than six hours before. "Yeah?"

"Yes."

"I miss you too. Can I see you tonight?"

"Yes, but I have my therapy appointment, so it will have to be later. Your place or mine?"

"I don't care, Tonya. I just wanna see you." Haley found the band aids and gauze. She even picked up some ointment.

"God, Haley."

"Yeah." Her heart was about to jump right out of her chest, but before they could go any further, the sound of someone knocking on Tonya's door came through the phone. Haley sighed. "You gotta go?"

"I do. You want me to call you later?"

"No, that's okay. I'll just see you tonight."

When she hung up, Haley felt like she could take on just about anything. Hell, she was already neck-deep in a relationship, something she'd sworn wasn't for her. But if Tonya continued to express herself like that, Haley knew she must be doing something right.

She got back into the car. Tang looked at her before muttering, "Thanks." He turned and lifted his shirt again.

Instead of touching the scratches, Haley squeezed out Neosporin on the gauze and taped it to his skin. "Did I miss anythin'?" She pulled his shirt up higher, but there was nothing.

"No."

Haley was already moving his collar aside. That's when she saw the bite mark. "Jesus." She slathered cream on a huge band aid and covered it. "You need to get that looked at. Human bites—"

"I know." Tang was firm.

"Does he do this to the nurse?"

"Sometimes."

"Was he like this before?"

"No. Can we just stop talkin' about it? Not gonna change it. Nurse is there during the day, and I'm the night shift. That's how it's gonna be until he fuckin' dies."

Haley didn't say anything.

"Shit, I didn't mean that. I'm just…tired already, and it hasn't even been that long." He undid his belt and pants to tuck his shirt back in.

"Eight twenty-two report of a 94 in progress at 8700 Edisburgh."

Tang sighed. "Just a lovely fuckin' day." He picked up the radio. "This is eight twenty-two. ETA five minutes. What's the word on backup?"

Another car in the vicinity chimed in.

When they got to the address, there were people standing in the street looking toward the house in question and talking. Haley got out of the car and asked the person closest to her, "Did you hear gunshots?"

The woman nodded. "There were a lot of them a few minutes ago."

"Thanks, ma'am." Haley stepped in front of the crowd. "For your own safety, everyone please move back to the other side of the street."

People grumbled, but they moved.

Their backup arrived, and Tang took charge. "We need one of you on crowd control and the other around back in case we get a runner." His expression was serious, but his eyes were unreadable again. "Rook, you and me to the front."

Haley nodded.

They approached the house. When they stepped onto the porch, Haley covered her nose. "Smell that?"

"Yeah, chemicals. Probably a meth lab. Be careful."

Haley rang the bell, then knocked. "NOPD! Open up!"

They stood on opposite sides of the door.

She leaned in slightly. Haley didn't hear anything.

Tang motioned that he was going to look in the window.

Haley knocked again.

She glanced at Tang. He shook his head, then stepped back and reached up to his shoulder, talking into his radio. "Waller, check in the windows back there."

"On it."

A second later. "I count three, all on the floor. No movement."

"Hold your position," Tang whispered.

"Understood."

He nodded at Haley and held up five fingers. She unholstered her weapon and he did the same. When he lowered the last finger, Tang kicked the door in. The wood split violently. The door hung off its hinges.

They hesitated.

Nothing.

Haley stepped inside quickly. She scanned the living room. The chemical stench was overwhelming. The French doors leading to the bedroom were ajar. She held up her hand, signaling Tang to stay back. Easing to the far right side, Haley peeked through the glass. Way in the left corner, a man sat slumped against the wall. Blood covered his chest. Haley watched him for a few seconds, checking for movement.

His arm twitched, and he groaned. That's when she saw the gun in his hand. Haley waved Tang inside and pointed toward the bedroom. She mouthed, "Ambulance," then squatted and slipped through the opening in the doors.

Haley stood tall and pointed her gun at the potential perp.

He tilted his head back and looked at her.

"Drop the gun," Haley whispered harshly.

He blinked but did as he was told. His legs were splayed. It fell between them. He probably didn't have the ability to fire a weapon anyway. Haley kicked it out of the way.

Tang came up beside her. "Is there anybody else here?"

"Dead. Kitchen." The man smiled and started to laugh but ended up choking instead. Blood oozed from his mouth. His chest heaved. His breathing was loud and liquid-sounding. He tilted his head to the side again, and everything just stopped.

"Shit. His day is a lot worse than mine."

Haley couldn't agree more. She reached in her pocket for gloves. After putting them on, she pressed her fingers against his neck for a pulse. There wasn't one. "Help me lay him down."

"Yeah, but it's better if Sims does first aid and waits for the EMTs while we look around. I'd rather have you with me."

Haley nodded. She could understand that.

Tang touched the radio on his shoulder. "Sims? Got your medic bag with you?"

"Affirmative."

"Get in here. We had a live one as of a minute ago. Looks like multiple GSWs to the chest."

"On my way."

"Waller, take over for Sims on crowd control."

"I was already on my way," Waller said.

Haley stood as Sims arrived.

"Ambulance should be here in a couple minutes. We're gonna have a look around. Vic said everybody else was dead. I'm not gonna take his word for it. I'll take the kitchen and whatever else is back that way. Look for the bathroom and any other bedrooms. Be careful." Tang pointed to the right.

"Sounds like a plan." Haley moved quietly but quickly toward the opposite side of the house. There seemed to be only one other room down a short hallway. The door was open slightly. She hugged the wall and listened for activity, but there was nothing to hear. Still, she yelled, "NOPD!" and kicked the door all the way open, keeping her gun low and ready.

It was the bathroom, and it was empty. She walked in, and if the contraption in the bathtub wasn't a dead giveaway that all of this was drug deal gone wrong, the containers of acetone, muriatic acid, and all the other crap was overkill. There were two black duffle bags sitting on top of the toilet. They were both unzipped. One was filled with at least a couple pounds of product. The other one was a lot smaller but had what looked to be more than ten banded straps of twenty-dollar bills stuffed in it. With usually two thousand bucks per band, it was safe to say there was potentially a shitload of money. "Holy fuck." There was no way to be sure. Without CSU and detectives on the scene, Haley couldn't touch the bag. She moved forward. That didn't mean she couldn't get a closer look.

"You find anything, Rook?"

She turned to see Tang standing at the bathroom door. He whistled.

"You could say that." She glanced over her shoulder.

"Yeah, looks like it. CSU and the rest of the gang shoulda been here by now."

"What did you find in the kitchen?" Haley asked. She heard an approaching siren. It was close.

"Dead bodies. These guys fucked each other over pretty good."

"It's a damn waste is what it is." She had to say the words out loud. Haley shook her head. The guy in the bedroom looked to be about her age.

"It's not called the Zoo for nothin'. Don't understand why they're killin' each other."

There were a bunch of reasons why. She wasn't stupid. "If you don't need any more help in here, I'm gonna go get some air."

"You okay?" Tang asked.

"Yeah, I just like it better when somethin' good comes outta shit like this." Haley walked toward the door and pressed the button on her radio. "Waller, I'm comin' out. Can you come cover the bathroom with Tang?"

Her radio crackled. "Be right there."

Tang went quiet and Haley stepped out of the doorway when she saw Waller.

"What's up?" he asked.

"Drugs and money. At least they didn't kill each other for nothin'."

Haley sat at an empty desk. She was few lines away from completing her report on the Edisburgh call.

"All right, Rook."

She glanced up. "Hey."

"I need to get outta here." Tang was in street clothes. His bag was slung over his shoulder.

"You gonna be okay?"

He shrugged. "It is what it is."

"I know. I'll call you later."

Tang sighed and looked heavenward. "You don't have to check up on me."

"I can do what I want." Haley stared him down.

He shifted his bag to the other shoulder. "Yeah, I'll see you in the mornin'." He walked away.

Haley watched him go and then turned back to the computer, where she checked to make sure his report had been filed. There were drugs, guns, and murder involved, so the paperwork needed to be dealt with sooner rather than later. It was there, but not submitted. She could at least do that for him. It wouldn't be the first time, especially lately. Doing so could get them both in big-time trouble, but Haley knew for a fact that the practice was commonplace.

She saved what she'd written so far, then logged out and back in under Tang's login. Maybe he didn't submit it because he wasn't finished. If that was the case, what the hell was he thinking?

Haley skimmed his report. In fact, he wasn't done. She picked up her cell phone to call him to come back. God, she really was his work wife. She breezed through the rest, and his account of the initial encounter was very close to hers, but he had additional information since he'd played a bigger part with CSU and stayed with the evidence. Haley stopped cold. He'd listed the money at twenty-four thousand dollars. There had been more in that bag. She had just taken a quick look, long enough to get a decent estimate to put in her report. Maybe she was wrong. Maybe...

She blinked. Haley's doubts didn't keep away the sick feeling that filled her stomach. She listened to her gut. Someone had sticky fingers. Haley pressed *three* on speed dial. Tang needed to know about this.

He didn't answer.

Money and drugs had to be guarded at all times by at least two officers. Before the place was crawling with law enforcement, she had been one of only three people who'd had extended time with the evidence.

Haley went over everything in her head as she texted Tang and waited. She'd been in the bathroom with Tang when Waller came in to take her place. Sure, she'd turned her back for a minute or two, but it was *Tang*. There was no way he would do something that stupid.

He didn't reply to her text.

Haley took a deep breath. She was overreacting. She had to be. There was no way he'd steal money from a crime scene. It had to be someone who came in later. She texted him again.

Okay, he was ignoring her, but that could have been because he didn't want to be bothered, especially five minutes after they just spoke. Haley took another deep breath. She used to doubt him all the time in the beginning, but not anymore.

She swallowed down a sudden gush of nausea. If the detectives investigating this whole thing found something wonky with the money, it would fall back on her since she'd made the initial discovery.

Alone.

"Shit."

Either that or IAB would think that they were both in on it.

"Fuck." She leaned back in her chair. A white-hot sliver of fear shot down her spine, and for a second, Haley couldn't breathe. When she could, she sucked in several deep ones until she felt less shaken.

Haley closed her eyes for a few seconds. She couldn't do any of this right now. There were too many unanswered questions and too much speculation. She'd talk to Tang in the morning and try to make sense of the whole mess. She logged back in under her own name and finished her own report.

As she got in her truck to leave, Haley tried like hell to clear her head. It didn't work. She needed a distraction, a tall, sexy one with curly hair. Nothing else existed when Tonya was around, and Haley needed that tonight more than ever.

Chapter 25

Haley couldn't sleep. She stared up at Tonya's ceiling and tried to quiet her mind to the point where she could doze. Tonya was draped over her and had her face pressed into Haley's neck. Her warm breath heated Haley's skin, reminding her that, in at least one thing, she was content.

Then, there was Tang. She'd hope to have everything cleared up by now, but he had taken the day off yesterday. His report still wasn't finished and submitted. That alone put him in deep shit, but that wasn't even the half of it. The fact that he was avoiding her screamed guilt. At first, she didn't want to believe it, but now it was hard to avoid. He still hadn't answered her calls or texts; hell, he wouldn't even answer his door.

Haley was way past angry. She was fucking livid.

The Tang she knew before would never have done something like this, but the desperate person he was now? Yes, goddammit, he would. Money would make his life a lot less complicated.

It made sense, but it also made him a thief.

And there was a little voice in her head, reminding her that Tang could throw all this shit squarely in her lap, playing it out as a nice little setup.

No, just no. But that voice wouldn't go away.

Tonya kissed Haley's shoulder. In return, she ran a hand down Tonya's back and pulled her closer.

"Are you ready to talk about it yet?" Tonya's voice was hoarse from sleep.

Haley didn't say anything at first. She couldn't talk about it, not right now. Things were way too sensitive, but she wasn't going to hold it all in for long. She couldn't. Not from Tonya. "No, it's—"

"Don't say things are fine when they're not."

Haley dipped her head to look at Tonya. "I wasn't gonna. It's just complicated as all hell."

"Work? Your friends?"

Didn't she just say she didn't want to talk about it? Haley didn't fight the irritation growing inside her. Lack of sleep and lack of answers were good fertilizers for it. She sighed. "Can you just drop it?" Her tone was a lot sharper than it should have been. She knew Tonya was just trying to help.

Tonya stiffened.

"I'm sorry. That wasn't called for."

"I shouldn't be prying. Obviously, there are places I'm not allowed."

Damn, Haley hadn't expected that response. It was kind of a low blow, but shit, tit for tat.

Tonya moved to the other side of the bed.

It got cold rather quickly. Haley needed to fix it.

"Maybe I should just go? I don't wanna keep you up."

That was so not what she'd meant to say. That was Aggravated Haley talking.

Tonya didn't respond. She turned on one of the lamps.

Haley glanced in her direction. She'd seen that look on Tonya's face before, hurt and confused. Mainly when she talked about her father. "Are you trying to pick a fight with me?"

"What? No." Was she? Shit, now she wasn't sure.

"If you are, it's ridiculous. If you're looking for an excuse to leave, leave. If you want to stay, stay. That needs to be your decision." Tonya crossed her arms over her chest, covering the logo on the T-shirt.

"Don't talk to me like I'm a kid." Haley's heart flipped over in her chest. Fuckity, fuck, fuck. What was she doing? She needed to just shut up.

Tonya's eyes widened. "I wasn't, but if this is going to turn into some kind of weird tantrum, I might have to."

Haley pressed her lips together to keep more crap from spewing out. She needed to get ahold of herself.

Tonya glared at her. This was not good, but it was nice to know that Tonya wasn't exactly in control of the situation either.

"Well?" Tonya asked.

Haley felt helpless, but she met Tonya's gaze. "I..." She paused and took a deep breath. "We need to stop. This is stupid."

"I already told you that," Tonya snapped.

Haley stared.

"Sorry," Tonya said.

"No, I'm sorry for bein' an asshat in the first place."

"God, I hope all the arguments we have end like this. That was almost easy."

"Wait. You expect there to be more?"

It was Tonya's turn to stare. "Some will even be as silly as this one."

Haley rolled her eyes. "Yeah, of course we're gonna argue."

"We are."

"I'm sure most of the time it will be my fault."

Tonya grinned. "Probably." Her smile slipped slightly. "And I don't need to know everything that goes on with you."

Haley nodded, but she felt guilty as hell. She had every intention of clearing the air after she confronted Tang. "I'll try to steer my irritation away from you."

There was a look in Tonya's eyes that Haley couldn't identify, but it was gone before she could get another crack at it. "Okay, you should try to get some rest. It's barely three."

Tonya turned over, away from her. Haley didn't like the distance. She scooted closer and pulled Tonya to her. She wasn't sure if she did it to give Tonya solace or herself.

She practically moaned when she took her first sip of coffee. Haley hoped it would banish any leftover cobwebs. She'd been able to sleep for a few hours, but the alarm and reality had interrupted far too soon. At least she'd brought her uniform, so she didn't have to leave early. Haley topped her mug off again before fixing Tonya's. She glanced over her shoulder when someone entered the kitchen.

Robert glared at her.

She hoped he was going to give her the silent treatment. Her emotions were way too close to the surface for anything else.

"Why are you here?"

Well.

Haley decided to ignore him. She put raisin bread in the toaster.

"I know you're not deaf."

She sighed. She could be cordial. She could, even in the face of his obvious dislike. "I thought it was rhetorical."

Okay, she needed to try harder. This was Tonya's father.

"Tonya wants me here."

"If she likes women who look like men, she might as well be with one." He spat the words out like they tasted nasty.

Haley bit the inside of her cheek, hard. Tonya did not need to walk in on this. She was so proud of the progress she'd made with him. Haley turned, leaned against the counter, and offered him a tight smile. "I don't think that's up for us to decide. She knows her own mind." She kept her tone light, conversational, which wasn't easy.

Robert shook his head. He crossed his arms over his chest, and Haley recognized the gesture for what it was: stubborn, willful blindness. "In most things. She was fine before you came along. Now she's throwing this mess in my face."

Haley focused on her breathing. Her heart was ramming against her chest. "Don't do this. All she talks about is how glad she is that you guys have made some progress. Don't ruin it. Let this go. You're gonna lose her."

His eyes widened, and he sneered. "She's not going nowhere. Yah heard me? She takes care of her family, and you don't tell me what to do. I live in a freak show. I tried, but I can't just let it happen."

"Try harder," Haley demanded.

"And what are you? Eighteen?"

"Daddy, that's enough!"

Haley closed her eyes. She hadn't heard Tonya come down the stairs. Her heart fell into her stomach, sending acid up her throat.

Tonya stood on the last step. Her eyes were wide and her face was red. She looked shocked and hurt. Haley couldn't blame her. "I'm sorry."

Tonya smiled softly at her, but she didn't look less tortured. "Don't, it's wasted on him. He meant what he said. Didn't you, Daddy?"

His jaw clenched. His expression was much like hers as he glanced at Haley and then back at his daughter. "How much did you—"

"Just about everything, and that's all you have to say? I thought we'd found some common ground."

"We did. I just can't—"

"All the pain I went through was a part of me, and so is this. It's who I am." Tonya was shaking.

Haley couldn't just stand there. She went to her. She didn't care that Robert was watching. Haley stopped in front of her, blocking Tonya's view. There were tears in her eyes. Tonya didn't wait for Haley to reach out for her. She grabbed hold, and Haley welcomed it.

Tonya's father left the kitchen.

A door slammed.

Haley sighed and pulled away slightly. So did Tonya. She wiped at her eyes. "Thank you for defending me, defending us."

"It was easy. You okay?"

"I'm going to have to be. I thought he'd get past this eventually, but I guess it was just wishful thinking. I can't believe I still wanted his approval after all this time."

"He's your father."

"And I have to love him regardless? He can't do the same for me."

"He's not you," Haley said softly. She brushed a thumb across Tonya's cheek.

Tonya slid her hand over Haley's and pressed it onto her cheek. "What do you see when you look at me?"

Haley tried to find the words. There were none. She just stared.

Tonya's breathing intensified, and she made this sound Haley couldn't describe.

"No one's ever looked at me like that before."

"But, I didn't say—"

"Yes, you did." Tonya kissed Haley's palm, then leaned in to do the same to her lips. "If my father could look at me a fraction of the way you do…" She paused. "Go to work. You have enough on your mind."

"Tonya—"

"No, there's nothing you can do right now. Just be there if—"

"You don't even have to ask." Haley hated this, and she'd already decided she was going to stay close to make sure Tonya got off to work okay.

"No, I don't, do I?"

Now that was rhetorical. Haley kissed her again, letting her lips linger.

"I'll be fine. He'll probably refuse to come out of his room."

He'd said some pretty shitty things. Hard to face up to that head-on, especially with a woman like Tonya staring at him. "I hope so."

Tang was at roll call, and Haley wasn't surprised that he wouldn't even look at her. She tried to burn a hole in the side of his head, and for the first time, she wished she had heat vision.

When it was over, they both sat there as everybody else started clearing out. Someone stepped in front of them. Haley glanced up. It was the lieutenant.

"You've been on the force what? Six years, Tim?"

Tang nodded, but he looked wary.

"So where's my report on Edisburgh? Your partner is shining. She got hers in on time." The lieutenant glanced at Haley, then back at Tang. "You know what? Let's save her virgin ears from this. Get in my office, now." He left and didn't bother turning around to see if Tang followed.

Tang stood. Haley grabbed his arm. "We need to talk."

He jerked away. "Take a fuckin' number."

Haley was waiting in the squad room when he came out of the lieutenant's office. His expression was virtually unreadable, but he nodded for her to follow. The questions burned her throat; she had to get them out.

He led them out back toward the dumpster, but she'd had enough. She was done following him. Haley grabbed his arm again.

Tang pulled away and turned. "Don't fuckin' touch me!" he whispered harshly.

Haley stepped forward. "I'll do what the fuck I want. You do. What the hell, Tang? You took the money, didn't you? You fuckin' ignored me. If I had any doubts, doin' that got rid of them really fast. I can practically smell the guilt all over you."

"Shhh!" His eyes widened and he looked around.

"Don't shush me. You're not even gonna deny it? The whole thing was sloppy and stupid."

He looked away. "There's no point in denyin' it. I knew when you started blowin' up my phone that you knew somethin' was up, and I didn't wanna lie to you. We can work this out. I'm the only person who could've done it. Unless you think me and Waller worked together."

"I don't know. Did you?"

"No. There was an opportunity and I took it."

"What did you do, stuff the money in your pants when my back was turned?"

"Around my waist."

She glared. "You know, when we first started workin' together, I was convinced you were dirty. Six years as a beat cop and no promotion? You're offensive. But you have a good heart, and you were a decent officer." Haley paused. She had to take a deep breath. She couldn't remember ever being this angry. "And a good friend. Now you got both of us lookin' like crooks. Either I was coverin' for you, we did it together, or you can pin it all on me!"

"I just needed time to think. I didn't know what to say to you." Tang wiped a hand over his face. "Look, it's really nothin' to worry about. Our reports match up to a point and Waller's will be the same as mine. You weren't there for the money count, and I read your report. You said yourself that it could have been between twenty and forty thousand bucks. We're in the clear. Nobody know—"

"I know! And we! What the actual fuck is this 'we'? I didn't do anythin'."

"Yeah, you did."

Haley tried to swallow past the sudden lump in her throat. She knew what he was going to say.

"You turned your back. We shoulda both had eyes on the evidence until Waller came in."

"It was you! I didn't think it was a big deal. I thought I could trust you, but as soon as I turned my back, you goddamn stabbed me in it."

"Rook, listen—"

"You're settin' me up to fall one way or another."

"It doesn't have to be like that!"

"You want me to lie. Keep all this shit to myself."

"Yes." Tang looked her right in the face.

"No, I can't—"

"Yeah, you're gonna have to."

"I'm not crooked, and I won't be for you!" Haley looked down at her feet. Her mind was in overdrive. "It'll look bad at first when I tell 'em my side of things," she muttered, "but they won't find anythin'. I'm not the one with the money."

Tang laughed. "You think they'll care? Damage will be done by then."

Who the hell was this person standing in front of her? Her mouth fell open, and she couldn't stop staring. How could she have been so wrong about him?

"Listen to me. It's drug money! And they're all dead, so what the fuck does it matter? I can't take this anymore. My house smells like a sewer! I'm tired of bein' thrown up on, scratched, and bitten! Do you know how many times I came close to just smotherin' him? He's not the man I knew. I wanna give him some dignity, but I don't even have any for myself. I can't take care of him, and I can't get him what he needs. Not like this. You said you wanted somethin' good to come outta that call. Let it. With what I took, I can get him into someplace nice for at least six months, maybe more. I don't think he's even gonna last that long. Please, Haley." Tang put his hands on her shoulders, and despite being furious and scared, the look on his face nearly tore out her heart. He was desperate, broken.

Still, Haley stepped away. She shook her head. "I get it. I do, but—"

"No, you fuckin' don't. When have you ever struggled? You don't know the first thing, so don't stand there and judge me. I'm tryin' to do right by him." His face was contorted, and he was actually snarling at her. "Let me break it down to you like this. You keep my secret, and I'll make sure the secret I know doesn't get back to your girlfriend. I did some diggin' on you, your friends, and Tonya, just in case you decided to go all goody goody no matter how much shit I could do to your reputation and career."

"What the fuck are you even talkin' about?"

Tang glanced away. His jaw clenched like the words he was about to say needed to be ground down. "Tonya's old man owned a neighborhood store, and back in 2007 he was questioned on suspicion of drug trafficking. The detectives were hot for some local up-and-comin' dealer. They intercepted a truck and found drugs hidden inside some merchandise, and traced everythin' back to her old man's store. The dealer even paid Preston to rent space in his store. He told the detectives some bullshit story about tryin' to help out the son of an old friend start up his own business. Claimed he didn't know about the drugs or anythin' else. Maybe they believed him 'cause he's old and didn't have a record, or they let it slide because they brought that dealer down when the truck driver sang his ass off."

He might as well have been speaking Latin.

"Bullshit. You're makin' this up."

"Yeah, you wish, but I came in early to make sure I didn't miss nothin'. The whole story is in black and white." Tang looked smug.

Haley went very still. "What's your fuckin' point? The case is closed, and he was probably innocent anyway."

"Yeah, maybe, but we don't really know what he does when Tonya's not there. It wouldn't take much to reopen the case, or get him wrapped up with some other dealer, maybe a whisper or two, 'specially since it could make those detectives look lazy. Even if he is innocent, investigations are nasty. They fuck up people's lives all the way to hell and back. It would be a damn shame for them to go through that."

Haley had never wanted to hurt anyone before in her life, but right now, she wanted to hit Tang hard enough to make his teeth cave in. "You fuckin' dick." He was a stranger to her. She took a step toward him. This would kill Tonya.

Tang's smug expression disappeared. He looked almost sad, regretful. "I didn't wanna do this, but I needed extra leverage."

"You fuckin' sick, backwoods, selfish son of a bitch!" Her hands clenched into fists and rage sloshed through her into every crack and crevice. She shook with it.

"So, you see, things aren't so black and white for either one of us right now," Tang said softly. "We'll all be better off if you just let this go."

"I could beat the shit outta you right now." Haley wasn't kidding. One punch and there was no coming back until she saw him bleeding and unconscious.

"I know." He cleared his throat and dropped his gaze. "Just take a few days and think about it. There's only two choices here. You can let it go, or we're both gonna burn for this one way or the other. I'm sorry I had to bring you in on this. I really am." Tang stared at her for a couple seconds before backing away. "I have to go finish my report. He wrote me up. I can't afford to get another one."

Then, just like that, he was gone.

Haley was drowning in a sea of shit and the person she wanted to reach out to the most would end up neck-deep in it too. That left her stuck between a rock and a dark, dank place.

Maybe it was a positive that her father had barricaded himself in his room. At this point, Tonya was sure that a confrontation with him would have completely obliterated her mood, such as it was. She was short on patience. Right now, she was short on a lot of things, and it had been reflecting poorly in her work. Her latest patient glared at her. Tonya waved at the tech outside the door, signaling him to come in. She didn't want the situation to get any more awkward than it already was. Tonya couldn't look at her patient. For the past twenty minutes, she had barely heard a word the woman said, and the patient knew it.

"Greg?"

The tech stopped at the door. He had one hand on the woman and one hand on the knob. "Yes, Dr. Preston?"

"No more…at least for a couple hours."

"You want me to divert to the social worker if need be?"

"That's fine."

Alone, Tonya leaned back in her chair and took a deep, cleansing breath, which didn't help all that much. The anger was still there, along with a sense of betrayal. But Tonya had to find a way to shut the door on all that until she could actively deal with it. She used to be good at that. Now it took a lot more effort. Opening herself up to the good things meant that she experienced the bad more acutely.

To top it all off, there was something going on with Haley. Tonya tried her best to beat back a growing frisson of insecurity. Was Haley getting tired of her, of them already? If her father could do this to her just when things were progressing, what was Haley capable of?

"No. No, don't even go there."

Haley would talk to her when she was ready, or she wouldn't. She had to be prepared for either eventuality. Maybe getting some of the crushing weight off her chest would help. She called Tracy.

"Hey, walking out of the classroom. Hold on."

Tonya waited.

"Okay, what's wrong?"

She closed her eyes and again tried to rein in some of her emotions. "It's Daddy."

"Oh God. What did he do?"

"I wanted to be a real family so much that I just kept throwing myself at him, hoping he'd see me and get it. I think he does in some respects, but while one door opened, the other, I think, is locked completely. I deserve everything, a family and a life."

"Yes, you do. What's going on?"

"Haley stayed with me last night, and when he saw her in the kitchen this morning, he practically jumped down her throat. I've never seen him be so nasty to anybody else." Tonya chuckled, but it was a dark, humorless sound. "Someone who wasn't me."

"Oh shit. What did he say?"

Tonya told her.

"Jesus, I'm so sorry."

"I am too. He can't talk to her like that. She doesn't deserve it. Being with her has…" Tonya searched for the right words but couldn't find them. "How can he not get that?"

"The other night when I called...the way you were laughing. You sounded so happy. I know we're working on it now, but we've never been close. Tonya, I've never seen you happy. You've always been damn good at being fake. I don't even know what happiness looks like on you. I get the feeling when I see you this weekend, I'll know then. Daddy can't see that, but I'm so glad I can."

Tonya let her sister's words sink in. "He'll never be able to accept me."

"I don't know."

"I can't live like this, Tracy."

"I don't blame you."

"I want to keep at least some part of us intact, but it can't happen with the way things are right now."

"What are you thinking?"

"Since I'm not paying for your school anymore, I can pay rent." Tonya paused as her idea took shape. "For Daddy." It made perfect sense, and some of that weight on her chest lifted.

"He's not going to take it well."

Tonya swallowed, but she had to ask. "Are you?"

"What do I...ohhh. Why would I be upset about that? He's been a dick to you. I can actually say that out loud now. He's still my father and you're still my sister. Nothing changes that."

"But he's getting older."

"That he is, and no matter what, we're going to take care of him in one way or another, right? Besides, when I'm done with school, it will be my turn. You've done enough."

No, it didn't feel like she had. It never did. "But—"

"Haley must really mean a lot to you for you to do this for her," Tracy said softly.

"It's not just for her. This is for me too."

"I hear you, but you want to know what I think? Don't freak out or anything, okay?"

"Why would I?"

"Because I think you're probably falling in love with her. I know you were going through some changes anyway, but I think this thing with Haley was the icing on the cake for you."

Tonya stared through the pane of glass on her office door. People shuffled back and forth as if life was moving at a slower pace out there. She'd always felt like she was on the outside looking in. Not anymore. Tonya had stopped being a spectator the first time she went to GrrlSpot; the second time she'd seen Haley.

Yes, she was falling in love.

The path in front of her was clear.

In her mind, Haley had proven herself a million times over with her touch, her words, her actions. Tonya's heart rammed against her chest. She tried to take a deep breath but realized that she couldn't. She tried again, and something tore open inside her, leaking warmth everywhere.

"You're speechless."

"I'm…something."

Tracy chuckled. "Do what you need to do to be happy. Now I need to get off here. I have a test in my next class and I want to look over my notes one last time."

"Please, you'll do fine. A 3.7 GPA in grad school is nothing to sneeze at."

"Regardless, I have to work to keep it."

"Okay. Hey, Tracy?"

"Yeah?"

"I love you." Tonya was feeling so much that she had to let it out, even though she couldn't remember that last time she'd said those words to her sister.

There was silence on the other end.

"Are you still there?"

Tracy exhaled shakily. "Wow." Her voice was thick. "I…" She laughed, and even that was filled with emotion. "I love you too."

Haley refused to release Tonya. She kept Tonya's legs splayed wide as she kissed the inside of her trembling thigh. Tonya's entire body quivered as if a high-energy current had passed through her. Haley's ears were still ringing from the way Tonya had cried out, uninhibited and desperate, a few minutes earlier. It was the best music Haley'd ever heard. She nipped at the soft skin under her lips. Tonya moaned and mumbled something Haley couldn't understand.

Being inside Tonya was one of the best things ever, but tonight Haley wanted to give, take, and have in a different, more intimate way. She could still taste Tonya on the back of her tongue; she coated Haley's lips, chin, and fingertips.

She closed her eyes and savored it all like it was the first time and not the hundredth.

This was her good place, her happy place, and she'd revel in it all night long and beyond if she could. Haley forced her own legs together and groaned. The sudden wave of pleasure was a reminder that she wasn't done.

She'd given, and now it was time to take, time to have.

Haley pulled herself up Tonya's body, leading with her lips and tongue, the rest of her trailing behind to make sure she touched every inch of Tonya's sweat-soaked skin that she could reach.

"Oh, God." Tonya's breathing had just returned to normal, but now, she was gasping again. She clutched at Haley's back and shoulders.

Haley dragged her sex over Tonya's thigh.

Tonya's answering moan was thick, breathless.

Haley pressed their foreheads together. "You...do this to me." She undulated her hips and groaned. The friction was incredible, and tonight, it was all Haley needed. With each surge of her hips, Haley flexed and pressed her upper thigh against Tonya's sex. She was still slick, swollen, and sensitive.

Tonya whimpered. With one hand, she pulled at Haley's hair. With the other, she dug her nails into the flesh of Haley's ass, urging her on.

"Harder." Tonya whispered the words into Haley's open mouth.

Sweat stung Haley's eyes, but she gave Tonya what she asked for.

"Yes!"

Haley's bed shook and slammed against the wall.

She felt her orgasm, hovering just out of reach, and Haley wanted so badly to touch it. Haley redoubled her efforts. With every thrust of her hips, she purged herself of all the anger, the fear, and the sense of betrayal. Even if it was only for a little while.

"God…I need—"

With no pretense and no warning, Haley slid three fingers deep inside her. Tonya cried out.

Haley drove into her relentlessly. She knew Tonya could take it.

"Fuck yes!"

Her orgasm was sudden and blinding. It ripped her open and left her feeling empty and full at the same time. Somewhere in between her hoarse, breathy moans, she called out Tonya's name. Tonya stiffened and fell apart in her arms. Tonya sobbed and bit into Haley's shoulder.

Haley was clear, weightless, and all she could feel was Tonya underneath her, inside her, around her. She was barely aware of where she was. It took her a few minutes to come back to the world. When she did, her head was pillowed against Tonya's chest. Her hand sifted through Haley's damp hair. Haley lifted her head and looked up at Tonya. Her gaze was so warm that it was hard not to leave it, but slowly, reality set in.

With a huge part of her world unraveling, it was a strange time to realize she was probably in love, but Haley was learning the hard way that life sometimes had no rhyme or reason. Tonya brushed her fingertips against Haley's forehead and cheek.

"What is it?" Tonya asked.

Instead of answering, Haley turned slightly and kissed Tonya's palm. Then she smiled and hoped it wasn't too sad or too confused, that it didn't give too much away.

Tonya's forehead wrinkled. She looked worried, but she didn't say anything.

Neither did Haley. She kissed Tonya again. Maybe it was best to enjoy the simplicity between them right now.

CHAPTER 26

Something was very wrong. Tonya could feel it. Not only that, she had evidence to back it up. She'd chosen to spend the weekend at Haley's, not ready to fight with her father, but Haley was barely talking to her. When she did, it was in a listless monotone. Although she was distant mentally, there had been plenty of angry, desperate sex. Haley had some demon she was trying to exorcize, and she was using Tonya to do it.

Tonya wasn't sure how she felt about that yet.

She should be offended and disturbed, but she wasn't. Haley was with her. *Her*. Not one of those nameless young girls from the bars she used to go to. That meant something. That meant everything. Tonya sat on the couch and watched as Haley aimed the remote at the TV and flipped through the channels.

Parts of Tonya screamed at her not to pry, but she couldn't help herself. She'd given Haley plenty of time, and her mood was only getting worse. Forcing the issue could help Haley feel better, less burdened. The problem may not be solved, but at least it would be loose and floating in the universe so they could look at it properly.

"You want to play zombies?"

Haley stopped and looked at Tonya like she was speaking in tongues. Her face scrunched. "No."

"Do you want to fuck me some more?" Tonya asked breathlessly. It did something to Haley to hear her talk that way. Aware that Haley's gaze was still riveted on her, Tonya licked her lips. "Or do you want me to do that thing with my tongue?" Haley *really* liked that too.

Haley's eyes darkened as she stared. "Always, but it—"

"Won't make it go away?"

"Yeah, that."

"This is me trying to be here for you."

"I know."

"Just talk to me. I know how hard it can be to do that sometimes."

Haley shook her head. "I'm sorry. I can't. Not until I get a handle on all my crap and everythin' else that's comin' at me."

Tonya held her gaze. "Your crap? You've been knee-deep in all my family drama. You made it your crap too. I don't deserve the same?" She wasn't sure if she was making sense. She stood.

"You do, but—"

"I've decided that my father needs his own place to live. I haven't told him yet, but I think it'll be best for everyone involved."

Haley got up as well and moved in closer. "You're not doing that for me, are you?"

"Yes and no. The responsibility is mine, but our relationship factored in. This is more about me and what I need right now."

Haley took Tonya's hands in hers and entwined their fingers. "You've already settled into the decision, haven't you? You feel good about it?"

"I have, and I feel as good as I can about the whole thing."

Haley sighed and stared. "Maybe it is for the best."

"I'll have to take a hard look at my finances. He has his social security, but I want him someplace nice." Tonya studied Haley as she let their conversation sink in. She pulled on Haley's hands until the final distance between them disappeared. Haley wrapped her arms around her.

"Is this what you wanted?"

"Yes." Tonya slid her arms around Haley's neck. "Do you even realize what you just did for me? Let me—"

Haley's nostrils flared. She took a step back. Her forehead wrinkled and her face flushed. "It's not the same. Trust me. I'm not tryin' to freeze you out. At least, not on purpose. It's Tang's crap too."

Tonya didn't like the sound of that. "But you're involved?"

"Yeah, unfortunately, way more than I'd like to be."

Tonya's anger flashed. "Did you know about all this the other night when we argued?" She had to ask.

"No, I just had a bunch of unanswered questions then."

"I don't like this."

"Neither do I."

"But I guess me hovering and trying to get in your head isn't helping much."

Haley didn't say anything, and her expression didn't give much away.

"Maybe I should go and give you some space."

"No, you don't have to. I'll pull myself together. I know I haven't been the best company. Give me a couple days to get things straight with Tang." Haley made a face. She looked disgusted.

"Are you guys fighting?"

"I'm not sure what to call it." Her expression didn't change.

Even with Haley's promises and reassurances, Tonya was worried and disappointed. She took in everything she'd been told, and for her, there was only one translation. "So you guys are in some kind of trouble, and you're trying to protect me from it." She didn't even try to hide the aggravation in her voice.

Haley closed her eyes, and her shoulders slumped. "Tonya."

Tonya wanted to scream; instead she reached out. She cupped Haley's face in her hands. "The more you talk, the scarier this sounds. I told you once before I don't need you to play the hero with me."

Haley gripped Tonya wrists and gazed at her. Haley's blue eyes were stormy.

"That's still true," Tonya whispered.

"I don't wanna be a hero. I just wanna be with you." Haley brought one of Tonya's hands to her lips and kissed it.

Tonya stared at her. Haley was pleading for understanding, and she wanted to give it. "You wouldn't take no for an answer. You called *me*, made me laugh, made me care, made me want you. I opened up to you…for you, and it was so easy, so simple. You can't unlock all those doors and then slam them in my face. I'll give you your space with this, but I've been pushed away most of my life. I'm not going to let you do it to me too. This involves Tim, but you're in the thick of it. That's what matters to me the most." Was her reaction a little over-the-top? Was she being selfish? Probably, but that didn't mean she was any less concerned.

"I hear you, and pushin' you away isn't even an option for me. At least, not on purpose."

"I believe you, but I'm still going home. You can come over later tonight. That'll give you a few hours to yourself unless you need—"

"I'll be there by nine o'clock. I probably wouldn't be able to sleep without you anyway."

"Me either." Tonya brushed her fingers over Haley's arm as she went to gather her things from the bedroom.

Before going to the Northshore, Tonya stopped at the store for creamer. She was almost out at home. There was going to be a lot of coffee drinking this week. She could feel it. The checkout line was long for midday, but there was only one lane open. Tonya listened mindlessly to the chatter around her until a child's voice coming from right in front of her caught her attention.

"I felt myself tippin' over, Momma. So I flapped my arms like a bird. My life depended on it."

"Did your life flash before your eyes?"

"Nooo." The girl laughed. "I'm only six." She was dressed in pink and blue, and thick locs fell past her shoulders.

The girl's mother laughed, and Tonya chuckled too.

"Well, I don't think you were in much danger skating on the sidewalk, but I'm glad you survived to tell that story."

"I'm glad she did too," Tonya said. She couldn't help herself. The whole thing was adorable.

The woman turned to Tonya and smiled. "I think I have a little writer on my hands. She has a way of tellin' a story."

"I agree."

"Momma! I'm standin' right here."

"I know, baby, but I was sayin' good things."

The girl rolled her eyes.

Tonya laughed some more.

The woman turned to empty her basket on the conveyer belt. She only had a few items. When the cashier was done, the woman took out her card to swipe it. The reader beeped in protest.

"It didn't read it. Try again." The cashier sighed and waited.

She swiped it once more, but it didn't work that time either. "Can you just punch the numbers in?"

The cashier stared and snatched the card out of the woman's hand when it was offered.

The woman didn't say anything, which was surprising because this was New Orleans. The people here weren't known for taking things lying down, but all she did was pull her daughter close.

Tonya was getting annoyed, but it wasn't at her new friends.

"You don't have enough to cover this," the cashier spat the words.

"Oh, I know. I'll pay the rest in cash."

"Fine." The cashier glanced at Tonya and rolled her eyes. Then, she mouthed, "Sorry, food stamps."

That was just enough to make Tonya's aggravation boil over. "I'm sorry. Did you just roll your eyes at me because she's using food stamps?" Would she have said something during this kind of situation months ago? Maybe, but not to this degree. These days she was way past hiding her feelings and walking away from a number of things.

"Uh, no. I was apologizing 'cause it was taking so long. People like her always have 'em."

"People like her...thanks for enlightening me, but I wasn't the one complaining." Tonya glanced at the woman and her child, then back at the cashier. "Marie." She read her name tag. "Did you think we were kindred spirits or something? Just because I *look* white like you and not black like them?"

The cashier sputtered.

"I'll take that as a yes."

Marie looked from the woman to Tonya and back again.

The woman handed her a ten-dollar bill. Marie kept her head down as she counted out change. "Sorry," she mumbled.

Tonya continued to glare. Someone touched her arm and she glanced to the side. The woman was smiling. "Thanks, friend. I didn't want to make a scene in front of my little girl. She didn't need to see me go off like that. If I'd been by myself..."

Tonya nodded in understanding.

The little girl was practically wrapped around her mother's leg. She knew something was wrong. It took the woman a minute to separate herself. She grabbed her grocery bags with one hand and guided her daughter out of the store.

By the time she got home, Tonya's nerves hadn't settled at all. In the kitchen, her father was in the process of making a sandwich on French bread. He stiffened and glanced up at her.

"Hello, Daddy." There was no need to be rude.

Robert's eyes widened, and he cleared his throat. "I'm surprised you even speaking."

"I'm not like you. Not anymore," Tonya said.

"I don't know what that means."

"I'm not hiding, and I won't be petty and pretend you're not here."

He pressed his lips together and stared. "I was starting to think you forgot where you lived. You gone more than you here."

She wasn't surprised that he sidestepped the issue. "That's going to change. Haley will be here more. As a matter of fact, she's coming over tonight."

He went back to fixing his sandwich.

Tonya headed upstairs. She'd made the right decision. She didn't have any residual guilt. They needed to be apart to have any chance at repairing what was broken between them.

Haley sat on the couch. Images flew across the TV screen as she whizzed through them once more. She'd spent the last couple hours on some mindless action movie, but it had ended a few minutes earlier. How the hell had things unraveled so fast? She had to be honest with herself. She should have seen the Tang thing coming, but it had smacked her in the face like a foul ball. That shit hurt. Was this some bullshit test the universe was shoving in her face just to see how she'd handle it?

Well, she wasn't going to let the universe win. Fuck it ten ways till Friday.

She hated the monkey riding her back. Damn thing had its claws in her, but she was sure that she'd figured out a way to loosen them a little bit. First things first, Haley needed to get away from Tang. With everything he was doing, she shouldn't have had the capacity to still care about him, but she did. Feelings didn't just disappear just like that. Haley had no doubt that he cared as well. That's why the whole thing cut so deep; they were partners, and he'd been fast on his way to becoming a part of her family.

And Haley wasn't going to be able to just get a new partner. Things didn't work that way. The lieutenant wasn't going to let her play musical chairs because of a disagreement; there had to be a pattern of behavior. But a transfer to another precinct was exactly what she needed. Hell, she'd bike-cop it in City Park if she had to. She had no seniority, and if another officer who'd been there longer wanted a transfer, he or she would get it long before Haley would. It was a chance she was willing to take, and Tang wouldn't know about it until she had one foot out the door.

Haley reached for her phone. She opened her email and typed a message. She had to make it good. She wrote that she needed new scenery, and a precinct with more diversity to increase her comfort as a woman. She even added a bit about being a lesbian and hinted that her current workplace was hostile. It was just enough to paint her as a potential problem but kept her off of any real shit list that would more than likely stagnate her career.

She absolutely hated keeping all this from Tonya, but once her plan was in the works, she'd tell her a majority of what was going on. The rest, no. There was no need to crush her. Haley was willing to sacrifice so that wouldn't happen. Tonya wouldn't approve, but the relationship with her father would still be intact, such as it was.

She'd *just* be a liar and an accessory after the fact. No big.

Haley wondered if this was what being stupid in love meant, because she'd do anything, *anything*. As far as she was concerned, there was nothing stupid about it. Tonya was such a part of her now, there was no looking back. Haley didn't want to. With Tonya was where she belonged. That was the one thing Haley was sure of right now.

The second thing Haley needed to do was check on Tang's story. What reason did she have to believe him? With all the shit he was pulling, Haley wasn't going to just take him at his word. She had to find out about Robert

Preston for herself. It was a big no-no to use the database for personal reasons, but there was no other way other than going to the source. If she got caught, Haley could get anything from a write-up to dismissal. It was a chance she was going to have to take. When it came down to it, she was doing the wrong thing for the right reasons. Haley almost snorted out loud at the irony. Tang was doing the same thing, but that didn't make any of it okay.

Her cell phone rang, and when she picked it up, Nate's goofy face flashed on the screen.

"Hey."

"Hey yourself. Sorry again we had to bail on you this weekend, but if we do this right, the restaurant could be in *Gambit Weekly* as part of their 'best of' series. It's just—"

"Nate, it's fine. Don't worry about it."

"Okay, but now I'm kinda worried about you."

Haley leaned back on the couch and tipped her head toward the ceiling. "What? Why?"

"Tim stopped by. He said you'd been actin' weird and wanted to know if we'd seen it too."

Haley's heart dropped to her stomach, and a combination of fear and rage rolled through her entire body. She was numb and on fire simultaneously. "What'd you tell 'im?" She wasn't sure how she kept her voice even, but she did.

"There was nothin' to tell. You're all wrapped up in Tonya, and that's a good thing. That's pretty much what I said. Did y'all fight or somethin'?"

"Yeah, it's hard to explain though. I'll tell you about it soon as I can."

"Okay, I'm gonna hold you to that. How's Tonya?"

"You just asked me that on Friday."

"Well, yeah, but so what? I like doin' it."

"Knock yourself out then."

"Uh-huh. How is she?"

"We're good."

"Not that I think you will, but I keep havin' nightmares that you fuck things up with her."

Haley could totally understand that, especially right now. "That's kinda disturbin' that you think about me that much."

"I'm bein' serious."

"I'm tryin' like hell not to screw things up."

"It shouldn't be that hard."

"Yeah, well—"

"Haley." Nate sighed.

"I'm doin' right by her."

"Glad to hear it. Ugh, okay I gotta go. One of the cooks just came outta the kitchen. He looks like he's about to cry."

"Okay, later."

Haley stared at the phone in her hands. She never thought she'd understand crimes of passion firsthand, but right now, she got it totally. She wanted to strangle Tang and inflict physical pain that was damn near equal to the mental distress he was dolling out to her.

Her hands shook as she called him. He answered almost immediately.

"You were able to get off diaper duty to go threaten my friends? Her voice was low, growly.

"I didn't threaten anybody."

"You might as well have. I know what you're doin'. Layin' down little trails of shit to lead to me."

"Why do you have to be so dramatic? I'm just tryin' to make sure we both come outta this okay and remind you that you have till Monday."

"No, fucknut. You're tryin' to set me up. Who are you? I trusted you."

"I'm me. We took a hit, but we can get back to where we were. I fuckin' hated you at first. Now, you're my best friend. Deep down, I know you understand why I'm doin' this. The only guilt I'm feelin' is all about you. I tried like hell to think of a way to leave you out of it, but this whole thing works better with you right in the middle."

Tang actually believed what he was saying. Haley could see that now.

"It's drug money. I'm not usin' it to buy a car. I'm gonna use it to take care of my family, and you're a part of that. There's no better cause than that."

When the holy hell did he get so articulate?

"I don't wanna fuck you over, but I will. Milt has to come first right now."

"You already have, and there's no fixin' this. You're delusional. I'll never fuckin' trust you again. I'm not stupid. It took a minute for my head to clear after all this shit went down. Settin' me up won't work. I don't have motive. You do. Internal Affairs might look at me first, but it won't stick. I'm squeaky-clean. You, on the other hand, barely have any friends, no promotion, every partner you've had left you, and you're livin' in a shitty situation. So your threat against me doesn't hold water."

"Yeah, well, fuck you. I'm still in control here. How about I put a bug in Tonya's ear? Give her just enough to look deeper, or would you rather I put that bug up a cop's ass?"

"Fuck you too. I'm not doin' this for you. You're not worth it. I'm doin' it for Tonya. But here's how this is gonna go down. I'm not a liar. I'm not the person you're tryin' to make me into. You're gonna give me some time to settle into this."

"Time for what? I heard all I needed to hear. You're keepin' your mouth shut."

"I can't be held responsible for what I do when I see you again. I'm just givin' you a heads-up. I'm gonna need time to get back to normal. If I say or do somethin' to piss you off, you're not gonna go back on our deal?"

"So you're askin' for a free pass to treat me like shit until you get over this?"

"Yeah, pretty much."

"I can do that. I know you don't trust me right now. You can consider this my way of tryin' to reestablish that."

Never. There was no way in hell, but it bought her time. It was a good distraction too. He would be too busy trying to make amends or some shit while she'd be trying to get the fuck away from him.

"Thank you for all this, by the way, and I mean that. Uncle Milt is gonna get what he needs. I already have the place picked out. They're gonna come get him on Saturday. The place has its own ambulance service. I paid for the first couple months already, and I gave them extra since they're doin' this on the weekend. I'm off on Saturday, so I can supervise the whole thing. And even though the time is gonna be shitty, I wanna spend it with Milt."

"Jesus Christ! You probably shoulda waited just in case."

"I can't take it anymore; a few days is all I have left in me. I'm gonna lose it if it's any longer."

He already had. Haley didn't want to hear anything else about it. His voice grated on her nerves. "Yeah, well, whatever. I'm hangin' up now." She didn't wait for more. There was no point.

She looked down at her phone. She couldn't believe a thing he'd said. He tipped his hand by going to Nate. What if he had plans to do the same with Tonya, or to go further just to stir the pot? Even if it was just part of this insane setup scheme? It would be a mistake for him to do anything else. He'd have no leverage at all.

She had to tell Tonya, at least most of it. She deserved to hear it from Haley, not Tang's fucked-up version. Without another thought, Haley called Tonya. She picked up after three rings, but Haley didn't give her time to say hello.

"We need to talk. I didn't have any control over the Tang situation before, but I've got a better hold of it now."

"Just like that in the past couple hours?"

"Yeah, but he helped in his own screwed-up way, and I don't wanna do this over the phone. Can I come over?"

Tonya released a long, shaky breath. "I'll see you in an hour."

That was all Haley needed to hear.

Just over an hour later, Haley was sitting in Tonya's living room. *Family Guy* was on TV, but it was just flashes and murmurs. While Haley talked, Tonya's expression went from shock to anger and back again.

When Haley was done, Tonya stared at her for several seconds. "The unintentional abuse from his uncle broke him."

"Yeah, I figured that. I feel like I should've seen it comin'."

"No, not really. Situations like this make people unpredictable." Tonya shook her head. "But that's not important right now. I'm sorry this happened to you. I know you guys struggled to get along at first and ended up pretty close. This must be killing you."

"He said I was his best friend." Haley paused and sat down beside Tonya. "He must've had some pretty messed-up relationships to think it's okay to treat people this way. He thinks we're gonna recover from this."

"Are *you* going to recover from this?" Tonya asked softly.

Haley reached for her hand. It felt good to be able to breathe a little easier. "Yeah, I think I'll be okay, but it's gonna take me a while. It's gonna be a long time before I stop lookin' over my shoulder."

"What he did is so muddled and gray. I mean, I know he broke the law, but are his reasons for doing it the biggest part of why you're going along with it?"

"It was a combination of that and his threats to frame me." Sitting here telling Tonya this made Haley want to be free from it all. She had to remind herself that she was doing the right thing, the best thing.

"You're right. It is going to take you a while to get through this. It's hard to carry a lie around, whether it's purposeful or inadvertent. I would know."

"I know it is, but it's a struggle I'm prepared to deal with. I'm doin' what I have to do." Haley held Tonya's gaze. Her eyes held caution.

"I don't necessarily agree with all this, because it's going to hurt you, but it's a catch-22 since the alternative will too. I'm with you no matter what. I do think it's best you transfer out of that precinct. You can have a new start, and I hope it goes through soon."

"Me too."

"I have to say, though, if he does come to me, it's going to feel good to beat him at his own game, especially after what he tried to do to you."

"I don't think he will. He's got what he wants now, but he's obviously unpredictable."

Tonya squeezed her hand and leaned forward, brushing her lips against Haley's. "Thank you for telling me. I hate that you have to go through this."

Haley swallowed down a surge of guilt. "I don't like it much either."

"I'm sorry for trying to push you to talk. I know it was a little selfish of me, but with everything that's happened with my father, I was expecting other parts of my life to implode too."

"There's no reason to apologize. I'm not goin' anywhere."

"I know."

Haley pulled Tonya close and sighed. She leaned back on the couch, and for the first time in the past few days, she actually felt that things were going to work out. That didn't make the whole thing any less fucked-up.

Tonya wrapped herself around Haley, and they stayed like that for several minutes. Despite the heaviness of the situation, Haley's eyes strayed toward the TV. Another episode of *Family Guy* was on. It was the one where Peter, Chris, and Brian drink ipecac syrup and end up throwing up all over the place. She snorted.

"What?" Tonya asked.

"Favorite episode."

Tonya glanced at the TV. "Jesus that's disgusting."

"I knooooow." Haley chuckled.

"Is this some kind of geek thing?"

"Probably."

Tonya pressed a kiss to her chin. Haley looked down at her. Recently, there'd been times when Haley was sure she'd been swallowed up by her feelings for Tonya. It was warm there. It was safe there, and she felt like she could do anything. Everything slowed down and sped up at the same time. This was one of those times. Haley was wide open. Tonya walked right in and made herself comfortable, and Haley wouldn't have it any other way.

"What? Why are you looking at me like that?" Tonya asked.

"Like what?"

"Some moony-eyed cartoon."

Haley smiled. "Is that right?"

Tonya traced Haley's lips with her thumb. "Mmm, how can you laugh and smile through all this?"

Haley was pretty sure that there were stars in her eyes now too. "You."

Tonya made a sound so soft that Haley could barely hear it. Her eyes darkened, and her expression was so unguarded that it made Haley ache. Tonya didn't say a word, but when she brought their lips together, she whimpered.

In the scheme of things, the moment was damn near perfect.

CHAPTER 27

"What are you?" Mr. Templeton sneered.

"Can you elaborate, please? Then, maybe I can answer your question." Tonya was crisp and professional. She schooled her expression to show nothing, despite the way her nerves suddenly jangled.

"I know you a woman, before you say something smart-ass."

"Yes, I am, Mr. Templeton." Tonya waited for clarification.

"Are you a nigger? Are you white or one of those muddied-up mixed people?"

"I'm just here to help."

"Ah, so a nigger, then. I decided to just pick one."

Already he'd reduced her to nothing but the perceived color of her skin. Tonya often wished work was the only place she had to deal with these types of situations. As Dr. Preston, her feelings were a little easier to brush aside. The anger, resentment, and disgust were still there, behind a wall for the time being, and Tonya wasn't going to give him the satisfaction of displaying any of it. "I have plans to treat you with respect, Mr. Templeton, and I expect you to do the same."

"A snooty nigger at that." He leaned forward in the chair and smiled while he stared.

More than likely, he was waiting for a reaction.

Tonya wasn't going to give him one. It was her job to be good at that, and she was an expert. Being in this position was commonplace; it wasn't even the first time this week. "I'm sorry about your wife. I know how difficult it is to lose someone you love. My mother died from cancer almost a year ago."

His smile dipped a bit. Mr. Templeton narrowed his eyes at her. "You don't know nothing about me."

"That's true. All I have are the reports from the emergency room that say you are violent, belligerent, and defiant."

He snorted. "You ain't gone add that I don't like niggers? Damn city is full of 'em, 'specially after Katrina."

"I can add that as well if you want me to, but is that all you are, Mr. Templeton?"

"What you mean?" He sat back in the chair and looked at her, his nose and forehead crinkled in confusion.

"You're a husband, a father, and a working man too." She kept her voice inquisitive and soft.

"Yeah, so?"

Tonya met his gaze. "Which roles are most important to you? Which ones are you anxious to get back to?"

Mr. Templeton looked away. His jaw clenched. "I ain't no goddamned husband no more."

"I disagree. I didn't stop being a daughter when my mother died, and you will remain Margaret's husband no matter where you go from here."

He turned back to her, but he was quiet. He didn't look away this time, and Tonya watched as a number of emotions chased themselves across his face: anger, loss, and sadness. His chin trembled.

His worldview was an important part of who he was. As a psychiatrist, she was taught not to disregard it, no matter how skewed it was from the norm or from her own. Was it difficult? Yes, and unfortunately, in her line of work, instances like these had to be endured. But she would never get used to them.

Right now, this man needed help. Tonya wondered if he was going to accept it from her. The last person hadn't, but threatening to commit suicide had to be taken seriously—especially since he had a plan, and a shotgun to bring that plan to fruition.

"Yeah, suppose you right." He cleared his throat. "I still don't like niggers."

Tonya nodded. "Okay, Mr. Templeton. I will still need to oversee your care, but the social worker was out sick today. I'm sure she'll be back tomorrow. You should be more comfortable with her for daily—"

"I ain't say I wanted that. You might be one of the good ones." He glared at her.

Tonya released a discreet breath of relief. "Okay, Mr. Templeton."

Hours later, Tonya was happy that the day was ending. Work wasn't particularly difficult, even though there were trying moments, but her mind continuously strayed to Haley during every free minute. Even when her time was occupied, those thoughts sat at the back of her mind. She was worried. How could she not be?

In an effort to help over the past few days, Tonya had been sending errant texts that were at times pithy, funny, and a little naughty. When she could, Tonya called just to hear the relief and contentment in her voice when Haley said her name. She was happy to provide those bright spots, but things were always better when they were face-to-face.

Seeing Haley in one piece was the highlight of her days and nights by far. The New Orleans streets were dangerous, even more so for a police officer with no one she trusted to watch her back. Tonya would eviscerate Tim with glee if anything happened to Haley. Her transfer was still pending but promising given she had an interview of sorts next Monday.

Through all this…Tonya didn't know what to call it, Haley had been incredible. She was stressed, angry, and disappointed, but that didn't keep her from being attentive. That didn't keep her from listening. That didn't keep her from laughing. And in return, Tonya listened when Haley had something to say and even when she didn't. When Haley reached out to touch, kiss, hold her, or more, Tonya was there.

She pushed away from her desk, stood, and gathered her belongings. Her cell phone rang just as she was about to drop it into her bag. It was Haley.

"Hey, you want somethin' special to eat tonight? I'll cook if you want. I'm goin' by the store to get beer, lots and lots of beer, so I thought I'd ask."

Tonya didn't bother to ask if her day had been difficult. "How about you get your beer and I'll pick up Five Happiness."

"Oh God, I love that place."

"I know." Tonya smiled.

"I'm gonna need two orders of salt-and-pepper calamari and Kung Pao chicken. I can eat that tomorrow."

"Veggie lo mein?"

"Yeah. You comin' to me?" Haley's voice was soft.

Tonya's heart rate increased. There was something about those words. She'd heard them many times before, but had usually responded without thought. She'd been moving toward Haley since they met, but the most important thing was that Haley had been meeting her halfway the whole time. "Yes, I'm coming to you." Tonya paused. "I'm going to be late. I—"

"You moved your therapy appointment. I remember. I'll see you when you get home."

"Okay."

Home. Yes, with Haley. Where she belonged.

There was a knock on her office door as she hung up. Tonya looked through the glass to see Stephanie. She walked in before Tonya had a chance to invite her.

"Walk down with you?"

"Sure.

A couple minutes later, Stephanie pressed the Down button on the elevator. "Ugh, I have a date with a pint of Creole cream cheese ice cream."

Tonya smiled. "Hope he treats you well."

Stephanie snorted. "He doesn't have a choice. And it could be a she, you know."

"Funny." Tonya glanced at Stephanie.

The elevator opened and the attendant stepped aside.

"I try."

"And you usually succeed."

"I really want him, but he just sits on my hips. I don't know if he's worth it."

Tonya chuckled.

A few minutes later, they were walking into the doctors parking garage. Tonya pressed a button on her key fob to deactivate the alarm and start her car.

"Nice job with Phil Templeton, by the way. It's amazing that you get through to anybody with that mentality. I had to give Greg a break. Mr. Templeton tried his best to rip him to shreds."

"I'm not always able to."

"Oh, I know. You know, we could just go out for a couple drinks to unwind, especially since you're used to being out on school nights now…"

That was true. Being with Haley had become her new routine. Tonya looked at her watch. "I'm sorry; I can't."

"Haley should come too. I think we've proven that we have fun together."

"I'm not seeing her until later. I have an appointment."

Stephanie stared at her over the top of the car. Her eyebrows were scrunched and her forehead wrinkled. "Okaaaay?"

Tonya sighed and eased into the driver's seat. Stephanie turned to look at her after she closed the passenger side door. "It's not…something medical, is it? I know some offices actually have late hours." She sounded worried.

"Well, it *is* a doctor's appointment." She couldn't think of any reason to keep it from her. Haley knew. Tonya wasn't a closed system anymore. She shouldn't have to remind herself of that. "I have a psychotherapy appointment. It's usually on Thursdays, but there's a lot going on right now—"

"The shit with your father. When are you going to tell him that he has to move?"

"This weekend, I think. Tracy will be home." She hadn't told anyone about Haley's predicament. It wasn't her information to share.

"Mmm. So has he helped?"

"She, and yes, she has."

"You've been seeing her for a while?"

"Yes." Tonya followed the exit signs and spiraled down toward the lower floors.

"Keeping it to yourself was a way of exerting some control over your own life."

Tonya smiled. It felt really good to be known so well, and she loved how the whole thing wasn't a big deal. Maybe she was the one making it bigger than it actually was. "Yes, exactly."

"Well, that was a stupid question before. She's obviously helped. Rain check on drinks, then?"

"Rain check, but just until Saturday. We'll make a night of it. I think I'll need to release some steam." Tonya was sure Haley would too.

"Sounds good, but this time we have to go to Oz. Those boys are so pretty, and you know I'm a sucker for the unattainable."

Tonya laughed.

"You requested an earlier appointment date. That's a surprise. I thought I misread my calendar when I saw it." Dr. Finn studied Tonya.

"Yes, your support staff was very accommodating."

"They know to give well-established clients some leeway."

"I should've expected my life to veer off course. Things were going so well." Tonya was tired of the small talk. She didn't even contemplate divulging Haley's situation, especially since it involved criminal activity.

"Off course? Really?" Dr. Finn stared.

Tonya almost smiled. "No, it was obviously a blanket statement."

"Obviously." Dr. Finn grinned. "But there have been some changes?"

"Yes. It's amazing how the good and bad can coexist at virtually the same time."

"It can be."

"Haley and I are closer than I thought was possible, and so are me and Tracy."

"Both are huge positives."

"That's not all."

"No?"

"No. I'm an open book, or as open as I think I can be. I've shared things, very personal things with Haley, Stephanie, Tracy, and even my father. It almost feels like I'm not capable of hiding anymore. I've become more…" She searched for the right word. "*Impulsive* doesn't fit."

"More demonstrative in the way you express yourself, carry yourself?"

"Yes, that's a good way to describe it. I can't sit idly by, but Daddy has never felt further away. He's within touching distance, and that's all we've been able to manage. I think I know why."

Dr. Finn remained silent, letting Tonya lead.

"He resents my sexuality and I resent his…resentment. We can't live in the same house with all that between us. There would be an argument every time Haley stayed over. I don't have the energy for that, and I don't think he does either. In order for us to build anything remotely resembling a bridge between us, there needs to be some physical distance. I won't stop living my life, and I won't tolerate him belittling it."

Dr. Finn smiled, but it was a small one.

"Is this for you, or is this about making Haley comfortable and less likely to walk away from the constant issues plaguing your family?"

Tonya knew that question was coming, and she didn't hesitate to answer. "It's for me, first. Secondly, it's for me and Haley, together."

Dr. Finn leaned back in her chair. Her smile widened.

Tonya returned it.

"How do you expect him to take it?"

"Not well. I suspect it will be one of our worse arguments to date."

"You're trying to prepare yourself. You can try, but I don't think that's possible. Despite the animosity between you, Tonya, you love your father; and because of that he's able to hurt you in ways that have been and could continue to be devastating."

Tonya sighed. "Yes, I know that."

"Are you also aware that your ability to deal with that pain, process, and move on has improved?"

Tonya opened her mouth to speak.

Dr. Finn held up a hand, stopping her. "Are you really aware of how full your life has become?"

Tonya's face flushed and she looked away. She wasn't ashamed, just overwhelmed, so when she glanced back up, Tonya was smiling again. "Yes."

"You're happy."

It wasn't a question. In spite of her father and the situation with Haley, yes, she was.

"You are also a realist," Dr. Finn reminded her.

That was true as well.

"You and your father may never be closer than arm's length."

She knew that. She did, but to hear it out loud from someone else's lips was difficult. Tonya swallowed. "I know."

"I know you're tired of this fight, but somehow you find it in you to keep going. That's something to be admired…to be proud of. You refuse to take the easy way out."

"I can't. Not anymore."

Dr. Finn nodded. "Let's look at where you were a little over two years ago and where you are now."

"I was angry. I still am, but I'm not consumed by it."

"Yes, and?"

"I pushed people away and had a fairly thick wall around myself."

Dr. Finn pressed her pen against her lips and continued to wait.

"Everything hurt."

"Does it still?"

"No."

"Two years ago, if you'd met Haley—"

"I wasn't ready for her then." She wouldn't have given Haley a second look.

"Are you now?"

Tonya explored her emotions. She didn't have to go deep to be surrounded by warmth that turned scorching whenever Haley was near. Her heart thudded. Her breathing shallowed, but she was the strongest she'd ever been. It all filled her with a heaviness, but she was lighter than air. "Yes, I think…I know I am."

"It is amazing that good and bad can coexist and occur simultaneously. You were nearly the victim of a violent crime, but look at everything that stemmed from it. All because you're not only a survivor, you're a fighter as well."

Something welled up in Tonya's chest and spread throughout her body. Her eyes burned and her breathing hitched. "Yes," she whispered. "I am."

Fresh from the shower, Haley downed her first beer in record time. She had no intention of finishing them all but wanted a nice buzz to take the edge off. She sat the remainder of the six-pack on the floor, reached for the remote, and put her legs up on the couch. Might as well try to laugh a little.

In the not-so-distant past, when she was in a shitty mood, Haley would have been out at some bar soaking up the attention. There was a time when that had made her feel on top of the world. That was before it started to get old. Funny thing was, Tonya hadn't lost one bit of her shine. Truth of the matter was that she gleamed a little brighter every time Haley saw her.

She'd grown up a lot the past few months. Some of that was because of the job. Some of that was because of Tonya, and some of that was because of Tim. He'd taught her a hard lesson about trust, friendship, and loyalty. Not everybody saw it the same way that she did, and from now on, Haley knew to be wary.

She'd hoped that he'd been lying about Mr. Preston, but he hadn't been. There was a record of an interview and even a transcript. Goddamn him. Haley wasn't sure where she got the strength to deal with Tim. Being in the same space with him was exhausting. Looking at him and acknowledging his presence took up her reserves.

Tim talked to her like nothing had changed. He looked her straight in the eye and laughed and joked, despite her silence or the occasional grunt she gave in response. It was pathological. It had to be.

Her doorbell rang.

Knowing it was Tonya on the other side boosted her energy. She really needed to get her a key. A smile tugged at her lips. She pulled the door open. "Good, I'm starv—"

Her words left her.

It was Tim. He smiled and held up a six-pack of beer. "I paid the nurse to stay late. I don't know why I didn't think about that before. We coulda been doin' this on Monday. We probably needed it."

The heat of Haley's anger burned her from the inside out. "Are you fuckin' kiddin' me?"

At least he didn't try to barge in.

"I'm not interruptin' anythin', am I? Tonya's not here, is she?"

"You have no right to even say her fuckin' name. Get off my goddamn porch!" Haley's voice was guttural, deep, and loud.

Tim flinched like he'd been slapped. She wanted to do a hell of a lot more. "Rook—"

"My name is Haley. I need to make sure you understand somethin' once and for all, *Tim*. There is no goin' back. You're a fuckin' dumpster fire, and just because I have to be next to you doesn't mean I wanna to smell the shit you're spewin'. Get your head outta your pathetic ass. There's nothin' you can say or do. You got what you wanted. Leave me out of the rest of your delusional clusterfuck."

By the time she was done talking, Tim was shaking and his face was red. He clenched his hands into fists.

Haley wanted him to swing. He was bigger, but she was fast. She'd try her best to beat the holy hell out of him.

Haley had hurt him, badly. She could see it in his eyes. They were glassy and dark with pain, as well as a lot of other emotions that Haley just didn't have it in her to identify. He'd blown her off before when she told him she could never trust him again, but Tim got the message this time, loud and clear.

She expected him to explode, but he just stood there, looking down at his feet.

"I'm closin' the door now." All the fight Haley left her.

Tim bent slightly and set the beer on the porch.

"Don't do this again." Her tone was soft. It was hard not to feel sorry for him.

He turned and walked away.

Haley had lost her appetite. She barely finished one order of the calamari before pushing the rest of it away.

Tonya put the lid back on the container and stacked it with the rest of the food.

"I mean, I just couldn't take it anymore. Has he lost his mind or what?"

"I don't think so." Tonya leaned back on the couch. She patted her lap and Haley went willingly, pillowing her head on Tonya's thighs.

"It's like some huge game of fake it till you make it."

"That may be more accurate. He really wants to believe that you'll both recover from this. The things he's done are so out of character, maybe this is his way of holding on to who he was instead of facing up to the person he's become." Tonya sifted her fingers through Haley's hair, making her shiver.

"Yeah, maybe. He apologizes, but it doesn't seem like he feels guilty at all."

"About taking the money, no, but toward you possibly. It's another way to explain his behavior tonight and the past few days." Tonya looked down at Haley. Her expression was caring but worried. "Why haven't you told Nate or Jen about this?"

"How do you know I didn't?"

"Because you haven't talked about it."

"I will after my transfer." Yeah, she had changed. She'd never kept anything from Nate and Jen.

Tonya sighed. "Haley."

"I'm coverin' up criminal activity, Tonya. The fewer people know, the better right now."

"I know that, but you were backed into a corner,"

Tonya didn't know the half of it. Goddammit she hated this.

"The more people you have in your corner—"

"Can we talk about somethin' else? It can't always be about me."

Tonya's gaze softened, and Haley just wanted to crawl inside. It was ridiculous the way even a small thing like that affected her. Haley reached up and trailed her fingertips from Tonya's cheek to her chin. "How was your day?"

She leaned into the touch. "Difficult at times, but nothing I couldn't handle."

"That's not what I asked." Haley stared.

Tonya smiled slightly. "There was a little bit of everything: sexism, classism, and racism. I got through to at least a couple of them. The racist man surprised me the most. The fact that he accepted help made dealing with him easier, but I'd rather you ask me about therapy. I can talk freely about that."

It was good that sometimes Tonya had to speak in generalities. It kept Haley from wanting to punch her patients in the face, but just barely. "Ugh, are you—"

"I'm okay. I'd tell you if I wasn't."

Haley held her gaze to make sure. "Okay, therapy?"

"It went well." Tonya's smile widened. "Especially when I talked about you. I think things are winding down on that front. No matter what happens when I talk to my father, I'm ready to deal with it."

Good news. Haley needed to hear some on a day like this. "You're so strong."

"So are you."

"No." Haley shook her head.

"Yes, you are. Look at what you do for a living. Look at what you're going through."

Haley tried to swallow down the huge lump in her throat. It didn't move. "Compared to—"

"It's not about that. There's no contest. You have to be strong to be who you are: open, caring, honest, and loyal. You're fierce. I want to make sure you know that. It's part of what drew me to you." Tonya's gaze was bright, serious, and completely beautiful.

With the information she was holding on to, it was hard for Haley not to look away, but she kept her focus where it needed to be, on Tonya.

Tonya's expression changed. Her smile was slow and wide. Haley couldn't help but be captured by it. She reared upward. She wanted to taste it, touch it. She brushed her lips against Tonya's. Haley needed to savor the goodness. She needed it to fill her so that nothing else could fit.

Breathing raggedly, Tonya pulled back. She was still smiling. "The tight T-shirts helped too."

Haley sucked in a surprised breath, blinked, and laughed.

CHAPTER 28

Haley wiped the condensation off the bathroom mirror. Her reflection looked distorted, fuzzy. That depiction was true all the way around. She didn't feel like herself. Well, when she was near Tonya, she was normal. Guilt wasn't sitting like lead in her stomach, and she had conviction that what she'd done had been right, had been necessary. Tonya was happy, and no one had the right to ruin that.

Not even her.

In time, Haley was sure that all this other shit would go away because she deserved to be happy too. Each moment Haley spent with Tonya, she felt deeply. She did her best to hang on to that natural high. Tonya had spent last night wrapped around her like she was protecting Haley from something. Maybe she was.

Haley peered at herself for a few more seconds. She was more in focus this time. She reached for her toothbrush and opened the medicine cabinet to get the toothpaste, moving like she had all the time in the world. She kind of did. Tonya had already left, and she was damn tempted to call in sick or dead.

She had no idea how she was going to face Tim today. She'd torn him to shreds. She wanted to believe it was only fair after everything he'd done, but the more she thought about the look on his face, the more awful she felt.

Before leaving the bathroom, she glanced at herself one final time.

A couple hours later, Haley looked out the passenger-side window as the local scenery whizzed by her. Tim had yet to say a word. The only sounds in the car were the crackle of the radio and the hum of the air conditioning and engine.

Haley couldn't even look at him. She was scared that the part of herself that was angry as fuck would claw his face off.

"Eight twenty-two, we have a 15 in progress at 2600 Holygrove Street. Neighbors allegedly caught him in a 62R, no weapons involved."

Haley whipped her head around. It wasn't every day that house owners caught their own burglar; it took balls on both ends. She watched as Tim answered the call.

"ETA ten minutes."

"Copy that, eight twenty-two."

They got there in eight, thanks to Tim's driving. He never seemed to care about the potholes. Maybe he thought the faster he drove, the less likely he was to hit them. That was bullshit. Haley was the first one out of the car. She waited for Tim at the bottom of the steps. Haley was pissed at him, but she wasn't stupid. This was a crime scene. Anything could happen.

She knocked on the door.

"Yeah, who dat?"

"Police. You called about a break-in."

"I got his ass. Hold on." The man's voice was muffled behind the door.

Haley heard the lock click. She stepped to the right, away from the door. Tim was on the left.

The front door opened. A man stepped out. He was short, stout, and looked mightily disgruntled. "Go on. He in there. He a little bloody, but he gone live. Taped his ass to a chair."

"Hey! Somebody help!" Someone inside the house screamed.

Well, this was interesting. Everything in her wanted to glance at Tim—he'd see the humor in the moment—but her gaze remained on the victim. "Are you hurt, sir?"

"Naw, I'm gone have me a cigarette out here while y'all do y'alls thing."

Haley nodded. She stepped in first, keeping her hand on her weapon just in case. The living room was clear.

"Heyyyy!"

The perp was still screaming. Haley followed the noise. She could hear and feel Tim behind her. When she got to the kitchen, she stopped and stared. It was a pathetic sight. A young man who looked like he hadn't seen the inside of a shower in a while stared back. He had a knot on the side of his head, and his nose was bleeding pretty badly. He looked emaciated, and his eyes were wild. Haley was sure it had nothing to do with his present situation. More than likely, he was a drug addict searching for something to sell or trade for a fix.

The man wiggled and kicked. "Help me out. Just help me out."

Grey electrical tape was wrapped around his shoulders, securing him to the dining room chair. Haley didn't say anything to him. She walked around the chair. "He's gonna have to be cut out of this."

They were the first words she'd said to Tim all day.

He looked at her. His gaze was just as wild as the perp's, and then it went blank. Tim nodded. Haley refused to be affected.

Tim reached into his pocket and pulled out a pocket knife. He handed it to Haley. She took it without looking at him. "Okay, sir. I'm gonna need you to stay still. This should only take a minute."

"Help me, please."

Haley flipped the knife open and started at the top. Before she knew what was happening, the guy was rearing back in the chair. Completely caught by surprise when it smashed into her, Haley went tumbling toward the stove behind her. The edge of it dug into her as she fell. Haley grunted in pain. Somehow, she ended up on all fours.

The guy in the chair was laughing hysterically. Asshole. She was trying to help him…to jail, but help him regardless.

Haley pushed up from the floor. She got a bird's eye-view of Tim's uniform pants as she stumbled once more. The pain in her back brought momentary tears to her eyes. When she glanced up again, Tim's hand was in her face.

His gaze was filled with concern.

She looked away from his face and stared at the hand he was offering. Haley was tempted to take it, but she didn't want him to see it as some tiny window to wiggle his ass back into her good graces. That just wasn't possible. Haley ignored him as she got to her feet.

Tim tried to help anyway. She arched away from him and glared.

Tim glared right back. A few seconds later, he turned to glare at the perp instead.

He was still in the chair, chuckling.

They stopped for lunch. Tim didn't ask her what she wanted. He pulled into the Wendy's parking lot on South Carrollton and got out. The Wendy's was right next door to a Popeyes and a Rally's, so she at least had a choice, but Haley wasn't feeling fast food. Hell, she wasn't hungry at all. Her back still hurt a little, but it was nothing she couldn't handle. There was going to be a bruise. It would heal. Haley eased the seat back and pulled out her phone. There were two new texts from Tonya as of twenty minutes ago. Haley smiled.

> *How many psychiatrists does it take to change a lightbulb?*

Haley rolled her eyes and went to the next message. This was going to be bad. She could feel it.

> *Only one but the bulb has to really *want* to change.*

She groaned, then chuckled, but it was cute that Tonya continued to try to distract her. It meant a lot.

U kno any cop jokes?

Haley waited. She looked out the windshield toward the restaurant. Tim was sitting down and had a tray in his hands. He looked her way. Haley concentrated on her phone. At least he'd left the keys in the ignition so she could keep the AC on.

> *A psychiatrist met a cop at a gas station. She turned out to be smart, sexy, and the psychiatrist doesn't know where or what her life would be without her.*

Haley stared at the words. Emotion clogged her throat, and her eyes burned. Her heart was racing, and it was hard to breathe. Instead of texting back, she called.

"Hey, I only have a couple minutes."

"That's all I need. You wanna know the punch line of your joke?" Haley wiped at her eyes with the back of her hand.

"Impress and enlighten me."

"The funny thing is that the cop feels exactly the same way," Haley said softly.

Tonya's breathing hitched. "Then they probably deserve each other."

"I think they do."

"She's sweet too, incredibly so."

"Don't tell anybody." Haley smiled. She couldn't help herself.

"I won't, but I'll definitely see you later."

"Yeah, later."

Haley looked into the restaurant again. Tim was shoveling fries into his mouth. She peered down at her phone and made another call.

"Hello?"

Ugh, she hated when he answered her mother's phone.

"Is that your phone?" Haley heard Cathy's voice in the background.

"Naw."

"Then why did you answer it? Were you gonna be rude to Haley right in front of me? That was her ring. We've had our discussion about that for the last time."

Jeb didn't say anything.

Haley smiled. He may be like an old pair of shoes, but there were obviously times when Haley fit better.

"Hey, sweetie. Sorry 'bout all that."

"It's okay, Mom."

"So what's goin' on? Not that I'm complainin', but I just talked to you on Sunday."

"I'm fine." Haley cleared her throat.

"Uh-huh. I didn't buy that bullshit on Sunday, but I didn't say anythin'. You ready to talk about it?"

Well, damn. "What—"

"I'm your mother, and at the risk of soundin' like some *Brady Bunch* episode, I can tell when somethin's botherin' you. I can hear it in your voice."

"Work stuff. Nothin' I can't handle." She hadn't hurt him yet, so Haley counted that as progress.

"Mmm, I know I asked this before, but everythin' okay with you and Tonya? I can't wait to meet her. I know she's gonna be somethin'."

Haley grinned. "Yes, we're okay, and yes, she is. I just got off the phone with her before I called you."

"I can hear you smilin'."

"Yeah, well." Haley smiled harder.

"Oh, baby. She has you wrapped around her finger, doesn't she?"

Haley laughed. "Yup." It was true. She'd do anything for Tonya, and had proven that to be true too.

"So you just called to chitchat?"

"I just wanted to hear another friendly voice."

"Ah, I see. Somethin's goin' on with your partner."

Haley sighed. "Yeah, I put in for a transfer to another precinct. I have an interview on Monday. Sorry I didn't say anythin' on Sunday."

"That's fine. It's that bad?"

"Yeah. It's easier to do it this way than to just try to change partners."

"I'm so sorry. I know the two of you were close."

The driver's side-door opened.

Haley almost dropped her phone. Tim had caught her by surprise. She should've kept eyes on him. "Okay, I gotta go, Mom. I'll call you this weekend."

"Oh, okay. Love you."

"Love you too."

Haley glanced at Tim as he started the car. He had the same stony expression he'd been wearing all day.

"So this is a surprise," Tracy said.

"Well, I know your schedule, and I meant to call this morning." Tonya leaned back in her office chair.

"It's fine. What's up?"

"I have an idea. I haven't talked to Haley about it yet, but I'm sure she'll go for it. If her friends and Stephanie are free on Sunday, how would you feel about going somewhere to watch the game?"

"Wait. The football game?"

"Yessss."

"You don't know a damn thing about sports."

"And your point is?"

Tracy laughed. "You've got it bad. This should be interesting. Yeah, I'll go, but what are we gonna do on Saturday? I'm sure you'll need some space from Daddy after you talk to him."

Tonya beat back a wave of sadness. It didn't belong. She'd made her decision and was sticking by it. "True, but Stephanie already beat you to it. We're more than likely going to Oz. We can get drinks there."

"Sounds good. Is Haley's gonna be staying over in the middle of that mess?"

"Probably." Tonya wouldn't have it any other way.

"She has it bad too."

Tonya certainly hoped so.

"Did you tell Stephanie the plan for Sunday yet?"

"No, but she'll be fine as long as she can drink." Tonya smiled.

Tracy chuckled. "Very, very true."

"I'll just be glad when this weekend is over. I'm tired of being tired of Daddy."

"I bet you are. Has he been giving you the cold shoulder?"

"He's tried, but I won't let him."

"You know, he could surprise us. We're expecting him to be angry about moving out. He could be relieved."

"I don't know, Tracy. Nothing with him has been easy so far. I don't expect this to be either."

"I see your point. If anything happens between now and Saturday, just call me. I should be home by noon or so."

"I'm sure it won't be anything I can't hand—"

"Just call me, okay? I'm your sister. We're in this together."

A ball of warmth invaded Tonya's chest. She smiled. "Okay, I will."

After Tonya hung up, she looked at the clock on her phone. Thank God it was time for the transition meeting with the next shift. She was ready to go. As if on cue, Stephanie tapped the glass pane on the door and waved her out. Tonya nodded and stood up.

Her office phone rang. She held up a hand, and Stephanie waved her away. Tonya picked up the receiver. "This is Dr. Preston."

The other end was silent.

"Hello?"

"I hate it when you think you know somebody and you really don't."

Tonya sat back down. Anger shot through her. "Tim."

"I like Tang better. She won't even call me that anymore, but it doesn't matter. I can tell by the sound of your voice that she's been talkin' to you."

"Then I'm hanging up now. There's nothing you can say."

"She tell you everythin', you think? I don't think she did. I know her. She can be all noble and protective when she wants to be."

"What do you want?" Tonya dug her nails into the leather armrests as something like apprehension filled her stomach.

"That daddy of yours is squeaky-clean 'cept for one little thing. Well, it's not little. I guess you were too busy with med school or somethin' to notice."

"I don't have time for this. If you want to play games, you called the wrong person. Get to the damn point."

"Oh shit, you got some fire in you. I knew there had to be somethin'."

"Good-bye, Tim."

"Okay, fine! Your father was questioned in 2007 because he was under suspicion of drug trafficking. Had good evidence on him too, but they let it go because catching the boss was more important than dealin' with an old man."

Everything in Tonya stopped, then whooshed back to normal working order. None of what he said made sense. She actually laughed.

"Haley didn't believe it either."

Tonya went cold as she put it all together. "What?"

"I could make things miserable for all of y'all. It doesn't matter that the dealer's in jail. All it would take is for a CI to come forward and say your daddy's name in the same sentence with a known dealer. It don't matter how old he is;

with his background, they'd be throat-fuckin' y'all with an investigation before you had a chance to breathe."

"Why? Why would you do something like that? I barely even know you."

Tim scoffed. "I guess that's a yes, then. She didn't tell you everything?"

"I've never done anything to you." Tonya was numb. She was feeling so much that there was no way to single out just one emotion.

"She's gonna try to leave. I heard her talkin' about it." Tim sounded tortured. "How do I know she's not gonna turn—"

Tonya didn't want to hear any more. She couldn't take it. She hung up the phone.

There was a knock at her door. Stephanie walked in. "Hey, we're wait... Tonya? What's wrong?"

She didn't know what to say. How do you put something like that into words when she didn't even understand it? "I...I have to get home. Can you handle things for me here?" Tonya stood again. She grabbed her things. Every movement felt jerky.

"Yeah, whatever you need. Is your dad okay? Did something happen to Haley?"

Tonya's stomach lurched. "No, nothing like that."

"Well, I'll take care of things here. Don't worry about it." Stephanie's eyes were wide and filled with concern.

Stephanie was somebody she could count on. Tonya grabbed her hand and squeezed on her way out the door. "I'll call you later." She didn't wait to hear Stephanie's reply.

Tonya was barely off hospital property when her phone started to ring. It was Haley. Her insides clenched and she couldn't breathe. Tonya couldn't talk to her. Not right now. She let it go to voice mail. By the time she reached the Causeway, Tonya was trembling and Haley had called and texted several times.

Shock, betrayal, and fury intertwined and sat in her stomach, slowly leaking poison to the rest of her body. Haley or her father. Tonya didn't know who was more responsible for what she was feeling. Tonya took some slow, deep breaths and tried to think rationally. He could have been making it all up.

She wanted to believe that, but she couldn't.

Would Haley keep something like this from her? The question had an easy answer. Yes, she would, if she thought she was protecting her. A surge of anger almost choked Tonya. How many times had she told her not to do that? She should have known there was more going on.

She should have known that the rug would be pulled from under her. Tonya had put too much stock in her own happiness. She'd put too much stock in everyone. And this information just confirmed that her father was a hypocrite. All those years, she'd felt like nothing, but he was hiding his own secret.

There was no way he ran drugs, then or now. He wouldn't put his family in jeopardy that way…but how could she say that for sure? Was there some other reason he'd lost the store? "No, no, no." She shook the thoughts free.

Her phone rang again. Tonya switched off the Bluetooth and put the phone on vibrate. She got home in record time. Her father was pulling out of the driveway as she pulled in. Tonya honked her horn. He stopped and waited.

She got out of her car and slammed the door. Any control she had gained left as soon as she saw him. Robert rolled down his window.

"We need to talk."

He sighed. "I don't have the energy to—"

"Now, Daddy!"

His eyes widened, and he stared at her. "Just because I live in your house. You don't get to order me around."

"We can do this right here. I don't care who knows if you don't."

He looked around. With controlled violence, he snatched the keys from the ignition. "Fine."

Tonya stormed into the house. She didn't check to see if he followed. She reached the kitchen and waited. It was incredibly hard to contain herself. She was shaking again. The psychiatrist in her encouraged calm. Nothing would be solved by a screaming match, but God it would feel good.

Her father walked in. He slammed the door and glared at her.

She didn't back down. "You don't know half of what I've been through." Tonya said the words slowly, softly. "I've been a million different people to try and please you, to try to make you proud."

"How many more times do I have to hear this!"

Tonya took a breath to keep from saying something unnecessarily nasty. "You have a secret too, Daddy. Are you who you pretend to be?"

"What the hell you talking about?"

She pulled out a stool and sat down, suddenly exhausted. "Tell me about 2007."

Robert stiffened. His eyes widened and his jaw clenched. He licked his lips. "What?"

"Drug trafficking." She stared at him, daring him to refute it.

"Did that freak show tell you about this? She's trying to ruin this family."

Tonya's eyes prickled with tears. She understood why Haley did it, but that didn't make her any less infuriated. "No, Daddy, she was actually trying to keep it together. This conversation isn't about her."

He walked toward her with his hands out in front of him in supplication. "It's not what you think. I would never do anything like that. It's not the kind of person I am. I've made some bad moves, a lot of them, and that one was one of the worst. I was doing a friend a favor. I didn't know there was drugs. As far as I was concerned, it was just bric-a-brac or some shit."

"I know you wouldn't, Daddy," Tonya said quietly.

His forehead wrinkled in confusion. "Then, what? I don't understand."

"You don't get to judge me or my life when you're holding back secrets of your own, especially since it could come back to bite us." She hoped Tim was bluffing. An investigation could put her job in jeopardy.

He took another step forward. "What? That's not the same thing. I was trying to protect you, all of you from that."

"I don't need anyone to protect me!"

He flinched.

"I needed you to be there. I needed you to love and accept me for who I am."

Their gazes held for a few more seconds. Then he looked away, just like she knew he would.

"I love you, Daddy. I was going to wait until Tracy was home to bring this up, but I can't. We can't live together like this. I'll help you find a new place. No matter what's going on between us, I'll make sure you're okay."

His mouth fell open. "You…kicking me out?"

"That's what it comes down to, yes."

He deflated right before her eyes. It was a sad thing to see, and it pulled at her heart.

Robert nodded. "I'll start looking around in the morning." He moved toward the hallway and his room.

Tonya was surprised he hadn't brushed off her offer to help.

He stopped and turned. "Tonya?" His voice quivered.

"Yes, Daddy?"

"What did you mean when you said come back to bite us?"

Tonya swallowed, but the feeling of apprehension remained. "I was told that there was a possibility of a new investigation, but I think Haley can help to keep that from happening."

He nodded again, but his expression held shock. "For what it's worth, I'm sorry."

Tonya remained quiet as he turned and disappeared down the hallway. She wasn't sure which issue he was apologizing for, but it was worth a lot.

She needed a drink.

Less than ten minutes later, the doorbell rang. Tonya wasn't surprised. She'd expected it. After ignoring the calls and texts, Tonya knew it was Haley at the door. She finished off her second glass of wine in one gulp and went to answer it.

Within seconds, Haley was wrapped around her. "Thank God! Are you okay? With everythin' that's goin' on, I was freakin' the fuck out. Did somethin' happen with your dad? Why were you ignorin' my calls?"

Tonya closed her eyes and sank into the warmth Haley provided. The feel of her, the smell of her settled Tonya just like it always did, but she couldn't let that happen. She stiffened and stepped away.

Reluctantly, Haley let her go and walked farther into the living room. Her face was crinkled in concern. "Tonya? What's wrong?"

"I got a call from Tim today." Tonya's voice was hoarse with emotion.

Haley's eyes widened and her face reddened. Anger spread over her features. "Fuck!"

Their gazes met. Haley moved toward her again. Tonya held up a hand and moved away. "Don't. I can't. Not right now."

"I'm not sorry. I did what I thought was right, but I am sorry that I hurt you."

"Why didn't you just tell me? My family would've been more prepared to deal with an investigation if we'd had more time."

Haley opened her mouth, presumably to speak.

"This was the real reason you went along with him, wasn't it?"

Haley nodded. She looked like she was in pain.

"I get why you did it. I really do, but I told you time and time again that wasn't what I wanted from you."

"I know, but I'd do it again."

Tonya's heartbeat rammed against her chest. "Was he really going to try to frame you?"

Haley stepped forward again. "That wasn't a lie. I kept some things from you, but I didn't lie. Yeah, he was, but he knew that it wouldn't hold water. He knew I'd figure it out too."

"He threatened to find a way to open up an investigation. You should've talked to me. We could have—"

"No. I hated keepin' all this from you, and I shoulda known my leavin' would trigger him somehow. I just didn't know he'd shoot himself in the foot like this."

"You're lying for me. If this gets out, your career and your freedom is on the line. I can't let you do that! Why would you do something like that?" Anger and fear whirled inside Tonya, vying for space.

Haley rubbed the back of her neck, but she didn't say anything. She wouldn't even look at her.

"Why?" Tonya asked again, just as loudly.

Haley met Tonya's gaze, and what Tonya saw there left her breathless.

"Because I love you."

Everything around them fell away.

"I'm supposed to protect you whether you want me to or not. I'm supposed to be there for you. I'm supposed to sacrifice for you."

"I thought I heard yelling."

They both turned to look at her father.

"I didn't mean to interrupt."

"There's somethin' I need to take care of anyway," Haley said.

"You can't just leave after saying all that!"

"I know, but I need to go talk to Tim before he does somethin' else crazy. The last thing y'all need is for cops to come sniffin' around."

"I'm coming with you, then."

"No, you're not." Haley's nose flared. Her eyes narrowed. She meant business.

"Why the hell not?" So did Tonya.

"Us gangin' up on him could make things worse." Haley closed the gap between them. She wrapped her hand around Tonya's waist. "Please, let me handle this."

Haley pressed her lips to Tonya's forehead. The burst of feeling that resulted sent Tonya's heartbeat back into a tailspin. Haley loved her, and she had feelings, so many feelings. But Tonya was still angry. They needed to talk, and soon. She took a deep breath and gave in. "Be careful, please, and call me when you get there."

Haley's lips trailed down to her cheek and then her mouth. "I will." Then she kissed Tonya like she was trying to rob her of breath.

Tonya watched as Haley drove away. She turned around quickly. She'd forgotten that her father had interrupted them, but he was gone. Haley's speech about sacrifice, protection, and being there reverberated. Even though his moving out was the right decision, maybe she had been too hard on him about the whole drug-trafficking thing, and maybe it would be good for both of them if she told him so.

CHAPTER 29

Haley's heart didn't start beating normally until she got past the tollbooth. She could have lost Tonya, but she hadn't. Then there was the expression on Tonya's face when she told her how she felt. She'd seen surprise, wonder, heat, and more. Haley was sure she could live a lifetime on that look alone. Her sense of relief was overwhelming. Plus, the monkey on her back was gone, and she allowed herself to feel the lightness of that for a hot minute. When the minute was up, she had some hard truths to face.

She'd fucked up.

At least she knew now instead of later that leaving would make Tim lose his shit. But this wasn't about him anymore. It wasn't about her either. Tonya and her family were the ones in the crosshairs, and she had to get them out.

If he'd already done something to make the police take notice, Tim had lost every bit of leverage he had with her. There was nothing keeping her from turning him in. Nothing. He had to be bluffing. He'd called Tonya to rattle her, to rattle them. The more she thought about it, the more pissed she got.

Anger wouldn't help her, though. He'd find a way to use it somehow and put them in deeper shit. She'd cancel the transfer if she had to. She'd even pretend that everything was fine, but first she'd try reasoning with him. She had to find some way to get in a reasoning mood first, and she had no idea how to do that. Haley was boiling on the inside. Didn't she have the right to be happy? Didn't she have the right to find a partner she could trust? Was Tim that fucking miserable that he wanted to pull everyone else into the black hole he was sitting in?

Haley's phone rang, and she snatched it up when she saw Tonya's name. "Hey."

Tonya's tone was low and soft; it felt like a caress. Haley let it wrap around her. "I'm not there yet. I wasn't gonna forget to call you."

"I know."

"Is everythin' okay?"

"No, it's not, but talking to you helps. It always has."

Something inside Haley melted. "I'm probably not in the right frame of mind to help anybody right now."

"See, I used to think your openness and the way you just put yourself out there was because you were young, but I figured out fairly quickly that it was you being you. I know you're angry right now, and you feel guilty too."

"Well, yeah. I shoulda thought things through. This wouldn't be happenin' otherwise." Haley gripped the steering wheel hard and hiked up her speed to eighty-five.

"Listen to me. This isn't your fault. You can't take responsibility for someone else's behavior."

"The whole thing is like some twisted game of dominoes. I do something, and he knocks things down around me."

"Haley, no. Tim started this. Even though his reasons were altruistic, he started this, and he pulled you into it. The fact that you're feeling this way means he got to you. It means he's already won in a way."

Haley went quiet.

"You have nothing to feel guilty about."

That just didn't ring true. "I hurt…you." Haley's tone was thick, hesitant.

"Yes, you did, and we'll talk about that, but I need you to listen to me. My family has been through hell and back, and we've been broken many times. We're still here, and we're still trying. A stupid, pointless police investigation won't pull us under again. I know we're hanging on by a thread, but it's a very sturdy one. Even with everything that's happened the past few months, I think we're stronger, and we're moving toward common ground despite our own stubbornness. Even if we don't get any closer, we'll survive this too."

Her breath stilted in her chest. "Tonya, I—"

"No, you need to know. No matter what happens, my family will be what it is. I know you're going to feel whatever you feel—"

"Tonya?"

"Yes?"

She'd heard everything Tonya said and did her best to internalize it. She didn't feel any less raw, but things didn't seem as dark. "I guess…I mean, I'm just realizin' that maybe I have a little bit of a hero complex."

Tonya didn't respond, but then Haley heard a chuckle.

"No kidding?"

Haley smiled. "No kiddin'."

"I'm mad at you."

"I know you are."

"But that doesn't change the way I feel."

Another wave of relief rolled through Haley. She knew that already, but to actually hear it was a completely different thing. "Thank God."

"Just remember what I said. No matter what happens, we'll all get through this."

Twenty minutes later, Haley put her truck in park. It was just starting to get dark. Tim's place was lit up like Christmas. His outside and living room lights were on. She could even see the commercial playing on TV. Maybe he was waiting.

Talking to Tonya had obviously helped because she didn't feel as much like strangling him. So there was that. This was probably as rational as she was going to get, and she hoped to God that he was there too. She sent a text to Tonya, and once she got a reply, she got out of her truck.

Haley rang the doorbell. Tim opened the door a few seconds later. They stared at each other. His eyes were hard, but they were sad as well. He stepped out of the way to let her in.

His living room looked like hurricane force winds had blown through it. Haley didn't say anything. She walked right past him and moved shit off the couch so that she could sit down.

"No point in doin' that. Just say what you gotta say and leave."

"It's like that, huh?" Haley turned to look at him.

Tim nodded. "It's like that."

Haley wasn't going to give up that easily. "All you're doin' is hurtin' a lot of people."

"Well, I'd say that makes us fuckin' even."

Rather than look up at him over the couch, Haley got up. She took a deep breath. "You started all this. Doesn't make sense to get pissy because the people you tried to fuck over didn't fall in line." She did her best to swallow down her rising anger.

He glared. "You didn't even give me a chance to try to fix things, so fuck you."

So much for rational. "Do you even hear what you're sayin'? You sound crazy. I swear to God, Tim, if you start this bullshit on the Prestons, I'll go to IAB and tell them everything. I might take a hit, but they'll come down on you so fuckin' hard. Then where will Milt be, huh? Supposedly this has all been about him. What would be the point?"

Part of her wanted to tell him that she would stay, and that they would work it out somehow, but it wasn't the right thing to do. She knew that now. They would just go down this road again if she did or said something Tim couldn't deal with.

He didn't say anything for a long time. Haley watched emotions on his face come and go: anger, fear, sadness, and resignation. Maybe she had him.

"That girl of yours is feisty as hell. Best fuck you ever had. Am I right? Gonna be kinda hard to do that when they start investigatin'. It'll look bad for both y'all. Damn shame." Tim smiled.

The fucker smiled, and before she knew what was happening, Haley was over the back of the couch and punching him in the face. His nose crunched under her fist, and it was so very satisfying.

Tim cried out and stumbled backward. He wiped the blood off his mouth and came at her. He telegraphed his swing toward her face, and Haley blocked it easily. She retaliated with a fist to his stomach. He doubled over.

Haley stepped back. Rage pummeled her, and she didn't want to let it win. This wasn't who she was. Slowly, Tim stood. She met his gaze. She saw his pain, but there was something else. His eyes gleamed with satisfaction.

Tim wanted this. Did he want to be punished? Did he want to punish her? She wasn't sure, but some of the anger leaked right out of her. She couldn't do this. It was wrong. All of this was wrong.

"I'm not doin' this with you. You were like family."

He wiped his mouth again and spat on the floor. His chest was heaving. "Bullshit. Family sticks together no matter what."

Haley shook her head. "No, if you thought of me that way, you never woulda done what you did to me. You don't treat people you care about that way. Don't you know that?"

"What you doin' to my boy?"

Haley turned toward the voice, and the floor fell from under her. Milt stood in the hallway. In one hand he had his cane. In the other, he had Tim's service weapon. He moved forward slowly. His cane scraped against the floor, and his hand, the one that held the gun, shook.

"Uncle Milt, I'm okay. This is Haley. Remember? My partner." Tim kept his voice soft.

Milt swung the gun toward Tim. "No, it ain't. Why you let him put his hands on you like that? Ya know how ta take a punch. Made sure of that. And ya know how ta giv 'em." He turned back to Haley.

The gun wobbled, his hand was trembling so bad.

"Git outta my house."

Haley didn't say a thing. Her heart was racing like it was going to pop out of her chest, but she did the best she could to breathe through it. Fear kept her alert, but the desire to live took over everything else. She held up her hands, palms out, and backed away, but she had no intention of leaving. There was a clip in the gun. She hoped the safety was on. With the way things were going, Haley couldn't be sure. She glanced at Tim. If he could distract Milt long enough, Haley could ease back around and disarm him.

"Give me the gun, Uncle Milt. I'll make sure she leaves."

"I ain't givin' you nothin'. I'm tryin' to clean up your mess." He lowered the Glock as he talked, but it was still aimed at Tim. He was wagging it like a finger.

Haley took another step. She brushed against Tim.

"Don'chu touch 'im!"

Tim stepped in front of her. "She's leavin'! Just give it to me. I'll get you back to bed, and this'll be over."

"Bullshit!" He raised the gun.

"Uncle Milt!"

A shot rang out.

Haley was pushed to the floor. She didn't stay put long. She crawled quickly toward the couch. When she got there, she peered around it.

Tim was lying in a pool of blood. Her heart sank, but she couldn't let her attention linger.

"Timmy, git up. Why ya on the floor?" Milton still had the gun in his hand as he looked around the room in confusion.

This was Haley's chance, and she took it. Moving as fast and as quietly as she could, she didn't stop until she was behind him. When he went to turn around, it was already too late. Haley knocked the gun out of his hand and kicked it across the room.

Her priority now was Tim.

Dread filled her. He wasn't moving. "Don't do this. Don't fuckin' do this." Haley felt for a pulse. It was there, barely. He groaned, and his head turned slightly. That was at least something. Haley didn't know she was crying until she tasted tears. "Try not to move. I know it hurts." Tim groaned again. He met her gaze. He was pale, sweaty, and his eyes were glassy. Haley grabbed whatever she could find to press against the wound in his abdomen and fished out her phone to called 911.

She did her best to ignore his cry of pain.

"Nine-one-one, what's your emergency?"

"This is Officer Haley Jordan, badge number 1264. My partner is down. I repeat, officer down. Gonna need two ambulances." She gave dispatch the address.

Haley dropped to her knees and continued to apply pressure.

Milton was behind her, sobbing.

"It's okay. It's gonna be okay." She said the words, but Haley wasn't sure if she believed them.

Haley stood around with fellow cops and detectives. As she gave them a preliminary report, she kept one eye on the EMTs working on Tang.

Milton had already been transported to Tulane.

"What happened to his face?" one of the detectives asked.

"I did that."

Someone from CSU walked up to her with a swab. Haley held out her hands. They were checking for gunshot residue.

"So really? You guys were fighting over a woman?"

"Yes." It was accurate, in a way.

"This is some story you're telling." The detective sounded doubtful.

"It's true. Once CSU pieces everythin' together, you'll see."

The EMTs wheeled Tang out.

"I'm goin' with him."

"I don't think so, Jordan." The detective stepped in front of her.

"Anybody here go by Rook?"

It was one of the best sounds she'd ever heard. "That's me!"

One of the EMTs waved her over.

Haley looked the detective in the eye. "I'm goin' with him. I'll be at the hospital if you have more questions." On the surface, it looked bad for her, but any evidence at this point was circumstantial. Besides, if she wanted to finish him, he had to know she wouldn't do it in front of two EMTs as witnesses.

The detective's jaw clenched, but he backed off.

A few seconds later, Haley walked beside the gurney.

"He's in and out of consciousness, but he asked for you."

Haley nodded.

"You riding with us?" the EMT asked.

"Yeah. Tulane?"

"Tulane," he answered.

Once they were inside, Haley pulled out her phone.

Just wanted 2 let u kno I'm ok. I'll call u in 10 minutes.

A few seconds later, Tonya replied.

U sure?

Yes. Will tell u everything I promise.

The technician hunched over Tang touched her elbow. "He's awake again and asking for you."

Tang looked at her. His gaze was tired, pained, and tortured. Haley leaned over him, turned her head to the side, and hovered close to his mouth.

"Sor…ry."

Haley wasn't sure, but she thought that's what he said.

She nodded, and when she looked down again his eyes were closed. The tech put the mask back over his nose and mouth. He'd done some unforgivable things to her, but Tang had also saved her life.

Haley walked back and forth in front of trauma room one. She tried to check on Milton a few minutes earlier, but they wouldn't give her any information. It was strange how calm she was even though she felt so lost. She pressed her phone to her lips. The trauma room door opened, and Haley moved out of the way.

"What's goin' on?" She aimed her question at the group of medical personnel crowded around Tang's gurney. He was still unconscious.

A young man was the first to speak. "He's stable, but his spleen needs to be removed. He's going to surgery now. Is there any family that needs to be notified?"

Haley closed her eyes and sighed. It wasn't pity she was feeling; she couldn't figure out what it was. "No, there isn't. His uncle is here too. He's not lucid enough to care what's goin' on." Haley paused. "Is he…gonna be okay?"

The doctor smiled. "His chances are really good."

"Thanks, Doctor."

He nodded, and they all disappeared down the hall.

Haley looked down at her phone again. She had another doctor to talk to.

She made her way to the waiting room and sat down. It was nearly full, but she found an empty section toward the back.

"Hey."

"I was just about to call you. Ten extra minutes is way too much leeway."

"Well…" Haley didn't even know where to start.

"Haley, something happened, didn't it?" Tonya's voice was shaky.

Haley released a long breath. "Yeah. I'm okay, though. I didn't get hurt. I'm at Tulane."

"Then, who…what's going on?" Tonya's tone was urgent, worried. "I'm on my way. We can still talk. Tell me everything."

Haley did, and by the time she was done, she was completely numb.

"This is so fucked-up."

"Yes, it is, but you're not alone, okay? Did you call Nate and Jen?"

"No, not yet."

"Click over and do that. I'll hang on. They'll get there faster."

"Okay."

Nate's phone rang a couple times before he answered. "Hey!"

"Nate," Haley said hoarsely.

"Shit. What happened?"

"Me and Tang got in a fight. His uncle tried to shoot me, but Tang jumped in the way. We're at Tulane in the ER."

"Oh God. Are you okay?" Nate sounded like he was running. "Just tell me you're okay."

"I'm not hurt." It felt like she'd repeated the same thing fifty times already.

"Thank fuckin' God. We're comin'. You call Tonya?"

"She's on the other line."

"Okay, good." He still sounded out of breath. Her voice was muffled, but she could hear Jen in the background.

"Is she—"

"Yeah, she's okay, and Tonya's on the other end."

"Tell her we'll be there in fifteen minutes," Jen said.

"Haley?" Nate asked.

"I heard. See you soon."

Haley said her good-byes and clicked back over. "I'm back. They're on the way."

"I had a dream a couple nights ago that I took you home for the first time to meet my mother."

"Yeah?"

"Yes." Tonya's voice was soft, soothing. "When you saw her, you whispered in my ear and told me she was hot. I pushed you away from me and glared, but you smiled and tried to look innocent."

"That sounds like me." Haley knew what Tonya was doing, trying to divert and relax her. It was working. She was completely focused on Tonya.

"It does. She was cooking, and you asked if you could help."

"What was she cookin'?"

"Shrimp creole."

"Mmm."

"I know, right? I sat down to watch. Within ten minutes, you'd totally charmed her. She was laughing so hard. She told me to hang on to you."

Haley smiled. She was suddenly so damn tired. "I'm not goin' anywhere."

"I know. Neither am I."

"I know." Haley covered her mouth as she yawned.

"You must be exhausted."

"Yeah, you gonna stay with me tonight?"

"Of course I will."

Several minutes later, Haley nearly jumped out of her skin when arms wrapped around her. She turned to see Jen, who untangled herself and sat down beside Haley. Nate took the other side.

He smiled and put an arm over her shoulder.

"Are they there?" Tonya asked.

Haley looked from Nate to Jen and back again. "Yeah."

"Let them take care of you. I'll be there soon."

"Okay."

Jen leaned into her and patted her on the knee as she asked what happened. She was surrounded by warmth and love. Haley tried to swallow and found that it wasn't all that easy. She tried to take a deep breath, only to find that it hurt. Her chest burned as she gasped. Her eyes prickled, and she let the tears come, telling them everything.

Tonya knew Haley wasn't hurt, but she had to see the evidence with her own eyes. That sense of urgency made her jog around the cars in the parking garage and to the elevator.

Her own heart slithered around in her chest. She dialed back her anger at Tim for putting them all in this situation in the first place, and whatever resentment she felt toward Haley went on the backburner. This wasn't about her or them as a couple anymore. This was all about Haley. Haley needed her, and Tonya was determined to be there for her.

The elevator was taking too long. Tonya moved quickly toward the door that led to the stairs. It creaked as it opened, and Tonya ran. By the time she got to the emergency room, she was breathless, but it had nothing to do with physical exertion. She scanned the waiting room, and for a few seconds everything stopped as she spotted them. Haley had her head on Nate's shoulder, and her eyes were closed. Jen's arm was around them both.

Tonya was nearly brought to her knees by the flood of emotions. Then Haley opened her eyes. Her smile was wide but sad. The world shifted under Tonya's feet. She didn't realize that she'd moved toward them. Nate stood and hugged her, and like it was commonplace, Tonya hugged him back. Jen took her hand and squeezed it as she scooted over, leaving a seat next to Haley free.

Tonya had the sudden realization that her family was much bigger than she thought.

She reached for Haley once she was seated, and their lips met. A sound rumbled in Tonya's chest, one of thankfulness and satisfaction. Haley tangled her hand in Tonya's hair, deepening the kiss. By the time she pulled back, Tonya was breathless again.

"Hey," Haley whispered.

"Mmm." Tonya's gaze went from Haley's eyes to her mouth and back. She brushed her thumb against Haley's lips and trailed it over her cheek.

"You not talkin' to me?"

Tonya smiled at the familiar words.

"Love those dimples."

Her smile widened.

"I love you."

Tonya shivered and her breathing hitched. It felt like fireworks were going off in her chest. There was so much she wanted to say.

Haley grinned, sincere and bright, like she'd discovered something. "And I gotta say, lovin' the way you're lookin' at me too." She paused and exhaled shakily. "Everythin's gonna be all right."

Haley didn't sound too convinced, but Tonya was going to try to rectify that. She kissed her gently. "Yes, it is."

Somewhere around them, a child started to cry. Tonya had forgotten they weren't alone. She glanced up, and people were staring. Nate and Jen had moved. She scanned the area to find them leaning against the wall behind their row of chairs.

Nate smiled softly.

Tonya nodded and wrapped herself back up in Haley.

It was almost four hours later when the doctor appeared again.

Haley looked up at him, eager for his report. She squeezed Tonya's hand, and Tonya squeezed back harder.

"We stopped all the bleeding. No other organs were affected, and we did some things to guard against infection. It went well. He's stable and strong. He should be able to go home in about a week, but the recovery time to get back to a regular daily schedule is four to six weeks."

Tonya turned to Haley, who stiffened for a moment and then visibly relaxed. Her eyes were watery but her smile was wide. It was obvious that despite everything, she cared for Tim a lot. Tonya was pleased for her, and thankful for a break in the chaos that had been surrounding them.

"Can I see him? He doesn't have anybody else."

The doctor nodded. "He's not awake yet, but you can have a few minutes."

"When he wakes up, can you let him know I was here?"

"I'll make sure one of the nurses passes that along. I'll take you to him."

Haley turned to Tonya. "I'll be back."

Tonya let her go.

Tonya blinked groggily. She wasn't sure why she was fighting sleep. She watched and felt Haley's chest slowly rise and fall. She thought Haley would've had trouble sleeping, but after she ate a couple bowls of cereal, she was dead to the world as soon as her head hit the pillow. It was a good sign, and Tonya was able to relax. She blinked again, and allowed the sound of Haley's breathing lull her to sleep.

Tonya woke up moaning. Her back arched as she chased the warm, wet suction surrounding her breast. "Haley."

All she heard was ragged breathing.

Haley trailed her lips up Tonya's torso, leaving the flesh in her wake sensitized and tingling. Tonya yanked at the T-shirt bunched up around her neck and tossed it to parts unknown. Haley whimpered as their lips met.

Their kiss was heated, desperate.

Tonya tangled her hands in Haley's hair and wrapped her legs around her waist. She moaned. Haley had already removed her own clothing. Skin met skin. Shamelessly, Tonya undulated her hips against Haley's stomach. She was already aroused and needy.

Haley rolled over, bringing Tonya with her.

It was then that Tonya realized what Haley wanted, what she needed.

"Touch me," Haley whispered into the kiss.

With a teasing swipe of her tongue, Tonya ended the kiss and sat up, straddling Haley's thighs. She continued to rub herself along Haley's abdomen.

Haley moaned, "Hurry."

She was powerful even like this. Strong, sleek, and wanton.

Tonya cupped Haley's breasts. The hardened points of Haley's nipples nearly burned the palms of her hands. She latched on to them aggressively, rolling and pulling at the aroused tips until Haley cried out and bucked beneath her. It was only then that she took one deep into her mouth. She went from one to the other.

"Fuck…please."

The urgency in Haley's voice made Tonya shiver. There was to be no waiting, no teasing. Not right now. Keeping her mouth where it was, Tonya moved to the side. She hooked her leg over one of Haley's powerful thighs.

Haley's hand slid down her own torso and went straight to her sex. "Yesss!" Her movements were frantic, hungry.

Overwhelmingly aroused by the sight before her, Tonya thrust against Haley helplessly, in search of friction. She whimpered when she found it. Needing, wanting to feel Haley's release, she slid her fingers between Haley's legs. The wetness and the heat she found there made her moan. She copied Haley's brisk, swirling motion and within seconds overtook it completely.

Haley turned her head toward her, and Tonya pulled her into a messy kiss, swallowing Haley's whimpers. When her body stilled and then erupted, Tonya drank in and shared in her cry of completion. But she wasn't done. As Haley continued to quiver, Tonya plunged inside her.

"Tonya!"

Her name was followed by a series of gasps and whimpers as Haley fell apart at the seams.

It was a long time later when Tonya lay back down to rest, and even then, she reached for the bedside lamp. She had to make sure that lost look Haley had left the hospital with had settled somewhat.

Haley blinked at her sleepily, but she held Tonya's gaze and smiled crookedly.

That was all Tonya needed.

It seemed like less than a few minutes later when they were jerked awake by the sound of a ringing phone.

"Dammit, that's me. I think that's me."

Haley fumbled around for a few seconds until she found her cell.

"Hello?"

Tonya sat up in the bed and turned the lamp on again.

"Tang?"

Tonya stayed silent. She didn't know what to think.

"Yeah, she's here. I'm gonna put you on speaker." Haley held the phone between them. "How are you? Are they keepin' you comfortable?"

"Yeah, good drugs. Only hurts like a bitch when I try to move. Who the fuck sleeps on their back anyway?" His voice was raspy and weak.

Haley looked at her and smiled. Something was right in the world.

"You'll be out in a few days. I'll make sure you get what you need. They wouldn't give me any information on Milt. I'm sorry."

"'S okay. I checked on him." He paused, then groaned slightly. "Rook, I won't be out in a few days. There's a reason I asked about your girl. Tonya? You there?"

"I'm here, Tim."

"For what it's worth, I-I'm sorry about all this. I had no right…no business bringin' you and your family into this."

"Thank you." There was really nothing else she could say.

"Wait. What do you mean you won't be—"

"C'mon, Rook. Think about it."

Tonya snaked an arm around Haley.

"You're turnin' yourself in," Haley said softly.

"Yep. I fucked up real bad, and it took you almost gettin' shot for me to realize it. I got lost. I wanted to fix my shit and I made other shit… worse." He paused. "I know you, Rook. You got integrity, and I almost messed that up for you. It's not right. None of it was right. I'm hopin' to get a plea, but I'll understand if I don't. While I'm inside, I need you to check on Milt. I know it's a lot to ask, but I don't want him dyin' alone." His tone was thick and tearful.

Haley's shoulders shook. "I will. I'll take care of it. I'm gonna come see you tomorrow. We'll start workin' stuff out."

"Yeah, okay. I-I need to go."

"Okay."

Tonya grabbed the phone and put it on the nightstand near hers. She turned the light off and leaned back, bringing Haley with her. She sifted a hand through Haley's hair as she continued to cry.

Epilogue

"Have you seen my belt?"

Tonya sighed. "Right here on the couch." She held it up and waved it.

Haley walked out of her bedroom. She looked good as always in her T-shirt and cargo shorts, but Tonya stared at the graphic on her shirt in confusion. "Who's J. R. and why did you shoot him?"

"Some soap opera guy from the '70s. Wore a ten-gallon hat. My mom dies laughin' every time I wear it in front of her. She got it for me. I like the gun on the front."

"Mmm, I'll have to ask for a better explanation when I meet her next weekend."

Haley was really lucky to have such acceptance. Tonya didn't have that, but at least now she had peace of mind. Despite her father's impending forced move, they were actually being cordial to each other. Maybe that, in itself, was a baby step forward.

"You do that. I'm sure she'll be full of stories." Haley bent down, and Tonya tipped her head back for a quick kiss. "It'll be interestin' to see how she reacts. You'll be the first woman I'm bringin' home, remember?"

"I remember." Tonya grinned. "Quite the honor."

Haley stopped halfway through looping the belt around her waist. Her expression was serious. "No, you honor me."

Tonya's heart stuttered before it started slamming against her ribcage. She felt weak. "Haley."

"I mean it." She kissed Tonya again. This time it was slow, deep.

Tonya whimpered when they parted. Her breathing was ragged and her stomach knotted. She stared at Haley, who looked back at her like she was about to pounce. Tonya beat her to it. She reached between them to unbutton Haley's shorts. "How much time do we have?"

"Enough." Haley growled.

Tonya watched as Haley smoothed out the wrinkles in her shirt. "Why aren't you wearing a Saints shirt?"

"Meh, I have on the colors. That's enough. I almost forgot. I got somethin' for you." Haley disappeared into her closet and came back out with yet another T-shirt. "This is for you."

Tonya took it from her and held it up. "Keep talking. I'm diagnosing you." She chuckled. It was cheesy, sweet, and cute. "I love you."

Haley froze and stared.

At the same time, some kind of parade was going on inside Tonya. It had confetti, a marching band, dancers, floats, and behind it was the second line, loud and strong.

"Uh, did you mean the shir—"

"No." She'd been trying to figure out these feelings, but Tonya knew she'd been trying too hard. There was nothing else it could be. "Not the shirt. You."

Haley's crooked smile widened. "Yeah?"

Tonya nodded and grinned. This person was who she wanted to be. This was who she was. While everything wasn't perfect, it was closer than she'd ever thought it would be. "Yeah."

Within seconds, Haley was kissing her like the world depended on it.

"How much time do we have?" Tonya gasped.

"I don't care."

Haley pressed her hand to the small of Tonya's back as they entered Cooter Brown's Tavern. The place was packed. It was game day. She hadn't expected anything less.

"We're late!" Tonya said.

"So. It was worth it."

Tonya grinned. "Maybe."

"Mmm, everybody should be here already. I'll text Nate and let him know we're here instead of tryin' to find them in all this." As Haley reached into her pocket for her phone, people started beating on tables and stomping. The Saints were coming onto the field. She wasn't surprised when somebody started chanting, "Who dat...who dat say dey gonna beat dem Saints?" It wasn't long before others joined in.

Just walked in. Near door.

Late ass. Everybody's here.
I'm comin' hold on.

Nate led them back to the others, but not before eyeing them both knowingly.

When they got to the table, there were plenty of groans and eye rolls. Tracy and Stephanie shifted to make room for them. Haley squeezed Tracy's shoulder as she sat down beside her. Halfway through drinks the night before, they'd become fast friends. She was like the bolder, more in-your-face version of Tonya. Haley winked at Stephanie, and she grinned in return. No one said anything about Tonya's T-shirt. That was a little disappointing.

The sound of Tonya's laughter grabbed her attention. She turned to see Stephanie and Tonya huddled together. As if knowing she was being watched, Tonya looked up, leaned toward Haley, and smiled. Haley couldn't help but feel that she was at the beginning of something great.

Tonya moved closer and whispered in her ear, "I love you."

God what those words did to her insides. When it came down to it, she should be floating. Haley grinned. When she looked up, Nate had his phone in his hand, taking a picture.

Haley's cell phone vibrated against her thigh during halftime. She pulled it out and recognized immediately that it was a call from Tulane. She answered and yelled for Tang to hang on.

"Tim?" Tonya mouthed.

Haley nodded and stood. "Be right back." She needed to get outside to hear. The Saints were actually winning. People were loud and excited. She weaved her way through tables to get to the door.

"How are you feelin'?"

"They're actually winnin', so not too bad. Hope they don't fuck it up."

"Hope not."

They both went quiet. She'd forgiven him. She had to, but he hadn't forgiven himself.

"You goin' to your interview tomorrow?"

"Yeah, but no matter how it goes, I'm takin' some time. I gotta deal with psych, so I figured I'd try to recharge."

"Sorry you have to do that," Tang whispered.

"Tim…just, how's Milt?"

"They're gonna transfer him to a nursin' home on Tuesday."

"I know you didn't—"

"Reap what you sow, Rook."

Very true. They were getting the best ending they could out of this. Regardless, Haley was going to have a hard time doing this again, trusting again. At least her love of the job hadn't been diminished. That gave her something to work with. "You'll call me as soon as you find out about the plea?"

"Yeah." His words trembled.

"I'm gonna come visit. You know that, right?"

"I know." Tang cleared his throat. "Look, I gotta go."

"Okay." Haley let him have whatever dignity he had left.

The door opened. Several people stepped out, and Tonya was behind them. Haley walked toward her. "I was just comin' back."

"Are you okay?"

"Yeah, I think so."

Tonya gazed at her a little longer.

"Promise. Now let's go see if they can hang on to this lead."

Tonya smiled. "Okay, but I have a football question. I think I get the offense and defense thing, but what is that bright yellow line that shows up?"

"Yellow line?"

"Yes, how do they draw it across that entire field so fast? Or is it some kind of projection?"

Haley stopped and stared. "You're…kiddin', right?"

Tonya stared right back.

Haley threw her head back and laughed. "It's just…just somethin' they do for TV, to show where the first down is." The disgruntled look on Tonya's face made her laugh even harder. Haley was starting to feel weak. She pulled Tonya to her and managed to contain herself, barely. "Uh, I love you, but I'm gonna have to tell everybody you said that."

Tonya pushed her away and glared, but there was a playful glint in her eyes. "Just Nate, then?"

Tonya stepped away and opened the door. She didn't bother to check if Haley was behind her.

Haley grinned and followed.

ABOUT KD WILLIAMSON

KD is a Southerner and a former nomad, taking up residence in the Midwest, East Coast, and New Orleans over the years. She is also a Hurricane Katrina survivor. Displaced to the mountains of North Carolina, she found her way back to New Orleans, where she lives with her partner of ten years and the strangest dogs and cats in existence.

KD enjoys all things geek, from video games to superheroes. She is a veteran in the mental health field working with children and their families for over ten years. She found that she had a talent for writing as a teenager, and through fits and starts, fostered it over the years.

CONNECT WITH KD WILLIAMSON

Blog: www.kdwilliamsonfiction.wordpress.com
E-Mail: Williamson_kd@yahoo.com

Other Books from Ylva Publishing

www.ylva-publishing.com

Blurred Lines

(Cops and Docs – Book 1)

KD Williamson

ISBN: 978-3-95533-493-2
Length: 283 pages (92,000 words)

Wounded in a police shootout, Detective Kelli McCabe spends weeks in the hospital recovering. Her only entertainment is verbal sparring matches with Dr. Nora Whitmore, the talented and reclusive surgeon. Two very different women living in two different worlds. When the lines between them begin to blur, will they run from the possibilities or embrace the changes they bring to each other's lives?

In a Heartbeat

(The L.A. Metro Series – Book 2)

RJ Nolan

ISBN: 978-3-95533-159-7
Length: 370 pages (97,000 words)

Officer Sam McKenna has no trouble facing down criminals but breaks out in a sweat at the mere mention of commitment. Trauma surgeon Riley Connolly tries to measure up to her family's expectations and hides her sexuality from them. A life-and-death situation at the hospital binds them together. But can there be any future for a commitment-phobic cop and a closeted, workaholic doctor?

Flinging It

G Benson

ISBN: 978-3-95533-682-0
Length: 376 pages (113,000 words)

Midwife Frazer and social worker Cora have always grated on each other's nerves, but they have to work together to start up a programme for at-risk parents. Soon, the unexpected happens: they tumble into an affair. However, Cora is married to their boss, and both know it needs to end. But what they have might turn out to be much more than just a little distraction.

Four Steps

Wendy Hudson

ISBN: 978-3-95533-690-5
Length: 343 pages (92,000 words)

Seclusion suits Alex Ryan. Haunted by a crime from her past, she struggles to find peace and calm.

Lori Hunter dreams of escaping the monotony of her life. When the suffocation sets in, she runs for the hills.

A chance encounter in the Scottish Highlands leads Alex and Lori into a whirlwind of heartache and a fight for survival, as they build a formidable bond that will be tested to its limits.

COMING FROM YLVA PUBLISHING

www.ylva-publishing.com

Falling Hard

Jae

Dr. Jordan Williams devotes her life to saving patients in the OR and pleasuring women in the bedroom.

Jordan's new neighbor, single mom Emma, is the polar opposite. Family and fidelity mean everything to her.

When Emma helps Jordan recover after a bad fall, they quickly grow closer. But neither counted on falling hard—for each other.

Under Parr

(Norfolk Coast Investigation Story – Book 2)

Andrea Bramhall

December 5th, 2013 left its mark on the North Norfolk Coast in more ways than one. A tidal surge and storm swept millennia-old cliff faces into the sea and flooded homes and businesses up and down the coast. It also buried a secret in the WWII bunker hiding under the golf course at Brancaster. A secret kept for years, until it falls squarely into the lap of Detective Sergeant Kate Brannon and her fellow officers.

A skeleton, deep inside the bunker.

How did it get there? Who was he…or she? How did the stranger die—in a tragic accident or something more sinister? Well, that's Kate's job to find out.

Between the Lines
© 2017 by KD Williamson

ISBN: 978-3-95533-825-1

Also available as e-book.

Published by Ylva Publishing, legal entity of Ylva Verlag, e.Kfr.

Ylva Verlag, e.Kfr.
Owner: Astrid Ohletz
Am Kirschgarten 2
65830 Kriftel
Germany

www.ylva-publishing.com

First edition: 2017

Credits
Edited by Sheri Milburn and Alissa McGowan
Proofread by JoSelle Vanderhooft
Cover Design by Streetlight Graphics

Printed in Great Britain
by Amazon